Julie Haydon was born in Adelaide in 1966. She has a degree in Media Studies and has worked as a publicist and sales assistant. Currently she lives in Melbourne. *Lines Upon the Skin* is her first novel.

GW00598137

LINES
UPON THE SKIN

JULIE
HAYDON

PAN
Pan Macmillan Australia

First published 1995 in Pan by Pan Macmillan Australia Pty Limited
Level 18, 31 Market Street, Sydney

National Library of Australia
cataloguing-in-publication data:
Haydon, Julie.
Lines upon the skin.
ISBN 0 330 356534
I. Title.
A823.3

Typeset in 11/13pt Bembo by Midland Typesetters, Maryborough
Printed in Australia by McPhersons Printing Group

*Lovingly dedicated to my grandmother, Phyl Fidler,
and to my parents, Robert and Diana Haydon.*

TIRAYI

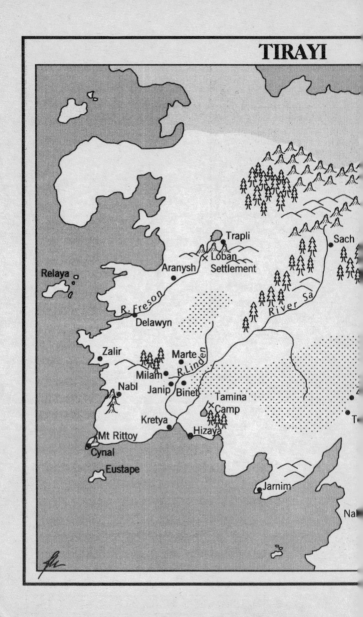

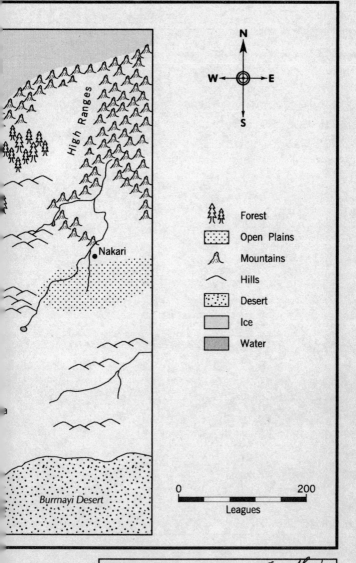

PROLOGUE

It was the summer the old king died. He went peacefully in his sleep and the people mourned him, grieving the passing of his honest, gentle rule. Yet though the funeral fires burned brilliantly now, lighting up the city with their eerie glow, all knew that the time of the prince would soon come. And once again fires would be lit, but this time in celebration of the enthroning of Cynal's new ruler. So the people could enjoy the festivies. A funeral and an enthroning always make for fun.

We had come to the city for work, promised to us by the king, but had stayed on, hoping, like so many others, for a chance to present ourselves to his successor. Besides, Cynal is a beautiful city, a harbour town on the west coast of Tirayi with green sloping hills and clear azure waters. So we stayed and had our fair share of the fish and the fruit and the wine. So much in fact that we nearly missed the funeral procession. It was only a man calling down to us from the top of the hill as he passed that told us it had begun. Only slightly the worse for the wine we had been sharing under the bright Cynalese sun, we climbed to the road and joined the crowds of people heading into the city.

As a harbour town, Cynal is used to foreigners. It does not command half the arrivals of Delawyn, the largest sea town on the west coast, but that is only to its benefit. The people who surged forward to see once more the body of the dead king were of all races. The dark Cynalese, with their nut-brown skin and glossy thick curls moved with ease amongst the visiting merchants and traders and sailors. We were just another five, come to bid the king well in his final moments on this earth.

The crowd cheered as the bier carrying the embalmed body appeared and a pathway was cleared by soldiers, their finely burnished buckles and swords flashing in the sunlight on their near-naked bodies. Where we stood the bier passed quite close and for a moment his profile was clear before me. I looked at this man, a man no longer, and wondered how I would have felt now if we had accepted his job in the spring as he had first offered. We had already signed for a small job with the Tamina and were forced to put him off, asking if it could wait one season. He had agreed to the summer, not knowing that he would never see the beautiful maps he had envisaged of his city and its land begun, if indeed now they were begun at all. The procession moved on and I lost sight of the bier amidst the crowd.

When the bearers reached the wooden platform, they carefully laid his body out, surrounding him with his precious possessions. A priest stood over the body invoking the spirits to make his passage one without trial. She was a tall woman in scarlet robes, a member of the peace-loving Mecla sect. When she had finished she stepped down and we waited for the pouring of the oil.

Nothing happened.

Curious, the crowd began to murmur. Once the priest had spoken the body should be sent to the spirits quickly, lest they forget him. I was not overly familiar with the rites of the Mecla but this I knew.

A shout was given behind us and the murmuring grew, then quickly dropped to an uneasy hush as a magnificent man rode unescorted into view and began to follow the path towards the pyre. Although I had never before seen him, I knew he had to be the prince, Lord Tarn.

He rode slowly through the crowd, looking straight ahead until he stopped his horse before the priest. He bowed to her and dismounted, then he turned to his father. There was not a sound now from the crowd. By custom this was the day for the dead king and his heir should view the funeral but not participate. His day would come soon.

Lord Tarn stepped up to the body then leant forward and kissed his father gently on the lips. He picked up one of the jugs of oil and handed it to the priest, then picked up another for himself and together they covered the body and the pyre. For one last moment Lord Tarn gazed at the king, before raising a burning torch and touching it to the pyre. The wood underneath, already soaked in oil, leapt into flame. Before stepping down and away from the fire he placed the torch across his father's chest and then I could see no more as the flames rose, consuming the human tinder.

ONE

OUR REPUTATION AS cartographers is something we have worked hard for. Now our maps are well known and command high prices. There are five of us, Chandra, Lilith, Alexa, Carly and myself, Ashil, though it had started with only Chandra and myself three years ago. It was in Binet, my birth city, that we first decided to map the world away from family and the complacent familiarity of home.

My father is a cartographer, though he works for the army at Binet where he too was born. My mother had always hoped that I would study at the university at Marte, as she had done, but her work as a city financier had never held me as had my father's maps and so it was to him I had turned once freed from school. In the cartography section of the army base, I spent those early days working under him like any apprentice to a trade, learning and studying and testing the skills of my profession. I learnt quickly, as one will who pursues something desired and rewarding, for I think I knew even then it would be my maps that would take me across the world, to places and people unknown and into cultures otherwise closed to me. In mapping them

I would come to know them a little and at times my very eagerness pained me.

My apprenticeship lasted two years and from amidst all the lessons and the repetitions and the off-hand advice, one occasion stands out as the most propitious of my career. It was the day I first saw my father's skill in diplomacy and the day I met Chandra.

The Futile War, which tore apart the twin cities of Zelia and Telish and which rages still, had finally become too fierce for even the nomadic tribes to ignore. It was no longer safe for them to travel their long-established routes with the tribal eye never looking outwards, so a group had come to Binet for consultation with the army's cartographers.

The nomads are an unusual sight for city-folk, yet my father possesses a pulsing curiosity for any world not his own and it was with genuine interest and warmth that he welcomed them to our city. They responded with polite assurance, finding much of merit in my father's words.

And it was from watching him, his face stilled in concentration, gently hearing then directing the nomads, that I realised my study of the cartography of Binet was not enough. I knew all about preparing the animal skins and covering them with intricate and precise lines and markings, but I knew nothing about talking of maps to people unfamiliar with my ways. So I hovered in the background, observing my father with these strange but marvellous people, learning, always learning.

The maps the tribespeople carried were crude by our standards, but their memories and understanding of the ways of the land put us to shame. They select their mapdrawers by their ability to remember and record accurately and it is a position of great importance and esteem within the tribe.

It was a small group which came to us, three women and three men, from four different tribes. I was fascinated by their colouring, the smooth skin like dark, dark syrup, soft and unblemished, and their black eyes, so large and alert. Their unruly black hair grew past their shoulders, curling in the tiniest spirals I had ever seen.

But I was not alone in my interest. The youngest of the nomads, a girl of my age, viewed my straight blonde hair and blue eyes with undisguised curiosity. She was tall and strong and she smiled at me confidently, showing impossibly white teeth, and introduced herself as Chandra.

On the afternoon of their arrival I was sent on an errand to fetch more ink cakes for the bench wells. I asked Chandra along.

We walked down streets that to me were common and unexciting, but I could not fail to notice the other girl's interest in everything and everyone that passed. She stared in the shop fronts, eyes gleaming at the sight of so many objects for sale, most of which I was sure she could see no use for. She paused at the food vendors, inhaling the strange and wonderful smells, and her fingers trailed the sides of buildings, her eyes following them up into the sky. At first I was silent, feeling unnaturally shy and reserved, and too involved in surreptitiously examining the exotic creature at my side. But finally I could stand it no longer and I began to talk, to explain what this was for and what one did

3

with that and she fed me with questions and gasps of astonishment and sometimes frowns of doubt.

So, knowing my father was in no hurry for the ink cakes that day, I took Chandra on a tour. First, I showed her the theatre.

We of Binet are particularly proud of both our theatre and our acting troupe, so it was with a sense of civic pride that I showed her the rows of curving stone seats that formed a half-circle around the beaten ground of the stage. She was distinctly unimpressed.

'It must have taken your craftspeople many seasons to arrange the stone in that way,' she said, frowning slightly, 'when the ground is just as comfortable.'

Having expected enthusiastic admiration, her flat denunciation momentarily stunned me.

'But the rows mean everyone has a good view,' I explained, and I waved my arm around the theatre, indicating the far top rows.

She followed the direction of my hand, studying the huge construction, then shook her head, the frown reappearing. 'So high up, the actors must appear tiny. It would be like standing on a cliff and looking down, or hovering in the air like a bird. If everyone was seated on the ground and the actors standing, all could see clearly.'

A thought came to me and I grinned suddenly. 'How many in your tribe, Chandra?'

'We are a large tribe,' she replied. 'There are over four hundred people.'

I laughed and she looked at me curiously. 'This theatre can seat over ten thousand people and many more can stand and watch,' I explained.

4

She tilted her chin slightly as she gazed thoughtfully once more at the rows and rows of carefully laid stone, then she turned her black eyes on me.

'And all can hear?' she asked.

'Most,' I demurred. 'But few come without first having read or being told the story and the actors wear distinctive robes and . . .' I stumbled to a stop. Ruefully I conceded she had a point. Deciding to leave that particular aspect alone, I asked what the plays of her people were about.

We moved to sit on one of the stone seats, quite alone in the enormous tiered edifice, the sky a clear blue ceiling.

'We gather to thank the gods for the hunt, or to praise them for new life and the season's change, or to present the child become adult. But they are not plays as you have described.' She leant back, resting her shoulders against the stone, a young panther at rest, strong, sleek and confident. She inhaled deeply and smiled at me, openly, and I wondered at the superb diet that kept her teeth so white and healthy. 'We dance and sing together,' she continued. 'Only the old and very young sit throughout. The priest recites the lore, and all must be able to hear it, for all must know it. Words are very important to us.'

The quiet of the theatre lent a strange stillness to the day, as though we had suddenly separated ourselves from the rest of the city, from its concerns and doings. It was a feeling I knew could not last. Soon some noise or action would intrude, returning us to the neverceasing stream of life that was the city.

'I would like to see,' and Chandra smiled as she added, 'and hear, one of your plays.'

5

'Yes,' I nodded, quite enthralled by her, 'I can arrange that.' Then I smiled. 'And one day I hope I can watch one of your tribe's ceremonies.'

As soon as I had spoken the words, I wished them unsaid, fearing to insult with my ignorance. It was possible that such ceremonies were sacred and private and so not open to foreigners. My relief was immense when Chandra assented.

'That would be good,' she said, not in the least upset by my words. 'Our gods have different names but perhaps the same ears.' She paused, obviously thinking, then gave her head a little shake. 'I have forgotten, what do you call your chief god?'

Religion did not play a major role in my family's life and was an area with which I rarely concerned myself, but her serious manner deserved an equally serious reply.

'Ruler of the Skies is the most common name for the paramount of the gods, although we offer to all the gods of the elements,' I chuckled. 'Just in case.'

She regarded me in astonishment and I decided it was time to move on.

'Our own actors are performing in Marte at the moment,' I said as I stood up and dusted the dirt from my clothes, ' but there is a visiting troupe from Milam due in a few days. They will perform on the Day of Rejoicing. If you like, we can come to see the play.'

Chandra nodded her agreement and we began to walk to the exit. 'What is the Day of Rejoicing?'

'It is when Binet celebrates the signing of the Premle Treaty with Marte, Milam and Janip. The treaty and the formation of the League marked the end of years

6

of warring.' In the queer stillness that surrounded us, it was hard to imagine an earlier Binet of blood and fire. 'Each year all four cities celebrate and each sends an acting troupe to a different League city.' I raised an eyebrow. 'Have you heard of Krotsaa?'

She frowned. 'No.'

'He was an evil man, bloodthirsty and cruel. He tortured Binet and we do not want to ever forget what our ancestors lived through. Now we each learn the tale so that the horror will never be brought to life again. Binet was once little more than a small cluster of villages. All that remains today of those villages is the sacred centre.' I pointed westward to where the centre now lay in the city. 'It was the hut dedicated to the gods in the middle of the cluster of villages. Only the priests were permitted to enter. When the fire that Krotsaa ordered raged through the fledgling city, only the hut, maintained by each generation, was left standing.'

'The gods protected what was theirs,' Chandra said very seriously.

I stayed mute. It had always seemed strange to me that any god would save a stone hut and not her people.

A moment passed and I continued. 'When the new city was built, the Plaza of the City Guardians was erected on the site of the sacred centre and the hut preserved. The Plaza's gallery will be opened on the Day of Rejoicing. I'll take you.' I grinned suddenly. 'I want to show you the tablets,' I added.

'What tablets?' Chandra queried, glancing at me.

I shook my head, smiling. 'No, you'll have to wait. I don't want to remove the surprise.'

Accepting this, Chandra asked, 'Do your actors tour often?'

'Yes, they have more invitations to perform than they can possibly attend to. They spend more than half the year away from Binet.'

Chandra gave a small grunt of envy and asked, 'Have you ever been away from Binet?'

We had reached the exit and passed under the stone arch into the cool dark of the short passage. 'Once to Janip, with my father,' I said, shrugging diffidently. 'I've been at school and then studying with the army, but when I've finished . . .' and I left the statement open.

Chandra nodded, looking straight ahead. 'Have you ever seen the sea, Ashil?' and the wistfulness was clear in her voice.

'No,' and the same longing filled that one word. The sea and its merfolk, how I had dreamed of them!

'None of my people has seen it, yet we have songs in the old tongue, the language of our rites, that tell us of it, and we have precious "shells" in the priest's tent.' She cupped one hand as though holding something small.

'I know them. Occasionally we have traders from Kretya and Hizaya set up in the marketplace and they sell them and other wonders from the ocean.'

We stepped from the passage into the street and the noise of the city pounced upon us once more.

'Our songs tell of so much we no longer see or know,' Chandra said, sighing deeply. 'Of the sea we once loved, the great sickness that killed so many, the tribe's wandering and our union with the Layar, the

People of the Stag, many many years ago.' She glanced at the activity around her then turned to me. 'I think that is how we learned your tongue, Ashil.'

I nodded and we walked on in silence, lost in our own thoughts, not speaking of the desires that gripped us. And I was glad, for although I had great plans they were still in their infancy, needing time to grow and develop strength. Only then would I and others be able to take them seriously.

If I had found Chandra's response to the theatre disappointing, it was nothing to her reaction to the city baths. On learning that the city's rich folk often bathed daily in the heated waters, taking hours having their bodies washed, oiled and groomed, she laughed outright. She inspected the tiny coloured tiles that form the blue-green mosaics with interest but then she wrinkled her nose at the powerful scents of passing women and men. 'Such smells would alert any animal on a hunt,' she said dismissively.

By now I had warmed to the girl's candour and utter lack of pretension. With delightful anticipation, I took her next to my old school.

On such a fine day, several classes were seated outside, so we sat at the edge of one group and listened to the discussion. With the Day of Rejoicing so close, I was not surprised to hear the subject was the Redu.

'They came from the east,' the tutor was saying, 'like a plague of locusts, the records tell us, sweeping over the land and devouring all in their path.

'The villagers were farmers, not warriors, and they quickly discovered that to disobey these wild ones was to die. The wild ones called themselves Redu, after

9

their vicious barbed spears. They were stocky and fair with long moustaches and braided hair which they wore held back by a dyed leather headband, carefully stitched with scenes of personal valour. The skin of their bodies was puckered with highly prized scars and their greatest warriors wore necklaces of human bones and,' he bared his teeth and made a sawing motion with his finger, 'filed their teeth to sharp points.' He leant forward and lowered his voice. 'For a Redu, the greatest honour was earned in killing.'

I heard several sharp gasps as the group stirred. Beside me Chandra was concentrating hard.

The tutor nodded and continued. 'The Redu warriors would pour the blood from their slain victims over their braided hair, letting it dry and harden, then with their own blades cut a stroke in their forearm to show yet another kill. They had travelled far and for long and they feared no-one and nothing. They made the villagers theirs.'

I knew the tale, and despite hearing again of the vileness of certain Redu customs I was finding it extremely pleasant sitting with the sun warm on my back and a soft breeze lifting my hair. I recognised several of the other students and, in another group, noted the young brother of one of my friends. Chandra was quiet beside me, listening intently to the lesson, and I wondered idly what sort of studying the children of her tribe did. Then I smiled to myself as I pondered what her reaction to this aspect of city life would be.

'Who can tell me what the Redu came in search of?' the tutor asked, obviously intending to lead into a group talk and garner what his students knew. When

10

no-one answered, I had to bite my lip to stop myself from laughing, memories of my own lessons returning when no-one was prepared to go first.

However, I was quickly jolted out of my reminiscent mood when it was Chandra who responded, and correctly.

'The Redu sought fertile land. They were weary of travelling and ready to settle.'

The tutor nodded. 'Yes, they were a warring race but they still needed food and shelter. But why did they keep the villagers alive?'

'To work the fields and to teach the Redu the ways of this new land.' Chandra again.

Indeed as the lesson progressed it was Chandra who asked the most questions,who queried certain statements and who probed deeply into the subject, even turning to another student to answer his question. She would lean forward when making a point or listening to an explanation, a slight frown creasing the skin between her dark brows. I was impressed at her knowledge and when finally the lesson ended and we made our way back to the army base, I asked, a little confused, where she had learnt of the Redu.

'Before today I had never heard of them,' and she grinned, pleased with the new experience. 'But the tutor led me along. He had hidden the answers in his tale. It was for us to find them.' She paused, reflecting. 'I think I would enjoy attending one of your schools.'

Our friendship grew during her short stay. I showed her more of Binet, always fascinated by her reactions to everyday aspects of my life, and on the Day of

Rejoicing, her last day in the city, I took Chandra to view the celebrations.

From early light, the city was crowded with people come to see the procession. They lined the main street in row after disorganised row, the people behind trying to peer over heads and shoulders and calling to those before them to sit down or remove offending head coverings or take children down from their shoulders. Some of the blunt replies they received clearly puzzled Chandra.

I did not stop to explain. Instead I grabbed Chandra's hand and held it tightly while I weaved amongst the crowd, heading towards one of the city's finest viewing spots—the roof of the army base. A small cluster of soldiers were already there. 'Good morning,' they called out, and 'You're late again, Ashil.' I laughed and shrugged exaggeratedly. It was a joke amongst us that no matter how early I came to the roof each year, I was never first. I led Chandra to the very front of the roof and we sat cross-legged, an unimpeded view of Binet's main street spread out before us.

'The procession is provided by the Plaza politicians,' I explained as we idly watched the antics of the crowd below us. 'They spend their own coin to pay for it and each year they choose young actors to play roles from different Binenese stories.'

The rumble of many hooves and wheels caught my ear and I pointed to the east, towards the city square. 'Look, it's started.'

It was a brilliant procession that made its way towards us amidst cheers and shouts of joy from the crowd. There were performers in masks and costumes as gorgeous as any found in the theatre, and musicians beating drums and blowing horns, as horses danced and skittered down the street, soldiers in uniform upon their backs. Banners flapped in the light breeze and jugglers and tumblers raced in and out, shaking bells and calling and throwing coins to the throng. When Binet's blue and red chequered flag appeared the roar of the crowd was deafening.

Before the noise had a chance to lessen, the first of the horse-drawn wagons appeared. It was heaped with animal skins and upon them, fierce and proud, stood a warrior.

'It's Sartcha,' I cried, unable to contain my excitement any longer and jumping to my feet. 'Eaglewoman. And there's Nark,' I yelled, pointing to the warrior riding alongside the wagon, 'her brother.'

Behind them came more and more of the Redu warriors, both mounted and on foot. All wore fur-lined vests and rough leather trousers, and as they passed below us they began to jump and run towards the crowd, screaming their war-cry and proudly thrusting their arms forward for all to see the many kill scars. I saw many in the first rows recoil and one or two of the children whimper with fright.

Chandra was standing beside me, avidly following the wagon and its wild escort.

'Why was she called Eaglewoman?' Chandra asked loudly, so I could hear her over the crowd.

I leant towards her to answer. 'She had eyes slitted and golden like a hunting bird and was fearless and cunning. She did not want the villagers as enemies. Others of the wild ones were already swarming over

13

the land, and if the Redu and villagers were to keep their fields they would have to join together. At first the villagers just laughed. All wild ones were their enemies, they said, it made no difference if the Hetir, the blood-drinkers, or the Grada, the swooping sword, replaced the Redu. So when the first attack came the Redu withdrew, leaving the villagers to fight unaided. The fields the villagers had so painstakingly replanted were trampled and ruined, villager blood ran everywhere and the villagers saw what the Redu had hoped they would see. The fighting with the Redu was over, with these new wild ones it would begin again. The villagers called Sartcha back and they talked. It was soon agreed that the Redu would defend the villages, but first Sartcha wanted a sign of the villagers' trust.'

I broke off as the crowd began to hiss and curse as another wagon rolled into view, following the Redu.

'Who is that?' Chandra asked, leaving my tale for the moment.

In the wagon were two men, one dressed in costly robes, the other in a pauper's garb. Both men's clothing and skin were streaked with blood as they wrestled and fought, their eyes gleaming like those of savage animals, both intent on murder. Surrounding the wagon were line after line of chained female slaves.

'It's Krotsaa and his brother Kraym,' I answered evenly. 'Years after the villagers had agreed to the marriages Sartcha wanted as a sign of trust, Krotsaa took power in Marte. The wild ones had settled now, spreading far over Tirayi and imposing on all a new language, what became known as the Middling Tongue. On both sides of the

River Linden the bloodlines of the wild ones had mingled with those of the villagers. Trade had been established and wars had been reduced to occasional raids. The hoe had replaced the sword. The villages were growing larger and the cluster of villages on the east bank had merged into one and was named Binet. Today, we Binenese believe we are made of the best of both the Redu and those early farmers.'

'The best?' Chandra repeated, lifting a lock of my hair. 'So no blood here?' she teased.

I laughed. 'Unlike the Redu, I don't have any enemies.'

Chandra smiled and turned back to the wagon. 'Was Krotsaa of the new blood?'

'Yes, but he was evil. Marte was very poor, with neither the timber of Milam nor the fields and pastures of Binet and Janip. Marte is north-west of the Linden, where the land is rocky and unproductive for leagues. Krotsaa told the Martines they were better than their neighbours and deserved whatever they could take. He gathered an army, intending on bringing Binet, Janip and Milam under his rule. Years of wicked war followed, worse than any struggles with the wild ones, for Krotsaa showed no mercy. He would kill any male found on land he took and send the women off to work as slaves in Marte's mines. Only Martines were allowed children.'

I shook my head at the madness of it all. 'So many died. He was a young man when he began, and it was twenty years later that his brother Kraym entered the tyrant's house late one night and attacked Krotsaa. He cut out Krotsaa's heart. Then Kraym cleaned off the

15

blood and put on one of his brother's robes and began walking home. He was seen and mistaken for the tyrant, thought to be out without guards, and Kraym was torn apart by an angry, hungry mob. By that time, even Krotsaa's own people hated him. Less than a year later a huge vein of silver was discovered in one of the city's mines. A council now ruled Marte, headed by a man called Premle. He convinced the councillors to allow some of the silver to be given to the peoples who had suffered under Krotsaa and with the rest they helped their own poor and built the first of Marte's famous schools.'

Another wagon had appeared, this one waving the striped and crossed green and yellow flag of Marte and carrying two Martines bearing a chest of silver. They flipped open the lid and dipped their hands inside, letting the coins run through their fingers, sparkling in the morning sun.

'Binet the city was begun with that silver. One of Krotsaa's last acts had been to order the fire that destroyed all but the priest's stone hut. Premle also called for the signing of a treaty which was agreed to by the four parties. That is what we celebrate today. The death of a mad one and the birth of freedom and respect amongst neighbours.'

The Martine wagon passed on and there was a short space. Then came the loud boom boom of a drum and the dancers ran forward, Binet's finest, their costumes twirling out around them as they spun and leapt, their faces glowing with excitement to hear the cheers of the crowd. Behind them walked the singers, their voices extolling the glories of our city.

16

Chandra and I stayed on the roof until the last member of the procession had passed us by, then we climbed quickly down and hurried to the Plaza. It would be open now and I wanted to show her the gallery.

We chatted as we walked. Chandra was very excited about what she had just seen. It was all so different to nomad celebrations and ceremonies and she had never seen so many people together at the one time. I laughed, enjoying my role as guide, and when we passed a group of corner musicians I had to tug her along when she would have stayed and listened. I was eager to show her the gallery's tablets.

Binet's Plaza is a magnificent building, with a grand portico held up by enormous sculptured pillars and reached by several dozen steps. It took more than five years to build, with ox-wagons shifting stone through the streets every working day of that time. My grandmother had told me that her great-grandmother had remembered the sound of the wagons and the dust their wheels would spin up from when she was a little girl. Now the stone of the building had darkened and mellowed, giving the Plaza a sombre, established presence. Chandra just stood and stared.

'It's divided into four sections,' I explained. 'The Hall of Discussion, where the politicians meet, the workrooms of the scribes and clerks who work for the city, the treasury and the gallery. The gallery is only opened three times a year. Come, let's join the line.'

People already stood waiting halfway down the steps. Chandra and I took our place and slowly the line moved. Step by step we climbed, until we were under

17

the portico. We eased forward into the hallway. Ahead of us the line turned a corner and, little by little, person by person, we reached it and turned it too. We waited, moved along another hallway, around one more corner, and the gallery door was now in sight. We stood watching as the people before us were slowly passed through. Finally, it was our turn.

The guards waved us forward and Chandra and I crossed over to the first display. It was a fine painted vase, almost as high as my shoulder, showing Neomaron, first son of the Ruler of the Skies, relaxing in his sun palace, his tiny children, the night stars, playing at his feet.

Next was a collection of three engraved gems, two set in pendants. They were city-gifts from our League neighbours. The first, from Janip, showed a handsome archer stalking a deer. The second, from Milam, was of a forest spirit, her hair and body draped with leaves, and the last, from Marte, was of a scholarly aged man talking with a young, athletic woman. Wisdom and Vigour in discussion. Each of the gemstones was no larger than my thumb and the detail of the engraving was exquisite.

We passed along rows of busts of various politicians who had held places of importance in Binet's history and Chandra gazed in fascination at a large bronze statue of Sartcha.

I showed her a Redu belt of beaten metal and a spear that had belonged to Nark, telling her that he had been called Death's Arm for his aim was always true. I pointed out a frieze showing Krotsaa's death struggle and the bone from the priest who built the sacred centre, the priest who, many said, was in fact the Ruler come to set up her place.

Through it all, Chandra walked wide-eyed, and when finally we reached the sacred centre, I stood back to let her see first.

When the Plaza was being planned, the spot where the hut that had survived the fire stood was noted, so it could be returned to its correct place when the Plaza was completed. The priests consulted with the gods and announced when the time was right for the hut to be moved. Now, as then, it was gently tended, masons fixing any weakness as it appeared in the blackened stone. Newer temples have since been built in the city, yet each week the priests continue to visit the sacred centre to honour the Ruler in her chosen place.

As in the early times of the villagers, only the priests are permitted to enter the hut, but I watched as Chandra squatted and peered through the open door. Inside were a small altar, scented candles and gifts for the gods.

'It is a little like the priest's tent within the tribe,' Chandra told me, standing again. 'The people of the tribe may only enter at the priest's word.'

'Is that where your records are kept?' I asked, moving along to my favourite display.

Chandra frowned. 'We keep no records. We have our songs, which the priest and elders teach the children, and our maps, no more. We do not carry what we do not need.'

Suddenly, I stopped. 'Then how do you learn to read?'

'We do not.'

I looked at her in astonishment. 'You can draw a map but you can't read?'

Chandra shrugged. 'Yes.'

I had noticed before that the nomads' maps used symbols and pictures instead of words, but I had not thought that it was because they could not read or write.

As though following my thoughts, Chandra said, 'What would be the point of drawing a map none of my people could understand?'

I nodded slowly and started walking again. 'We lost many of our early records in the fire. If the priests hadn't also had a temple a day's ride from here we would have lost all.'

Then I grinned, seeing what I sought before me. 'But something very precious did survive the fire, other than the sacred centre,' and I waved my hand at the display.

Chandra stepped closer to the cabinet, bending to peer at the tablets. Then she stood up and threw her head back, laughing gaily. 'Maps, Ashil,' she crowed with glee. 'They're little clay maps.'

'Yes,' I beamed, stepping forward. 'Aren't they wonderful? Some early Binenese cartographer drew rough sketches on clay to copy from later, but any skins she may have used burnt, while the clay baked in the fire.' I paused, a small, sad smile on my lips. 'They're the earliest maps we have. Who knows what other ones burnt in that fire?'

Chandra's sigh echoed mine.

That evening I took Chandra to see the Milam theatre troupe. They performed a short satire, which was cleverly amusing and made even more engaging for me as I watched Chandra scowl at the veiled jokes that set the rest of the audience howling with laughter. I would lean over and try to explain the context. But the politics and power struggles that were the subject of the piece are not easy to grasp at the best of times, and Chandra's basic knowledge was almost nil. Despite what I had told her of Binet and the League's history, Chandra could not understand why corruption and deceit would be tolerated. So with a sigh half of enchanted delight and half-exasperation, I was forced to give up.

The following day, as the nomads expressed their thanks and bade us goodbye, Chandra took me aside and pressed my hand in friendship.

'Farewell, Ashil,' she said calmly, 'until we next meet.'

I smiled, not questioning her certainty that we would meet again. The nomads' belief in the continual life of the spirit was known to me. If we did not see one another again in this lifetime, then we undoubtedly would in another. It was a vaguely disturbing thought.

'Farewell, Chandra. Take care.'

Her teeth glinted before me as she grinned broadly. 'I will take care and I will remember what you have shown me of Binet. And I will think too of your actors, your city nomads.'

'Not only actors, Chandra,' I told her, thinking of my own plans.

'No, I understand that,' she replied softly.

I watched her go with mixed feelings. She was an

exciting companion, invigorating and tirelessly curious, and my love of cartography was something I could share with few people my own age. Yet it meant I could return to work with full concentration and fewer interruptions, for there was still my apprenticeship to complete. 'Finally,' my father grunted as I sat myself before a set of freshly prepared skins and began work that had been neglected during Chandra's visit, but I knew that truly he was pleased with the friendship.

In fact, the words of Chandra's leavetaking were soon to be fulfilled, for we were to meet again before the end of my apprenticeship. I had been included in a mapping party doing preliminary sketches for a secluded area directly east of the city that was being considered as a training base. It took several days riding to reach it so we had prepared for the isolation and brought supplies to last the week. We were aware that this area was part of the wider country the nomads sometimes crossed. So, as we concluded our work on the second day, we were delighted when a lone nomad rode up to our camp to offer the hospitality of his tribe, Chandra's tribe. We accepted gratefully and were surprised by the extent of the welcome we received as we rode behind him into their circle of tents.

The entire tribe was there to meet us, overwhelming in their joy at seeing us. Our horses were led away and we were escorted as part of a noisy, unruly procession towards the centre of their camp, where huge cooking fires offered both warmth and light. Game roasted above the fires, sending delicious smells to us on each breath of wind.

Unconstrained by artifice, the nomads talked freely to us, warming us with their refreshingly open gazes and broad smiles. Chandra found me early in the evening and took me to sit with her, showing off her city friend. When the food was ready we were served first and, after our dull rations, my mouth watered at the smell and sight of the roast deer and the fleshy tubers and sweet berries.

After the meal a group of young nomads jumped up from the circle and began a brisk whirling dance around the fires, their only accompaniment a single drumbeat and the tribe's encouraging clapping. The fire-glow threw their shadows into a blurred imitation of their movements and I sat back on the animal furs given us as visitors and watched in delighted absorption. One of the young men pulled Chandra to her feet and led her around in the curving chain the dancers were forming, and as they came around again Chandra grabbed my hand and I fell into place behind her.

Finally, the chain slowly broke up, and gasping and laughing we collapsed onto the furs, the young man reluctantly relinquishing Chandra's hand. I watched him walk away and grinned in amusement. When Chandra noticed she wrinkled her nose with distaste.

'His name's Larr,' she told me, glancing over in his direction, then quickly away. 'He's one of our finest hunters.' She sighed, almost angrily, and looked at me. 'Once, we were great friends, but no longer. Now he wants a tent-mate.'

She stretched her long legs out before her, crossing

them casually at the ankles and leaning back on her hands. 'He's happy here so he can't understand why I refuse him.' She snorted. 'And neither can my family.'

Around us parents were starting to lead their young children away towards the tents and drinkskins were passed around. We filled our bowls and I sipped at mine gingerly. The nomads' beer was made from wild barley and had a bitterness and strength I was unaccustomed to, but it had an enticing smell and the meat and the dancing had left me thirsty.

I wanted to spend more time talking to Chandra and hear what else she had to say, but we were not given the opportunity. Kray called me over to where he and the others from Binet were discussing cartography and the training base site with the tribe's other mapdrawer. Chandra joined us and we talked maps until late in the evening. When finally we broke up, I was so tired my eyes were beginning to shut of their own accord. All I desired was sleep.

The following morning, Chandra joyfully shook me awake. 'I have good news for you,' she said.

Rousing myself with an effort, I glanced around the dim interior of the tent, taking a moment to remember where I was. I was in Chandra's tent, where I had spent the night sleeping, cosily wrapped in soft, thick furs. We were alone. As mapdrawer, Chandra was given her own tent.

I gave an enormous yawn and looked beyond Chandra, through the open flap of the tent. All I could see was the cold grey of the sky. I pulled the furs closer. It still looked like the middle of the night and I felt as though I had hardly slept at all.

'What time is it?' I asked groggily.

'Nearly dawn,' she replied impatiently. 'Get up. Today we present to the gods and the priest has said you and your companions may join us.'

'Present to the gods?' I echoed, not moving and wondering if this had something to do with Chandra being up so early.

'Yes, those children whose bodies began to change two seasons ago are now ready to be presented to the gods as adults. It is very exciting but you must hurry. We do not want to miss the song to the sun.'

'No, of course not,' I murmured and reached for my clothes.

The song to the sun was one of the most beautiful ceremonies I had ever witnessed. I had followed Chandra out of the tent and across to the eastern side of the camp where most of the nomads had already gathered, sitting in a rough half-circle around a clearing, facing out to the open plains. The day was still, there was only the slightest of breezes in the air, and I stared at the vastness of the land around me and the sombre dull sky with a growing feeling of excitement. Something was going to happen, I could feel it. My skin felt taut and I shivered suddenly, tiny chill-bumps skipping over my flesh.

I was not alone in my feelings. There was a sense of expectancy amongst the nomads and when they spoke to each other it was in hushed tones. As I walked behind Chandra, I saw my companions dotted amongst the tribespeople and waved to them. Kray was sitting talking amongst the elders but he nodded in acknowledgement as I passed, and I wondered how much work we would do today.

Dawn was not far away now. Already the restless twitterings of birds could be heard amongst the long wild grasses, preparing to fill the air with their own dawn song at the first sight of colour in the sky.

Chandra steered her way through the crowd, stepping nimbly over outstretched limbs until she reached the front. It was already crowded here, but when the nomads saw that I was with her they happily made room. We sat down and I looked around. At the edge of the clearing, to the left, a large tent had been erected. Unlike the plain skin of the camp tents, this one had been dyed a warm ochre and decorated with the figures of mortals and beasts and a number of symbols I did not recognise. Nowhere could I see the children who were to be presented today.

'They are inside the priest's tent,' Chandra said, aware of what I was thinking. Suddenly, she grasped my hand and squeezed it tightly. 'Look, here comes Lelarni.'

The priest stepped out of the tent. He was a tall man, surprisingly young, with a graceful, erect bearing. He wore a long loosely woven skirt, of the same ochre as the tent, that reached to mid-calf. The rest of his body was bare. Bare that was, except for the startling array of necklaces, wristbands, anklets and earrings made from bones, teeth, claws, grasses, dried seeds, strips of leather and what looked like hair. As Lelarni walked towards the centre of the clearing, his jewellery swung and danced with each step. I watched enthralled. There

26

must have been more than ten necklaces alone lying against his chest and I felt certain that each was more than just whimsical decoration.

'See the hair around the fingers of his left hand,' Chandra said.

I looked at his hand and saw the thin black strands of hair that formed slim rings, almost indistinguishable against his dark skin. I nodded.

'The hair is from each of those who are to be presented today. We believe that some of a person's spirit, both the good and bad, exists in each strand. The priest will raise his hand to show the gods. If the gods do not reply in anger by burning away the hair, the priest will call the youths from the tent and the ceremony will begin.'

'What happens if the hair is burnt away?' I whispered, as Lelarni turned to face the east, his back now to us.

Chandra frowned. 'It is an ill sign. The youth has angered the gods in some way and they refuse to accept her. She must go through many rites of cleansing and hope that the gods will accept her after the next cycle.'

'Have you ever seen it happen?'

Lelarni had begun to sing softly as the first ray of light spread out in the east, his voice a low accompaniment to the shrill ecstasy of the birds.

'Yes, once,' Chandra replied, her voice a low murmur. 'The girl was strange. She had few friends because she was cruel and unfeeling, and once she had been found trying to start fires on the plains. The elders were angry and upset and wondered if she should be presented. Finally, they decided to let the judgment lie with the gods.'

Chandra scowled. 'I can still remember the smell of the burning hair and the way she laughed when the priest showed her his hand.' She shook her head sadly. 'I think her mind was not whole. Not long after, she drowned herself in the river. We prayed she would find more peace when next she returned and that no more of the tribe would be found unworthy.'

The voice of Lelarni had risen and we fell silent, listening. The words were unfamiliar to me. The nomads speak the Middling Tongue, the common language of Tirayi above the Burrnayi Desert, though their accent is strange to me. But they also have their own language, used in ritual, as Chandra had explained. It is a series of low, haunting sounds, long and melodic, that to a stranger were impossible to understand. Yet the feeling behind the words was clear enough. Lelarni was singing a paean to the sun, both hands outstretched in welcome and homage. My eyes were drawn by the dark strands around his left fingers. Chandra's tale, so simply stated, so horrific, had shaken my earlier scepticism and I watched every move the priest made until his brief song was over.

It stopped abruptly and the priest spun around and held his hands out to the nomads, showing them the untouched hairs. A ripple of delight and relief washed over the tribespeople and excitement built as Lelarni turned towards the tent and pulled back the flap.

The sun was just creeping over the horizon so the four youths, or, to my mind, children, walked out slowly into half-light, their heads bowed, looking neither left nor right. They were dressed in long un-adorned cloaks that covered them from neck to foot and their heads, hands and feet were bare. They lined up facing the crowd, trying hard to retain their solemn expressions, but I saw at least one bite back a smile as he saw someone he knew and I supposed the hardest part was behind them now, they knew the gods had accepted them.

The priest walked to the first youth and laid a hand on her shoulder. As she stepped forward before the crowd Lelarni spoke her name and she bowed to the elders and her tribespeople before turning to face the east. This was repeated for the two other girls and a boy, until all four were facing east. Then at a sound from Lelarni, they dropped their cloaks and everyone gasped.

Under the cloaks were simple robes, entirely covered with tiny pieces of polished, shimmering shell that shone and dazzled in the brightening light. It was a stunning sight, turning the youths into glittering, breathing, dancing, iridescent flames that blinded the eye.

Lelarni began to sing once again, and this time the youths joined him, swaying gently with the rhythm of the song, the joy in their voices plain to hear. Lelarni swept his arms up and as one the tribespeople rose to their feet and added their own powerful voices to the song. It was a roar of pleasure that celebrated living and it was a soft croon that spoke of their reverence for the gods. It was a fast, racing song of the hunt that caused feet to stamp and hands to clap and it was a calm tale of wandering, year after year. It was the story

29

of their lives, life and death, the great cycle that the gods control, and they sang to them all.

I stood beside Chandra, aware of her voice raised joyously beside me, and I felt the meaning behind their words. I had become a part of the tribe for that short time and it moved me more than anything I had ever experienced.

When the song ended, the four youths were led back to the tent. Until all the gods had been honoured they were neither child nor adult and so could not yet return to the tribe. Chandra smiled at me and we moved to where others had already begun to prepare a morning meal. The food smelt delicious and I realised I was hungrier than I had been at this hour for a very long time.

We ate in near silence, busy concentrating on the food, and when I was finally satisfied I put aside my empty bowl and asked Chandra what came next. I was already looking forward to whatever else the day held.

'We offer to the god of death.' She tore a piece of the flat, rough bread and used it to scoop up another mouthful of the thick soup from her bowl. She had not noticed the expression on my face.

I swallowed and asked casually, 'How?'

Chandra looked at me and grinned suddenly. 'We kill one of our cows and burn a part of it for the god. The rest we will eat tonight. What did you think?'

I gave a small, embarrassed laugh. 'I'm not sure.'

After the meal, the youths were brought once more from the tent and a docile, plump cow was led forward. It died simply and quickly, though I dropped my eyes from the sight of the blood spurting from its throat. It was the first time I had seen an animal die in such a way and I was not sure I could trust my stomach.

A solemn, dour chant was sung by the tribe as they sat watching the priest cut away four portions of flesh and hand them to the youths. The chant rose, an eerie sound so early in the day, and the four stepped up to a large fire that burnt now in the middle of the camp and offered the flesh to the flames. As the smell of roasting meat wafted through the air Lelarni raised his arms and the chant ceased. He spoke briefly, his voice rich and compelling, and when he fell silent the tribe rose to its feet and watched as he and the four left the fire and turned towards the river. When the last of the youths had passed the tribe, the nomads began slowly to follow. I glanced over my shoulder at the carcass of the cow, already being skinned and gutted for dinner that night, and then I too turned and walked towards the river.

We waded together in tribute to the god of water. The water was icy and the flesh on my legs turned blue, but I did not consider staying on the banks. I had become a part of this ceremony and I would see it through.

Next, to honour the god of the earth, the nomad drummers began pounding out a slow, throbbing beat on their waist-high instruments. The tribe encircled the drummers, stamping their feet to the beat in clever patterns and clapping their hands, some closing their eyes as their bodies bobbed and pulsed to the strong rhythm. As the beat of the drums quickened I did my best to copy the intricate steps Chandra made, feeling my blood pound in my veins until, laughing, I fell to the ground exhausted, happy that I could sit and quietly watch the honouring of the next god while my breathing slowly returned to normal.

It was a silent play that followed, dedicated to the god of the air. The actors wore bird feathers and elaborate headdresses. They moved imaginary wings and soared through the heavens until they spotted prey and dived mercilessly upon it, resting to preen their wings after the kill. Smaller birds skipped and flitted across the ground, searching for worms and seeds, their movements quick and jerky, always alert and ready for flight.

Lelarni spoke before each god was honoured, and often the nomads sang or spoke replies. Even the very young knew most of the words. It dazzled me a little to see such enthusiasm and belief amongst so many.

When the play had ended we paused to eat once more. The youths gave specially prepared feed to the tribe's animals in praise and thanks to the god of beasts, who was also the god of the hunt, and then returned to the tent for their own meal. There was an unmistakable buzz of excitement amongst the nomads now and much laughter and joking.

'What gods are left?' I asked Chandra, smiling in query.

'Only one, the god of life.' Chandra was excited too, I noted. She looked at me, her eyes bright. 'You will enjoy this, Ashil.'

The trouble with pale skin like mine is that even the faintest suggestion of colour will show in it, and hiding a blush is all but impossible. So, while the god of life was honoured, I sat watching, sitting painfully still, aware that my cheeks were burning red for all to see.

It had begun simply enough with a parade of little children, skipping around a small group of pregnant women before the priest's tent. There had been a happy song and a merry dance, with women and men pairing off. Then the four youths had stepped into the centre of the clearing, naked.

They stood tall and proud, exhibiting proof of their adulthood, and then a single drumbeat commenced and they began to dance. At first it was a slow, lazy series of turns and spins, as they wound gently around one another, their skin just brushing. Then as the drumbeat became faster, so too did their movements, until they were running and jumping and whirling crazily. Their faces reflected the joy they were feeling, their eyes shining, their lips curved in wide, ecstatic smiles. The drummer stopped and they fell to the ground, their chests rising and falling rapidly.

Lelarni carried a bowl to each of the girls and they drank from it. Whatever was in the bowl was not offered to the boy. While the youths remained seated on the ground, Lelarni spoke again. This time Chandra whispered the meaning of the words in my ear.

'He is saying that now they are adults before the gods, the gift of life passes to them. It is one of the greatest gifts ever given to mortals by the gods and one that can bring great pleasure and joy. It unites woman and man and fills the tribe with children.'

Lelarni paused and Chandra fell silent beside me. I

was aware of the feelings of anticipation and eagerness that emanated from the tribespeople seated around me, though I was at a loss to understand it. I glanced at the faces near me, but all eyes were on the priest and the youths. Obviously something was soon to happen. Puzzled, I watched Lelarni as he looked down at the four at his feet and smiled. He lifted his hand to indicate they should rise and they turned to face the crowd, their faces filled with nervous excitement. Lelarni said one short, sharp word and the youths stepped forward as though suddenly released from a restraint, searching the faces amongst the crowd.

'What did he say?' I asked Chandra quickly, as one of the girls passed close by.

'He told them to choose now. They each seek a partner.'

'A partner?' I queried.

'Yes, for the joining.' She watched as the girl found who she was seeking and held out her hand to a young man. An expression of delight shone from his face as he accepted her hand and walked with her back into the clearing.

Chandra was smiling softly. 'It is a great honour to be chosen,' she said to me.

Suspicion grew in my mind but I told myself there must be another meaning to Chandra's words. The four had all returned to the clearing with their partners, who quickly removed their clothing, and once again the solitary drumbeat began. They began to dance and my skin began to burn.

Skin brushed against skin, feather-soft and blood-warm. Young, supple muscles rippled and tensed under

34

firm flesh. They barely touched as they danced around and around, their heads thrown back, their long dark throats exposed, their strong white teeth flashing with the escalating thrill and passion. The beat quickened and the dancers joined hands, spinning around their partners, their eyes dark with excitement, the air around them pulsing with purpose.

The tribe was humming a rich accompaniment to the beat and the sound seemed to rise and swirl around us. Suddenly over the powerful pounding of the drum there came also the sweet trilling of a pipe and the dancers were in each other's arms, writhing as their sweat-slickened bodies touched and they continued to move to the beat. I swallowed hastily as their arms reached around each other, pulling themselves closer into the swaying embrace, their feet rising and moving, their chests pressed together, legs braced slightly apart.

It ended suddenly and there was silence. The dancers stopped, still curled in each other's arms, their breathing the only sound in the clearing. The tribe stood and silently spread out on both sides of the ochre tent to form a wide passageway. With Lelarni at their head, the four youths, their arms entwined with their chosen partner, walked along the passage towards the tent entrance. The priest held the flap open and one by one the couples disappeared inside.

TWO

'LET'S RIDE. I can show you some of the plains,' Chandra suggested.

The tent flap had fallen into place and the nomads were beginning to disperse. Many, I noticed, with the mood of the dance still upon them, walked arm in arm towards their own tents. My cheeks still pink, I thought Chandra's idea an excellent one and agreed quickly.

Cleo was glad for a run and kept pace easily with Chandra's horse, Ray, as we cantered out of camp. Once free of the tents, we kicked them into a gallop and rode out into the long grass, our hair flying with the motion, our mouths open with delight.

It was mid-afternoon and we rode north-east, roughly following the route of the river. It was the first month of autumn and the water level was still low, but the bed was wide and, come winter, the river would swell to more than twice its present size.

Trees and shrubs grew along the banks, the dusty green of their leaves the only point of colour in the otherwise golden landscape. We led the horses down to the water and dismounted to let them drink, flopping down on the coarse stumpy weeds that grew at the water's edge.

The sound of the running water was soothing and as we sat there I became aware of the voices of insects and birds that had made their home nearby. Near us, two small birds dropped to the ground and began searching the moist soil for a meal. Their quick, sharp movements reminded me of the play I had watched that morning and from there other thoughts began to fill my mind.

'Chandra,' I said, recalling something that had puzzled me. 'What was in the bowl Lelarni gave to the three girls?'

Chandra had been watching Cleo and Ray, who were now tearing at the tough grass with their teeth. She looked around at my question.

'It is a special drink,' she explained, 'so they will not bear a child from their time in the tent. All women of the tribe may drink it, although it is rare to do so once you have a tent-mate. The girls would have been first given it mid-summer.'

I was silent a moment, pondering what she had said. How different her life was to mine! 'Do you drink it?' I asked tentatively.

'Yes,' she replied, 'much to my family's and Larr's disgust.' She saw my frown and smiled as she elaborated. 'I chose Larr for my joining. You can choose any adult in the tribe who does not have a tent-mate. After that first joining in the priest's tent it is usual to have several lovers before one chooses a tent-mate, and then the woman puts away the bowl. I was presented to the gods four full cycles ago. Many women wait only two before they take a mate, and now my tribe grows impatient with me.'

I thought I understood but I asked anyway, to be sure. 'If it's not Larr, is there another you want?'

'No, no other,' Chandra answered, shaking her head, and I heard her sigh. She glanced upstream and I followed her gaze. 'Do you know where the river begins, Ashil? I have often wondered.'

I thought about it for a moment, calling to mind my father's maps. 'In the mountains behind Sach,' I answered. 'It's the River Sa. It flows to the sea.'

Chandra nodded and smiled bitterly, turning to me. 'I did not know. Our maps are of the plains, of the tribal routes. Our excursion to Binet was most unusual and only happened because there was such need, now that the war threatens the eastern tip of the plains, but we were not even sure we would find the city. We only heard of Binet by chance, from a group escaping from Telish who were passing through the plains. They told us Binet is famous for its mapdrawers and they offered directions. Without their help we would never have known of such a city.'

I did not know what to say, so I said nothing and Chandra gave a short laugh. 'You are wise to stay silent for there are no words that would console me. Soon, the tribe will cross the river and move southward in preparation for winter, and I must make my decision. You see, Ashil, I do not want to stay with the tribe and find the tracks within the same borders season after season, but when I say this my family and elders look confused and hurt. They think it is them I am trying to leave.' She shook her head. 'I cannot make them see that this world is so large and my tribe so little. For them the tribe is all.'

I could sympathise with Chandra's pain. She loved her family and her people but it was no longer enough. I watched the river flow past, carrying leaves from the overhanging trees.

'Where do you want to go?' I asked.

Chandra answered without hesitation. 'Everywhere.'

I nodded, turning back to stare at the river. It was the same with me.

The feast that night was lively and merry and the four new adults, having the places of honour, shone with happiness and importance. While we sat around the fires, eating the celebratory dishes and watching the dancers perform energetic jumps and leaps, I shared with Chandra my plans of travelling and working. She listened avidly.

'When will you leave Binet?' she asked, too interested in our discussion to notice Larr join the dancers.

'I finish my apprenticeship in less than a year, so I hope to leave shortly after that.'

She mulled this over, ignoring the amazing flips and twirls Larr was performing with an eye in our direction.

'If you decide to leave the tribe, you could join me and we could work together.'

Chandra grinned. 'I would like that, Ashil.' She sobered. 'I have decided I must leave. I have known it now for a long time.' She shook her head. 'But now I can say it to myself I must do it quickly. I cannot wait several seasons until you finish your apprenticeship.'

'Fine,' I replied, feeling excitement welling up inside. 'Come to Binet now and work for my father. We're busy now with several projects and I know he would love to have you work with us. You could learn a lot, too.'

I could see almost every tooth, all of them perfect, in Chandra's mouth as she smiled in delight. 'What a wonderful idea!' she exclaimed. 'I will do it.'

When I made that casual remark to Chandra about her learning much, I had not realised how true my words would prove to be. In fact Chandra not only had to adapt to a totally new style of cartography in Binet, but she had to learn to read and write.

Although Chandra knew all about finding a path and drawing it up on the skins, she lacked the finesse to present the type of maps demanded in cities. The technique and equipment I used were different from those she was accustomed to, but were at least understandable to her. So she quickly grasped our sketching routine, taking a blank mapping sheet and, using her symbols where I used words, filling it with measurements, selected scale, directions, notes and sketches of the land's features.

However, it was the symbols she relied on that ultimately failed her, for after the sketching came the drawing of the map and the labelling of most, if not all, of its prominent features. Not knowing how to read or write, Chandra was unable to do this. She listened while I gently explained this, then, without any fuss, set about learning. She was voracious. I taught her late each afternoon when our work at the army base was completed and her eagerness and natural intelligence made her a brilliant student. Her success was also aided by the fact that she regarded anyone else in sight as a potential tutor when I was not around.

Not only maps and letters consumed her. All subjects left her wanting to know more and my father, who had thought me full of questions, was sometimes left speechless by Chandra and her turn of mind. She let nothing pass and he and the others at the base soon learnt to speak carefully around her.

Another nine months passed in this fashion, by which time my apprenticeship was completed and Chandra was able to read and write with a startling fluency. Even her speech had changed slightly as she learnt different ways of combining and using words she already knew. She had also mastered all aspects of map presentation, the labelling, edging, illustrating, colouring and so forth, though she would always refer to it as 'prettying' the maps. There was now only one thing to prevent us from leaving. My family. I feared nothing more than hurting them with my plans. Chandra's painful leavetaking was something she had briefly mentioned and I spent long hours pondering how to deliver what I feared would be equally painful news, but it was all for naught. In the end it was my father who relieved me of the dreaded task.

I had come into the workroom after completing some final details on a particularly difficult map, my head full of the praise the officer in command had heaped on me. My father was at the storage racks, collecting several maps, and he looked over as I entered and called to me. I followed him into his workroom and sat in the seat he indicated. I was keen to repeat the compliments I had been given, but I sat quietly, knowing he would ask me how the work had gone.

He did not sit down but leant back against his workbench, toying with a stylus.

'How was this morning?' he asked as expected, and I launched into my report. He idly twirled the stylus from finger to finger while I spoke, not stopping until I had finished, when he nodded and laid the stylus down on the bench.

'You deserve the praise, Ashil. You've been working hard and it shows in your maps.'

I flushed with pleasure. He was not a hard man to work for, but nor was he lavish with his praise.

'Now your apprenticeship is over it's time you started thinking about your career. You won't want to spend your entire life working in Binet.' He smiled ruefully at me and sat down. 'And the Ruler knows, neither will Chandra.'

I grinned back at him, relief and excitement churning within me. It was finally beginning to happen. I had to force myself to stay seated, so great was my rapture.

He picked up the stylus again, his elbows on his workbench, and resumed twirling. 'Cartography by its very nature invites travel. It is one of its greatest attractions and cartographers trained in Binet are recognised as some of the finest in Tirayi.'

Such wonderful words! I had one leg crossed over the other and I leant forward and hugged my raised knee, my delight thrumming through me.

'That, and the fact cartography is properly taught in only a few cities, means that those with the skills and the inclination can move from job to job, city to city, making a good living while seeing the world at the same time.'

His face, so familiar, so loved, held a certain wistfulness as he spoke. 'When I was your age I was already married. Your mother had her work here and I had joined the army. That made the possibility of such a lifestyle impossible. It is my one regret.' His expression lightened, his blue eyes warm as he gazed at me. 'But there are no such restrictions on you. So go and see the world. Then come back to this old man and tell him all about it.'

Unable to contain my excitement any longer, I jumped up to hug him. 'I will, I promise.'

'Good.' He laughed at my enthusiasm, holding me close to him for a moment. 'What have you and Chandra planned?'

'Nothing specific,' I admitted.

He nodded thoughtfully. 'The two of you make a good team. You are a particularly skilled drawer and Chandra sketches well and fast, but most jobs will require at least three people.' He cocked one pale eyebrow as he looked at me. 'I suggest you look for another partner, one who can both sketch and draw and who seeks adventure as you two do.'

We were interrupted then by a knock on the door. A young soldier entered the room, saluted and told my father that the captain wished to see him. My father nodded and, waving her forward, he began piling her arms with maps from his workbench. When both he and the soldier had their arms full, he turned back to me.

'Think about what I have said, Ashil,' he counselled softly. Then he and the soldier left the room, leaving me alone.

'Think about what I have said, Ashil,' my father had told me, and in truth I thought of little else for many days. Chandra complimented me on having had the good sense to be born to a marvellous father and then set to working out the numerous tasks to be completed before we could actually leave Binet.

We organised ourselves with the speed of those eager to be away and then fortune came knocking at our door. The hardest aspect of all our planning had been finding another cartographer. We were fussy. We wanted someone near to our own age who was interested in travelling, would work well with us and, most importantly, was a good drawer. Chandra and I could sketch an area quickly and competently, but despite a healthy confidence in our own abilities we knew we needed another for the precision drawing required for several maps.

It was the end of the school year and again my father was having to turn away students in search of employment. Mostly they were without any recognisable talent and my father had enough recruits from the army to fill any need he had for untrained workers. Yet occasionally he would see one he thought had potential and give the youth a chance over a short period. He was pleased to have discovered one such lad, a young brash boy with a stunning cap of red hair, whose progress had been excellent, so when another came looking for work my father had no choice but to say he had no vacancies. However, Chandra and I did.

Her name was Lilith. She was very young, fresh from school and painfully shy, but her work was superb. The drawings she had produced from her small amount of study were so skilled that my father looked more closely at his new boy's work and frowned at what he discovered in the comparison. But Lilith was ours. Chandra and I drew her aside into a corner of the workroom and sat her down, trying to contain our excitement at our providential find.

'Lilith,' I began, 'Chandra and I are planning on seeking work outside of the city and we need another cartographer.' I outlined our ambitions, turning to Chandra for her bold words, trying so hard to convey our eagerness, our desire to succeed and what it could mean for all three of us.

Lilith sat quietly, listening courteously to all we said, her slender hands folded neatly in her lap, her doe-brown eyes fixed on our faces. When Chandra and I had finally run out of breath she smiled. 'Is there a job arranged?' she asked in a gentle, expectant tone.

We admitted there was not. 'We cannot apply for work until we have a third person,' I explained.

'Yes,' she concurred softly. Wisps of her white blonde hair, loose from her simple braid, stirred around her cheeks as she nodded. 'Have you worked outside of Binet and the tribe?' she asked.

Again, we admitted we had not and I began to fear we were losing her. She lowered her eyes and toyed with her fingers. She finally said, 'I have been offered a job with the library, copying old works.'

'No,' I gasped. 'You can't do that. It would be such a waste.'

She surprised me by laughing at my horrified expression, a rich little chuckle. But it was a quick flash of humour, soon gone, and her young face became once more grave and subdued.

'A waste?' she queried.

'Yes, you're too talented a drawer. Why choose a small, stale library when you can travel across the world?'

This pale, delicate creature would be forgotten in such a place, left alone in some small corner, month after month, year after year, stunted, like a babe denied nourishment. It would be an atrocity.

'It would not be that bad,' she protested. Her voice was low, totally lacking in conviction, and she would not meet my eye.

Chandra snorted in disgust. 'You could never say that of what we are offering, so why consider the other?'

'Because it is a secure position,' Lilith answered in little more than a whisper.

'Utt!' Chandra dismissed that argument with a sharp grunt and a corresponding wave of her hand. 'Once we are known our work will be in great demand. You will have security.'

Even I smiled at Chandra's lopsided logic, but then she could not understand poverty. For her, there was always an open sky to sleep under and food to be found on the plains. Even to Binet she had brought her bow and quiver. Life was adventure, to be embraced with both arms. But I was grateful for her words, for their short exchange had revealed something to me.

'Lilith,' I said, 'we may have failed to mention earlier that Chandra and I are prepared to pay the third cartographer out of our own earnings until we find work out of the city.' I glanced warily at Chandra, having just committed her coin without her prior approval, but she was looking at Lilith, nodding at my words. 'Though, of course,' I added brightly, 'I agree with Chandra when she says our maps will be in great demand, and the sooner we get started the sooner it will happen.'

Lilith was regarding me with astonishment, then she smiled a little. 'Thank you,' she murmured.

Delighted that I had discovered the reason for her reluctance, I smiled back. 'Does that mean you'll join us?' Totally unaware of what her living arrangements might be, but wanting to tip the balance in our favour as much as possible, I told her she could stay with us until we left Binet. Chandra was already a house guest, but I knew my parents would understand what had prompted me to extend such an invitation.

She shook her head. 'Thank you, but there is no need.' She looked at us both, first Chandra, then at me, took a deep breath and then spoke in her gentle way. 'And yes, it does mean I will join you. I will be your third cartographer.'

The three of us anxiously sought employment in neighbouring cities and the surrounding countryside, but we were unknown and inexperienced and nothing had been offered. We continued with my father and the army, but minds lost in dreams of other places do not do the best work. We used the time to get to know Lilith and I was gratified to discover she was as quick to learn as Chandra had been, if not as insatiable.

My father had been following our planning from a discreet distance, and I sensed that he was almost as excited as we were. When a month had passed he asked if we had had any luck and I was forced to admit that we had not. He grunted but made no comment.

To aid us in our search for work he would occasionally free us from the workroom for the afternoon. On one such occasion I had arranged to meet Lilith at her home to discuss some equipment we needed to buy. I knew now that she lived with her parents, her only living relatives, but I had never met them. As I climbed the stairs of the old building where they lived my mind was full of our plans, not the imminent meeting.

An old man answered the door. I introduced myself and asked to see Lilith. With a shy smile, he pulled the door open and I saw that the skin on his hands and arms was deeply stained. He politely invited me in.

'Lilith has gone to the bakehouse,' he said almost bashfully. 'Would you like to wait for her?'

'Yes, thank you,' I replied. Then realisation dawned on me that this man, this old man, must be Lilith's father.

He led me to their small salon, where his wife sat with an embroidery frame in one hand and a threaded needle in the other. He introduced us and I sat down with them, amongst a pile of delicately embroidered cushions. Smiling like a fool at this little grey-haired couple, I said, for want of a better topic, 'These cushions are lovely, did you do them?'

Lilith's mother smiled and nodded, then offered me wine and fresh fruit pieces.

I looked around at the room, searching for inspiration, but all I saw were a couple of worn but still attractive rugs on the floor, some simple furnishings and, arranged by their window, rows of clay pots containing green plants and brightly petalled flowers.

'Is it difficult to grow plants inside?' I asked, hoping it was not Lilith who tended them.

'No,' her mother replied, gazing fondly at the window arrangement, 'not if you are careful with watering.' Then she fell silent once more.

It was apparent that Lilith had inherited her shyness so I gave up any attempt at conversation with her parents. Instead I ate their fruit and smiled at them and looked out the window onto the street below, watching people enter the cloth shop on the ground floor.

Shortly after, I spotted Lilith coming up the street carrying a loaf of bread. When she came into the room her parents promptly excused themselves and left us alone to talk.

'I'm sorry I wasn't here to meet you, Ashil,' Lilith said, pouring some wine and settling herself on the couch her parents had recently vacated. She shrugged apologetically. 'It's Papa's mealbreak and we had no bread left.'

'That's all right. I haven't been here long.'

Satisfied with that, Lilith asked, 'Do you have the list of materials we need to buy?'

'Yes,' I replied, just as a soft knock sounded at the salon door. A moment later Lilith's father entered with a tray containing slices of the fresh loaf and some soft cheese. He smiled at me as he put the tray on a table before us, then left without saying a word.

I watched the door shut, then surprised both Lilith and myself by asking suddenly what her parents thought about her working away from Binet.

She almost dropped her wine goblet and her face paled, 'Why?' she gasped in a breathless whisper. 'Have they said something to you?'

'No,' I reassured her, alarmed by such a drastic reaction. 'I was just curious. It's really none of my business.' Not wishing to upset her further, I pulled out the writing tablet to pass to her. 'Here, take a look and see if you think we need to make any changes.'

She put the goblet down and took the tablet from my hand, but she did not try to read it. Instead she lowered her hand to her lap, still grasping the tablet. She gnawed on her bottom lip, avoiding my eye, and I cursed myself for a fool for ever having raised the topic.

'They said they understand and that they do not want to stand in my way,' she told me finally. Her voice was small and tight.

'That's good,' I mumbled inadequately.

Lilith smiled unhappily. 'I'm everything to them, Ashil. I'm all they have.'

She glanced away and sighed, then turned back to me. 'Did you notice my father's hands?'

'Yes.' I saw no reason to lie. 'It looked like dye.'

She nodded. 'It is,' she said softly. 'He works as a dyer downstairs in the cloth shop, where he has worked all his life. My mother is an embroiderer. She is employed by a garment-maker but she works from home. They rarely leave the building.'

The hand holding the tablet was slowly kneading the edge of the soft wax coating on the tablet's upper side, but Lilith was unaware of what she was doing.

'I would come home from school and they would want to hear all about my day and the other students. Now I'm working it is the same. Through me they hear what is happening in Binet. Without me,' she paused and swallowed and now her voice was little more than a whisper, 'without me, I don't know what they will do.'

'Oh, Lil,' I said, wishing there was some way I could make it easy for her. 'They would want you to do what makes you happy.'

'I know, but it's so hard, Ashil. Part of me says I should stay and comfort them, while another part demands that I have my chance while I'm young and before the fear that I see in them begins to rule my life.'

I leant across and took her hand. 'I'm sure that is what they truly want too. They're proud of you, you have their blessing and their love.'

'Yes,' she nodded, wretched in her misery. Slowly she began to smooth out the wax, pressing the edge smooth with her thumb, careful not to erase the words I had written in the middle of the tablet. She stopped and raised her eyes to me and they were full of pain. 'I want to go so badly, Ashil,' she told me hoarsely, 'just like you and Chandra, but I hope we get work soon, for if they were ever to ask me to stay I don't know that I'd be strong enough to tell them no.'

It was soon after this that my father called all three of us into his workroom and introduced us to a Skar Linon. He was a short, stocky man with longish blond hair and a jolly expression on his pleasant face who had come to ask my father's advice on a set of maps he wanted drawn of his land. Skar owned a vast area to the west of Binet which was divided into farm holdings, hunting grounds and his own castle and its land. Having seen some of the work my father and his people had done for the army he wanted to hire him to do the job. His face fell when my father told him he was not permitted to take private commissions.

'This of course does not apply to any of my people who are not in the army.'

Skar's face lit up. 'Will you recommend someone, and let them come to work for me?'

My father did not reply. Instead he turned to me. 'Ashil, bring me the maps of the new army training base.'

I rose quickly and left the room to find them. Of course I knew exactly the maps my father wanted as Chandra and I had worked on them together. I returned and handed the skins to my father, who unrolled them before Skar.

'These were done by two of my best cartographers. One map shows the base site on a large scale, the other

52

shows it in relation to Binet and the Rivers Sa and Linden.'

Skar looked at them eagerly, nodding with satisfaction. 'They are very good.' He glanced up at my father. 'And would these cartographers be free to work for me?'

My father smiled at Skar. 'Yes, I think we can probably arrange something.'

Skar Linon grinned with pleasure.

And so it was that we got our first job.

THREE

WE WERE ANXIOUS to impress so we worked like fiends on that first assignment. Skar was a friendly hovering presence in the background, always eager to help in any way he could, seemingly fascinated with the slowly enlarging web of lines on the skins that represented his holdings. We were still new to so much, and at times too eager or too careless, so it took months to complete his maps. But he did not care. He knew little of cartography and happily accepted us as part of the small retinue of his castle. We often dined with him and his family and those of his friends and tenants he had selected to make up a party. Although only a minor land baron, his castle was never still, buzzing with activity and geniality.

Even when we had finished and had presented the maps to a beaming Skar, he insisted that we stay on for his upcoming name-day celebrations. Skar's generosity and good nature ensured a large crowd, with people arriving from as far away as Eustape, an island to the south. His friends were warm and eager to enjoy themselves. They hugged and slapped Skar on the back, wishing him well, and their talk ranged from family life to politics and farming. This was the ideal opportunity for Skar to show off his new maps and he exhibited them proudly, pointing out the skill of our work with great confidence. His fellow landowners were suitably impressed and before the end of the celebrations we had our next two positions all arranged. Everyone agreed it was a fabulous event.

From that time on we never looked back. Our work for Skar's friends took us even further west, and when those maps were completed we had a further two positions in the offing. Needing a base where we could be contacted, and wanting to satisfy our curiosity, we chose Delawyn, the largest city on the west coast. With coin to spend and the promise of the foreign and stimulating ahead of us, we felt jubilant.

It was late afternoon when we rode into the city through its ornate south-east gates. The wide paved boulevard before us was tree-lined and edged with beautiful houses, elaborate temples, and neat, prosperous-looking shops. And the boulevard was thick with people.

'It's like Binet on a festival day,' I commented as we walked forward dazedly and as yet another person bumped against my leg, forcing my heel into Cleo's side.

'It's like a swarming ant hill,' Lilith said, looking about warily and stroking Timi's neck to calm him.

Lilith was right. The Delawese did resemble a colony of ants, all bustling business as they marched along with their heads down, paying little heed to anyone else about them, though I did notice one or two give us and our horses strange looks and clear wide paths around us.

'Why do they walk so fast?' Chandra asked, puzzled. 'They move as though they are all running late.'

Just then a loud, brusque voice, impatiently ordering people to move, caught our attention, and two Delawese soldiers strode angrily towards us.

'Good afternoon,' I said cautiously, wondering how and why their anger could be directed at us.

'Show me a cuff or a pass that permits you to be riding in the city during daylight hours,' the soldier who had barked at the crowd demanded.

I glanced hesitantly at Chandra and Lilith, then turned back to the soldier. 'I'm sorry, but we are visitors here and are not familiar with any laws concerning riding.'

'Dismount!' he snapped.

We slipped from our horses' backs.

'By order of the Circle House, in consideration of the inhabitants of this city, no vehicle or animal of transport may use the streets of Delawyn between sunrise and sunset. The exceptions are the vehicles and animals of the Fifty and those people issued passes from the House to conduct essential business.'

'No wagons or horses?' I cried in surprise. 'What do the traders and merchants do?'

'They work at night,' the other soldier answered, using a milder tone than his friend. 'The city streets become busy with such traffic in the hours before dawn.'

It seemed a hard lot, but I said no more. It was not for me to protest against the laws of a foreign city. Their ways were not mine, though I knew this did not make either of us wrong.

'What do we do with our horses?' Chandra asked. 'We wish to stay in Delawyn and see the city.'

'You may leave now and return with them this evening and stable them at your hostel for the remainder of your stay,' the more amiable of the soldiers replied. 'Or you can leave them at the travellers' stable outside the city. It is run by one of the Fifty and your horses will be well tended and safe there. The fee is quite small.'

'We can't continue to the nearest hostel now?' I asked, hopefully. 'There must be one very close by.'

'No,' the snarly one bit out. 'You must go back through the gates and wait until sunset.'

I sighed. 'I see. Very well, we'll go now.'

'The travellers' stable is two leagues to the south as you leave the gates. You will find it faster to re-enter the city through the southern gates,' said the other soldier. 'Special passenger wagons owned by members of the Fifty run across the city four times a day. You can use those to move about Delawyn while visiting.'

'Thank you,' I muttered, feeling anything but grateful, and we turned and led our horses through the melee, knowing that the soldiers watched us until we passed out through the gates.

'Are we going to use the travellers' stable?' Lilith asked, as we mounted.

'Let's have a look at it first,' I said, kicking Cleo into a trot and heading southward. 'After all,' I added dryly, 'we have several hours to fill before sunset.'

The travellers' stable was situated behind a high wooden wall, with an open paddock attached, filled with dozens of horses. The grazing was low and the wood of the stable building was old and weakening in places. As we rode up, we saw a groom distributing meagre feed.

A middle-aged woman greeted us as we dismounted. Like those around her, she wore working clothes of a dull, practical brown, except for the small grey cuff on her left sleeve. The contrast was very odd. She had small features and a pinched look to her face and quickly told us what the fee bought, reciting the details in a bored voice, like a daily litany. When she mentioned the figure, I almost choked. It was exorbitant.

'So, do you want to leave your horses here or no?' the woman asked impatiently, only moments after finishing her recitation. 'It be cheaper than stabling them anywhere in the city.'

I raised my eyebrows at the other two and they nodded. We were not happy with the arrangement but it appeared the best we could do. We let two grooms lead our horses away and then the woman demanded we pay half the fee at once. She must have seen my incredulous look. After all, we were hardly going to run off and leave our horses.

'For their feed,' she told me huffily, and reluctantly I handed over the coin.

The stables were quite close to the city's southern gates, so we entered Delawyn for the second time that day, once again almost overwhelmed by the sheer mass of people.

'Let's find a hostel,' I suggested, for now we carried our packs and I wanted to relieve myself of the weight.

We paused and looked about us. The streets and buildings around us were well maintained but did not have quite the same air of prosperity as those we had first seen. I could smell the salt of the ocean in the air but I could see neither it nor the River Freson that split Delawyn in half. I was keen to see both, but if it must be without our horses then the morrow would be soon enough.

It was clear we would have to ask for help locating a hostel. We could not see one amongst the buildings around us and we did not want to walk down street after street aimlessly searching.

'Good afternoon,' Chandra called to a man as he brushed by. 'Could you please tell us where we can find good lodgings?'

The man paused, glared at the three of us as though we were his bitterest enemies, and walked on. He did not utter a sound. We watched him pass on in amazement.

'Perhaps I can help you,' a voice behind us said and we turned to see a small, smiling blonde woman. 'Are you visitors here?'

'Yes,' I replied, glad to have finally met a friendly Delawese. 'We're looking for a hostel.'

The woman nodded and stepped closer, pointing eastward along the road. 'Try the Singing Eel. It's about five blocks from here. You'll . . . ' but we never did hear what we would do, for just then a crazy man came out of the crowd, singing a ludicrous song about the coming of a white panther and the Blessed One, and bumped heavily into the woman. She gave a little cry and fell forward into Lilith, cracking shoulders. The woman's hands quickly grabbed Lilith to steady herself. It was all very fast and very blurred and by the time the woman had straightened and assured us that she was all right the crazy man had disappeared.

'I'm sorry,' she told Lilith, her voice breathy with embarrassment. 'I hope I didn't hurt you.'

Lilith was flushed. 'No. Not at all.'

The woman stepped back. 'Aye, well, good luck finding the hostel, I hope you have a pleasant stay.' And she pivoted quickly and was gone.

I rubbed Lilith's shoulder and we shared a bemused smile at the speed of the woman's departure. Resettling our packs, we began to walk along the road, doing our best to stay together and not to knock anyone or be knocked.

We stared about us quite openly. The Delawese style on their buildings seemed to lean heavily towards elaborate carvings and masonry. I was fascinated by the many delicate and delightful animals and dreamcreatures that seemed to scamper above their doors and windows and around their pillars and roofs.

It was a shock then to see the groups of scraggly men and women sitting on the steps of the temples or clustered by the side of shops, holding out bowls and begging. Our appearance, our packs, our surprise on seeing the beggars were like a bloodied sheep before a pack of starving wolves. Unlike the Delawese, who simply grunted and elbowed the beggars aside with the impatience of familiarity, we were still susceptive. Several leapt up and scurried towards us. 'Coin, please, we need food, coin, please,' they implored in whining voices. 'I have children, they eat dirt, please, coin.' 'We have no work, no home, please.'

They thrust their bowls under our noses, almost

blocking our paths, and were soon joined by others of their companions, all encircling us and hindering our walking. I did not like it. Their unwashed bodies bumped mine and they rattled their bowls before my eyes, all the while beseeching us for coin.

I frowned, trying to step around them, but they only seemed to close in tighter. Beside me, Lilith reached for her pouch and they swarmed towards her, only to fall back disappointed when she cried in dismay, 'It's gone! My pouch is gone!'

Horrified, I stopped, unmindful of the beggars. 'You've lost it?' I asked incredulously. It held all her payment from our last assignments. 'You would've felt it fall.'

Lilith's expression was pitiful. 'I don't think I lost it, Ashil,' she told me in a small voice. 'I know I had it when we came through the southern gates.' She patted her hips once again, as though hoping the pouch would miraculously reappear.

As I realised what she was trying to say, I let out an anguished groan. 'The Singing Eel woman?'

Lilith nodded, looking woeful. 'I think so,' she muttered.

'The wicked woman,' Chandra exclaimed. 'She tricked us.'

I said nothing, feeling both anger at the woman and self-reproach for our own gullibility burn within me. I checked my pouch and was relieved to find it was still there. Chandra, who always carried hers beneath her clothes, did the same.

The beggars had dropped back a little, following our exchange with indifference, but when they saw that both Chan and I still had coin, they moved back in and resumed their pleading. 'We need blankets, it's so cold at night, the babies cry.' 'Our clothes are torn and dirty, please, please.'

I fished out a few small coins and threw them in the bowls. 'Now go,' I ordered sharply, my good humour all but gone. 'You'll get no more,' and I stepped determinedly forward.

They followed us for a little longer, but they had learnt to read people well. Our bad news had spoiled their chances for the day, so they quickly latched on to another group when the opportunity arose repeating their unhappy tales with renewed vigour.

'Do not worry, Lilith,' Chandra said, turning consolingly towards Lil. 'We have plenty of coin for the three of us.'

'I know,' Lilith replied, though her voice was dull and flat. 'It's just that she seemed so friendly, when she must really have planned it all along.'

A little further on, a sign proclaiming a large, colourful hostel called the Cat and Fish caught our eye, and happy to ignore the recommendation of a thief, we decided to enter.

An hour later, the warm meal and good wine had gone a long way towards dispelling our gloomy mood. It was too early for bed, yet we felt no desire to go wandering the city streets. The way our luck was running, we feared being knocked over by some wild horse or laden wagon as the city's second shift began.

So we sat idly at our bench at the rear of the hostel, continuing to eat and drink too much and watch the other patrons. When three men rose from a table across from us, I noticed all wore a cuff of yellow and blue stripes on the left sleeve of their shirts. Though these cuffs were larger than the one worn by the woman from the travellers' stable, they too made the men's garb appear very strange.

As the three reached the door, the publican scuttled over to open it for them, an ingratiating smile on his face. When his daughter came around to offer us more of the freshly baked bread, I asked her what the significance of the cuff was.

She regarded me as though I was simple. It was not a nice look. 'It means they're one o' the Fifty,' she told me, and she tore off a large chunk of the bread and dropped it on our table.

'The Fifty what?' I asked, disliking the idea of being too ignorant in this city.

'The Fifty families, o' course,' she answered shortly. 'The ones tha' make up the Ring of Advisers tha' sits at Circle House. Only the Ethnarch's more powerful. If you're a member o' the Fifty, you wear the cuff with your family's colours. The higher your family sits in Circle House, the larger the cuff.' She looked at me to see if I had any more daft questions.

I did. 'Is the Ethnarch elected from amongst the Fifty?'

She actually laughed. 'The Ethnarch inherits the Three Keys of Power. It's always the oldest child of the First family.'

She swung her trencher around and made to leave, but I had one more question. 'Do the passenger wagons leave from nearby?'

'Aye,' she nodded, taking another step away.

'There's one tha' leaves from round the corner,' and she pointed to the west wall. 'It travels all round the city on this side of the river. It'll take you to the palace if you want to see it.' Clearly not wanting to answer any more questions, she turned her back on us and walked to the next table.

We did see the Ethnarch's palace the next day. It was an immense, cold-looking monstrosity, topped by mighty spires and towers and rimmed with guards in the city's south-east. The Circle House was not far from it, a large circular building covered by a high dome and surrounded by exquisite gardens which, we soon discovered, the cuffless, such as ourselves, were not permitted to enter. We had ridden there in a pas-senger wagon and the journey had been uncomfortable to say the least. The wooden wagon seats were badly made, the passengers were crowded almost atop one another and the cost of the trip was unjustifiably high. I watched the green- and black-cuffed arm of the driver extend to take coin time and time again from poor Delawese and I found my dislike for the city and those governing it growing. The sight of the glossy horses and shiny carriages gathered before the palace and Circle House did nothing to diminish this dislike.

While in this polished and wealthy district we walked to the home of the Binenese diplomat, where we had arranged to leave details of where we would be staying in Delawyn. She was not in when we called and the Delawese clerk who took our message did not encour-age us to linger. We caught another passenger wagon and continued our journey around the city.

This wagon took us near to the River Freson and

we glimpsed the many bridges that spanned the cold water. When Chandra asked the cuffed driver if any passenger wagons took visitors across the bridges, she guffawed. 'Aye,' she said, 'for it's such a pretty sight,' and she laughed again.

Never one to be put off, Chandra did find a wagon that would take us early the following morning. To our surprise and delight, the wagon was almost empty and we had the most enjoyable experience of our visit while crossing that river. For seated so that we could see the huge harbour ahead of us near the river's mouth, we also had an unimpeded view of something extraordinarily wonderful that none of us had ever seen before. The ocean.

Its sheer size and force were overwhelming. It defeated the mortal eye like the stars or the sun. I was mesmerised, and could not wait to stand at its edge and search its waters for a sign of any scaled inhabitants. I had heard it said that the merfolk sometimes swam close enough to touch, and such a thought gave me chill-bumps. My father had always warned me about believing tales of such fanciful creatures, but staring at the liquid vastness before me, my hope grew.

The wagon driver pulled up as soon as we had crossed the bridge. We had been too absorbed by the ocean's immenseness to have paid any attention to our destination. The smell of the place reached us first.

As we jumped down from the wagon, we almost gagged. On the bridge, the sea breezes had kept the stench from us. Now it was so strong I had to cover my nose as I turned to find its source.

To our left were the extensive river docks with their

enormous warehouses, most owned by members of the Fifty. Beyond them were the homes of Delawyn's poor. It was a smaller ocean of crumbling, decaying shelters that housed the starving, the diseased, the ignored. Those who could work were scrambling aboard the wagon now in their pitiful rags, their skin plastered with sores, their long grimy fingers gripping the wagon's seat like an eagle's talons clutching its prey. Their desperation kept them silent as they watched us listlessly. The wagon, so full now that I pitied the poor horses, began to move, rolling back towards the bridge. In shock, we watched it go.

We did not stay there long. All we saw was awful and our powerlessness was disheartening. We walked back across the bridge, then headed west towards the harbour, hoping to lift our spirits.

The harbour was crowded and rough, the workers and fishers unpleasant, sniggering at our innocent questions. Just as we crossed to stand before the beautiful expanse of water, it began to rain heavily. Wet, cold and miserable, we plodded back to the hostel.

We stayed in Delawyn for three more days, our viewing of the city hampered by a spate of late summer showers and the surly, contemptuous nature of the people. The city was infected with gloom, a gloom that seemed to be growing. People muttered in shadows and watched all foreigners with suspicious eyes. Those that did speak to us asked strange questions about religions I knew little about. We did meet one or two Delawese with pleasant dispositions, but I fear they were a minority.

I had always known that I would encounter cultures

that I would not like, or could not understand. The existence of the Fifty appalled me. Delawyn was wealthy, its colossal harbour trade alone would have been enough to feed and clothe all its inhabitants, but the wealth belonged to only a few, and those few wanted more. As Chandra described it, 'Delawyn is rotting from the inside, like a shiny apple with a maggot eating at its heart.'

We could do nothing other than rejoice that we were not of its poor and were free and able to leave.

When we received two firm offers of work, we were well pleased. We departed early one morning, walking towards the southern gates in the soft light of dawn. Our first job offer had come from the Loban in the north-east and I was excited by the prospect of working for the priests.

We had just crossed the road close to where Lilith had been robbed that first day, in view of the southern gates, when Lil gave a soft cry. 'Look.' She was pointing to a small stall, doing a thriving business selling taffy sticks.

Lilith, Chan and I knew, had a weakness for sweet confectionery, so we strode happily towards the stall.

There was quite a crowd forming a rough line, so we waited patiently for our turn. More people collected behind us, but the vendor waved them away. 'There's no more sugar today. Don't be waiting.'

In fact, as Lilith stepped up, there were only three sticks left. Lilith smiled with pleasure and handed over her coin from the new pouch Chandra and I had partially filled. The vendor was just about to pass the sticks to Lilith when an imperious voice commanded him to wait.

A black-lacquered carriage had pulled up behind us and a woman descended from it slowly, hampered by her enormous bulk. She was followed by two plump children. The red and silver cuffs on their left sleeves went halfway up their arms.

'I'll take those last sticks, vendor,' she cried, bustling up to push Lilith aside.

Lilith stepped back. Since joining Chandra and me, she had been becoming daily more confident and less reticent with us, but she was still far too timid to gainsay a stranger, especially a forceful one.

So I protested. 'Wait a moment. They've already been paid for.'

The woman raised one eyebrow almost to the line of her hair, but in no other way acknowledged my presence.

'There's no more sugar,' Chandra explained, 'so there are no more sticks today. We have bought the last ones.'

The woman heaved a huge sigh. 'Vendor, quickly,' and she held out her left hand, wiggling her fingers at him impatiently. 'I do not have a morning to waste.'

The vendor glanced from her to us and handed her the sticks. With a satisfied grunt, she took them and passed two to her children, keeping the other for herself. She slapped the coins down and returned to her carriage. Not once had she even glanced at us.

Before we could protest any more, the vendor slid Lilith's coins back to her. 'She's o' the Fifty,' he told us in a low voice. 'You do no want to anger her.' Then he too turned from us and began to pack up his stall.

I shook my head and hooked my arm through

Lilith's. 'Never mind. Just think, we get to leave here and she has to stay.'

Lilith gave a small chuckle. 'And she's not a cartographer,' Chandra added. What more needed to be said?

It was a long but pleasant journey to the Loban priests' small settlement. The season was changing, and as we progressed even further north we could feel the cool breath of autumn against our skin and smell the moisture in the air. Our horses' heads were up and they lifted their hooves nimbly, invigorated by the dry, cooler weather. It was pretty country we rode through. A low mountain range jutted out over the land, surrounded by shallow, wild hills and the rich pastures the local farmers had claimed for their livestock. There was plenty of water and the land was covered with magnificent trees.

As we rode, we could not help but stare at those trees, for they were covered with leaves of every shape and size and, it appeared, every colour. We rode slowly beneath and beside them, gazing with delight at the deep plums, bright oranges, the crimsons and pale golds that adorned the branches. The trees had begun to reluctantly yield only a few of the leaves, letting them fall into small piles at their roots for the wind to toy with.

We met with the Loban and agreed to deliver the map within a month, only to discover, much to our chagrin, that we could not find the pathway we had agreed to map. But determined nevertheless, we went in search of help, looking in the most sensible of places, the nearest inn.

The inn was a large wooden building set at the edge of a small village and served both as a local meeting place and a resting point for travellers. It was half-full when we pushed open the sturdy wooden door and stepped inside, the warmth from the blazing fire prickling my wind-roughened cheeks. The locals looked us over curiously, then the innkeeper bustled over and we explained what we needed, a guide.

The pathway did exist but it was difficult to follow as it climbed through the foothills and up and across the mountain range, saving days of travel around the mountain base. We asked the innkeeper if she knew of any guides who could take us across, and to our relief she nodded earnestly.

'Had a young girl in here a few weeks ago who's taking a group of hunters across,' she said, then shook her head at the notion. 'They wanted to follow a herd of deer. Seems they've some sort of wager on the leader but they lost the trail.' She smiled then. 'Well not that I mind what brings them here, as long as they drink my ale.'

In the pause that followed we ordered a drink each and found ourselves a table while the innkeeper brought the drinks over to us.

'She'll probably be back soon, that guide, maybe tonight. Seen her around before though she never stays long.' And she smiled again and asked us what we wanted to eat.

The girl did not return that night or the one after and on the third night, the last we were prepared to spend waiting for her, we began discussing where else we could try in the morning. We were at what was now our regular table, drinking wine and talking softly and still waiting, hopefully, for the guide to show. The innkeeper had described her to us briefly, 'Young, long curly hair with eyes like ice. Can't miss her.'

She came in late that third night. We had already convinced ourselves that we had missed her and were just about to go to our room when the door opened, letting in the cool night air and a dark figure. She was wrapped in a long cloak that covered her from head to toe and she flung it from herself in a deft movement as she took a seat near the fire. The innkeeper nodded at us as she went to take her order and we waited until she had left before we approached the girl.

She was staring into the fire but turned as we stood beside her table and arched one golden eyebrow. 'Yes?'

Her voice was low and calm, with no accent that I could trace. She appeared unperturbed by our appearance as I introduced our group, explaining that we were cartographers with a total lack of the self-consciousness, a mixture of pride and diffidence, that had once plagued me.

She nodded politely and invited us to sit down. The description the innkeeper had given had been fair enough. She was about our age, with wild honey-coloured curls falling down her back and eyes of a vibrant crystal blue. She wore leather trousers stuffed into knee-high boots with a white shirt and leather vest. Around her waist on a plain leather belt hung a dagger and short sword and a small pouch of coins.

I explained that we needed a guide for the mountain path. The innkeeper had returned with her drink and she filled a goblet with the cider, offering the flagon to us.

'Why do you want to map it?' she asked, her steady blue gaze on me.

'We've taken a job with the Loban,' I answered, then paused, wondering if I needed to explain about the priests, but the girl nodded so I continued. 'They want a map of the pathway so they can save time when they cross for their winter festival.'

The girl sipped at her drink, then returned her goblet to the wooden table. 'The mountains are low,' she said, 'but even so winter can be a dangerous time to cross them.'

Chandra leant forward, resting her elbows on the table as she spoke. 'The Loban already know this. They travel around the base every year so they are familiar with the weather. And although it is their winter festival, the first of their rites begins next month.'

For the first time the girl smiled, coolly, wryly. 'It doesn't leave you with much time then.'

Chandra smiled too, her gorgeous gleaming smile. 'No, that's why we want to hire you.'

We had wondered earlier if the girl would be keen to make another trip back over the mountains so soon after leading the hunters.

'We can pay you well,' I quickly added. 'The same as the hunters.'

To our surprise she laughed outright at that, then raised her goblet. 'All right,' she said. 'I'll take you.'

Chandra, Lilith and I grinned in delight.

The innkeeper brought another flagon of cider to the table and placed a large bowl of thick, steaming soup and several generous slices of bread before the girl. The innkeeper then turned to us and enquired hopefully if we were feeling hungry, despite the fact we had eaten a huge meal only a few hours ago. Her face fell when we declined and she moved on to the next table, her smile miraculously reappearing.

There was a low chuckle from the girl as she picked up her spoon and took a mouthful of soup. She looked up, still amused, and as she tore off a small piece of bread she told us her name was Alexa. 'When do you want to leave?'

'Early tomorrow morning,' I replied. We had already lost several days trying to find the pathway ourselves and then waiting for our guide at the inn. We could not afford to delay any longer.

Alexa nodded. 'It will be colder the higher we climb and there is no shelter along the pathway, so we will have to camp out until you have all the sketches you require. Pack warm clothing and blankets and bring plenty of food.' She smiled then, her crystal blue eyes alight with humour. 'I'm sure the innkeeper will be more than happy to oblige you there.'

'Yes,' I agreed, laughing. 'We'll speak with her tonight.'

A cool gust of wind blew in through the door as several of the locals headed home, reminding us of the late hour.

'Do you have a room?' I asked Alexa. 'If not you're welcome to share ours.'

'I have my own, thank you.'

I nodded. Her answer did not surprise me.

'Well, it's late,' I said, glancing in enquiry at Chandra

73

and Lilith. They both nodded and put down their goblets in silent assent. We all rose. 'We'll say good night, Alexa. Until the morning.'

'Good night,' she replied, her cool gaze following us as we left the room.

We met early the next morning in the stables. We were filling our packs with the food the innkeeper had provided when Alexa entered.

She greeted us and quickly saddled her horse, wielding her generous supply from the innkeeper's stores. She mounted and we followed her out into the crisp morning air and kicked the horses into a trot.

Riding slowly, the foothills were several hours away and although we would have liked to go faster, the irregularity of the terrain made only short bursts of speed possible. The morning passed quickly, without incident, and after one more short, fast canter we eased the horses to a walk as we began to climb the first of the foothills. Alexa was just ahead of me but she had turned to look back and I caught her eye as I leant forward to pat Cleo.

She smiled and slowed her horse so that we were soon level. 'It's not far now. We'll stop to eat soon, before we start on the path.'

'Fine.' I looked around me and took a deep, contented breath. The weather had stayed fine and I was feeling quite exhilarated. I eyed the summit ahead of us with pleasure. 'This will be the first mountain we've ever mapped.'

'How long have the three of you been together?' Alexa asked.

I shrugged, thinking back. 'Our first job was a little

over a year ago now. We set out together from Binet, Lil's and my birth city, and we've been working in the west.'

Chandra and Lilith had drawn up on either side of us as the land opened out. 'You may have heard of us,' Chandra said, looking at Alexa expectantly.

'No, I'm afraid not.' If Alexa was amused by Chandra's rather misplaced optimism she did not show it.

On my left, Timi lowered his head and tried to pull at the sweet grass. Lilith gently tugged at his reins and he raised his head and walked on. Lilith had until now said nothing to Alexa, though she had watched her with great curiosity all morning. Evidently this curiosity had become too much even for her, for she spoke up now, asking Alexa quietly if there was much work for a mountain guide in this area.

Alexa looked kindly at Lilith and shook her head. 'I only work in these mountains from time to time. I track and guide elsewhere, depending on my plans.'

'So we were lucky to meet you,' I said.

'No,' Chandra disagreed, before Alexa could reply. 'The gods must have meant for it to happen.'

Instead of laughing at such a notion, Alexa nodded. 'Perhaps,' she said.

We reached the top of the foothills soon after and stopped for our midday meal. As we distributed our food, Alexa briefly outlined the direction we would be taking.

'It's a simple path. It cuts right across the range almost in a straight line. The hardest part is finding where it begins.' She pointed towards the highest peak which stood stark and cold against the sky. 'If you join

75

the path too early, you'll hit a false trail and it will take you up there. That's why most people think it's impossible or too difficult to try the crossing.'

She unwrapped her food. 'Of course it will be harder when the snows come, so I hope the priests know how to read a map.'

After our meal, we climbed up to the range and our work began.

Alexa was a thorough and resourceful guide, leading us through the path slowly and showing us the signs and landmarks which indicated the beginning of the true pathway, explaining how they would change with full winter.

Chandra was disgusted with herself for having missed the true pathway, which appeared amazingly easy to find once it had been revealed. Alexa laughed good-naturedly and said wasn't that always the way.

We worked hard during the day, then relaxed around a large blazing fire each night, talking and eating. The food the innkeeper had provided was more than enough to keep us well-fed and Alexa was a fascinating companion. Extraordinarily well travelled, she had even been to Binet and was full of amusing tales and useful information about the land.

She seemed genuinely interested in our lives, our plans and our work, looking on quietly as we sketched, filling our mapping sheets. She was evidently no stranger to mapping and her familiarity with our methods and equipment surprised and impressed me.

Around the fire, while Chandra and I looked on in amazement, Alexa drew Lil into our conversations and soon had her chatting about life in Binet and the jobs we had taken. She was generous and kind, and stimulating company, and I grew to like her very much. Yet, for all her warmth and helpfulness, she gave little away of herself and in that short time we spent together on the mountain she managed to intrigue me as no other person ever had.

We soon had all the information we needed, so we began the trip back to the inn where we would stay and complete the map before delivering it to the Loban. I was feeling smug. This job was a success and we had an even more exciting job ahead of us. I smiled to myself as I trotted alongside Chandra, idly watching Alexa and Lilith chatting several lengths ahead of us, their fair heads turned towards one another, their long hair blowing gently in the breeze.

I glanced across at Chandra, who was being uncharacteristically quiet, but she seemed immersed in her own thoughts so I rode on, quietly cheerful until we reached the inn.

The innkeeper beamed us a welcome and hurried to place steaming plates of stew before us before we could decline dinner. We ate in companionable silence, finishing the meal with warm honey cakes and rough red wine.

The innkeeper came to clear our plates and pulled a key from one of her many pockets.

'I'm sure you're all tired after that long ride, so I've saved you one of my best rooms where you can draw your map in peace. It's got plenty of light and four large beds.' With a satisfied clunk, she lay the key in the middle of the table, and beside it she placed another, unasked-for flagon of wine. She grinned at us then moved on to the next table, another flagon in her hand.

Lilith picked up the key. 'I'll take our work upstairs,' she said, smiling, 'before it gets doused in red wine.'

I laughed. The three of us had celebrated the completion of the first of Skar's maps by sharing a very good flagon of wine in our workroom. Fortunately we had not shown the finished map to Skar, for I had reached for the still-drying map at the same time Chandra had reached for the flagon and our arms had collided, knocking the flagon and its contents all over our beautiful map. It was totally ruined and we had to start it all again. Still, we had learnt a lesson from that disaster. We never allowed food or drink in our workroom and we were always very careful when reaching for a flagon, especially if it was not our first for the night.

With our work bundled up in her arms, Lilith headed for the wooden stairs at the back of the room and disappeared upstairs. I sat eyeing the plate of honey cakes the innkeeper had left on the table, debating whether or not I wanted another one. I had just decided I did when a cold gust of wind announced the entry of another traveller. He was a stranger to me but Alexa obviously recognised him, for she excused herself and went to join him at his table.

I ate the cake, then lolled contentedly in my chair, the warmth from the fire and my full belly conspiring to make me drowsy.

'It shouldn't take long to draw up the final map,' I said dreamily to Chandra.

She nodded mutely, stretching out fully, her legs

crossed, her arms behind her head. She was watching Alexa and her friend so I poured myself more of the wine and filled her goblet. She lifted it idly and took a sip.

'Our next job is our biggest yet,' she said, without taking her eyes from Alexa.

I smiled happily in reply.

'It will be hard for three people,' she continued.

I looked at Chandra sharply, jolted out of my complacent mood. Was she worried we could not cope? I was rather surprised. Of the three of us, Chandra was the least likely to suffer from such thoughts. Perplexed by her words, I sat up straighter.

'It will take longer than any of our other jobs,' I said, 'but we wouldn't have been offered the position if there was any doubt about our ability.'

'That's not what I meant.' She shook her head without removing her hands and still without taking her eyes from Alexa. 'I know we can do it, but wouldn't another person make it easier?'

Finally I began to understand and relaxed a little. 'By another person you mean Alexa?' I asked.

Chandra nodded.

I looked across at Alexa. She was laughing with her friend and, seeing us watching, flashed a smile.

I shrugged. 'She seems happy working the way she is. She may not want to work in a group.'

'Then she'll say no.' And Chandra finally turned to face me. 'But do you agree we ask her? You and Lilith draw beautifully, but you have little tracking or path-finding experience.' She nodded at Alexa. 'She has. And she knows maps.'

Chandra was stating what I had thought myself. It

was only a matter of time before we would have to start looking for another cartographer as the assignments we accepted became larger and more detailed.

'I agree,' I said. 'We'll ask her if Lilith has no objections.'

Lilith was not long in coming down and Chandra sat up, dropping her hands flat on the table. 'Lil, what do you think of asking Alexa to join us?'

Lilith didn't hesitate. 'I'd like to work with her.' She pulled out a chair and sat down. 'I like her and I think we could learn from her.'

'Good,' Chandra said. 'We'll ask her as soon as she's free.' She drank more of her wine, then placed the goblet on the table and pushed it away. 'But first, I must answer another call,' and she strode off in search of the washroom.

I too pushed my goblet away, I did not want a thick head in the morning when it was time to draw. 'Well, Lil,' I said, turning to her triumphantly, 'we've climbed our first mountain.'

'Yes.' For a brief moment her face was aglow with our success, but her joy did not last long. She lowered her eyes to the table and her smile slowly faded, to be replaced by a pensive, rather sombre expression.

'Don't look too overjoyed with the accomplishment!' I scolded. 'Just remember that in Binet the closest thing to a mountain is the steps before the Plaza of the City Guardians and they're swept clean every day.' I drew my goblet over, forgetting that I had decided not to drink any more as I mused aloud, 'No nasty clumps of rock to trip you or bruise your shins, and no deceptive clods of dirt that look safe enough to step on, only to crumble under you and send you flying. No interminable slopes that seem to go straight up to the heavens . . . '

Lilith laughed. 'You can't fool me, Ashil. You loved every moment.'

'And you didn't?' I asked.

She frowned and shook her head. 'Of course I enjoyed it. I was just thinking how strange it is that what you might think is an extremely difficult task actually becomes easier when you start to do it. It makes you wonder how much of life you miss because you're afraid.'

She tilted her head, slanted a look at Alexa and sighed. 'And then you meet someone like Alexa, who is so undaunted by life, and it makes you want to be like that. The longer you are with her, the more you start to believe that perhaps it's possible.'

She met my gaze and I smiled sympathetically as I pushed the goblet away once more. 'It is possible, Lil, and you are doing it. You didn't stay in Binet and settle for climbing the nice, clean steps. You're here with Chan and me in this inn. We've just sketched a mountain path, seen the ocean at Delawyn and soon we'll be working in Nalym, on the very edge of the Burrnayi Desert. It's the doing that makes you strong.'

She touched my hand lightly. 'You're right. Thank you. I do feel stronger. It's just that sometimes . . . '

'It's just that sometimes you think too much,' and I retrieved my goblet and handed her hers. 'And you don't drink enough wine.'

Chandra rejoined us and we chatted amongst ourselves. I was glad to see Lilith brighten as we began to tell silly jokes we had heard amongst Skar Linon's friends.

It became very late, but as Alexa appeared quite engrossed with her friend we decided to put off speaking with her until the morning, so we wished her a good night and retired to our room.

When I awoke the next day I was delighted, and amazed, to discover my head was clear. Chandra had already risen and had begun sorting the mapping sheets out on her bed, but was nowhere in sight. Alexa's bed was untouched and Lilith was still sleeping, so I dressed quietly and went downstairs to breakfast. Alexa was waiting at the table, looking fresh and well-rested and she called good morning to me as I crossed the room.

I returned her greeting and sat opposite her at the table, looking around the room for her friend but I could not see him among the other patrons.

'He's already left.' I turned to see Alexa watching me, grinning in amusement. 'Do you want the milk?' Slightly abashed, I took the jug from her. I had not meant to be so obvious.

Chandra suddenly appeared at the door, carrying several goatskins. She saw Alexa and me and waved them at us, flashing a blinding smile as she moved towards us eagerly.

'Look at these, Ashil,' she crowed. 'There's not a mark on them.' And she handed me one of the skins.

I examined the raw skin, checking for rough patches or blemishes, but Chandra was right, they were in excellent condition. I glanced up at her and said approvingly, 'They're fabulous, where did you get them?'

Delighted, Chandra sat down. 'I came downstairs this

morning, you and Lilith were still asleep, and the inn-keeper called me over and introduced me to her brother. He breeds goats and he was wondering if we needed any skins. I knew you would sleep for a while yet, so I went with him to his farm and bought all of these.' She patted the pile in her lap.

I leant over and fingered them, shaking my head at our good fortune. 'That pile should see us through our next job. You're a marvel, Chan.'

'Yes,' she agreed.

In the excitement of the find, I had momentarily forgotten Alexa but she chuckled now. 'Only a very few would be so thrilled by the skins of dead goats,' she said dryly.

'Don't laugh,' I responded. 'A wash and a scrape and these skins will become soft, flawless parchment for us to draw on. It can be extremely difficult to find good quality parchment.'

Chandra nodded and put them down on the chair beside her. 'The preparation is messy, time-consuming work but we do it better than most parchment-sellers.'

At that moment, Lilith came down the stairs and joined us. The innkeeper brought us an especially large serving of warm nutbread, evidently well pleased by our morning's purchases, with a pot of honey, and a bowl of porridge each for Lilith and Chandra.

Deciding this was a good time, I asked Alexa what she was planning to do.

'I'm heading south,' she replied simply, biting into a piece of the bread.

Chandra said, 'We're going south as well. We've been offered work by Lord Maltra of Nalym.'

This did interest Alexa. She raised an eyebrow and cooed, 'Lord Maltra, that's quite an offer.' She put down the bread and looked at Chandra. 'Nalym can be a difficult city to visit, uninvited.'

We knew what she meant, of course. Without an invitation from the ruler, it was doubtful we would be permitted past the gates. Nalym's inhabitants were very selective about who they would admit to their city, for they saw enemies everywhere. Not that it was a dangerous city, or so the representative who had brought us the contract in Delawyn had assured us. Once inside its walls, far from it. We had not failed to notice his qualifying 'once inside its walls'. He had been Abroni, the first I had met, and, like us, found Delawyn a cold and friendless place. We had invited him to sit and share a meal with us at the Cat and Fish and he had gladly accepted, willingly telling us a little of his city's history.

Five generations ago, the Abroni lived in their tents and shelters amidst the shady trees and waterholes of the oasis they called Nalym. There they made the pots and weaved the blankets they were famous for all over Tirayi. They had little wealth, only their craft pieces, their few sheep and the small crops they grew, but still the nomadic tribes would come from the Burrnayi Desert each year and raid the camp, killing and stealing. As their religion forbade the taking of another's life, the Abroni would not fight back. They would stand and watch the destruction, then, after the tribespeople had left, they would gather what remained and begin again.

Further north, the Futile War, whose beginning is

hazy even to the inhabitants of the twin cities, was raging in all its ferocity, forcing many to leave Zelia and Telish, searching for new land and a new beginning. Those who headed south called themselves the Bramkari, the Scouts, and they came to Nalym and were welcomed by the Abroni. The Bramkari had never known peace and the gentle, uncomplicated ways of their new friends soothed and gladdened them. Until the desert raiders came again.

Only this time they met opponents equal to them. For the Bramkari were seasoned warriors and this was a fresh fight and they were angry. They defeated the desert nomads and from that day a new alliance was born between the Abroni and the Scouts.

The Scouts built huge walls and buildings, barracks sprang up in every corner of the new city, where the men and women, married or not, lived apart, training and making their bodies hard. Children were desired, they would defend the city when their parents were old or dead, but family life was discouraged. It was believed to weaken a soldier. So the children were taken young from their mothers and put into their own barracks, where small swords as well as writing tablets were put into their hands, the swords to remain long after the tablets had been discarded.

For their part, the Abroni put aside their pottery and their looms and turned their hands to the soil, for they would feed the soldiers who would defend them. To this day, the Bramkari, led by Lord Maltra, continue to defend the city and the Abroni continue to feed it. The Bramkari are the soldiers and they rule the city. The Abroni are the farmers, the traders, the artisans who supply the city and bring in Nalym's coin.

Over time, the fire of creativity has died in Abroni veins. For many years they had no time for their beautiful pottery or blankets. The Bramkari wanted swords and helmets and uniforms and boots from the artisans, and scorned the purely decorative. Now the city is settled and secure, the Abroni are more merchants than artists, and they seek outside Nalym for whatever the city requires. And so we were found. Cartography was too advanced a skill ever to be taught in Nalym, so using the coin they now had in plenty, the Abroni brought foreign mapdrawers to the city to draw Lord Maltra's maps. Mapdrawers found far from the Burrn-ayi Desert and Nalym's traditional enemies.

'What sort of maps does she want?' Alexa queried, and I wondered how much of the history she knew.

'To start with, some simple maps of the city,' I answered. 'There's a possibility she may want the outer farms and the Doma where she lives mapped later.'

Alexa smiled. 'When she has determined she can trust you not to sell any defence secrets. A map in your enemy's hand can be a dangerous weapon.'

I frowned and, beside me, Chandra bristled.

'We are not fools,' Chandra said, chillingly. 'We have turned down bribe-coin before.'

And indeed it was true. Despite our relatively short time as cartographers we had already encountered our profession's darker side. Maps are information and as such are powerful, for people will pay well for a cartographer to draw false markings on a map or slip details of their foe's holdings to them. But we had never been tempted. We took too much pride in our work to ever corrupt it in such a way, and coin had never been an overriding love for any of us.

Chandra snorted, sitting tall and magnificent. 'Bribe-coin is for greedy idiots,' she declared with rich contempt. 'Not only would we be in trouble with some powerful people if we accepted such dishonourable payment, once word passed we would never be able to work again.'

'We have a reputation for quality and discretion that we intend keeping,' I explained.

'An unusual combination,' Alexa murmured softly, 'scruples and foresight. Such will serve you well, as long as they're not kept too rigid.'

When no-one replied—I think even Chandra was struck dumb—Alexa asked if we had ever seen Nalym before. None of us had, we had never been that far south. That was half the attraction.

'Have you?' I asked.

'Yes. It's a very interesting city.' Alexa smiled at me then, her eyes the colour of a summer sky, warm and inviting. 'Which is precisely the reason you do this work, isn't it?'

I grinned. 'Well, you've been to Binet,' I said dryly, and she laughed lightly.

'The work in Nalym will be demanding,' Chandra said, judging this to be an apt moment. 'We could use another cartographer.' She paused dramatically. 'Would you be interested?'

There was a collective hush at the table as the three of us watched Alexa expectantly.

She smiled coolly. 'You don't know much about me.'

Lilith spoke up, protesting gently. 'As much as you

know about us, Alexa. You know we are good cartographers and we know you understand maps and tracking.' Her pretty face was delicately flushed. 'You could always try the one job with us.'

Again that cool, enigmatic smile as Alexa sat silently for a moment, her calm expression revealing none of her thoughts, then smoothly she spoke one short, soft word. 'Fine.'

'You will?' I asked in surprise.

'Yes, at least for Nalym,' and she raised her mug. 'A toast, to your new partner and to my new job.'

Our mugs clinked in approval.

The Loban were thrilled with their new map and eager to try the mountain path. We smiled, collected our coin and set out for Nalym.

It was a long journey to the desert city. We rode south, away from the mountains, passing to the east of Binet and along the western edge of the plains. Often as we rode, I gazed west, towards my birth city, wondering about my parents and my brother, Thoma, and hoping all was well with them and that they missed me too.

Lilith's thoughts were also of her parents and our longing for home grew stronger the closer we came to the city. As a result, I fear that we subjected Chandra and Alexa to more tales of Binet than they ever wanted to hear.

We were also approaching the territory of the nomads. Chandra made no comment but I knew it could not have escaped her notice and on the day we crossed the River Sa I asked her, tentatively, if she wanted to see her tribe again.

She shook her head. 'No,' she replied unequivocally, 'not yet. Perhaps one day I will go back, but I do not think it will be soon.'

I said no more to her and we continued in silence.

My father had generously given us several maps of Tirayi to refer to as we moved from city to city, job to job. They showed the south to the Burrnayi Desert, the west, and some of the north in much detail, but left most of the east, beyond the High Ranges, uncharted. It was a constant tease for a cartographer and my eye was drawn to those blank eastern spaces each time I unrolled one of the maps.

As we rounded the southern side of the plains, we drew close to a city called Netla. I knew little of it and Chandra, Lilith and I gladly thought to rest there before completing the final stage of our journey. We longed for the comforts of a city, a bath, fresh food, a soft bed, entertainment, but to our surprise Alexa counselled against it.

'Netla is a foul city,' she stated, peering eastward with a look of repugnance. 'Three powerful families rip it apart while they battle for supremacy. They profit from the Futile War and they bleed the farmers and crafts-people white.' She shook her head sorrowfully. 'The poor line the streets and there is crime and death everywhere.'

She had shocked us and she looked at our faces and smiled without amusement at our expressions. 'There is much danger in this area,' she told us softly, 'and a life is not highly regarded. You have heard that Nalym is a tough, hard city, yet Lord Maltra is strong and rules uncontested. Her city is well guarded and her laws are obeyed, by both the Scouts and the Abroni. She has held Nalym from desert intruders and the filth of Netla for thirty years, and she has order and respect. Netla has no order, there is only greed and despair.' She turned away and said finally, 'We would do best to ride on to Nalym.'

Alexa's words rang in my head as we rode wide of Netla, leaving it well behind us, and headed towards Lord Maltra's city.

We saw the enormous stone wall that surrounded Nalym when we were still one haul's distance away, one haul, three thousand paces. It was a daunting sight.

As we approached, we were soon able to discern movement at the two sets of gates on the wall's eastern side. We rode forward, the moving mass distinguishing itself as a huge swell of people moving unhurriedly in and out of the wide-flung gates. Guards stood above the people on the stone wall, well armed and alert, but clearly unconcerned at the sheer number of people entering their city.

We walked our horses onto the hard-baked dirt of the outer road and I looked curiously at the brightly robed figures around me. Most wore swathes of cloth wrapped around their heads, some with small veils attached.

'The flowing robes and head-cloths protect their bodies from the heat and the veils keep the sand from their faces,' Alexa said, bringing her horse, Drella, alongside me.

'They're desert nomads?'

She nodded.

Many were urging livestock along, or carrying large packs upon their backs. Those on horseback were covered with pouches and rolls of woven material and large, straining bundles that bounced against their thighs as they rode.

'What are they doing here?' I asked. 'I thought Nalym and the desert tribes were at war.'

Alexa smiled. 'Continually, but they don't let that interfere with trade. The nomads are the only ones who trade with both the lands above and below the desert. Other people have tried, but,' and she shrugged, 'without the help of the nomads it is impossible to cross the desert and they guard their role as traders ferociously. As I understand it, the Abroni hold an open bazaar once a month. It seems we've arrived in the middle of one.'

Just then three desertmen came up from behind us, driving four of the strangest beasts I had ever seen. The beasts were heavily laden, with long legs, a solid body and a thick, curved neck, topped with a head a little like a deer's. But it was the huge lump upon their backs that startled me the most. If I had seen just one such animal I would have thought it to be suffering from some sort of ugly growth, but all four were the same and all moved easily as though in good health.

Another desertman rode up, this time upon the back of one of the beasts. He passed us and entered the city.

I met Chandra's eye and she grinned at me. 'What was that, Ashil?' she called.

I opened my hands and shook my head.

'Camels,' Alexa told her, slowing Drella so that Lilith and Chandra could catch up. 'Wagons don't travel well over sand, so the nomads use those beasts. They're hardier than horses and they need little water. When they're well fed, their hump fills out. You need a knack to control one, though, they can be vile-tempered.'

I caught Lilith stroking Timi's neck and we both laughed.

Surrounded by the nomads, we rode into the city, our eyes dazzled by the colour and flurry that was everywhere.

It was not at all what I had expected. Where were the neat, ordered streets I had envisaged the Scouts building? All I saw was a wild, confusing jumble of wooden shops and stalls, animal pens, soothsayers, tricksters, streetcooks and more. Winding pathways veered around the displays, often abruptly ending and forcing us left or right. It was noisy, crowded and frantic. Still, I reflected, the crowd's excitement reaching me, it was as far removed from the clean, planned streets of Binet as possible, and I felt a shiver of delight run along my spine.

The bazaar was enormous, larger than any other I had ever seen, and seemingly every article ever made was for sale here. There were precious silks, incense and perfumed oils, spices, gems, goblets and plates and jewellery of gold, silver and copper, ornate weaponry, grain, dates, almonds, melons and other vegetables and fruit, livestock, horses, goat-hair rugs and rope, camel-skin sandals and water pouches, woven tents, piles of linma leaves for chewing, wooden chests and stools, delicate glassware, instruments of music, and more and more, filling the shaded stalls and displays so that they almost overflowed.

We were not the only foreigners here. I saw many looking over goods, chatting to the sellers, arguing prices and placing orders. Others I saw sat at makeshift tables under awnings, watching the crowd while sipping drinks supplied by roving drink-sellers with large plump water- and wineskins slung across their backs. It was as though Nalym was one huge meeting and bargaining place and not a city after all.

I did see a few of the grey-clad Bramkari soldiers walking amongst the crowd. They did not seem very interested in the wares about them and I suspected they were there simply to remind the people that the Scouts still ruled this city. Not, I thought, that they seemed to be doing it the way their ancestors had. And then I saw the second wall.

Alexa had been leading us towards the centre of the city, taking us through the bazaar towards what I now saw was another huge set of gates in another huge stone wall. Between the wall and the bazaar was two hundred paces of cleared land. Not even a rock interrupted the flat smoothness of that dirt surface. Now, I realised, rather impressed by their diligence, we were approaching the true home of the Scouts.

The gates were shut and as we stepped our horses onto the cleared land, an order from the wall told us to dismount and state our business. We called back our names and reason for being there and the gates opened and a group of guards stepped forward. They reached us and took the contract to examine, while other soldiers on the wall held bows at the ready. Even knowing that we had legitimate business in Nalym, my belly quivered with nervousness, for I could see the large barbed heads on the arrows.

We were expected and were quickly passed through, the gates shutting behind us. An escort immediately surrounded us and led us towards the Doma where Lord Maltra lived.

The streets we crossed were exactly what I had imagined. They were well laid out, well cleared, the buildings all of stone and neatly maintained. There were more shops here and comfortable, affluent homes and large, long dwelling houses I took to be the Bramkari barracks. We passed several busy training grounds.

All the Scouts, even the children, wore the grey uniform, and the Abroni were easily identified, for they shaved the sides of their heads between ear and temple and wore pale, flowing robes similar in style to those of the desert nomads.

It was very quiet and people moved about their business unobtrusively, it was hard to believe that the bazaar going on just beyond the wall was a part of the same city.

We did see some of the desert nomads here but these were the unfortunate ones who had fallen prisoner to the Bramkari and had been handed over to the Abroni slave-keepers. The slave-keepers sold some of the captives back to their tribes and to other Abroni for their homes but most of the prisoners they kept, for the slave-keepers' task was to keep the city clean and in good repair and they had long since learnt that slaves made their work far easier. I winced when I saw the ugly brands these slaves wore across their foreheads.

Our escort took us directly to the Doma, from where Lord Maltra and the chief amongst her Bramkari ruled the city. It was an elaborate fortification, totally enclosed in stone walls, with guards along its every face. There was not a fat belly or grey hair amongst them and they each had ugly-looking weapons which they carried with accustomed ease.

To our surprise, Lord Maltra greeted us personally in what was to be our apartment. It was simple but comfortable, with an enormous central archway dividing the sleeping area from the salon and work corner. A curtain had been pulled back from the archway, revealing five curtained beds beyond. But we were given no chance to explore for introductions were barely over before she began outlining exactly what she wanted, with very precise instructions.

That was to set the pattern for the rest of our stay in the city. Lord Maltra was a hard-working, shrewd ruler, who met with us regularly to check on the progress of her maps. We were provided with a small retinue of guards to escort us or, as Alexa said, 'to watch us' as we worked in the city. There were slaves to tidy and care for our rooms and provide our meals, and any requests we had were granted immediately. In exchange we were expected to work hard and quickly and produce excellent maps.

It did not take long for the four of us to settle into a successful working pattern, Alexa and Chandra would do most of the sketching and Lilith and I would draw the maps. At first we all spent days trekking through the city streets, but as the filled mapping sheets began to pile up it became more common for Lil and me to find ourselves left behind with blank pieces of parchment before us and ink pots by our sides.

The Doma, I soon learnt, was the original city of Nalym, but as the city's population had grown it had soon outstripped the walls and new ones were built. When the Abroni had approached Lord Maltra about opening their marketplace to the desert nomads for trade a third set of walls, with only two openings to the east, had been built. Within these walls, through which the desert nomads could pass freely once a month, all had to be built in wood. This way if ever the desert tribes tried to attack the city, the Bramkari could simply shoot flaming arrows from the second wall, burning down the stalls and exposing the tribespeople for slaughter. The Bramkari's position was further strengthened by the fact the outer wall joined with the second wall along the western side, containing the bazaar area within three sides, like a 'U' around the city. This meant any attacking force would be caught in a burning inferno between two stone walls with the eastern gates their only chance of escape.

Still, the desert tribes continued to attack, raiding the outlying farms with their clever irrigation systems and heavy patrols, and so providing the Abroni with more slaves each time.

We enjoyed the work, sketching and drawing throughout the warm and clear winter and into the south's blazing spring, until there was only the 'prettying' left. We became quite familiar with the city and its strange dichotomy and we had been accepted as trustworthy for we were now permitted to travel the streets without our escort.

One afternoon, following another raid on Nalym's farms, Chandra, Lilith and I left the Doma to buy some supplies at the monthly bazaar. We were well pleased. Alexa had told us only that morning that she would stay on as our fourth cartographer when we left Nalym. She was not with us now. While dressing that morning, her belt had snapped so she had gone to visit the leather-workers and select another one.

We had been very busy the last few days, so the three of us relaxed now, chatting idly as we walked our horses towards the bazaar, enjoying the novelty of a ride without the necessity of measuring and assessing the streets we passed.

We tied up our horses inside the second wall and walked out through the gates, across the cleared land. The bazaar was never the same, so we wandered amongst the traders, through the colossal crowd, looking for the dyes we needed. It was not something that either the Abroni or the tribespeople would have in abundance, so we followed the seemingly endless lines of stalls around the city's south side.

Here, the stalls ended abruptly to be replaced by an open square, filled with a large, noisy crowd. The people's backs were to us, all looking at something that we could not see from this distance. Yet there was a contained, hungry excitement about the throng that I found disquieting and I hesitated. Chandra, however, who did not have a cautious bone in her body strode forward determinedly.

Lilith and I hung back for a moment, then I shook my head and gave a small, exasperated laugh and we began to follow.

Up close, it was easy to see the large wooden platform which stood at the front of the crowd. Chandra's dark head had been swallowed up by the sea of bodies, so Lilith and I stood near the back and watched in morbid fascination as the slave sale continued.

The slaves were desert nomads taken in the previous day's failed raid. Some wore rough bandages over still oozing wounds. I had never witnessed a sale before and I was feeling distinctly uncomfortable. It was difficult accepting the service of the slaves at the Doma, but this was far worse. I turned to look for Chandra, to suggest we leave, just as the crowd took in a collective gasp of surprise followed by murmurs of excitement and soft coos of appreciation. Despite my reluctance to stay, I stood and stared like everyone else at the platform and then gasped myself, in horror.

An Abroni slave-keeper was pulling a woman onto the platform and she fought him all the way. She was dressed in the remnants of what must once have been an expensive silken wrap and, her long black hair flying, she kicked and hissed and bit the man who held her. He ducked as she swung at him with her free arm and then quickly grabbed it before she could try again. Holding her tightly by both wrists he dragged her before the crowd and the bidding began.

She was very beautiful and the crowd shouted enthusiastically, hurling exorbitant figures at the man who yanked the woman around to give the people at the sides a better view. I was feeling rather ill at the sight of such an uproar and, grabbing Lilith, I searched once more for Chandra. The price had already passed that normally paid for two female slaves and it was still climbing.

I found Chandra right at the front of the crowd and tugged at her arm. She nodded absently, not budging, then pointed at the woman and said, 'Look she has green eyes.'

I turned and for the first time really looked at the woman. She was tall and slim with dusty-gold skin and waves of black hair falling down her half-exposed back and across her face. Then she moved and her hair was flung from her eyes and I saw that Chandra had been right. Her eyes were not the dark colour of the desert nomads but a deep emerald green. That explained the incredible prices. She was a stranger and a rarity, and very, very beautiful.

The crowd had quietened as the price rose. Most of the initial bidders had been forced to drop out and now everyone was wondering who would finally buy the woman. She had stopped fighting the man and stood with her head up, looking disdainfully at the people below her. She ignored her shouting captor who spun between the two sides of the platform where the final bidders were.

I could see the one on this side. He was a large, well-dressed Abroni, a merchant I guessed from his style, whose eyes roamed slowly over the woman's body. I turned to seek the other, but he was somewhere far to the left and I could not see him through the crowd.

The amount offered was already more than I would earn in a half-year and I shivered at the force of the desire that drove anyone to bid so much. At one stage the merchant faltered but as he stared up at the woman she chanced to turn her head and for just a moment their eyes met. Her glance passed over him as though he was not even there and he immediately raised his hand. I made no move to leave now. All such thoughts had been replaced by a curiosity to see this through to the end.

Finally the merchant could not better his rival's offer and the sale was made. Her fate, it seemed, had been sealed by the tinkling of gold. Chains were placed around her wrists and she was taken from the platform and led away to a small wooden hut behind it where the exchange would take place. Now all the fun was over the crowd quickly dispersed.

I stood with Chandra and Lilith and for a moment no-one spoke. Workers were already starting to pull the platform down and we stepped back to give them room. Chandra was peering at the hut, trying to see into it but the door faced away from us.

'I didn't see who bought her,' she said, glancing questioningly at Lilith and me. We both shook our heads.

She nodded and moved towards the hut and looked back at us over her shoulder. 'Coming?' she asked and she walked to the door without waiting for an answer. Lilith smiled at me and shrugged. I took a deep breath and once more we followed.

As Chandra pushed open the thin door, three people looked up.

The slave-keeper, who quickly glanced away again and spoke to the new owner. 'I can brand her now,' he offered. 'I didn't do it before to show she was a new captive. Fresh,' he added with an explanatory grin.

The green-eyed woman, standing silently beside him. She ran her eyes over us swiftly then returned her attention to the third person, who leant indolently against the table, holding a bulging bag of coins.

And Alexa, who glanced at us and smiled calmly before coolly refusing the man's offer, 'No, no brand.' She picked up the slave tag and key and tossed the bag onto the table, just out of his easy reach. 'Leave,' she said dismissively to the man.

His eyes lit up at the sight of the heavy bag and he stretched eagerly to grab it. Once it was in his hand he grinned widely, no doubt pleased with his day's work, and moved towards the door, the green-eyed woman now totally forgotten. He nodded at the three of us as he stepped around us to reach the doorway and then he was gone. Alexa had not bothered to watch him leave. Instead she had stepped up to the woman, relaxed and smiling, and unlocked the chains that held her wrists. I stood in a state of disbelief, trying to come to terms with the fact that Alexa had just bought herself a slave.

Once she had the chains off she dropped them onto the table with a loud clang. The woman's green eyes were studying Alexa with a mixture of wariness and relief. I found myself watching her too, in mystification. I had just remembered the final price.

Alexa met the woman's gaze. 'I am Alexa, this is Chandra, Lilith and Ashil,' and she waved a slim hand easily at each of us as though making introductions at a dinner party.

The woman had turned to us as Alexa spoke our names, her eyes skimming over each of us, bright and alert, and we murmured hellos, still unsure as to what exactly Alexa was doing.

Alexa then drew her dagger from the shiny new belt around her waist and deftly split the slave tag in half, dropping the leather scraps carelessly onto the hut's floor. She slid her dagger back into its sheath. 'We are cartographers working for Lord Maltra,' she explained pleasantly. 'You are free to leave. Or, if you wish, you can come back with us to our rooms and bathe and have something to eat.'

For the first time the woman smiled, a slow, pleased, sensuous smile, and she was truly beautiful.

'I've never seen the Doma before,' she declared in a low, husky voice, her eyes solely on Alexa.

For a moment their gazes held, ice blue and emerald green, and Alexa's lips curved with delight. Then she turned to Lilith. 'Can we have your vest, Lil?' she asked.

Lilith was the only one wearing anything over her thin pale shirt and she murmured a shy 'Yes' and handed it to Alexa with a timid smile for the woman. The woman pulled her wrap around herself as best she could and slipped the vest on over it. It looked strange but covered her.

We headed out into the bazaar and Alexa asked me if I had any difficulty getting the dyes.

With a jolt I realised we still had to buy them. They were important, as our supplies were very low and we would need more before we finished the Nalym maps.

'We haven't bought them yet,' I confessed. I looked at Chandra and Lilith. 'We'll go now.'

Alexa nodded. 'We'll see you back at the Doma.'

Leaving Alexa to take the woman back to our rooms alone, the three of us returned to searching the stalls. We were in luck and found a vendor just north of the inner gates. She had all we required and we made our selection quickly. Laden, we returned to our rooms.

The woman was stretched out asleep on the fifth bed, her long hair still damp from her bath, wrapped in one of Alexa's robes. Alexa was working, but she stood up to help us with our purchases.

'How is she?' Lilith asked quietly, gazing gently at the sleeping woman through the open archway.

'She's exhausted. Her name's Carly and she's going to work with us.' Alexa smiled cheerfully and began to put away the dyes.

FOUR

Occasionally, during our stay in Nalym, we would be invited to dine with her lordship. That evening, with cartography for once not at the forefront of my mind, we received one such summons. It is, of course, not politic to refuse Lord Maltra, so we left Carly sleeping soundly, with a message by her to explain where we had gone, and went to join her lordship's table.

When we returned several hours later, Carly was still fast asleep and we were all too tired and too well-fed to discuss the day's events, so we put it off until the morning and fell into our beds.

The first sound I heard upon waking was Chandra's deep laugh overlaid by a lighter, huskier one. I roused myself and leant up on one elbow, able to see two figures through the thin material of the bed curtain. I reached over and pulled back the curtain and stared through the archway at the two women sitting at the table, eating from the fruit bowl.

Chandra saw me. 'Good morning, Ashil,' she called. 'Come and join us now, before we eat all the figs.'

Her companion turned too and smiled at me. 'Good morning.'

This morning, Carly was dressed in a pair of green trousers I recognised as Chandra's and a plain white shirt of Alexa's. Her hair had been brushed recently and hung with lustrous beauty down her back, soft and thick. Now, relaxed and well-rested, her face shone with good humour, the white of the shirt showing up the warm natural glow of her golden skin. I immediately felt very self-conscious, imagining I looked rather thin and pale, and I smiled back while I reached quickly for my robe.

As I padded over to the table, Alexa stepped out of the washroom in her robe and pulled her hair free of the topknot she had tied it in while bathing. 'Sleep well?' she enquired cheerily as she shook her hair out and began loosing the curls with her fingers.

'Yes,' I replied. 'Like a milk-fed babe.'

'Or a wine-filled cartographer?' Alexa gibed good-naturedly.

There was a knock at the door and two slaves with our breakfast, and another fruit bowl, entered. I pulled out a chair and sat down at the table, watching as the plates were laid before us, but my interest in the food was feigned for, to tell truth, my mind was churning with questions for Carly, particularly concerning her mapping experience.

I did not wish to appear too inquisitive or discourteous, so I held my tongue. I added a chunk of goat's cheese to a thick slice of bread and bit into it, thinking about this beautiful stranger in our midst. Although I was curious to know how she had become a slave, I was loath to just come out and ask. I believed it was a matter that required some delicacy.

'How did you become a slave?' Chandra asked, with a small frown, as she poured herself a drink of milk. Horrified at her lack of subtlety, I glanced hurriedly at Carly, but she was not at all upset and she answered equably, leaning back in her chair.

'I had just concluded my work at the camp of one of the desert tribes. When they said they would be riding to Nalym, I accepted their offer to accompany them. Little did I know that the nomads planned to raid the city's farms, hoping to add to their herds before the bazaar. Three other northerners were with me when the Bramkari struck. One escaped on his horse with a handful of the nomads, two were struck by Bramkari arrows, and I was taken.' She shrugged, as though dismissing the whole incident. 'That was the day before yesterday, when I was given to the slave-keepers. The rest you know.'

Lilith had joined us at the table from the work area and I could see my own horror mirrored in her pale face.

Chandra, however, was clearly disgusted. 'The tribes should not raid and the Bramkari have a right to be angry, but slavery is a wicked thing. Lord Maltra should stop it.'

There was a hard note to Carly's replying laughter. 'People do not always do what they should. They are either unable or do not want to. Without the slaves, the Abroni would not be able to service Nalym and the Bramkari's training routine would be affected. Lord Maltra will never allow that. The raids are nothing. It is when all the desert tribes band together and attack Nalym, trying to force out the Scouts and reclaim the waterholes, that the Bramkari prepare for. These wars occur every few years and are bloody and long, worsened by Netla's self-seeking support of the tribes.'

'What about your friend?' Lilith asked, her brown eyes huge with compassion for the woman who had survived such an ordeal. 'The one who escaped. Will he search for you?'

Carly shook her head. 'We had only just met and although he saw my horse get shot and me fall, he did not stop to see if I still lived. I am not his concern.'

I was astonished with the ease with which Carly could say such things. She appeared truly untouched by it all. Such violence and savagery staggered me. 'What about your family?' I queried. 'They will want to know you are safe.'

Carly nodded. 'I have a brother in Sach. But I have not been gone long enough to alarm him. I will send him word before we move on.'

'Sach?' I repeated softly, mulling over what I knew of the city and its cartography, and realising it was not much.

'Sach,' Chandra echoed excitedly. 'The musician who played last night for Lord Maltra was from there. He had a strange instrument.' She formed a rounded shape with her hands. 'It had a long neck and strings,' and her fingers plucked at imaginary strings. 'The music was so beautiful.'

Carly laughed, this time with true pleasure. 'It's called a gitar. The Bramkari call many of life's pleasures "frivolous" but even Lord Maltra enjoys the sound of good music. What was the musician's name?'

Chandra shook her head, regretfully. 'I do not know. He did not play for long,' she complained.

'I think his name was Demran,' Lilith offered in her quiet voice. 'I heard one of the other guests comment on his talent.'

'Ah, Demran,' Carly said. 'He is well-known. His skill is great. There is one piece that is my favourite.' She tapped her fingers on the table and began to hum a soft tune.

'Yes!' Chandra exclaimed with excitement. 'He played that one. You know it. Are you a musician?'

'No,' Carly replied, raising eyes filled with amusement to Alexa, who, now fully dressed, took a seat at the table, 'I'm not a musician. But I had a tutor who believed life was sadly lacking without an appreciation of music.'

Chandra nodded earnestly. 'She was right. I wanted to speak with Demran last night, but Lord Maltra was too keen to hear all about her maps.'

Alexa smiled and patted her consolingly on the shoulder. 'Speaking of which. Are the maps dry, Lil? If so, the four of us can work on the "prettying" today.'

'Yes,' Lilith replied, 'they're dry enough to work on.'

Carly looked at Lilith. 'I noticed those maps this morning,' she said. 'What part of Nalym are they of?'

I nearly dropped my mug. To anyone with any knowledge of cartography, those maps, though still unlabelled, would have been easy to read. When Carly had said she had been working in the desert I just assumed she had meant as a cartographer or possibly a tracker. Now, I carefully set down my mug and asked her if she had much experience with maps.

'No,' she smiled, 'I'm afraid not. I'm a dancer.'

I shut my mouth and stared at Alexa in disbelief. What could she have been thinking to offer her a job? Our group did not need a dancer!

'How wonderful!' Lilith gushed. 'Were you dancing for the nomads?'

'Yes, my troupe had travelled from Sach to perform at a large celebration. When our leader decided to accept an offer to perform in Netla I decided to stay longer with the nomads and make my own way home to Sach. That's why the other three northerners were strangers to me. They were not from the troupe.'

'Don't you want to rejoin your troupe?' I asked hopefully. I did not dislike Carly but could not see how a dancer could be of much assistance to us.

'No,' she answered, as I feared she would. 'I have had enough of dancing. I'll happily work with the four of you.'

I could not think of anything to say, so I settled for an ambiguous 'Oh.' I darted a glance at Alexa, who was eating her breakfast, but she only met my eye and smiled.

'Where does the next job take us?' Carly asked me.

I opened my mouth in shock, then quickly closed it. 'We do not have the next position arranged,' I explained, 'it's hard to get news of work this far south and we want to head back north once we have finished in Nalym.'

Carly pushed her plate away and smiled brilliantly at me. For a moment, engulfed by the warmth of her smile, I forgot what we had been discussing. 'Fine, leave it to me,' she announced, quite pleasantly. 'I'll leave you to work. I'm off to the Abroni shops. Do you need anything?'

All morning as we worked, I found myself wondering just exactly what Carly had meant by that casual 'leave it to me.' After all, arranging and signing contracts for maps was a detailed and difficult procedure. And Carly knew nothing about maps.

She returned several hours later, her arms full of her purchases which she dumped on her bed before joining us at the table for our midday meal. Afterwards, she followed us as we moved from bench to bench, asking us dozens of questions about our work, how we filled the mapping sheets, the way we drew, the materials we used, the time each task took, the 'prettying', and so on. She was intelligent and quick to learn and, at times, quite undeniably charming, but I was still confused. Carly could never become a cartographer by watching and talking to us. It would take months of training and practice before she could even begin to attempt a rough sketch. So, what was she doing?

Her purchases, it was revealed, were a half a dozen or so elegant outfits. She dressed in one the following morning, a full jade silk skirt with a matching bodice. Long silver earrings dangled from her ears and a thick silver wristband flashed at her wrist. She had touched her eyes with kohl and darkened her lips so that they looked like ripe berries. She smiled, wished us a good day's work, then disappeared out the door and we did not see her again until late that evening.

This continued for three days. Then late on the fourth, as we relaxed on our couches, the maps almost completed, she came in and sat down with a very satisfied grin.

'The Tamina want you to draw for them,' she said off-handedly, as she took a goblet of wine from Chandra.

Chandra, Lilith and I gasped in delighted surprise while Alexa chuckled softly. 'Here is the contract.' Carly threw a thin piece of parchment onto the table. 'It will take us through to the end of spring and take us back north.' Her grin had spread, her own pleasure in our reaction evident.

Chandra picked up the contract and read it with relish, as she loved to do now with each contract we received. Beaming, she handed it to me. I scanned the words, wonder and astonishment and chagrin running through me as I realised it was all true.

'Carly,' I began, feeling very contrite, but she held up her hand.

'It gets better, Ashil. After I had arranged that contract, we received another offer, also for the spring, but I explained that we had already signed and I asked if the job could wait one season. The party was very keen and a contract was offered today. After we finish with the Tamina, we draw for,' she paused, baiting us, her low, husky laughter filling the room as she gazed at our expectant faces, 'we draw for the King of Cynal.'

The room erupted in amazed exclamations, excited cheers and loud talk. Cynal was a beautiful harbour town on the south-west coast, so very appealing after months of scorching desert winds and heat.

'Carly,' I began once more, softly, but she shook her head, smiling.

'You're right, Ashil, I know nothing about maps, but I can be of use to you. I know cities well and I know people well. Nalym is full of diplomats. It has to be because it's the crucial link between the trading desert tribes and all the cities above the Burrnayi Desert. Nalym's bazaar is famous all over Tirayi. In addition to organising trade agreements, part of the duties of the diplomats is to arrange work contacts and I, of course, represent a group of world-renowned cartographers.' She laughed at the incredulous look on my face and patted my cheek. 'It's simple really, because, you see, I made a very interesting discovery. I may know nothing about maps, Ashil, but diplomats know even less.'

We completed the Nalym maps, including those of the outer farms and the Doma, and a very satisfied Lord Maltra gave us our final payment, with a little extra. So that afternoon, when Carly was out of the room, I suggested to the others that we use the extra coin to replace the horse Carly had lost during the raid. The others agreed with enthusiasm.

Chandra and Alexa went to make the purchase, while Lilith and I began the packing. When both tasks were completed we led Carly to the stables with a great deal of foolery and teasing. We had no fanfare, so I gave a high-pitched hoot and Cleo reared and neighed as she had been taught. Carly laughed, then quietened as she saw the pretty piebald mare that Chandra was leading out from the stall behind Cleo. Carly was touched beyond words and promptly named her Flir. So it was in fine spirits that the five of us rode out of the city of Nalym and headed north towards our next job.

It is strange how events occur. If anyone had asked me, I would have said that the risk of danger would decrease as we moved further away from Nalym, Netla and the desert, and I would have been very wrong. For with the Tamina, not only danger but great pain awaited us, and we rode towards it cheerful and unsuspecting.

The Tamina, or the Rovers, as they are also known, are a passionate, nature-loving people. They have little wealth, though amongst their numbers is a seer so famed for his skill at foretelling the future that his name is spoken with awe and reverence throughout Tirayi. Kings and rulers have tried to lure him to their courts with offers of great riches and luxury, but always he refuses. He knows his place. All who wish to speak with him must come to the caravans of the Rovers and pay, whether pauper or prince, one piece of silver. For such a price one may enter the seer's caravan and ask him one question and hope, while he enters his trance, his fingers moving beads in his sand tray, to hear news of good fortune.

We met Brai, the seer. He was old and small and full of warmth and soft smiles and gentle laughter. He could not see, his eyes were cloudy and dull, like a white clump of agate a trader had once shown me, and he had long ago lost his two front teeth, so that at times, smiling, with his pale hairless scalp and unfocused eyes, he appeared like a babe. He liked to tell silly jokes and hear the stories of the children's antics and, when he could, he liked to sit and chat with us, finding the stories of our lives fascinating.

Coming to know him like this made the events of our meeting all the more horrible.

It was early in the afternoon of a hot day. We had encountered no problems on our journey from Nalym and knew we were within a league or two of the Tamina caravans. We had told them to expect us this day or the next, so we were moving at a leisurely pace, confident of arriving well before nightfall. Carly had spilt her water pouch earlier that day and when we came to a small creek we paused so she could refill it. The bank was steep and soft and we had to dismount to water our horses. Cleo was not thirsty and stood, head raised at the water's edge, so, moving out of Alexa's way, I climbed back with her to the track, standing beside her, idly stroking her warm snout. Moments later, Chandra came up beside me, already mounted.

So close to the caravans, we were not alarmed when we heard loud voices and cries before us, then the sound of horses racing. I assumed it was some of the Rovers come to meet us. They were reputed to be a noisy, frolicsome bunch. But the people who came charging through the trees before us were not Tamina and they were neither frolicsome nor friendly.

There were six of them, riding four horses, the riders

all so heavily robed in hooded cloaks that it was impossible to see their faces. The attack was so quick and unexpected that neither Chandra nor I ever stood a chance.

Unprovoked, the riders charged forward, one kicking me solidly in the chest so that I dropped the reins and fell, rolling awkwardly down the bank and coming to rest against Flir's hooves, the ends of my hair floating in the creek.

Shocked and angered, Chandra drew her hunting knife and was immediately faced with two swords. One was raised high and would surely have killed her had not an arrow come flying through the air and pierced the attacker's side. The robed figure gave a strangled cry and dropped the sword, bending forward, to be grasped and held up by the rider behind. The other sword came swinging through the air and Chandra managed to deflect it skilfully with her knife so that, instead of taking her head, the blade slid and hacked deep into her chest and cut across her shoulder. Chandra screamed and was toppled from Ray's back by the sheer force of the blow.

Yet before she fell, her own knife had run along the edge of the sword and flown up into the face of her attacker, tearing the hood. For a moment, the rider's face was revealed before the hood was hurriedly put in place. Another arrow came from behind and pierced another rider's arm. Hastily they kicked at their mounts, leaning to grab up Cleo and Ray's reins. They tugged at the two confused horses and galloped away. Moments later the Tamina archers arrived.

As I was lifted slowly from the creek's edge and

carried to the track, trying to ignore the unbelievable pain that bit at my chest with each movement, I saw Carly come up beside and open her mouth to speak. I shut my eyes, waiting for her words. When none came, I opened them again to see her staring beyond me towards the area where the attack had occurred. Rolling my head very gently to the side, I watched her walk over and stoop to pluck something from the ground. Curiosity now fighting pain, I stayed alert as she brought it back to me and showed me a small plait of chestnut hair.

'It must be from the rider,' Carly said, holding it up to the sunlight. Then suddenly she grinned. 'Amongst my people,' she said, 'a lock of hair in your enemy's hand is considered very bad luck. I wonder if the rider knows that.' She tucked the plait inside her silver wristband.

At the caravans, all was chaos. Chandra and I were carried in, Chandra barely conscious, to discover that we had not been the only ones to feel the sting of the riders' blades. An old blind man, with blood streaming down his cheek and dripping from a mangled hand, had been the first. He was Brai the seer and one of the hooded riders had tried to kill him. Such a thing was unheard of amongst the Tamina and their confusion, disbelief and fury were great. It was true that many left the caravan of the seer with heavy hearts and worried minds, having found no solace or pleasure in his words, but none before had tried to punish him for speaking of what he saw. Angered and betrayed, the Tamina closed around him protectively, sending away all other petitioners who had come to see him. He sat calmly while his people ranted and screamed and wept around him until they led him to a caravan for healing and Chandra and I were taken to another.

I was lucky. No bones had been damaged in my chest, though it was painful just to breathe for many days after and I learnt to take small, shallow breaths, hoping to cheat the pain. Almost all movement was a torture so I spent the days lying still on my back, willing my body to heal and my mind to dwell on other things. My chest swelled with bruising and the skin changed from black to purple to yellow. I felt awful but I knew it would pass. Not so for Chandra. She was in agony.

They had placed her on the other side of the caravan with a curtain between us and the healers came to her often. Above her breast, the bone had been cracked and exposed and the muscle torn, while the cut to her shoulder was deep and ugly. The Tamina healers were skilled and gentle but nothing they gave her could remove all the pain and I wept to hear her anguished moans as they set the bone and stitched the skin together.

Alexa, Carly and Lilith sat with us for hours, repeating idle chatter and stroking Chandra's brow, trying as best they could to ease our suffering. It was another blow to hear that Cleo and Ray were lost to us. Alexa explained that the Tamina, with their short, sturdy ponies had quickly been outdistanced by the hooded attackers and, returning disheartened, had been eager to accept her offer to track the six riders. The tracking had gone well, taking the Tamina far beyond the point where they had first lost the six, but then the riders had taken to water and try as she could to find where the tracks re-emerged, Alexa had been forced to admit defeat.

The attack had a strange effect on our group. Just as the Tamina had closed ranks, the five of us were drawn more closely together. Lilith was concerned with our comfort, always present to fetch us water, adjust our blankets, talk softly to us or just sit companionably in silence. She rarely left us.

Carly was furious, cursing the riders ferociously, her green eyes hard and brilliant, saying that she hoped whatever it was that Brai had spoken of came true and was painful, terrifying, debilitating and continued without end. I found her anger warming, amusing and exhausting.

Alexa was angry also but she did not swear and curse like Carly. Instead, calmly, quietly, coolly, she spoke with the Tamina, trying to discover all she could about the six. There was not much to know. Brai would not say what he had read in the sand, only saying that on hearing it, the rider had risen, enraged, screaming 'Liar', and drawn a long dagger and made to plunge it into his chest. Brai had raised a hand to protect himself and the blade had passed through it, the tip emerging to scratch his cheek. Fleeing from a rear door, Brai had escaped and the rider had rushed from the caravan, calling hurriedly to the other five as they waited nearby. They were mounted and riding by the time the alarm was raised and the Tamina managed to kill two of the horses and wound one of the riders before the six fled the camp. The rest of the tale we knew.

'If Cleo is gone,' I said, 'then so too is my sketching kit with all my equipment.'

Alexa nodded. 'We can get replacements. Your father's maps are safe, I was carrying them.'

I looked up at her from my bed. 'I loved that horse,' I said flatly.

'I know.' Her voice was soft.

While Chandra and I were recovering, the other three began on the map. The Tamina followed a similar route each year and had several small maps that they used. One of these maps had been recently lost and we had been employed to replace it. Our mapping progress was slow but soon improved when I became able to move about once again and assist with the sketching.

We completed the map without Chandra. The pain grew less as she slowly mended, the bone strengthening and the scar tissue forming, but the healers insisted she remain still so as not to undo their painstaking work. Gradually, as the weeks passed, Chandra was able to take small walks around the camp, her upper body heavily strapped. She regained her appetite and slept less. When the healers suggested it was time to begin moving the arm and shoulder gently so it would not stiffen permanently, she agreed with enthusiasm.

Brai was not so fortunate. His hand had been permanently damaged by the blade. Tendons had been severed and the hand was now ugly and near useless. And a thin, raised scar ran along his cheek. He, however, paid little attention to his wounds, acting as though his disfigured hand was no hindrance. He came to visit Chandra and me, though his talk was never of the riders. I thought I understood this, though one thing puzzled me, and one day I asked it of him. If he could see the future, how had he not foreseen the attack?

He had smiled, unsurprised by my question, and answered simply, 'Some things must be. If you alter one step, the whole pattern of the dance changes.'

'But your hand,' I protested.

'There are worse fates.'

Spring ended and we completed the map. It was time to plan our next move. We were fortunate in that Carly, not knowing exactly how much time to allow with the Tamina, had been overly cautious and had not signed us to begin in Cynal for several more weeks. We were close to Binet, though it lay to the north and was not on our route west to the harbour city. Both Lilith and I thought of it with ill-disguised longing, and all five of us knew that we could easily buy the horses and packs Chandra and I needed there, so it was soon decided that we would head to Binet next. The Tamina lent us two ponies, saying we could leave them with some friends they had in the city, and we said our goodbyes, setting out at a moderate pace that Chandra would not find too taxing.

It had been almost two years since I had been home and as we entered my birth city along its main street, all around me felt at once familiar and yet strange. Lilith edged Timi closer to me and I smiled across at her, sweet anticipation animating both of us.

We had planned it so we would arrive on free-day, for neither Lilith's nor my parents would be at work. I had written home many times but this visit would be a surprise as my parents knew nothing of our contracts with the Tamina or the Cynalese. I glanced at Chandra but she was sitting tall on her pony, looking around with interest, her hands loose on the reins. She was no longer troubled by constant pain and said she felt stronger every day.

The main street runs straight through Binet from east to west and cuts directly through the city square and the marketplace. West of the square one finds the city baths, the courthouse, the Plaza of the City Guardians and the houses of the rich. East of the square, where we now rode, was full of shops and factories and the homes of artisans and workers. One block from the square Lilith pulled up. Her parents' home was three blocks away to the left. She would go alone and the other three would come with me. I knew my parents would be eager to meet my workmates.

We waved goodbye to Lilith and continued on, walking our mounts slowly through the marketplace as we dodged people and livestock in varying degrees of liveliness. The army was based midway between the western gate and the square, with a small rotating contingent at the eastern gatehouse. My parents lived as close to the base as they could afford, in the city's north-west near the schools and within comfortable walking distance of the theatre. It had always been my favourite part of the city, as it thronged with students, actors, young orators practising for the courts or Plaza, and cafes and wine shops with street tables overflowing with customers and talk.

My parents live in a thin two-storey beige house in a quiet cobbled street. The house gives straight onto

121

the road but there is a stable and a small walled garden at the back where my father tends his scented flowers. In the spring I would take my home-lessons and sit in the garden, revelling in the solitude and the delicious perfumes.

We led the ponies and horses through the side gate into the stable. My father's mount whinnied a greeting, sniffing eagerly at the newcomers, while my mother's looked up, his mouth full of hay, and regarded us solemnly for a moment before returning to his eating. Although it was early, I was not surprised to see Thoma's horse was already gone. My brother had always risen with the sun.

We settled the animals, my stomach churning with excitement, and walked out into the garden. It glowed like green glass in the clear sunlight but I barely spared it a glance as I hurried to the rear door. I pulled it open and stepped inside and called out a loud hello. I heard my mother's joyous shriek from above, then seconds later she was running down the stairs and embracing me tightly. My father had followed at a more sedate pace and he greeted Chandra and the others with a broad smile while waiting for my mother to release me so he too could enfold me in his arms.

My mother took a deep contented breath, her eyes roving hungrily over my face as she reached out to touch me once more. 'Darling, what a delightful surprise,' she said on a loud, happy sigh, her hand squeezing mine.

The other three had hung back but now my father, who was behind me, with his hands resting on my shoulders, greeted Chandra and asked how she was.

'I am in excellent health,' Chandra replied, beaming happily, and Carly, Alexa and I stared at her in astonishment.

My father raised an eyebrow and I shook my head.

'I'll explain it all later,' I said. 'First I'd like you to meet Alexa and Carly.'

After the introductions we moved to the salon and I looked around the room in fond remembrance. Not much had changed. There was a new vase by the window full of the last of the garden's blooms and there were several more rare books on the shelf, and in the centre of the floor was the soft mat my mother had just started weaving before I left for Skar Linon's. But it was still the room I had grown up with. My father brought in a tray with drinks and cakes then sat between Carly and me on the long couch.

'You've missed Thoma,' my mother said, as I sipped at a cool drink. 'He's gone to visit Sarra for the day.'

I had heard of my brother's romance from his and my parents' letters. Apparently I had met this paragon of loveliness years before, but she cannot have been quite as striking then for I could not remember her.

My father had not said much yet, but once we were settled with food and drink, he leant forwards, his expression keen. 'And how goes the world of cartography?' he asked.

I grinned with pleasure. 'We're on our way to Cynal, to draw for the king,' I announced.

But instead of my father's face showing the delight I had anticipated, his forehead creased in a frown.

'You've heard that he's ill?'

I nodded. We had heard something of it from the

Tamina but they had called it a spring cold so we had not given it much thought. 'Yes, but it is only a cold.'

My father shook his head solemnly. 'So they thought at first, but he is not a young man and it has grown worse. There are doubts he will pull through and even if he does he will be considerably weakened. It is rumoured he will step down for his son, Lord Tarn.'

An uncertain silence fell over the room as Chandra and Alexa broke off from chatting with my mother and Carly, on my father's left, lowered her wine goblet to stare at him in dismay. Aware of our plummeting spirits my father laughed.

'Don't despair. Ill or not, Cynal has not ground to a standstill. I'm sure your maps will still be required.'

In the silence that followed, mother offered more drink and cake but Alexa refused politely and stood up. 'If you don't mind, we' her glance included Carly and Chandra, 'were thinking of visiting the market and having a look at the city.'

Alexa had an uncanny ability to say the right thing at the right time and this was no exception. Her words were like the opening of a window, bringing with them a refreshing, gentle breeze, exactly what was needed to remove the last stubborn traces of my father's unwelcome announcement. Alexa's tact pleased me too, for it meant I could have my parents all to myself for the day and we could talk freely, and I saw by the broad smile that appeared on my mother's face that she shared my thoughts.

I turned to Chandra. 'Unless you want to rest,' I offered hesitantly.

Chandra gave me a withering look and, saying no

more, I rose and walked my friends to the front door, repeating my parents' invitation to dinner that evening. They accepted and waved goodbye to me as they stepped onto the street and I watched them until they disappeared around the corner. Then I returned eagerly to the salon and my parents.

'What happened to Chandra?' my father asked immediately and I was forced to give a brief, softened, description of the attack at the Tamina camp.

Both my parents were horrified and my mother insisted on examining my chest, though I assured them both I was fully recovered. After finding no trace of damage, my mother kissed my cheek.

'You were very lucky. Any or all of you could have been killed,' my father said solemnly.

I was over the shock of the incident now. 'It was the horses they wanted, not us,' I replied, with a small shrug.

He grunted. 'People will often kill to get what they want, Ashil. You should think about learning to defend yourself. I could arrange for one of the officers to give you some lessons while you're in Binet.'

'We won't have time. We leave for Cynal at the end of the week.'

He gave a brisk nod and I could see how worried he was. 'Well, give it some thought,' he murmured.

'I already have,' I answered honestly, throwing my arm around his shoulders and giving him a quick hug. It was nice that they were so concerned. 'I can't afford to lose another horse,' I added lightly, hoping to ease the tension.

This successfully changed the subject, my mother

asking if I was short of coin and saying that if I wanted to buy another horse in Binet she had a client who ran a large, well-respected stable.

From this topic we drifted to other harmless ones, gossip about people I knew in Binet, tales from my travels, cartographic news and problems we had encountered. During a natural pause in the conversation, my mother cut me another piece of the rough grain cake, she knew it was my favourite, and passed it to me. 'Did Lilith come back with you?' she asked.

I plucked out a thick nut from the dense mixture and crunched it between my teeth. 'Yes, she's spending the day with her parents. She'll probably visit tomorrow.'

'How are the five of you getting along?' my father asked, settling back against the couch.

'Wonderfully well,' I replied. 'One's weakness is another's strength, so our working routine is quite efficient. We give each other time alone when we need it and accept that we all have different pasts.' I thought in particular of Alexa, about whom we still knew very little. 'We all share a genuine respect and liking for each other, so it makes sitting down to share a meal at the end of the day very pleasant.' I sighed contentedly. 'It's delightful having such friends and knowing that they are there for you in moments of difficulty.'

An amused look passed between my parents and I looked at them questioningly.

My father laughed. 'It's just that that used to be our role. You've grown up, Ashil. Your mother and I will need time to adjust.'

I kissed his cheek. 'I'll always need you. After all,

you can't buy grain cake like this anywhere else in Tirayi.'

They both laughed and my father playfully swatted my cheek.

Dinner that night was a jolly, relaxed affair, made all the more pleasant by the arrival of my brother Thoma. My parents had aged slightly since I had last seen them. There was still no grey in their hair and they stood straight and strong, but there were more wrinkles around their eyes and deeper grooves from nose to mouth, but in Thoma the change was drastic.

Two years ago he had been a slightly built fifteen-year-old boy. Now I stook looking up at a broad-shouldered giant with shadowed cheeks and a deep voice. My astonishment lasted all through dinner, tempered by my amusement at his obvious admiration for Carly, who was in fine spirits, flirting with him gently and I am sure quite making him forget Sarra for the evening.

My father was engrossed in a conversation with Alexa about the upcoming Plaza elections. I had long since passed the point of surprise where Alexa was concerned. Nothing she could do or say could astound me and I was glad to see this was not yet the case with my father, who sat and listened to her opinions with unfeigned admiration. I could just see him thinking that if Chandra had been a dry well in need of filling, Alexa was a deep spring quietly overflowing. It pleased me that now when I wrote, my family would be able to picture the faces of the people I spoke of. Not that

I told them everything. They knew we had met Carly in Nalym but they were ignorant of the circumstances, for they were right, I had matured a lot in the past two years and there were aspects of my life I would no longer share with my parents.

We visited Lilith at home, briefly, and Lil introduced Alexa and Carly to her parents. She also spent time with my family and I noted my father watching her curiously. I raised an enquiring eyebrow. 'Lilith has grown up too,' he remarked pithily. Then he ruffled my hair affectionately and left the room.

I turned to look at Lil with new eyes. She had not even turned sixteen when we took our first job with Skar Linon, and now, two years later, she had indeed grown up. She had filled out in body, though she was still slight, and would always be, but I was sure my father was not referring to any physical changes. It was simply that Lilith, like me, had matured. She was more sure of herself now, comfortable in her role as carto-grapher and traveller and, best of all, her voice and laugh were more often heard.

It was a discovery that pleased me and I repeated my father's words to her. 'I had not really noticed it until he pointed it out,' I said.

A pretty smile lit her face. 'My parents said the same thing. I see them looking at me sometimes in awe, as though they're not quite sure what happened to the daughter who rode away from Binet that fateful sum-mer's day.' She sighed softly. 'They have not changed.'

Then she smiled and shrugged her shoulders. 'I had hoped that perhaps they would have discovered more of the world once I was gone, but their routine is just the same. And the strangest thing, Ashil, is how I feel when I am with them and in my home. It is as though I had never left, and I can feel myself returning to the way I was.'

She sighed again and looked away. 'I love them very much, but returning to Binet has made me realise that my leaving was the right decision and it makes it easier to leave this time. I find myself looking forward to Cynal.'

I too was looking forward to Cynal and, with Chandra, spent a day at the marketplace purchasing new equipment to replace what had been stolen. We were fortunate that Lilith and Carly had been carrying the two large mapping packs and so it was only two sketching kits that needed to be replaced. Still, each had contained blank mapping sheets, sketching styluses and ink pots, a pair of wooden dividers, wooden rulers and angle squares, a rectangular protractor, a circle tracer with a specially tapered stylus attached and mathematical charts. It was a long list to fill and both Chandra and I were enormously relieved when we were once again able to sling a kit over a shoulder, happy to feel the familiar weight.

We returned the Tamina ponies and bought new horses from my mother's friend. My gelding, Lukar, was handsome and well-mannered, but it felt strange to be on any horse other than Cleo and I knew it would take time before I came to cherish him.

All too soon, it was time to leave. We made our farewells and, with a very satisfied feeling, I rode out of my birth city, surrounded by my friends, with the prospect of another exciting job ahead of us and the knowledge that I was leaving my family safe and well behind me.

We arrived in Cynal to the news that the king had died and the city was in mourning. There could be no talk of maps or contracts until after the funeral, so we set ourselves to enjoying the weather and the wine and resigned ourselves to waiting.

FIVE

CYNAL MOURNED FOR two weeks. Black banners flew from houses and buildings, the palace walls were covered in black and silver silk and the soldiers wore black and silver ribbons in their hair. Funeral fires burnt throughout the city, there was no public dancing or singing and inns closed immediately after serving their evening meal. The streets were empty and even the marketplace was subdued, with many vendors not setting up stalls at all. It was only at the harbour that activity did not cease, for not even the death of a king could slow the arrival of the trading ships.

Cynal is very beautiful, full of delights both natural and hand-hewn, but the time of mourning left us with no heart for anything other than the most desultory investigation of the city, and we took to spending most of our time on the beach.

It was an old fisher who told us about the cove. We had been watching the fishers unload their catch late one morning at the upper harbour, enjoying the play of light on their glistening, tanned skin and flirting with them quite merrily, when Chandra began to chat to him.

'Will all those fish get eaten?' she asked, staring in

amazement at the number being unloaded. She had only caught a glimpse of the ocean at Delawyn and now, in Cynal, she was free to examine and exclaim over its many marvels.

The fisher gave a dry, croaky laugh. 'I hope so, otherwise we should've left them in the sea.'

Chandra grinned, agreeing entirely with that sentiment. She watched as the huge nets were slowly gathered and replaced on the boats, then asked how the fishers knew where to find the fish.

He gave a curt nod in response to her question, his greying curls blowing about his lined face. 'You learn to look for the signs and sometimes,' that dry laugh again, 'if you're lucky, you have a little help.'

I had been smiling at a particularly gorgeous fisher who was standing aboard one of the boats, gathering the nets. He was grinning back at me, his task nearly complete, but at those words I suddenly broke our gaze and turned to the old fisher.

'The merfolk?' I whispered, hope and incredulity robbing my voice of its strength.

He looked at me, his eyes gleaming like polished wood amidst skin almost as dark. 'You're not from nearby, are you?'

I shook my head slowly. 'No,' I murmured, 'I'm from Binet.'

He raised his eyebrows as he considered my answer, then peered out to sea, far beyond the anchored boats and their crews, to where there were only the seabirds, diving and calling effortlessly, flying off to become tiny silhouetted specks against the burning morning sun, before disappearing from sight.

In fact he was so quiet I feared he had forgotten my question. I could hear Carly and Alexa laughing gaily behind me, amid the deep sound of male voices, and, not far ahead of where Chandra and I stood, I could see Lilith shyly allowing two Cynalese children to play with her white blonde hair and run their chubby, tanned fingers across her pale skin. I had forgotten the handsome man at the nets as I stood and stared at the old fisher, wanting desperately to know what he knew.

Finally, softly, his eyes never leaving the ocean, he spoke. 'They're out there now, playing.' He turned to me. 'But you can only see them if they want you to. They're as fast in the water as any dolphin. They lead us to the fish sometimes and they follow the boats, jumping and swimming around and around. They've been known to help fishers and sailors who've fallen overboard.' He smiled, his tone becoming gentle, almost admonishing. 'But their ways are strange to us and it's impossible to call them. They're choosy about who they'll befriend.'

He gazed once more out to sea. 'They rarely come into shore. They're the most beautiful creatures I've ever seen or heard. They can speak the Middling Tongue you know, if they've a mind to.' Then softly, wonderingly, his eyes misted with memory, Chandra and me all but forgotten, 'I heard them once.'

The pang of envy I felt astonished me. All my life I had heard garbled tales of these folk. How exotic and foreign they had seemed to me in my landlocked birth city! The fishers in Delawyn had been dismissive of my questions, saying the merfolk no longer visited their waters and were nothing more than a nuisance when they did. But they were a surly bunch, infected with the city's gloom, and I refused to take their words to heart. Now, after having heard that the marvellous folk did exist and swam in Cynalese waters, I looked out to sea, crestfallen, for the fisher's words had also made my cherished hope of ever seeing the merfolk appear foolish and childishly unrealistic.

He had resumed talking to Chandra. She was explaining what had brought us to Cynal, standing tall and relaxed, her head back as though welcoming the caresses of the sun on her face as she told the fisher of our hopes that Lord Tarn would honour his father's contract.

'Until we know this,' Chandra concluded, 'we must wait patiently in Cynal. So today we have come to watch the fishing boats return and perhaps to swim in this water full of salt and merfolk.'

He laughed. 'I wish you well with your maps. Lord Tarn is an honourable man. He is a good friend of the fishers. His father gave him the harbour as one of his duties and he looks after us.' He gave an emphatic nod. 'He is fair and knowledgeable.'

Then he grinned. 'As for coming here today, well, you have seen the boats and many fish, but here is not the place to swim.' He shook his head. 'It is too crowded. There is a cove south of the city which is well hidden. It is known to the fishers but it is small and a long way to carry the fish, so it is mostly left undisturbed. If you wish to swim in peace you should go there. I will tell you how.'

The fisher gave us directions and we stayed on the beach, talking to him and other fishers and sharing their midday meal. Afterwards, we walked along the water's edge, the many-sized fishing boats bobbing at their moorings on the short simple pier. Leisurely, we walked on until the sandy beach ran out, the wall of the lower harbour now jutting out ahead of us into water deep enough for the large trading ships. The noise of the place reached us but we went no further. Instead we turned to retrace our steps, the afternoon effortlessly slipping away.

At the pier once more, we stopped to watch the sun lower itself into the water, appearing to melt gently into the waves. Such a beautiful, simple sight has the power to relax and cheer and we returned to the subdued city streets, speaking of our day in hushed and peaceful tones, looking forward to our venture for the morrow.

We followed the directions the fisher had given us the next morning, after first stopping at the market-place to buy food and wine. If we failed to find the cove, we would stop elsewhere along the coast for a leisurely picnic.

But the cove was easy to find and it was exactly as the fisher had described it. Well hidden by the tall, wild trees that grew on its three sides and by the slope of the ground towards the ocean, the pale half-moon beach, when we stepped down onto it, was breathtak-ing, a delight to treasure. It was barely twenty paces across, and we could neither see nor hear anything other than the cry of the birds and the song of the sea. It was as though we were alone in the world.

We settled down beneath a clump of the trees, their shade offering delicious respite from the searing summer sun, feeling the warmth and the calmness enfold us, looking about us with pleasure.

I was curious to swim in the salt water. My swimming experience was limited to the city baths of Binet, where my mother had taught me as a child, and although I was not a strong swimmer the ocean appeared tranquil and inviting and I was soon feeling too hot to sit still. I stood up and began to strip off my clothes.

'Who wants to join me?' I asked.

Chandra rose instantly. 'I will.'

Alexa smiled. 'So will I. It's been too long since I swam in the ocean.'

'Carly? Lil?' I asked, turning to them.

Carly laughed softly. 'I can't, I don't know how. Water in Netla was scarce so,' she shrugged, 'I never learnt.'

I stopped in the act of folding my shirt. 'Netla?'

She nodded. 'My birth city.' She smiled up at me. 'Never go there, Ashil, it's one huge midden.'

'I can't swim either,' Lil confessed, with an apprehensive glance at the ocean, 'I've never been in water deeper than my knees.'

Alexa had just finished pulling her long curls into a single thick braid. 'Never fear,' she said, 'we'll teach you. This is the perfect spot to learn.'

Lilith hesitated but Alexa spoke to her gently. 'We'll take it slowly, Lil, and no-one will force you to go any deeper than you feel comfortable. None of us was born knowing how to swim. We all had to learn it.'

'Yes,' Chandra agreed, 'and it's fun.'

That brought a small smile from Lil and a loud laugh

from Carly and they both stood up and quickly dropped their clothes to the sand. Loving the warm breath of the wind as it skipped over our bare flesh, we padded down to the water's edge, where tiny ripplets ran up to kiss our toes.

The water was so clear and pure we could see our feet beneath us as we waded in.

'I can see fish,' Chandra exclaimed. 'Look,' she pointed, 'they're everywhere.'

Indeed, tiny schools of fish were darting around our legs like so many streaks of silver and we laughingly tried to catch them, laughing even harder when they effortlessly escaped our hands.

We waded in further until the water was to our waists, our fingers trailing behind us.

' I always won the river races at home,' Chandra said, her mouth open as though to drink in the blue beauty that encircled us, below and above, 'but this is better than any river.'

Alexa dived in neatly, entering the water with barely a splash, to re-emerge moments later, pushing stray wet curls from her face. She lay back in the water, floating gently, her body bobbing with the movement of the sea.

'How are you doing that?' Carly asked, staring at Alexa, perplexed.

Alexa smiled and rolled over to swim a few strokes towards Carly. 'I'll show you.'

Lilith watched too, fascinated, as Alexa began to explain. Chandra tugged my arm. 'Let's go for a swim, out there,' she said, waving an arm out to sea.

'All right, but not too far.' The ocean, so vast and

peaceful, had a strange allure that was difficult to resist.

'Good,' and Chandra dived into the water and began to swim with easy, powerful strokes, only a slight dipping of her scarred left shoulder acknowledging her wound. I crouched down, letting the water flow over my body, then dropped my head under the water as I pushed off with my feet, breaking through the surface and into a slow, relaxed stroke. I found my rhythm quickly and was soon enjoying the feeling of freedom and movement as my naked body plunged through the water and the sun warmed my back and neck.

I caught up with Chandra, who was using her hands and feet to keep herself stationary in the water. I copied Alexa and floated on my back, squinting up at a flock of seabirds as they flew overhead. The lapping of the water at my ears blocked out all sound and I shut my eyes for a moment.

It was the dripping of water on my forehead that roused me and I opened my eyes to see Chandra beside me, grinning, her cupped hand above my head, full of water.

'Wake up, Ashil, or you'll float out to sea.'

I glanced back to shore and was surprised to see how far I had come. The other three were still close to the shore and I thought I saw Lilith floating.

'Alexa has got Lilith and Carly diving too,' Chandra told me, following my gaze. 'Let's go and help.'

We swam back together and spent the rest of the morning in the shallows, dissecting our swimming styles, while Lilith and Carly made marked progress. Before the sun reached its zenith, I rose out of the water.

'I'm going in before my skin burns,' I said, holding my arms out before me to see if they had reddened. 'You should come in too, Lil,' I suggested. 'You're even fairer than I am.'

'Yes,' Lilith nodded and Carly stood up beside her, the water streaming off her golden skin.

'Learning to swim is great fun,' Carly said, 'but right now my body is demanding sustenance.'

The mention of food was too much for us all, so the five of us returned to the shade of the trees where we unpacked our morning purchases and passed around the wineskin, eating and drinking hungrily.

Our skin was dotted with tiny droplets that dried as we sat and our wet hair hung down our backs. All except Chandra's, which was curling even tighter than usual, dusted here and there with sand grains.

We had none of us bothered to dress and I eyed my shirt undecidedly, knowing that to put it on with my hair still damp would mean a wet back, when Chandra suddenly burst out laughing.

'Ashil,' she exclaimed with glee, 'I remember when your cheeks would redden at the sight of nakedness. Now,' she grinned happily, 'you sit and eat first, before deciding whether to cover yourself.'

I smiled, recalling the nomad youths' dance to the god of life and how my cheeks had burnt. I shrugged, mildly amused by the memory, and wondered if Chandra realised that it was not just the youths' nakedness but the raw, celebrated sexuality of the dance that had so shocked me.

'We've all seen each other naked before,' I offered as explanation. 'Besides,' I added, 'we're all female.'

139

Carly chuckled. She was as stunning undressed as dressed, flawlessly beautiful with the pliant strength and grace of a dancer. She was also the one most likely of us all to walk around our apartment unclothed on her way to bathe or as she searched for an item of clothing. I no longer felt too embarrassed to be seen by her. Friendship had cured me of that, friendship and because, as I reasoned, it did not truly matter. A cartographer does not need to be beautiful to be successful, just skilful.

Carly was lying on her side now, on the blanket we had brought to cover the sand, her elbow causing a small indentation where it pressed against the wool, her head resting on her hand.

'My first lover was a woman,' she stated simply, with a reminiscent smile. 'She was a perfumer in Netla.'

'A woman?' I repeated softly, incredulously. Carly?

Unperturbed, she nodded. 'It's common in Netla for your first lover to be of the same sex. Sometimes you lose interest as you grow older and turn to the other sex, sometimes you don't. My brother in Sach is still living with the same man that he escaped from Netla with years ago.'

Chandra was clearly fascinated. 'It happens in the tribe too, though it's discouraged when you are older because that way there can be no children.' Then, blessed Chandra, she asked outright what I dared not. 'Do you like men now too?'

'Very much. I like the feel of strong, hard muscle under my hands, and other things besides.'

I turned and reached for the wineskin. Here I was feeling so smug because I could sit naked amongst my friends, yet Carly's words had brought the fire back to my cheeks. I took a deep gulp and handed it to Lilith, for she looked as if she needed a drink as well.

'Did you escape from Netla with your brother?' Alexa asked, taking the wineskin from Lilith.

'Yes,' Carly nodded, 'the cursed triad left us with no choice. They had already killed my mother and sister and left my father in the fields to die slowly. Our house and farm had been burnt, there was nothing to hold us there any more.'

'The triad?' Chandra queried, turning to Alexa. 'Are they the three families you spoke of?'

Alexa nodded grimly.

'Why did they hurt your family and burn your farm?' Chandra asked, frowning unhappily.

Carly gave a bitter laugh. 'We were an example to others. We owned a large cotton farm outside the city, in an area that had long been under the control of one of the triad, the Alenit clan, to whom we were forced to pay peace money. But the Geron clan had long been growing in power in the area and wrestled control from the Alenit and demanded that we pay peace money to them instead. All my mother cared for was getting the crops in and my father just wished to continue his dance teaching, so they complied.'

Carly sneered. 'Of course the Alenit and the Dezla clans became alarmed at the increasing strength of the Geron, and joined together to break their hold of the area. Once the Alenit were back in power they made an example of several families, saying we aided the Geron and gave them money that belonged to the Alenit. My mother and sister were killed trying to fight

141

the soldiers who came to burn our fields. My brother and I were not on the farm and only discovered what had happened when we returned that evening. We could not find our father anywhere. He was not at his school and several of his students said they had not seen him all day. We found him late that night, amongst the burnt fields, too weak to move. He could barely speak. If it had not been for the rings he wore on his hand, I would not have known him under the burns.'

Carly's voice was controlled and unemotional but I could feel tears welling in my eyes. For a moment I tried to imagine how I would feel if I had discovered my mother's corpse and the dying, burnt body of my father. My world would end, I thought. I was no longer aware of the beauty of the summer day or the calm, blue sheen of the ocean. My throat felt choked and at Carly's next words I feared my tears would spill over.

'In a painful whisper, my father told us both how much he loved us and how proud he was that we were his children. Then he told us where we would find money that he and my mother had hidden over the years. We all knew he would not live till morning and the pain was unbearable, so he asked my brother to draw his dagger and kill him. It was done and we buried him amongst the fields. After, we stopped long enough to collect the money and my brother's friend and we left Netla that night.'

She took a deep breath. 'We have never been back. My brother and his friend now have a tiling business in Sach and I joined a dancing troupe in the city. I travelled often with the troupe but after performing with them in the desert I refused to accompany them to Netla. Instead I planned to visit Nalym.' She laughed suddenly. 'And what occurred after that, you know.'

Chandra shook her head mournfully, almost, I thought, uncomprehendingly, then I glanced at her scarred chest. 'Such wickedness, to kill for coin and power. When life can be so magnificent without them.'

'It is a sickness, Chandra, that fills the heart and mind until there is no longer any room for rationality,' Alexa said sadly.

'Did you hate them?' Lilith asked Carly softly.

'Oh yes,' she said, almost fiercely. 'I wanted to raise an army and destroy every last Alenit soldier and clan member and those of the Geron and Dezla clans too. But I don't have an army and my parents and sister are dead and I will never see them again no matter how many people are punished for their deaths. Besides, Netla is fouled beyond repair now and should any of the clans fall, another will simply rise in its place. I will not waste my life on such a place.' She paused for a moment, then smiled coldly. 'Though, should I ever meet an Alenit soldier on a dark quiet night, best she be alert.'

Silence fell amongst us and I was no longer grateful for the feeling of isolation and quietness that the cove offered. We needed the distractions of a city street or harbour to take our minds from Carly's tale, other noises and voices to fill our ears with happy sounds.

Then Carly gave a light chuckle. 'Ah, there is nothing like the talk of misfortune to dampen spirits.

Here,' and she hefted up the wineskin and passed it to Chandra, 'have another swig of wine each. My pain has had years to settle, so let's talk of happier things.'

For several days we returned to the cove, to swim and play and laze in the sunshine, white skin turning golden as we lay on the fine white sand, the grains clinging to our damp flesh as we succumbed time and again to the whispered invitation of the crystal clear water to come cool ourselves in its gentle aqua depths.

Chandra spent hours wandering over the sand, collecting handfuls of the tiny, rough shells. She was amazed and delighted at their abundance and would sometimes sit beneath the trees, plucking a shell from the small mound in her hand and idly dropping it back onto the pile while she stared out to sea. We left her alone at such times, for we knew she was wondering about her people's past, and remembering the songs of the sea in the old tongue of her tribe.

On our fourth morning at the cove, Carly surprised us by producing a pig's bladder. She and Lilith had taken to swimming with delighted zeal and she laughed outright now at the expressions on our face.

'I got it at the market this morning,' she explained. 'I saw children playing with one at the harbour and thought it looked like fun.'

She tossed it lightly to Alexa, who caught it easily.

'Let's play then,' Alexa said, and we raced down to the sea, even Chandra, who had put away her shells, throwing the bladder to one another as we went, laughing at the crazy direction of some of our throws.

Once in the water, we copied some of the games Carly had seen the children playing, forming teams and trying to keep the others from claiming the bladder.

We splashed and dived and jumped in the water, chasing and grabbing the slippery bladder, our yells and screeches of laughter loud and joyful, knowing that no-one could hear us.

Finally, Carly caught the bladder and hugged it, panting exaggeratedly. 'I'm exhausted, and Lil and I haven't even had our swimming lesson for the day.'

'I'm ready when you are,' Alexa said. 'What about now, Lil?'

Lilith nodded and smiled happily. 'Yes, I want to do ten strokes without stopping before lunch.'

'Great,' Alexa grinned. 'Ten strokes it will be then. Give Ashil the bladder, Carly. She needs to practise her throwing.'

They all laughed. I had been rather too zealous with one of my earlier throws and it had sailed over Alexa's head and onto the sand. I caught the bladder now and with a sidelong glance at Alexa that made her laugh even harder, I waded out deeper, calling to Chandra to come join me.

In the deeper water, the game of catch and throw became more difficult and to tease Chandra I threw the bladder way over her head.

'Jump!' I cried.

She sprang up out of the water, her ebony arms outstretched above her and the bladder sailed past, a finger's width above her hands. She paddled towards the bladder, lifted it from the water and turned to me with a wicked grin.

'Here, Ashil,' she called. 'Dive!' and she heaved the bladder to my left, forcing me to fling my body sideways in the hope of catching the bladder. I missed it.

I shook the water from my face and scooped up the bladder and stood weighing it in my hands. 'Ready Chandra?' I queried, grinning as she stood waiting, beaming her broad white smile and I laughed at her enthusiasm. This time I made the throw short and she dived forwards, landing with a large splash, the bladder bobbing innocently just out of reach.

Chandra flicked the water from her curls. 'Be prepared to move in a hurry, Ashil.' And she raised the bladder above her head with both hands. Her intent was immediately clear and I began to paddle backwards, watching as she drew her hands back for extra force, knowing I would not be fast enough if she threw with all her might.

She did. I saw her release the bladder and I began swimming in the direction it was headed, hoping to beat it before it hit the water, but it landed far beyond me, riding the small waves and bobbing in and out of sight. Fine, I thought, next it would be Chandra's turn to swim out to sea and I took several strokes towards the bladder, watching as it disappeared from sight behind another of the small waves.

Only to come sailing back through the air towards me.

I stopped, my mouth and eyes open wide in disbelief, and swallowed a mouthful of salt water. I coughed to clear my throat, moving my arms and legs enough to stay afloat as I glanced warily around. There was no way the bladder could have returned to me other than if someone or something had thrown it. A sudden chill crawled over my scalp and down my back. The water no longer seemed as friendly or inviting.

I could see nothing above the surface and I glanced fearfully into the blue depths, unable to discern anything beyond the reach of my arms. I was debating whether to fetch the bladder or turn for shore when Chandra's strong voice called, 'Ashil, I'm going in.'

I turned to see her wading towards the shallows where the other three were swimming. It made my mind up. I swam quickly towards the bladder and pulled it close to me in preparation for the swim back, but before I could even take one stroke towards shore, I heard a sweet voice trill.

'Throw it, Ashil.'

I released the bladder and spun around, my heart pounding unpleasantly in my chest and there she was, smiling as she swam easily before me, a merwoman.

She swam closer until I could see the glimmering pink and gold and aqua of her tail. 'Throw it, Ashil,' she said again, 'I'll catch it.'

I was too startled, too amazed to be scared any longer. I had dreamt of such an encounter for so long that I just watched her in shocked fascination, fearing that a careless word or expression would drive her away and I would lose what I had only just found.

As though aware of her impact on me, she floated effortlessly in the water before me, her head slightly tilted to one side as she watched me patiently, still smiling happily. Joyfully, mutely, I smiled back.

She gave a little trill of laughter then flipped up in the water, flicking her long, tapering tail up into the air as she slipped under the water. Horrified that she might swim away, I turned quickly, trying to follow her flitting form under the water.

She swam past me and I saw the bladder move as she reappeared, holding it in her small webbed hands. 'Now catch it, Ashil,' she directed gaily, and she tossed it lightly through the air to me.

I caught it and she laughed with pleasure. 'Now throw it, Ashil. Throw it to me.'

Because I did not wish to alarm her, my throw was light and gentle, but I misjudged it and it fell short. Unconcerned, she swam forward, closer to me, catching the bladder effortlessly, her small, pink mouth open wide in delight, showing tiny perfect teeth. Without a doubt, I thought, she was the most wonderful, exotic creature I had ever seen.

As she fingered the bladder, trying unsuccessfully to push it under the water and laughing as it resisted her attempts, I examined her closely. She was about the size of girl on the verge of womanhood, with tangles of long pink hair streaming down her back and into the water. Her upper body, with its small, high breasts, was palest cream, though it seemed to gleam with myriad soft muted colours as she moved, like the glazed inner coating of a large shell. And beneath the sea, swaying slowly, almost lazily, was her magnificent multi-coloured tail. It appeared aqua at the edges, deepening in places to a deep, dusky blue, overlaid with pink and lilac and yellow scales.

'What's your name?' I asked softly, speaking for the first time.

She raised her head and looked at me with enormous sea-green eyes. 'Raeyiyilarala,' she said, then tapped the bladder to me. I caught it reflexively, my mind too busy contending with her name.

'Rayi . . . ' I began, frowning slightly.

She squealed delightedly, repeating, 'Rayi, Rayi,' evidently quite pleased with the shortening. 'Ashil and Rayi,' she said, pointing at me then herself, and chuckling. 'Chandra and Alexa and Carly and Lilith and Ashil and Rayi,' she recited.

'You know all our names,' I blurted in astonishment.

'You're very loud,' she replied, simply, innocently. Then, 'Throw it, Ashil. Far away. I'll catch it.' Her small nose crinkled as she smiled with childlike expectation, watching my hand as it held the bladder.

With all my strength, I threw the bladder as far away from us as I could, and Rayi gave an ecstatic little crow, then dived under the water and darted away. She resurfaced directly beneath the bladder and jumped up and clasped it to her chest, while it was still airborne, falling back into the water with a gleeful laugh.

She swam back to me, cradling the bladder, and stopped before me, but it was not I that held her attention. She was gazing over my shoulder, her eyes open wide with interest. Before I could turn to see what held her, she lifted the bladder.

'Catch it, Alexa,' she called.

Rayi's throw fell easily into Alexa's open hands. Beside her was Chandra, with Lilith and Carly following more slowly behind. Without any prompting from Rayi, Alexa returned the throw, aiming beyond the merwoman, and Rayi sped happily away after it.

As Alexa and Chandra drew abreast, paddling gently

in the deep water, I broke into an enormous grin. 'Her name's unpronounceable, so I call her Rayi. She already knows our names. She's a merwoman,' I added unnecessarily, feeling a resurgence of my earlier excitement and disbelief as I spoke.

Alexa smiled at me, then turned to watch Rayi as she swam back towards us. 'She's so fast,' Chandra exclaimed in admiration. 'Like a snake through grass.'

'No, Chan,' I disagreed softly, 'faster.'

Rayi stopped and grinned at her two new admirers, throwing the bladder to Chandra. Then she stared across to where Carly and Lilith had paused. 'Come and play with us,' she called eagerly to them.

They waved but hesitated. 'It's too deep for them,' I explained. 'They're not strong swimmers.'

Rayi appeared momentarily surprised by my words, then she smiled widely. 'That's because you have legs,' she said. Then she dived, slipping into the water and swimming between Chandra and me, her tail brushing our legs playfully as she passed.

Laughing, Alexa, Chandra and I followed the merwoman into the shallow water. Rayi's pink head had popped up ahead of us and she was speaking softly to Lilith and Carly, who were listening earnestly, their faces alight with pleasure.

The merwoman heard us approaching and pushed up out of the water, her pearl shoulders glistening, her strong tail moving in easy, slow strokes below her. She faced us with a joyous grin. 'Throw it, Chandra,' she called out, to no-one's surprise.

• • •

That afternoon, exhausted from a long morning's playing and replete after a large midday meal, we lolled in the shallow water, waiting for Rayi to return. She had left us when hunger and the burning sun had forced us from the water. Unperturbed by our departure, Rayi had responded to our queries with a blithe promise to return shortly. So now, we lazed in the water, talking quietly amongst ourselves while our eyes scanned the ocean for any sign of the merwoman.

I was feeling anxious as I idly fingered the bladder, fearing she would not return after all. There was so much I wanted to ask her, to know, all morning I had found great pleasure in just watching her, seeing her delight and enjoyment as she played with the bladder, ordering us around imperiously, ingenuously. Yet it was not enough. I wanted to speak to her, to learn. I had caught a glimpse of another world, a stunning, awesome, splendid world, and standing on the threshold, straining to look in, I dreaded the thought that the door might slam shut, locking me out forever.

A high, merry chirrup to my left broke through my reverie and I glanced over to see two young merchildren staring at us excitedly. They saw me looking and instantly dived, their small tails giving a jaunty wave as they slipped quickly under the water. I heard the others stir beside me.

'Where did they go?' asked Chandra.

Two little pink heads popped up again, this time to my right. I laughed, heady exhilaration filling me. 'Hello.' They both tilted their heads at the sound, their green eyes open wide, before disappearing once more into the safety of the ocean.

Before us two other heads appeared, one aqua, one lilac, mermen. They stared at us curiously, commenting on us to each other with incomprehensible trills and chirps and high-pitched calls while we looked on in astonishment.

Rayi swam up, grinning, and called a greeting. 'My friends,' she explained, turning to utter several high short trills that drew the attention of the two mermen. They ceased their conversation and regarded us silently for a moment before slowly gliding through the water towards us.

Rayi glanced out to sea and gave another clipped chirp. The merchildren instantly appeared, responding with a timorous chirrup of their own. Rayi repeated her short, commanding chirp and they dived and began to swim towards us, halting a short distance away.

'They have never seen Likiliyanarali before,' Rayi said. 'They are uncertain.'

'What did you call us?' Alexa asked, with a perplexed smile.

'Likiliyanarali, the Ones Without Tails. They wish to see what legs look like, but think you are very large.'

'Tell them we want to be their friends and will not hurt them and that we would like to see their beautiful tails.'

Rayi grinned and faced the merchildren to deliver Alexa's message. The merchildren became very excited and chattered quickly to each other. Then, eyeing us carefully, they began to approach, slowly, tentatively.

The mermen meanwhile had obviously accepted Rayi's assurances that we were harmless and were drifting before us, grinning happily. One surprised us by speaking.

'Hello. Can we play?'

It was the lilac-haired one. His long hair floated around him in the water and his broad, muscular torso gleamed like pale marble.

'Of course,' I replied. 'I'll throw it to you,' and I raised the bladder in one hand.

It was all that was needed, the merchildren saw me lift the bladder into the air and gave delighted squeals, much like human children, and raced forward, ready to jump for the bladder the moment it left my hand. I tossed it to the merman, as I had promised, but slightly off-centre so that it breezed past the merchildren. Undaunted, they both sprang up, their tiny bodies leaving the water entirely so that for a moment they appeared suspended in the air. Then both grasped the bladder and they fell together back into the water, landing with a loud splash and an ecstatic croon of satisfaction.

All doubts about the Ones Without Tails now apparently vanquished, the merchildren threw the bladder back to me with huge grins, waiting to see where I would throw it next.

It was soon evident that the merfolk have an insatiable appetite for playing and it was only by taking turns passing the bladder that we managed to keep the game going. The mermen told us their names, which we shortened to Kioik, of the lilac hair, and Finikra, of the aqua. The merchildren were Litissa and Epuoinil.

The merchildren grew bolder during the afternoon.

They would wait until one of us had moved away on her own, then swim over and quickly dive to stare at our legs underwater, occasionally darting a webbed hand out to touch the skin. The first time they did this with Carly, they erupted out of the water, chirping and clicking and screeching loudly to one another, their small faces expressing their amazement and wonder at encountering this strange marvel.

They approached each of us in the course of the day and when Chandra wiggled her fingers under the water at them, as they stared at her dark skin, they hesitated for a moment before touching her fingertips with their own, sliding their webbed hands curiously between her fingers.

My turn came and I cautiously dropped my hands under the water and stroked Epuoinil's iridescent tail. It was surprisingly compact and smooth and I could feel its strength through my hands. Epuoinil watched me under the water but did not pull away and when I smiled and ran a finger lightly down his cheek he grinned and rose to the surface to gently touch my face, pursing his lips and cooing softly.

Far away, another of the great ships heading for Cynal's harbour could be seen. Out of respect for the dead king, a black mourning sail fluttered in the breeze high up upon the mast. The merfolk gazed at it with interest but it was a common sight these days and they made no move to leave us. We tried to ask them about their home but they could not understand our questions, saying only that it was far away, below the water. When we asked how many merfolk lived there, they nodded and said a great many, then Epuoinil grabbed the bladder and called, 'Catch it, Ashil,' and the games began again.

We left the merfolk with some reluctance when the sun hung low in the west, its rays covering the ocean with pathways of glittering jewels. Epuoinil and Litissa watched us leave the water, their voices loud and incredulous as they saw us step out onto the sand, walking properly for the first time. We heard Rayi call to them and they dived and quickly sped after the adults, going to their home far away, below the water.

After that day, the cove took on a special significance for us. The city withdrew into the background and the small crescent-shaped beach with its calm water and merry tailed inhabitants absorbed most of our energies and time. One day, hoping to thrill the merfolk, we brought our horses to the water's edge, but Rayi and her friends took one look at the large four-legged creatures that snorted and shook their fierce heads and lifted and pawed their hooves in the wet sand and fled out to sea, ignoring all our calls that they would come to no harm and refusing all attempts to coax them back until we had taken the horses from the water and out of sight.

The merfolk's conversational skills did not improve, but from comments dropped it was clear they were aware of the death of the king and that Lord Tarn would soon be upon the throne. They liked the royal family and Rayi called them friends. 'Cynal is a good place,' she said, 'full of good people.'

'What about other cities?' I asked, curious about why they no longer swam near Delawyn. 'What about Delawyn?'

'Err, nasty place.' Rayi's little nose wrinkled in distaste as though my question had upset her and she swam off to play.

The day of the funeral came and from first light Cynal's streets were made nearly impassable with mourners. Funeral fires burned throughout the city, despite the fierce, unrelenting heat of the white, hot summer sun. To my mind the heat only added to the general feeling of suffocating oppression that enfolded us, making it difficult to draw a clean breath. The funeral would occur in the afternoon and, in an attempt to escape the mawkish unpleasantness of the crowd's mass pain and hysteria, we collected several skins of wine, in order to drink farewell to the king's spirit, and headed for the cove.

I do not think any of us truly expected to see the merfolk that morning but I waded into the water, my clothes hurriedly dropped in a messy pile behind me on the sand, and called out to them, 'Rayi, Kioik, Finikra, Epuoinil, Litissa.' The water was deliciously cool and refreshing after the crush of the city streets.

There was no reply and I did not call again. Instead, I immersed myself in the water, swimming several strokes under the water until I could no longer continue without drawing breath. I surfaced and inhaled deeply, just as Epuoinil popped up before me, chittering and screeching agitatedly, his green eyes wide with fright. Then, just as suddenly, he was gone, a sleek darting underwater shape that disappeared from sight.

Bemused and a little alarmed by his behaviour, I shouted after him.

'What is it?' Alexa asked, wading in behind me and looking out to sea.

I turned to her and shook my head. 'I don't know. Epuoinil appeared, but he was upset and I couldn't understand what he was trying to say, then he just sped away.'

She moved up beside me and we both scanned the horizon.

'Perhaps one of the merfolk has been hurt,' I said worriedly.

Alexa frowned. 'It's unlikely he'd come to us. He knows we are weak in the water, we're the Ones Without Tails,' and she flashed me a reassuring smile.

I nodded. 'You're right. Then what could it be?'

'Perhaps Rayi can tell us,' and Alexa pointed across me. 'She's over there.'

I followed the direction of Alexa's hand and saw the familiar pink head bobbing amongst the waves. 'Rayi,' I called, 'do you need help?'

Rayi lifted herself slightly out of the water and then I noticed that she was not watching Alexa or myself or the others drinking on the sand. Instead she was scanning the beach warily, as though checking it was safe to approach the shallows.

'We're alone, Rayi,' Alexa called to her and she gave me a worried glance.

The merwoman swam swiftly towards us, breaking the surface before us, her small face drawn with fear.

'What's wrong?' I asked, reaching out to touch her shoulder.

'Evil,' she said, with a small fearful moan. She pointed towards Cynal. 'In the city.'

I swallowed, unsettled despite the fact I knew the merfolk found much that was normal in mortal behaviour strange and sometimes menacing.

'What sort of evil?' Alexa asked calmly, but Rayi did not answer, for just at that moment Kioik surfaced beside her and began to berate her, tugging at her arm and trying to drag her back out to sea.

Rayi answered him with a series of high, protesting chirps, but he continued to pull at her, his own voice rising. Finally, Rayi nodded and said something to him that seemed to pacify him. Now, almost quivering with anxiety, Rayi looked directly at us, her eyes concerned.

'Last night, we felt a great evil pass over the water,' she said quickly. Her voice shook and her eyes darted once more towards the shore. 'We fled and hid and the evil passed over onto the land and,' again she pointed at Cynal, 'into the city.' She gazed at us imploringly, her voice sad. 'Do not go back there, friends.'

That was all. Kioik tugged at her again and this time she did not resist. They dived together under the water and sped away, leaving Alexa and me speechless in the shallow water.

'What could they have meant?' Lilith asked, as we gathered our belongings and left the cove. Alexa and I had just finished relaying what Rayi had said and we were all confused and somewhat disturbed by her news.

'It's impossible to say,' Alexa replied. 'But whatever

it was the merfolk felt last night, it certainly scared them.' She paused and looked over her shoulder at the gleaming ocean. 'I don't think we'll be seeing much of them any more.'

We moved from the cove to a small hillside outside of the city and settled down to share the rest of the wine. I was feeling particularly depressed. Rayi's warning had upset me and as I pondered Alexa's words I managed to feel even worse. To me, Cynal and the merfolk would always be intermeshed, and the thought of never seeing the merfolk again lessened my enthusiasm for the work we were hoping to begin here. I almost found myself hoping Lord Tarn would not honour his father's contract and we could leave. I knew I was being irrational. I felt like a child who had been promised a special treat and then, having had that treat denied, sulkily rejects any others offered. I grasped the wineskin and drank heavily, one recourse a child does not have.

Carly took the wineskin from me. 'There is no way of telling what the merfolk even consider evil. They are simple folk,' she said, shrugging her shoulders. 'They were frightened of our horses, after all.' She drank and held out the wineskin questioningly and I took it again.

'Yes,' Alexa agreed, 'but they did not call them evil, and once the horses were out of sight they were happy to come back and play with us. This is something else.'

Chandra spoke. 'The old king was a popular ruler. Perhaps he had strange friends who have come to send him to the gods and who are not friends of the merfolk. The little ones only know water.'

Alexa nodded. 'Perhaps.' She did not sound convinced and I took another draught. 'At least we have no reason to fear. There will be guards aplenty today, should there be any trouble.'

'You realise,' Carly said, 'that the funeral almost ends the time of mourning. Soon we will see a city unveiled and we will be able to enter the palace. All this swimming and eating and drinking,' and she nudged me as she spoke the last word, 'are all very well, but soon we will be busy. There will be interesting people to meet and fascinating places within the city to discover. It will be exciting.'

Chandra laughed. 'That's usually Ashil's speech.'

'I know, but she's so unhappy now, dwelling on the departure of the merfolk, that I thought I better say it for her.' She grinned as she tapped me on the leg. 'How did I do?'

I put the wineskin down on the coarse grass before me. 'You forgot to mention the maps, Carly,' I replied with as much dignity as I could muster. 'They, after all, are why we're here.'

Her eyebrows rose as her face took on an expression of feigned surprise. 'Are they?' She glanced at the others and they all burst out laughing.

I opened my mouth to protest, then realised there was nothing I could say and shut it again. Lilith, smiling prettily beside me, gave me a gentle squeeze.

'Don't fret, Ashil,' she said. 'The merfolk will come back and in the meantime we've got our beautiful maps to draw. Maybe the palace of Lord Tarn will contain something as marvellous and exciting as the merfolk.'

160

That set the other three off laughing again.

'Thanks, Lil,' I said. 'You may be right.' But I shook my head disgustedly at the other three.

Carly leant over and slapped my thigh, her eyes full of mischievous delight. 'And Ashil, because I know how much it means to you, I'm prepared to make a big sacrifice.' She paused, trying to keep a straight face, and said very seriously, 'Consider the pig's bladder yours.'

They all laughed, and this time I joined in.

We nearly missed the funeral procession. After Carly's magnanimous offer, our talk turned to lighter things and we took little notice of the passing of time. It was a friendly shout from a passing fisher at the top of the hill that alerted us to the fact the procession had begun. We climbed to the road and made our way into the city, part of the huge crowd come to bid the king well in his final moments on this earth.

I do not like funerals. They make me uncomfortable and I find myself allowing my mind to wander in an attempt to check the sounds of distress and the bitter sadness of the occasion. Yet even now, when I think back on that hot afternoon, standing solemnly with my friends in the blazing sun, watching the bier pass close by, I can still clearly see, as though I am gazing at a picture, three powerful images.

The first is the sight of the dead king, this stranger who was so loved by his people, lying still and quiet on the bier, his body cold and leaden while all around him near-naked bodies sweat and strain in the heat, small grunts and puffs of warm breath accompanying their movements. The second is the striking vision of the Mecla priest, Rianne, standing so tall and resolute, the focus of all eyes as with arms outstretched she invokes the spirits, her scarlet robes falling gracefully about her. And, thirdly, as clearly as though it was only yesterday, I behold once more the magnificent prince, Lord Tarn, as he rides unescorted through the crowd, proud and vibrant, to take his place beside the priest, as they, with a kiss and a prayer, light the fire that sends the king to the other world and his final resting place.

That evening, the mood of the funeral still upon us, we returned early to our inn and ordered a light meal. The inn was a sturdy, squat building on the fringe of the harbour district. The upper level was given over entirely to rooms for rent and the lower level, reached from the road by entering and climbing down several steps into cool dimness, was one large room where food and drink were sold. All the patrons were subdued that night and we ate quickly, talking little, and climbed the stairs to our room. The inn was neat and comfortable, we had stayed in far worse, but due to the influx of mourners into the city we had been forced to share the one room and it was a tight squeeze. The room could only hold four beds, so we had been taking it in turns sleeping on the floor under the window. That night it was my turn.

We moved about, preparing for bed and trying not to get in the way of one another. I had just begun to undress when, true to her word, Carly brought me the pig's bladder.

'Keep it safe,' she said, handing it to me with a warm smile.

I took it from her and placed it amongst my things, neatly stacked in a corner. 'Thank you,' I whispered, my throat closing on further words, but Carly understood, for she nodded and squeezed my arm silently before moving away towards her own bed.

When I had finished undressing, I lay down. I had left the shutters open and I stared out into the night, up into the star-filled sky. Distantly, I could hear the rhythmic movements of the sea, the low, rumbling rush of the waves towards shore and the calming sough of their retreat. I listened for other night sounds, the cry of a night bird, the flapping of a mourning flag, the hushed voices of people passing below the window, the patrol of the city guards. I rolled onto my side, all seemed normal, and I shut my eyes, willing sleep, for I was eager for this day to end.

SIX

At the end of the two weeks we presented ourselves once more at the palace, which we viewed for the first time without the black and silver mourning silk. Like many of Cynal's buildings, the palace is a gleaming white, sharply contrasting with the bright blue cloudless sky. It spreads out comfortably in one corner of the city overlooking the azure waters, its assorted domes rising gently above the cityscape, the peak of the huge fire mountain, Mount Rittoy, a dramatic dark shadow in the background.

Since the departure of the merfolk we had turned our attention once more to our prospective job. The first task in mapping any area is to become familiar with it, particularly the framework from which we would work inwards. The framework for the city of Cynal was to be its outer walls, so we spent many hours walking our horses around those walls, discussing where we would begin. To map Cynal we would divide it into numerous triangles. At first these triangles would be large and, because of the distances covered, we would measure angles as well as lengths on the ground. Later, with the framework in place, we would divide these triangles into even smaller ones filled with detail.

We showed our contract, signed by the diplomat in Nalym, to a guard at the outer palace gate. He was deliciously handsome, tall and olive-skinned, dressed in the lightweight three-quarter-length trousers of the army, with his sword belt wrapped across his flat belly. On his feet were strong leather sandals and a gold earring dangled from his left earlobe, glittering brilliantly when it caught the sun. He seemed unaware of our appraisal as he read the contract thoroughly, unhurriedly, and checked the wax seal. When he had finished and was satisfied, he looked up and handed it back.

'Please follow me,' he said politely, smiling slightly, revealing beautiful white teeth, good enough even to rival Chandra's. As I wondered how anyone could ever not follow him I caught Carly's amused grin as he signalled for two guards to take our horses. I knew she was thinking the same.

He led us through the gate and stopped briefly to report to another soldier. We stood patiently, glancing around greedily at the sights, glad to be finally within the palace walls.

From the gate the path divided into three, going straight ahead and to the left and right. Straight ahead the path soon disappeared from sight as it curved and was swallowed by the gardens. Beyond it I could see the brilliant white walls of the palace proper, gently rising before us like some cool exotic bloom.

To the right, beneath the high outer wall, soldiers were exercising with great verve and skill in the training ground. I could hear the sounds of their wooden practice weapons striking with resounding cracks and the accompanying noise of sandalled feet crunching and scattering the tiny white shells and pebbles that covered the ground. Beside the training ground, on the eastern wall, sat a large building which, from the look of the women and men going in and out, I assumed were the barracks. I knew from talk in the city that there was a second, smaller gatehouse on that wall, often used by traders and merchants bringing their goods for the royal kitchen or storerooms, but I could not see the gate from where we stood. I turned back to see our guard nod to his companion and step over to rejoin us. He gave us another engaging smile then led us, without hesitation, onto the left path.

This path took us around the edge of the gardens as we followed the line of the southern wall. We passed the smithy, where dark plumes of smoke were picked up and carried away by the sea breeze and the regular cadence of hammer striking anvil filled our ears as we strode by. With our guard's bare muscled back a constant distraction, I looked around at the gardens and when a breeze blew up quickly I was delighted to feel cool water on my face. But although I could hear the tinkling of a fountain, I could not see it from the path.

Despite the heat and salt air, the gardens were beautifully tended but with none of the manicured prettiness I so detested. It was a hot day, but even just on the edge of the extensive gardens it was noticeably cooler than in the city streets.

Ahead of us was one of the four main towers that sit at each corner of the outer walls, but I could see no guards on the high stone gallery and doubted the towers were ever used except in war, which Cynal had not known now for many, many years. The tower, however, had been neatly preserved, not allowed to fall into disrepair despite the long period of peace. A walkway wide enough for three soldiers abreast was atop the outer walls that enclosed the palace and its environs and linked all four towers and the two smaller ones that sat either side of the main gatehouse. It would give an astonishing view of the surrounding city and ocean and I wondered how long it would be before our work took us there.

I smiled to myself as I realised such a thought assumed we would soon be working in Cynal. It seemed impossible to me now that I had once hoped the Cynal contract would not be honoured. I still missed the merfolk, their carefree playing and lazing in the sea at the cove, but Cynal held other attractions and I dearly wanted to map this beautiful city. My old eagerness had returned and now I only wished to begin. I told myself not to get too excited, for we could still be turned away, but the smile stayed with me as we walked on.

The path turned and we continued along it, the western wall now to our left. The palace is situated on a flat-topped rise that runs down to the ocean. While not so high as to give one the feeling of dangling over a precipice, it is high enough to make it almost impossible for the palace to fall to an attack from the sea. It also meant that the west and north walls, those facing the ocean, were in fact lower than the palace, giving its occupants a clear view of the beautiful sparkling water.

Between the western wall and the path was a huge pasture full of grazing horses and before that, with five different coloured doors opening on to the path, were the five stables. They were large buildings, currently alive with the activity of mortals and beast. Beside them, rather incongruously, sat a small, single-storey house.

'Flir will be happy,' Carly said beside me, gazing across at the pasture. 'She's already made it clear that she hates being locked up in a stable for hours on end when the weather's fine.'

'We haven't got the job yet,' I pointed out, in an attempt to tease.

Carly seemed unconcerned. 'We'll get it, Ashil, never fear. The hardest part is behind us.' Her glance rested idly on the rows of colourful flowers that lined both sides of the path. 'We're inside the palace now. It's unlikely we'll be turned down.'

'You don't know that.' I looked at her in astonishment, forgetting that I wanted to believe her. 'We could be turned away for any number of reasons. Lord Tarn may not want to be bothered with cartography so early in his reign. After all, he'll have plenty of other more important details to attend to.'

'Yes,' Carly agreed, then she shrugged. 'But we can work unsupervised and the new king will not deal with us directly anyway. He can easily assign someone to the task. Besides,' and she grinned at me, 'mapping Cynal was one of the last projects his father had planned and we all know how excited the old king was by the prospect, so I don't doubt for a moment his son will honour the contract. Seeing his father's dream through is one way of expressing that love and shedding some of his pain.' She bent and brushed a bright yellow flower with her fingertips, then pursed her lips and blew the gold dust from her fingers, smiling as she watched the dust disperse. 'It's too perfect an opportunity for Lord Tarn to let pass.'

We had now reached the white walls of the palace and I looked up in awe. The Doma in Nalym had been large and imposing but it had held little beauty, its whole intent being defence and strength. Cynal, while retaining its defence capabilities, was also a delight to the eye, a lustrous, shining pearl amidst the blue-green setting of the ocean.

Our path led to one of the side entrances, where other guards, almost as attractive as ours, stood attentively, checking each of the passers-by before allowing them through the door. We had no trouble, our guard taking us through with only an acknowledging nod for his fellows and we stepped onto the cool marble walkway, shaded by a low portico, and through an archway and finally into the palace.

My initial impression was of a great cool quiet space as we walked along a wide corridor with silk hangings in aqueous greens and blues on the white walls. People passed us, guards, servants and other palace inhabitants, all dressed in light casual clothing, eyeing us pleasantly but not speaking. I caught glimpses of rooms as we walked. Many were obviously workrooms, the type we hoped to inhabit should we still have the job. In them an assortment of people moved about calmly but purposefully, some even carrying maps. Other rooms we passed were partially screened from view by white woven screens, and soft murmurs of voices rose from behind them.

The corridor opened out suddenly, with several off-shoots and a staircase. At first I thought we were going to climb the stairs but instead we passed by it and took one of the smaller corridors. Our beautiful guard pushed open a door on the left and stood back to let us walk in. He stood at the threshold.

'Please make yourselves comfortable. I'll let the chancellor know you are here but she may be a few minutes. In the meantime I will have cool drinks sent to you.' And with a slight nod and bow he left us.

The room was medium size, pleasantly furnished with fat-cushioned seats around a low wooden table. A large white sheepskin, freshly combed, lay on the floor and more of the silken hangings decorated the walls. They lifted slightly in the breeze that blew through the square holes in the woven screen at the window. The wooden shutters that enabled the room to be locked from the inside were open.

Carly fell back into the plump cushions with an exaggerated sigh. 'That guard was gorgeous,' she said to no-one in particular. We all laughed and Chandra and I sat down with her.

Alexa walked to the window, pulled back the screen and inhaled deeply. The view of the ocean was breath-taking. Lilith looked over Alexa's shoulder and gave a happy sigh of appreciation. 'It's so beautiful.'

There was a knock at the open door and a servant carried in a tray of drinks, poured them and left without saying a word. We took one each and for a moment there was silence as we drank thirstily.

When I had finished my drink, I stood up to study the silken hangings. The first was an underwater scene of the merfolk, laughing and fooling beneath the green ocean. The colours were soft and muted, the blue-green of the water, the pearl of their faces and the pinks and lilacs and blues of their hair and tails. On the opposite wall was a hanging of a Cynalese fishing boat in the early morning, already heading for home. The colours were glowing and layered, as the golden rays sparkled on the lightening waves and the burgundy of the sails turned red in the growing light. On the bow stood two figures, emblazoned by the fiery rising disc, and in the far left corner the silver arcs of dolphins could just be seen breaking through the water as they followed the boat silently home.

There was another knock at the door and our handsome guard and a pretty, middle-aged woman stepped into the room. Around the woman's waist was an embroidered cotton belt holding a huge ring of keys. When she moved the keys jingled musically.

She smiled broadly at us. 'I hope you haven't had to wait too long.' And she held out her hand to me, for I stood closest to her. 'I am Neesha, the palace chancellor. Welcome to Cynal.'

We all stepped up to her and introduced ourselves, clasping her wrist in our hand in the Cynalese style of greeting. When we expressed our sorrow over the death of the king she accepted our condolences with a slight nod.

'Thank you,' she said very seriously. 'It is a great loss for Cynal. Although we are fortunate the late king, may his spirit soar, left a son worthy to rule after him.'

A servant appeared and we all seated ourselves and accepted another drink.

Neesha waited until the servant had withdrawn and she had wet her lips with her drink before she spoke again. 'I have reviewed the mapping agreement you made early last spring and presented it to Lord Tarn and I am pleased to say that he is keen to continue with his father's plans.'

Her voice had a soft lilt to it and the sunlight streaming in through the open window gave a rich sheen to her dark curls. 'The captain of the guard, Varl, will be helping you. We have set aside rooms and Varl will arrange any additional furnishings you may need.' She smiled quite charmingly as she spoke. 'The enthroning is in ten days time so the palace will be quite chaotic for a while. If you have any difficulties, Captain Varl will help you. He will be waiting for you tomorrow morning to settle you in.'

She paused and looked at each of us, 'Do you have any questions?'

No-one did, so she stood up and indicated the guard standing by the door. 'Rarnald will take you back to the gate.'

On the walk back through the palace I was next to Alexa. Rarnald of the bare and beautiful back glanced openly at her several times, but she either did not notice or chose to ignore it. I was far too happy to mind and turned to her with a wide grin.

'Well, it seems we have the job after all.' It is a marvellous feeling being employed.

Alexa smiled at my enthusiasm. 'Yes, we're lucky.' Her voice was low and contemplative. 'The enthroning and change of rulership should make Cynal a rather exciting city for the next few months.'

172

'I wonder what Lord Tarn is like?' I mused, recalling the rather dashing figure we had seen briefly the day of the funeral. 'Everyone seemed very fond of his father.'

Alexa nodded. 'The king was reputedly just and kind and competent, so I imagine his son has a lot to live up to. Though I'd say it's a good sign he's going to continue with the mapping.' She grinned. 'It's certainly good for us.'

I laughed cheerily. We were once again nearing the staircase, and as we began to follow Rarnald across its base a small group of people came down the stairs. Rarnald halted suddenly, putting out his arm to prevent any of us passing him, his movements so quick and unexpected that we each pulled up short. Then he surprised us even further by dropping into a deep obeisance, one knee touching the ground and his head bent.

'Your Lordship,' he murmured reverentially.

Stunned, I glanced past the Cynalese guards and the others who made up the group, to look at the man who stood at their centre. He was tall and well-muscled, dressed in similar fashion to the soldiers but in trousers and vest of the finest cotton. His brown skin and long dark curls, held back in a leather tie, glowed with health and vibrancy, and his eyes were of the deepest brown, dark enough to appear black. On both hands he wore large jewelled rings and around his neck hung a large medallion stamped with the Cynalese royal crest. The silver looked cool and bright against the warm breadth of his chest. I raised my eyes and felt my breath catch in my throat, for those brown eyes, so intelligent and assured under thick straight brows, were in turn regarding me steadily. I blushed, feeling my skin burn, and bowed low.

Lord Tarn stepped forward, his companions parting to make way for him, and stopped before us, indicating that we could rise. 'Who do you have with you, Rarnald?' he asked, his voice beautifully deep and rich.

Rarnald flushed with pleasure at being recognised. 'The cartographers, Lord, come to map Cynal. We have just come from a meeting with the chancellor.' He half-turned to us and with an open hand introduced each of us to Cynal's lord.

Lord Tarn's gaze had rested on each of us as the introductions were made, his expression one of polite interest. When they were over he gave a small half-smile.

'Welcome to Cynal,' he said. 'I look forward to seeing your work.' His eyes moved over us once more, pausing, I thought, a little longer at Carly, then finally coming to rest on me. 'Perhaps,' and he smiled wryly and qualified, 'when I can spare the time you could instruct me in some of the ways of cartography. It is a fascinating field and I have often considered that it might be in Cynal's interests to have our own resident cartographers. I would like to learn more.'

Not once did he lift his eyes from my face, and as I looked up at him I became aware of numerous tiny details, even while I took in every word he spoke. I saw the black lashes that fringed his eyes, thick and curled, and the tiny lines that spread when he smiled and his eyes lit up. I saw the pale scar that cut across his top lip, straight and slightly raised, and the strong line of his jaw and the glint of his clean, white teeth. And I reminded myself he was the Lord of Cynal, soon to be crowned king, and I was a cartographer employed to draw for him. I dropped my eyes, just as he stopped talking, and I inclined my head.

'It would be our pleasure, Lord,' I murmured.

He watched me silently for a moment. 'Good.' He spoke softly. 'I'll look forward to it.' He paused a moment longer, then he turned and strode away without another word, his guards and companions following.

Our encounter with Lord Tarn had left me feeling slightly disoriented, a rather disturbing feeling. Rarnald led us back to the gate and our horses were sent for.

'You will be met here tomorrow,' he said when they arrived. 'Until then, cartographers.'

We mounted and rode out onto the street, surprised at how much traffic now flowed towards the palace.

'It's easy to see mourning is over,' Carly observed. 'All eyes will now be on Lord Tarn.' She slid her eyes over to me. 'Won't they, Ashil?'

Stung, I protested loudly. 'What could I do? He was standing there addressing me. I could hardly look at my feet.'

'Indeed not.' Carly laughed. 'Who'd rather stare at a pair of dusty feet than at such a handsome man?'

'I think he liked you, Ashil,' Chandra said, grinning. 'That's why he was staring.'

'He's just interested in cartography that's all,' I replied shortly. Then, turning in the saddle to face Alexa and Lilith, who were forced by the traffic to ride slightly behind us, I raised my voice to ask if we were still going to the market.

'We need more ink cakes and parchment,' Lilith called back.

I nodded. We had not bought extra supplies in Binet, other than what Chandra and I needed for our sketching kits, as we had been confident supplies would be freely available in Cynal's marketplace. This was not always the case, and when we were uncertain we carried supplies over hundreds of leagues, but it was not our favourite way of travelling. Supplies were heavy and damage occurred, costing time and coin. Now the job was assured it was time to replenish our supplies.

'And,' Alexa called, 'we need to buy hats.'

I smiled. Hats in Cynal, during the period of mourning, had proved extremely elusive. All the hat-sellers were shut, even though it was the midst of summer and the demand was high. On the day of the funeral alone, vendors could have made a small fortune if they had opened their stalls, but the Cynalese deemed it disrespectful to think of coin on such a solemn occasion. Most follow the Mecla religion, which promotes humility, generosity and peace, and the Cynalese take these tenets to heart, which is why Cynal is, for the most part, such a pleasant and happy city. The people are raised from birth to think of others.

'Good,' Chandra said, beaming. 'Today all the stalls and shops will be open. We can visit them all.'

Carly groaned good-naturedly and I gave a small exasperated laugh. Chandra was generally indifferent to much of city life, but her love of markets was well-known.

'Chandra,' I said, 'it's a big market.'

'Yes,' she replied happily, 'I know. They're the best.'

It was early afternoon and the city streets were humming with activity. All the mourning colours were gone and the brightness of people's clothing as they passed and the brisk purpose in their step was a delight to see. As we rode nearer to the market, the traffic did not lessen, as people came to buy what had been unavailable for the past two weeks.

'I think this is the beginning of the chaos Neesha was referring to,' Carly mused, glancing around at the people milling about.

I nodded. 'We'll have to leave mapping the marketplace until after the enthroning.'

'Yes, but today we don't have to sketch, just look,' Chandra interrupted eagerly. 'Let's begin at the east corner.'

'Chandra, it's full of livestock!' Carly protested.

Cynal's marketplace has three distinct sections. The east, where Chandra wished to go, was given over entirely to the sale of livestock and is the noisiest and smelliest part of the market.

'Yes!' Chandra answered Carly enthusiastically, not the least deterred by her tone.

'We'll have to see it at some stage,' I said, 'and it will be easier when we come to work here if we have an idea of the marketplace as a whole.'

Carly sighed and looked heavenwards. 'Okay, but let's make it quick.'

I called out our destination to Alexa and Lilith and they called back their agreement. We rode to the beginning of the livestock pens and dismounted, leaving our horses in the care of an old man who made his living this way. On foot, we began to weave our way amongst the makeshift pens that held the animals, careful where we placed our feet.

We were not as quick as Carly had hoped, for Chandra liked to stop and watch the animals and had a habit of falling into conversation with every seller. Carly stood by impatiently, incredulous that Chandra could be interested in so many animals, most of which reeked.

The southern end of the market contains the shops of the artisans. Here are the tailors, shoemakers, leather-workers, carpenters, cabinetmakers, knife-sellers, metalworkers, ropemakers, silk-sellers, glass-makers, mirror-sellers, jewellers, perfumers, druggists and parchment-sellers who supply the city with goods. We walked past the shops, along a cobbled pathway that was swarming with people and looked curiously at the artisans' work, displayed artfully outside their shops. The colour and noise were overwhelming. Everywhere people haggled over items or paused to discuss them with friends, fingering the goods and checking for faults while coins clinked all around. We walked on, enchanted by it all and by the sheer quantity of goods on display as they shone and swayed and gleamed and fluttered in the sunshine.

We found the parchment-seller, between a perfumer and a mirror-seller, and entered his shop. The smell was at once familiar, the smell of skins soaking in lime to remove the fat, and I was glad that this time we would be able to buy the skins prepared. While the seller unwrapped a selection of parchment for us to see,

I watched an apprentice at the rear of the shop as she finished scraping and shaving one of the fat-free skins, stretched taut before her. Satisfied the skin was now clean and smooth, she picked up her pumice and began to rub powdered chalk onto the skin to soften and polish it. She glanced up and met my eye and smiled tentatively. I smiled back warmly, for I could sympathise with her. Preparing the skins is one of the first tasks any apprentice under my father learns, and I could still recall how my wrist would ache from pushing the pumice stone.

The seller was helpful and obliging. The sale would be a large one for him and when he learnt who the maps were for he brought out his best skins. Happy with the quality, we made our selection quickly and he wrapped the skins carefully. We could buy ink cakes, the seller told us, from the druggist two shops down, and we thanked him and left his shop.

Before the druggist sat a scribe, available, for a small fee, to write or translate letters, for even in such a fine city there were still the poor and illiterate. The scribe was busy now, composing a letter for a young woman who sat before him, watching absorbedly as the scribe's stylus flowed over the parchment.

Chandra grinned at me. 'She should go to Binet and learn how to do it for herself,' she whispered.

I grinned back, knowing Chandra was only half-joking. She still found it difficult to understand that anything or anyone could hold a person from their dream.

We passed them both and bought the ink cakes, then moved on in search of a hat stall before we stopped for a meal.

The hat-sellers, as expected, were trading briskly. It was like watching so many birds converge on a small pile of seed. Around the stall with the largest and best variety was a large group. Sailors, I gathered from their talk, with the golden tan of pale skin that has been long under the sun. There were over a dozen of them and those who had already bought hats were looking around openly at the other buyers. Many halted their glances at Carly, running their eyes over the stunning combination of her long dark hair, dusky skin and slim, supple body. One sailor, a trim, well-muscled woman with long sun-yellowed hair and blue eyes, caught Carly's eye as we approached the stall and winked. Carly flashed her a smile and the woman grinned back and quickly walked over.

'Greetings,' the sailor said.

'Greetings,' Carly replied, casually. 'Where are you from?'

'We arrived yesterday afternoon from Delawyn with a mixed cargo and a hundred passengers.' While speaking the woman glanced around at us all but her eyes quickly returned to Carly.

'That's a full ship then.'

'Aye,' the woman smiled. 'Everyone wants to be in Cynal for the enthroning. The captain charged high and made a fortune on selling passage.'

'I'd heard that those from Delawyn are a wily bunch.'

'True, but he must've been asking too much for some. We discovered when we docked that we'd had a stowaway.' She laughed. 'That she got past us is amazing, the captain runs a tight ship. Do you know our city?' she asked Carly.

'No, I've never been there.'

'You should come,' the woman suggested. 'I could show you around.'

I smiled to myself and tried on a hat. Carly might tease me about Lord Tarn, but just wait until we were away from the sailor. I found a hat I liked and helped Lilith try on several. Alexa and Chandra chose what they wanted and Carly, the sailor watching on, tried on three before quickly making a choice.

'We're going to buy a meal at the market,' Carly said to the sailor, indicating the north section where the foodstuffs were sold. 'Like to join us?'

'Aye, indeed,' the sailor replied eagerly, and she bowed slightly. 'My name's Lindsa.'

Carly introduced everyone and, as we walked towards the north end, Lindsa asked what we did, exhibiting surprise and curiosity when we told her.

'Must be interesting work.' She looked at Carly. 'Have you ever worked on a ship? There's always work for skilled navigators.'

There was genuine amusement in Carly's laugh. 'I don't think I'd be of much use.'

'We only map land,' Alexa explained. 'Our methods wouldn't work at sea.'

'Pity,' Lindsa murmured.

We had left the shops of the artisans behind and were now walking amongst the stalls of the food vendors. Fresh fruit and vegetables were laid out in large baskets or on rugs under awnings to keep the worst of the sun off. Then there were stalls selling spices, fresh flowers, wine, confectionery, pastries, breads, meat, poultry and, of course, fish. Without hesitation, we moved

181

towards the wine-seller. The easiest purchase would be made first.

With a wineskin in hand, we approached the food stalls, staring at the delights on offer. Chandra and I chose a fish pie, while Alexa, Lilith and Lindsa all bought a vegetable-filled pastry. Carly chose spiced chicken on a stick and we added a loaf of the light bread we liked so much, a handful of pears and, just for Lil, some taffy sticks, and went to sit on a step in the sun.

'How is Delawyn reacting to the death of the king?' Alexa asked as she tore off a piece of bread.

Lindsa shrugged. 'To tell truth, I don't think many people are upset. He was a good king, and a fair trading partner, but we all know his son will take the throne and life will go on as usual.' She gestured wide with her hands. 'There has always been rivalry between the two cities and to many the Cynalese royal family and the success of Cynal are the same, so it follows in their thinking that any blow to the royal family must be to Delawyn's benefit.'

'That's crazy,' Alexa said, frowning.

'I know,' Lindsa agreed. 'But remember, Delawyn got most of the trading business before Cynal became an important harbour town.'

'That was generations ago,' Alexa pointed out.

'Aye, but people have long memories. There are people in Delawyn, particularly amongst the Fifty, who still begrudge Cynal the trade. The death of the king seems to have stirred up a whole lot of talk about Cynal. It's brought it to the fore of people's minds.' She shrugged again. 'It's just talk, Delawyn's abuzz with such things of late, like all this nonsense about the white panther reappearing. The one that appeared to Meclan from the gods.'

'The gods?' Chandra queried. 'Who is Meclan?'

Lindsa laughed. 'Don't say that in front of too many Cynalese. They take their religion very seriously. Meclan's the man all the Mecla follow. I don't know much about it, it's not my religion. All I know is that the white panther was sent to Meclan as a symbol of his power and to mark him as the true voice of the gods.' She picked up a pear. 'And now there's talk that the white panther is coming again.'

I confess that I was surprised by Lindsa's friendliness and openness. From what I had seen, both were rare qualities amongst the Delawese. Then I realised that, as a sailor, Lindsa probably spent more than half the year away from her birth city, and travel has a way of nurturing tolerance.

As Lindsa bit into her pear, I caught Carly's eye and pursed my lips into a silent kiss, for the sailor's interest was evident. Carly grinned and repeated the gesture back to me, just as Lindsa turned to her. She saw the kiss and misinterpreted it. Her face fell.

Carly chuckled and squeezed Lindsa's arm. 'Ashil is thinking of a certain handsome, young man we met this morning, who quite dazzled her.' Chandra and Alexa laughed and even Lilith, nibbling on a taffy stick, smiled. 'I'm just giving her some advice on how to impress him. Do you have any for her?'

Relieved, Lindsa laughed. 'Not me,' she replied.

'I don't need any advice, Carly,' I said. 'Thanks all the same.'

'Fine, then I'll just say the one thing. If your feelings are ever strong for anyone, let him know how you feel, because you never know when there will be a raid on your farm.'

Moved, I stared at her for a moment, then nodded. 'I understand what you're saying,' I said quietly.

'Good!' She slapped Lindsa on the leg. 'Feel like going for a swim?'

'Aye!' Lindsa had been following the last part of the conversation with difficulty, but now her face cleared and she rose with alacrity as Carly got to her feet.

We returned together to collect our horses, paying the old man for his care.

Carly mounted Flir and helped Lindsa up behind her before kicking the horse into a trot.

'I'll see you back at the inn later,' she called, and waving, they rode off.

SEVEN

We had eaten at our inn almost every evening since our arrival, but with the lifting of official mourning came the revival of Cynal's nightlife and we were eager for some fun. We decided to leave the harbour area alone as the constant arrival of itinerants gave it the reputation of being a rough district, and with all inns once again open and the wine flowing freely we felt no desire to go courting trouble. Instead we selected an elegant restaurant which several of our new-found fisher friends had said bought and served the best seafood in Cynal. We arrived just in time to secure the last table.

The evening was still warm and we had dressed in our best, buoyed as we were by the morning's news and the lightening of the city's mood.

I wore a simple white shift with a corded tan leather belt and a bright beaded necklace. Beside me, Lilith had on a similar style but with elbow-length sleeves and a soft rounded neckline in a pretty pale blue. She wore her white blonde hair up, tied with a blue ribbon, and in her ears were tiny pearl earrings. She was chatting with Chandra who, in typically subdued style, was dressed in a short blood-red skirt and summer bodice with skilfully dyed red leather sandals.

Opposite me sat Alexa in midnight-blue silken trousers and short-sleeved top. Her over vest was embroidered with bright blue and gold thread and plain gold loops hung from her ears and matched the thin bracelets on her arm. They tinkled playfully as she lifted the wine goblet to her lips and regarded the other patrons with her cool gaze. And on my other side was Carly, who had returned from her afternoon with Lindsa saying little, other than she had had a most enjoyable time. She looked stunning in an emerald green sheath with slim straps that tied behind her neck. Her glossy black hair fell loose around her bare shoulders and silver rings shone on her fingers, matching her silver wristband. Our skin, from Lilith's pale gold to Chandra's matt black, glowed with health. We were young and lithe and bold and I knew we had never looked so beautiful.

The other patrons were a mixed crowd, young sailors, grey-haired Cynalese, soldiers, dreamy couples and a smattering of exotic visitors. The pleasant murmur of conversation filled the room as the servers glided quietly across the polished floor, the spicy tang of the ocean blowing through the open windows. A small group of musicians sat against the far wall, strumming softly on their instruments. Before them was a small tiled dance area, still empty so early in the evening.

Beside us was the only table still unoccupied. It was set for five but as yet there was no sign of the party. I was discussing the particular merits of various local dishes with Lilith when vibrant scarlet caught my eye and I looked up as three robed Mecla priests and two Cynalese soldiers were escorted to the table.

They settled themselves and a server greeted them eagerly, displaying great pleasure at being so near the priests. I had been so fascinated by the Mecla that I had ignored the guards, so I turned in shock when Carly nudged me. 'Look, it's Rarnald,' she said. And indeed it was. Our handsome guard had yet to notice us as he was intent on giving his order to the server. Once this was done and the server had left, he glanced idly around the room and when he reached our table I saw his look of surprise quickly turn to a delighted smile which Carly, Lilith and I returned.

As we watched, he said something to the priest beside him and then stood up and walked to our table. He wore a short-sleeved shirt and the sword was gone. He stopped next to Alexa's chair and rested his hand lightly on its back.

'Good evening.' He smiled at all of us, his earring swinging slightly. 'Could we offer you a drink to welcome you to Cynal?'

There was a pause in which I glanced quickly around the table. Everyone nodded except Alexa, whose eye I could not catch as she had turned to look at the Mecla.

'We'd be delighted,' I replied.

Rarnald stepped back and pulled out Alexa's chair. 'Perhaps we could join the tables?'

Alexa, who had stood up and was watching the priests with interest, half-turned to Rarnald and smiled breathtakingly. 'That's a good idea.'

The priests stood as the tables were moved, their robes sweeping the floor, and looked up in interest as we approached with Rarnald. When it was time to be seated, priests and cartographers intermingled by tacit consent. Rarnald took a chair next to Alexa.

'We should introduce ourselves,' Rarnald said to the table in general, and he turned to the priest on Alexa's right. 'Kira, these are the cartographers who will be mapping Cynal for Lord Tarn,' and he gave our names.

The priests and the other soldier greeted us and then Kira introduced the Mecla.

'As you heard Rarnald call me, I am Kira and this is Damin, and Laibi. Do you know Nikol?' And she indicated the soldier.

Servers came with wine and we chatted. Aside from their robes, the Mecla looked like any other Cynalese you could pass in the city streets. Kira was a short plump woman, not many years older than us. She had flawless olive skin and a calm open gaze and her dark hair was cropped short. She was questioning Alexa on cartography.

Damin sat at one end of the long table and was the oldest of the three. His grey curls were thinning, covering his head sparsely, and his face was noticeably lined, but his eyes were alert and he laughed a lot as he spoke to Chandra and Lilith and the young priest Laibi. Laibi was just out of boyhood, with the fresh-faced appeal of so many young Cynalese. He was slight and very tanned with long glossy curls and deep-set dark eyes.

Carly sat beside me and across from Rarnald, and between them at the end was Nikol. She was a tall, strong woman with a crazy sense of humour and a wicked laugh. She kept leaning over and topping up Carly's goblet while she spoke to her about various people and places in Cynal, stopping occasionally to nudge Rarnald, who was torn between listening to her stories and jokes and following the conversation between Alexa and Kira.

Although I found Nikol's jokes very funny I could also hear Alexa and Kira and I was fascinated listening to Alexa's modest and concise description of our time in Nalym and with the Tamina and Kira's interested comments. It was not long before they started on religion. It was Alexa who introduced the topic.

'I don't remember seeing any Mecla in Nalym. Do you practise there?' she asked, regarding the priest with her cool blue gaze.

Kira nodded. 'We have a small following and a handful of priests in Nalym, though you would not be able to pick them as they don't wear the robes. It's partly the heat though there are other reasons as well.'

Alexa raised an enquiring eyebrow and Kira responded with a half-smile. 'I'm afraid our preaching of humility and peace does not sit well with Lord Maltra or her style of ruling.'

Alexa laughed softly. 'Yes, I can understand that.'

Kira paused as the server came to ask what we wanted to eat. Once more I was struck by the combination of deference and delight in the server's behaviour when faced by the priest. Kira was polite and gave the server her full attention but, after we had ordered, she quickly returned to her discussion with Alexa.

'Although we practise elsewhere,' she continued, 'Cynal has always been the sect's home.'

Alexa reached across the table for the wine flagon and filled her goblet. Then she held it over my goblet and glanced at me. I nodded and she poured the wine. Seeing Kira's goblet was already full, Alexa returned the flagon to the table and turned to the priest. 'Sect?' she said. 'Are you part of the Menlin religion?'

'Yes,' Kira replied, 'there are three main sects. The Mecla, the Meran and the Melcran. At one time, the priests of the Meran and Melcran were spread far over Tirayi and their power was considerable, but the Meran have little power now, in part due to the influence of the Mecla, and the Melcran are now found mainly on Eustape and keep much to themselves. Meanwhile, the Mecla continue to grow.' She looked directly at Alexa. 'Do you know much about us?'

Alexa smiled. 'A little. I've read some of the writings of Meclan though I am not familiar with your ceremonies.'

Kira shrugged, dismissing that. 'It is the premise that counts.' Then, with real interest in her voice, she asked Alexa what she thought of the writings.

'I was impressed by most of them,' Alexa answered, lifting her goblet to take a mouthful of wine. Then she smiled at Kira. 'Particularly the emphasis on taking enjoyment from the present and not just looking for it in the future.'

'Yes,' Kira said happily. 'Meclan writes, "Today is the future of yesterday." Too many people forget and so they never live their dreams, they only plan to.' She paused and nodded seriously. 'It is important to act.'

The server returned with plates of steaming fish pieces and an assortment of different sauces. They were laid out before us and Alexa picked up a piece of fish and dipped it in a white sauce. 'Do Mecla priests work outside the House?'

Kira and I tried the brown nut-based sauce and the priest nodded.

'Most do, some choose to spend their time studying the writings but it is a very secluded and solitary task that suits only a few. The rest work in the city as tutors, scholars, fishers, physicians and so on, and most contribute some time to running the free-houses for the poor. We must allow time for prayers and House duties, but Cynalese employers are very accepting. The House subsists on donations and a small amount of the coin we earn. The rest goes to the city's poor and sick. We try to help these people by encouraging schooling, teaching them how to care for themselves and, of course, by example.

'We have regular meetings for our followers and of course the Mecla ceremonies.' She turned to Alexa, waving her free hand to emphasise her point. 'We try to encourage humility, generosity and peace. We don't believe you should have to impoverish yourself to help another, just share what you have.' Kira indicated the fish and the wine. 'As you can see we don't go without good food or wine, and we allow ourselves time to spend relaxing with friends. It is a great success for us when we introduce even one more person to our beliefs.'

Alexa had stopped eating. 'I can understand how that could happen in a city like Cynal,' she commented.

'You are well-known here, and respected, but it must be considerably harder in places where the people know little of you. Why should they spare the time to listen to your words?'

Kira nodded. 'That is true, unfortunately. Deaf ears and closed hearts are our greatest barrier to spreading the word and message of Meclan.' She shook her head and sighed. 'It is a pity, the world would be a far better place if there were more who followed Meclan.'

Amused, Alexa said, 'I believe that is what most priests would say of their religion. And as there are dozens of different religions in the world, not all can be right.'

'How could the world suffer from our teachings?' Kira asked, but gave Alexa no chance to answer her. 'It is because we believe this that the followers of Meclan work so hard. We will work towards such a goal until our deaths.'

Alexa studied Kira silently for a moment. 'Other people have different goals,' she said.

The Mecla priest gave Alexa an indulgent smile. 'Yes, you are right, but can I ask you, do you earn more than you spend?'

Alexa nodded. 'Yes, far more.'

'And do you keep it all to yourself?'

'Not all, but quite a lot.'

'But you do share with others less fortunate?'

'Yes, when I can.'

Kira smiled warmly, pleased. 'Then you are already helping. You see how easy it is. It only takes a little.'

But Alexa was doubtful. 'Unfortunately a little from a few is not much.'

Kira shook her head. 'Most people want to do good, they want to help, they just don't know how to. It's one of the strengths of the Mecla. We show people how.'

The server arrived then with individual plates and Kira, Alexa and I sat back while they were placed before us. When the server had departed, Alexa leant forward, twirling the wine in her goblet, her food untouched. 'Do you believe there is good in everyone?'

Kira paused, glancing quickly at Alexa, before answering carefully. 'I like to think everyone has the capacity for good, and I believe most people have. It's really more a question of encouraging the good side to take a stand over the doubt and laziness and greed. If all followed the good of Meclan, what a wonderful world it would be.'

'But do you believe there are evil people?'

'I don't believe anyone is born evil, though circumstances in their life can make them so if they turn from the gods. What do you think?'

Alexa put down the goblet. 'I'd like to believe in the good in people, and most of the people I have met have been good and kind, but I think sometimes people pass a certain point and that once past it there is no return.'

'Well that's where we disagree.' Kira frowned as she spoke. 'I believe all people can change.'

'Oh, I don't doubt they can change. I just doubt there is any inducement great enough to make them want to change.'

For a moment both were silent, then Kira spoke.

'Can I ask you what you value most in your life?'

Alexa smiled her cool smile. 'My health, my freedom and my friends.'

'Do you think everyone has the same values?'

'Of course not.' Now it was Alexa's time to frown. 'That barely deserves an answer.'

Kira laughed. 'Not everyone would disagree. And that is much of the problem. If a miser sees the rest of the world as potential misers, coin for the poor will never be given.'

'So what is more important, getting coin from the miser grudgingly so the poor don't starve, or trying to change the values of the miser so that the coin is given freely?'

Kira grinned. 'That is the crunch.'

The meal was as delicious as we had been told to expect, and as the evening progressed and more wine was served Nikol's and Carly's jokes were getting louder and funnier. At the far end of the table, I could see Laibi and Lilith talking softly while Chandra discussed tribal ceremonies and nomad music with Damin, looking up from time to time to gaze with interest at the musicians. They had begun to play soft dance music, audible over the low hum of conversation in the restaurant, and couples were now moving to the dance tiles.

Rarnald stood up and, to my amazement, walked to my chair. 'Ashil, would you like to dance?'

He was an excellent dancer and he held me close as we swayed and turned to the music, which was louder now that more people had joined us on the pale tiles.

'How do you like Cynal?' I could feel his warm breath on my cheek as he spoke.

I smiled. 'What I've seen is very beautiful. Though we haven't had a chance to see the city at its best, this is the first day we've been here that it hasn't been in mourning.'

'Well you'll get a chance with the enthroning. Cynal will sparkle.' He laughed softly in my ear.

His mention of the upcoming ceremony reminded me of our brief meeting that morning with the man who would be Cynal's new king. Curious, I asked if a Cynalese king has total power. It was something I still found strange, coming as I did from a city that voted in its politicians.

'Yes, total power but he has many advisers. Experts on trade, soldiers from the army, though his closest adviser is a Mecla priest.' He leant back so he could see my face. 'Did you attend the funeral?'

'Yes.'

'Then you would have seen Rianne. She performed the ceremony.'

I nodded, remembering the priest in the scarlet robe. 'I wouldn't have thought that religion and politics would always mix well.'

Rarnald smiled down at me. 'No, but the king of Cynal is ruler first and Mecla second. Otherwise we may as well have a priest on the throne.' He chuckled at the thought. 'Cynal has room for all people of peaceful beliefs. We Cynalese expect no less.'

The tempo increased as the musicians began a jaunty dance tune and Rarnald and I swung around, laughing in sheer delight, no longer trying to talk. When the music slowed once more, neither one of us made any move to return to the tables. Instead we rocked gently within each other's arms. He began to question me about our group, asking how we had met, and I answered happily. He stopped me for more details about the inn where we had first seen Alexa, obviously curious about our meeting, and then he wanted to know where we had worked previously and exactly what it took to draw a map. I prattled on until it seemed he had no more questions for the moment and we were both silent.

I had my head down against his chest when he said softly, almost musingly, 'You are all very beautiful.'

And so are you, I thought, and tilted my head up so I could see his face. But, of course, he was not looking at me, not, I am sure, even thinking of me, as he watched Alexa over my shoulder.

I managed to suppress a sigh. So now we had it. The real reason he had asked me to dance and why there had been so many questions. Not that this was the first time I had been cast in this role, particularly since Carly had joined us, and I was not greatly upset. It was not as though an attachment had been broken, but I had enough pride to feel a moment's irritation with Rarnald. Did he have to be so transparent?

But to tell truth I was more amused than annoyed. Oh, I confess I have thought at times how exceedingly pleasant it must be to be the object of another's attentions. To be seen in some light other than approachable, but I console myself with the thought that my role does have its advantages. For once assigned it, I often become the keeper of confidences and, what is far better, I make a great many friends. And as I have always believed that one can never have too many friends, particularly when leading a travelling lifestyle, this pleased me.

At the end of the dance, we returned to our table and resumed our seats. Almost instantly Rarnald turned to Alexa.

'Ashil was telling me that you worked as a tracker before becoming a cartographer,' he said with feigned casualness.

Alexa smiled her cool smile. 'Yes, I did.'

Rarnald showed her his startlingly white teeth in an engaging grin and leant closer to her. 'How does one become a tracker?'

Alexa put her goblet down and her ice-blue eyes looked for a long moment at the man beside her. Her regard was warm now as amusement lightened her features, and I hid a smile as I listened to her reply, watching as Rarnald hung on her every word.

'It is like most professions, Rarnald. You discover you have a skill and knowledge that people will pay for and you go on from there.'

Rarnald nodded, obviously hoping she would say more. When she did not, he asked if she enjoyed tracking.

Alexa laughed now and Rarnald, delighted by her response, if not quite sure what had elicited it, laughed with her.

'I enjoyed it very much.' She raised her slim shoulders in a shrug. 'Otherwise why would I have done it?'

He took her question as I believed Alexa meant it

to be, as one not requiring an answer, but Kira frowned and offered a serious comment.

'Often there are numerous reasons why a person chooses their type of work,' she said almost didactically. 'Unfortunately enjoyment is not always one of them.'

Alexa nodded. 'True, Kira, but then it depends on the priority you give to each reason.'

Displeased with that answer, Kira shook her head. 'But it is not as simple as that. It's all very easy to say such people put enjoyment behind other factors, but if you can find no other work, or have a sick parent at home, or a debt to repay, then what you earn, how far you work from home, when you work, all must be considered.'

Alexa smiled. 'Exactly, and that is because the job, the parent or the debt are given a higher priority than one's own enjoyment.'

Clearly Kira did not like this argument. 'And you think that is wrong?'

'No.'

Bemused, Kira paused for a moment. 'Then being in a position to choose work that you find both rewarding and pleasurable, don't you think you are particularly lucky?'

Alexa raised an eyebrow. 'Lucky?' she mused. 'No, I refuse to consign my achievements to such an impalpable notion. Perhaps it has played a part in my chosen lifestyle, but by acting as a complement to it, not by being the cause of it.' She smiled wickedly. 'For, you see, I agree with Meclan when he said "Today is the future of yesterday."'

Kira looked taken aback at having the words she

had spoken earlier used in argument against her, and seeing her stricken face, Alexa touched her gently on the arm.

'Kira, I do not deny that life is a struggle for some, and a struggle not of their own making, and we should all offer them what help we can. But that means easing their suffering, not sharing it.'

'Yes, indeed I agree, but first one must be able to recognise their pain as genuine. And just as the healthy do not always understand the cries of the patient when no broken bones or pustules are evident, so those who have never experienced hardship sometimes find it hard not to scorn and criticise the sufferers, calling them liars, good-for-nothings and cheats.'

Alexa frowned. 'Tell me, do you enjoy your life as a priest?'

Uncertain as to where this would lead, Kira nodded tentatively.

'And as a Mecla do you suffer in any way?'

'No, indeed not.' A half-smile curved Kira's lips.

'Yet you can devote your life to recognising and appeasing the pain of others, as though you were a healthy woman attending a patient.' Alexa turned her brilliant blue gaze on the priest. 'How is that?'

The dialogue between Kira and Alexa continued, with Rarnald, determined not to be forgotten, contributing the odd comment here and there, but I was unable to go on attending to it as Carly nudged me and I turned to listen to what Nikol was saying about the upcoming enthroning ceremony.

Nikol first insisted on filling my goblet. 'Dancing is thirsty work,' she said, winking at me. I smiled my thanks and she poured more of the pale liquid for herself and Carly before setting the almost empty flagon on the table.

After she had taken a long draught, she smacked her lips together with pleasure. 'I love the soldier's life, but there are days when I eagerly await the end of my round, so I can experience the mellow delight of Cynalese wine slowly running down my parched throat.' With that she put the goblet down with a satisfied sigh.

Then she smiled suddenly at Carly and myself. 'But to taste the finest wine this wonderful city can produce, look to the palace. In ten days time Cynal will play host to the biggest party since the old king, may his spirit soar, celebrated his son's maturity almost a decade ago.' She laughed loudly. 'And the music and the dancing and the feasting and the drinking will go on all night.'

It was hard to resist her merriment, and I chuckled to hear her talk with such relish about the upcoming festivities.

'The new roster begins tomorrow. How I pity the poor sods who've drawn rounds that night.'

Carly laughed, I could see she was interested by the news of a party, and her question to Nikol confirmed it. 'So, besides the formal reception at the palace, where else can we attend the celebrations?'

But Nikol shook her head. 'No, you told me you were staying at the palace, and all palace inhabitants, including servants and soldiers and now,' she nodded at us and laughed happily, 'cartographers, have been invited to the feast—Lord Tarn's orders. So we're all going to dine in style that night.'

I looked at Carly and she grinned, delighted. She leant forward in her seat, her elbows resting on the table, her fingers laced together under her chin.

'How wonderful!' she said in her deep husky voice. 'I've never been to an enthroning before.'

And of course, neither had I. Taking a slice of melon from the platter of fruits that the servers had just brought to the table, I bit into its tangy flesh. I was beginning to think this was going to be our most exciting job yet and, smiling happily, I finished the melon in one more bite and reached for some grapes. Carly took a handful of blood-red berries and tapped me lightly on the arm.

'Why the grin, Ashil?' And she lowered her voice so that no other could hear. 'Contemplating an evening with the handsome Lord Tarn?' Then she chuckled softly at the shocked expression on my face.

'No,' I protested, torn between laughter and indignation. 'I'm sure his lordship will have things other than cartography on his mind that night. I was just thinking that it all sounds so marvellous.'

Carly laughed and turned to face Nikol, who had heard my last comment. 'Ashil has unfailing optimism where our work is concerned. Every job we complete has been a delight and every prospective job is only going to be better.'

'Well and good,' Nikol said, raising her goblet at me. 'Look for delights and you'll be bound to discover some.' Then she drained her goblet without stopping for breath.

201

Carly nodded and, laughing, imitated the soldier by lifting her goblet and saying, 'Well and good, Ashil. Well and good.' And then she too drained her goblet.

My own goblet was still over half-full but I stuck to the chilled fruit pieces, for I agreed with Nikol that Cynalese wine slid down smoothly, too smoothly, and I wanted a clear head when we made our appearance at the palace in the morning.

Nibbling on some more berries, Carly returned to the subject of the party. 'So tell me, Nikol, what does one wear to an enthroning?'

Nikol shrugged. 'As a soldier of the city, I wear my best uniform. You can wear anything you think appropriate but no sea green, it's the colour of the royal robe and it's thought in poor taste to appear in it before the king on such formal occasions.' She paused, considering. 'Oh yes, and no animal fur. The King of Eustape will be attending and in her religion they believe the only place for animal flesh and fur is on the animal itself. The Eustapeans can just accept others eating meat and fish, but not wearing pelts.' She shrugged again. 'It's all very well when you live in Cynal or on such a warm island as Eustape, but I wonder how the Melcran religion would fare in cooler climes.'

Carly had been listening attentively and Nikol turned to her and pointed to her emerald green sheath. 'Something like that would be fine in any other colour, but try not to look too beautiful or royal cousin Leah may not be too pleased.'

She obviously expected Carly to enquire as to just who royal cousin Leah was, but Carly already knew how to deal with women of all ranks who were jealous of her beauty. It was other information Carly wanted.

'Tell me more about the guests attending from other cities,' she said as she leant over to fill Nikol's goblet.

Chandra stood up and asked Rarnald to dance. He politely agreed, but I did not miss the swift backwards glance he gave Alexa as he stood up and walked with Chandra to the dance area. Smiling to myself, I picked up my goblet and left Carly and Nikol to discuss the guest list while I moved to take Chandra's seat beside Damin.

His eyes almost disappeared from sight when he smiled at me, so wreathed in lines was his face, but the smile was warm and welcoming and his voice steady and deep. 'I hope you have enjoyed your meal, Ashil.'

Pleased that he had remembered my name, I nodded. 'Yes, very much,' I said. 'It was a pleasant change from the hearty but rather limited choice of meal at the inn where we are staying.'

'Well you must be our guests at the House one day and we will serve you some of Cynal's traditional courses. Laibi is one of our finest cooks,' he turned to look at the young priest, 'and I must confess we hoard him shamelessly for fear some restaurant with a large, well-stocked kitchen and boisterous patrons will lure him away.'

Laibi smiled at Damin's gentle teasing, then courteously turned to Lilith and myself as he spoke. 'It would be my pleasure to cook for you and your friends.' We thanked him. 'And don't let Damin's words fool you,' he added in a deceptively mild voice. 'You'll find no noisier crowd than hungry Mecla priests awaiting their dinner. My kitchen is already one of the best stocked in Cynal.'

Enjoying their banter, I asked Damin if he worked in the House, also.

'No, I am an animal healer, so my work takes me all over the city and often to the farms outside the walls. Sometimes, I do not even make it back to the city before dark and must depend upon the hospitality of the farmers.'

My initial reaction was that it was strenuous work for one so old, and as though he knew my thoughts, he chuckled. 'Hard work for an old priest, you think?' Embarrassed, I said nothing and he patted my hand. 'I have an assistant, who is young and healthy and together we manage very well.'

One of the servers paused by Damin's shoulder to ask if there was anything else we required, but we were all well satisfied and said there was nothing.

I could see Chandra and Rarnald on the dance tiles. Chandra was chatting away confidently and Rarnald appeared to be enjoying himself. I wondered if Alexa was the topic of conversation.

'Were you a priest before you became an animal healer?' Lilith asked Damin softly and, interested in the answer, I returned my attention to the table.

Damin smiled. 'No, I trained at the House while I served my apprenticeship. There was no need to separate the two.'

'It is not so with the priests in Binet,' Lilith said. 'They work only within the temples.'

'All religions and all priests are different,' Damin

replied. 'Even just within the Menlin religion, the ways of the three sects vary enormously.'

'How?' I asked, perplexed. 'When all follow Meclan?'

'Ah,' Damin exclaimed, 'there is often more than one truth and the writings of Meclan mean different things to different people. The Mecla interpret them in one way and so we promote generosity, humility and peace. The Meran and the Melcran see it differently and so there is, unfortunately, a history of much anger and dispute between the sects, particularly the Mecla and Meran.'

'Dispute?' Lilith echoed. 'But surely you want the same things?'

'Perhaps we once did,' Damin replied, 'but time has changed that. Now there is little similarity between any of the sects.' He noted the look of confusion on Lilith's face and began to explain.

'Meclan preached of many things and his words were wonderful, filling people with joy and hope and love. He spoke of a balance between all things, a balance between life and death. Now the priests of Mecla interpret this to mean that, in order for one to occur, so must the other. One animal dies in the forest to feed another, an old woman dies just as a child is born, a dead tree falls to the ground and another springs up in its place in the rich earth. It is a cycle and one the Mecla believe should not be disrupted. The Meran see it differently. To my Mecla eyes one of their faults is their impatience, and early on they began seeking ways of altering the balance, trying to control it, and so they began to sacrifice the living.'

Lilith gasped and I swallowed, shocked by the unexpected words.

Laibi nodded. 'It is customary in certain other religions to perform such sacrifices of mortals,' he said in a low voice, 'but the Meran do it under Meclan's name and so it is doubly abhorrent to us.'

'What about the Melcran?' I asked.

'No.' Damin shook his head. 'They are different again and, to tell truth, we know little of their ways, though their respect for all things living is well-known. That is why they will eat no flesh.'

'Is it because of the sacrifices that the Mecla and Meran drew apart?' Lilith asked.

'Partly,' the old priest replied, 'though that was just the beginning of the separation. One of Meclan's greatest powers was the ability to talk to all animals and he offered to share his gift with his followers. Greedily, the Meran sought such knowledge in the hope of distorting it to touch mortal minds. The Melcran too developed the mind power, though I do not believe they ever set out to control a mind as the Meran did. The Mecla saw the way the Meran handled the power and refused the gift, though the Meran laughed at us.' Damin shrugged expressively. 'Yet today it is the Mecla who spread the word of Meclan and not the Meran.'

'What happened to them?' Lilith asked. Her face was pale and her brown eyes fixed on Damin. How unlike this was to the religion we knew at Binet. Indeed, I reflected, it was far more like the manoeuvring that occurred amongst the politicians at the Plaza of the City Guardians.

Damin explained the Meran downfall. 'They thought

to force their beliefs on many people by use of their powers, as I said they were impatient and did not want to wait for people to come to them, but resistance grew amongst the people and they rose up against the priests. The Meran appealed to us to speak to the people, to calm them, for it was well known that the word of the Mecla could be trusted, but we refused to lie and would only aid the Meran if they agreed to give up the mind powers. They refused, cursing us, and were all but destroyed. The few that remained, fled. It was at this time that the Melcran withdrew to Eustape.'

I was reminded of something that Lindsa had said that afternoon and tentatively, not wishing to appear a fool, I asked if this was the time of the white panther.

Both Laibi and Damin exhibited surprise and then displeasure at my question.

'So you have heard the talk,' Damin said, sighing loudly. 'It is nonsense of course. It is true that a white panther came to Meclan and became his companion, and it is true that many believed it was sent from the gods as a symbol of Meclan's power and goodness.' He frowned. 'But this talk of another white panther reappearing is a canard. There is no priest living who has the knowledge or wisdom of Meclan, and the white panther that was Meclan's companion would choose no less.' He shook his head sadly. 'Such talk is senseless and deceitful and will only serve to excite and then disappoint many people.'

The subject obviously distressed him, for he finished speaking and stared down at the table, frowning unhappily.

Alexa came up behind him and gently touched his

shoulder. 'Damin,' she asked, 'would you like to dance?'

His face softened as he looked up at her. 'I would be delighted,' he murmured. Rising from his chair he took Alexa's proffered arm and they crossed to the dance area.

They met Chandra and Rarnald just quitting the tiles and the four of them paused to have a few words before Rarnald returned to his seat beside Nikol and Chandra took Damin's chair at the end of the table.

We topped up our goblets once more and, the white panther now forgotten, Lilith asked Laibi what made him decide to become a priest.

Laibi grinned at the memory. 'At first, when I was very young, I wanted a scarlet robe and to be able to walk down the streets wearing it and have people greet me from all sides with warm smiles.' He smiled at our laughter. 'It was only when I was older and began attending the Mecla ceremonies with my family that I understood it was the priests and not the robes that brought such joy to people. I would listen as the priests preached, hearing the words that filled a person with hope and happiness and I would feel as though all that was bad in the world had suddenly diminished in size and strength. I knew that I always wanted to feel that way and to share such a feeling with others, so I began to read the writings of Meclan. The words were wonderful but they left me consumed by questions and so one day I approached a priest as she walked in the street and we began to talk. She invited me back to the House and I met other priests and we talked for many hours. That evening I went home to tell my family I had decided to become a Mecla and I joined the House as an acolyte the next day.'

'And now you have a scarlet robe,' I teased.

'Yes,' he said, nodding with pleasure, 'and people greet me in the streets.'

'Are you happy?' Lilith asked gently, her expression very serious. In fact there was an intensity to her this night that I had not seen before.

'Yes, I am very happy. There is still a striving to my life but there is also a serenity and a contentment that I did not know before. I would choose no other lifestyle.'

'That is good,' Chandra stated. 'Priests are good, they help us to honour the gods.'

'Not all priests, Chandra,' Lilith protested, no doubt recalling Damin's words. 'Some are corrupt.'

Chandra raised her eyebrows in surprise, then beamed a smile at Lilith. 'You are right. There are always exceptions in cities, so I'll say most priests are good, and those that are true help us to honour the gods.'

Laibi chuckled softly at this small exchange.

'Are you the only priest in your family?' I asked.

'Yes, I come from a fisher family. I have four brothers and three sisters and they have many children and several boats between them. My eldest niece is only a few years younger than I am and is proud to already have a place at the nets.' He shrugged and grinned. 'I do not envy them, I do not mind cooking fish but I do not like catching it.'

Chandra was immediately curious as to how one caught fish from a boat and soon had Laibi describing the process in detail. I was not as curious and I glanced around the restaurant, my gaze lingering on the other tables' occupants. As I turned towards the door, a blur of grey caught my eye and I glimpsed a pale-haired man staring at our table. The light was dim and it was difficult to see his features from such a distance, but there was something very strange about his appearance. I only saw him for a moment, for he noted me looking and swiftly pulled his grey cloak around him, covering his face with his hood. I frowned at this, just as he spun around and quickly slipped out through the door, his grey-clad figure merging with the darkness beyond. Bemused, I gazed at the empty space where he had just been, wondering what it was about our group that made him stare so. Just at that moment, Carly's husky laugh rang out from the other end of the table and I turned to see her beautiful face alight with merriment. I smiled, I had my answer, and I turned to listen just as Laibi was concluding his explanation to Chandra.

'And once the nets have been emptied, the fish are sorted and then the delightful job of gutting and cleaning them begins before they are sold.'

Chandra nodded. She was an expert hunter, able to kill her prey cleanly with or without weapons, but I had never known her to fish. 'I'd like to try it.'

Laibi looked surprised. 'It's not easy work. Physically it's very demanding and it can be difficult for a beginner. There is more skill involved than there often appears.'

'Yes.' Chandra nodded again, delighted by the prospect. 'Could you arrange it?'

Laibi chuckled. 'Of course I can if you really want to.'

Chandra gave him one of her blinding smiles. 'Yes, I would like to,' she said eagerly.

Damin and Alexa had finished their dance and Rarnald promptly stood and met Alexa as she stepped from the tiles. She laughed at something he said and turned back with him and they began to dance closely together. Damin smiled at them and walked over to meet Carly.

The evening grew late, the conversations at our table continuing while all around us tables began to empty as the other patrons headed home to their beds and the servers came to clear away the plates and wipe the tables clean. Finally, the wine finished and the restaurant empty of all but us, we paid and thanked the servers then walked outside with our new friends and took our leave of them. They wished us well in our start at the palace and we waved and called good night to them before we began our walk back to the inn.

The night was mild and still and we were pleasantly relaxed by the good food and wine and the excellent company. We chatted casually amongst ourselves, talking of the Mecla, our voices low and lazy as we walked through the city streets. We were not alone. Cynal was full of those who had celebrated the end of mourning. Some passed us by quietly, their voices low contented murmurs, while others gave us friendly shouts, raising their arms to us as they weaved their way along the road.

The number of such loud greetings increased the closer we came to the harbour district. The inns were still open and, to judge by the inebriated state of many we passed, doing a wonderful trade. We walked on, feeling delightfully drowsy, responding with amusement to the greetings and laughingly refusing various invitations. Our own beds were not far away.

There was a large inn, called the Blue Dolphin, on a corner three blocks from our inn. It was renowned throughout Cynal for two reasons. One was the pair of lifesize blue dolphins which framed either side of the doorway. Skilfully carved from wood, they stood on their tails, their long noses nearly meeting above the portal, seeming to watch you as you entered. The second reason was that of all the city's inns, it was here that the most patrons had died. Wise Cynalese stayed away from the Blue Dolphin and warned their friends to do the same. Those who insisted on visiting the infamous place were advised to carry a weapon.

From the safety of the lit roadway, I gave it a curious glance. Through its open windows I could see figures moving and the din of many voices and the sound of raucous laughter floated out to us on the street. I gave Chandra a nervous glance but she was repeating Laibi's description of net-fishing to Alexa and we passed it without incident, turning the corner.

At the rear of the inn there was a small space for those patrons with horses to leave their mounts. Under the solitary light that hung above the rear door I could see several horses tied up and I was looking at them, wondering how difficult it was to ride when drunk, when I saw a familiar grey-clad figure move amongst them. I narrowed my eyes, puzzled, following his movements, then recognition came to me. It was the man from the restaurant, the one who had been staring so intently at our table. As I watched, he stepped up to two of the horses, set slightly apart from the others, and ran his hand down the neck of one. Its ear twitched at the contact and it turned to gaze at him. The man leant forward, one hand still touching the horse, and began to stare deeply into its eye. I stopped walking, expecting the horse to toss its head in annoyance, and was greatly surprised when it did nothing.

Noting that I was no longer keeping pace with them, the others had halted and now searched to find what held my attention. They spotted the grey-cloaked man, half-turned towards us, as he continued to stare soundlessly into the eye of the horse. Frowning, Chandra wondered aloud what he was doing.

I shrugged. 'I don't know.'

'Let's ask him,' she suggested, taking a determined step forward.

'Wait,' Alexa said, grabbing Chandra's arm. 'Let him finish.'

Both man and horse were as still as statues, their gazes locked, as though in some strange, silent communion.

'He was in the restaurant,' I said softly. All four of them turned to me. 'By the door, watching us. I thought he was staring because of Carly.'

'Why isn't the horse moving?' Carly wondered. 'Flir hates it when I stare at her.'

'Most animals do,' Alexa said. She looked at me. 'Did you see his face clearly?'

'No. He fled when he saw me watching him. I didn't think anything of it. All I saw was that he is very fair, both his skin and hair.'

'He looks strange,' Lilith whispered, 'even so far away.'

'Yes,' Alexa agreed, 'but it's hard to say how.'

'Let's ask him,' Chandra repeated. 'He can tell us who he is.'

'He may not want to answer,' I murmured.

Chandra shrugged and strode from the road. The man had not noticed us, so intent was his concentration on the horse, and it was only Chandra stepping on a loose pile of pebbles that caused him to start visibly and spin around. The horse neighed protestingly as the contact was suddenly broken and the man stared at Chandra uncomprehendingly for a moment, as though dazed.

Chandra smiled. 'Hello,' she called in a friendly tone. 'What are you doing?'

In reply, the man took a step back, pulled his hood up over his face and ran from the horse's side and around its rear, escaping into the night.

Carly laughed as we came up. 'That was beautiful, Chan. Do you always have such an effect on men?'

Chandra frowned. 'Why was he so scared? I would not have hurt him.'

'He didn't know that,' Alexa said, and she ran a hand down the neck of the horse the grey-cloaked man had been so interested in. 'I wonder what he found so fascinating about this horse?'

'Some people are like that,' Carly said with a grin, and Alexa smiled and dropped her hand.

Lilith had wandered over towards where the cloaked man had fled, a tiny gap between the side of the inn and the next building which led back to the main roadway.

'Did you notice he didn't make a sound?' she said softly to me. 'Just like a cat.'

I nodded, peering into the gap. It was in total darkness. 'You'd have to be very game or very scared to
run down there,' I mused, 'and you'd certainly need
the eyes of a cat. I can't see a thing.'

The other three had left the horses and moved back
to the road. They called to us, then turned away to
talk just as the rear inn door opened and two very
drunk, heavily armed brutes stepped out. They spied
Lil and me at the end of the horse lines and sauntered
over towards us, reeking of wine, their faces flushed,
their eyes alight with interest.

Lil and I made to walk around them but they
blocked our path and one, a tall, battle-scarred woman,
leant forward.

'It's more fun with four,' she whispered loudly.

Her companion, a beefy, lank-haired man, laughed
loudly. 'Aye, more fun,' he repeated, laughing hilari-
ously as though he had told a great joke, his breath
rank with drink.

'Excuse us,' I said and once more Lil and I tried to
pass.

'There's no hurry,' the woman said, moving across
in front of us, and this time there was a hard edge to
her voice. She smiled nastily. 'Why don't you come
along with us?'

I was not scared, yet, though they were armed.
There were five of us and only two of them and they
were very drunk, but I was beginning to feel distinctly
uncomfortable.

'No, thank you,' I told her, my voice firm. 'We have
to be going.' I grabbed Lilith's hand. 'Come on, Lil.'

'Lil,' the man crooned, 'give me a kiss,' and he took

a step closer to her, his thick, moist lips making tiny kissing sounds.

Lilith recoiled and I took a step back in alarm. Both brutes laughed, a horrible sound, and the man reached out and stroked Lil's cheek while the woman came up close to me and cruelly squeezed my breast.

'Stop it,' I screamed, shocked into anger, realising that in a moment we would be backed up against the wall and would have to force our way out. I swallowed, alarmed, for I had no idea how we would do that.

The woman sneered. 'Stop it? What's to make us?'

The sneer quickly disappeared when she was answered with the sound of four knives being drawn. She pivoted unsteadily, coming face to face with Alexa, Chandra and Carly. Chandra held her hunting knife and Alexa her dagger, while Carly casually twirled two slim, pointed daggers between her fingers.

'Five against two,' Alexa declared, smiling coolly. 'I rather think the odds are in our favour.'

Both brutes were wearing swords as well as daggers, and the man struggled to draw his, but the woman stayed his hand. Not quite as drunk as he, she was sober enough to realise that their reflexes were dulled by drink.

She stared at the three before her for a moment, then turned and patted me on the cheek. 'Another time, my pretty.' And with the man still blowing kisses to Lilith they walked off, not quite steadily, towards the horses.

Lil and I joined the other three and we crossed to the road as the two brutes came riding out. The woman reined in before Alexa and pointed at her, swaying a little in her saddle.

216

'I hope we meet again,' she said, her expression ugly, 'and then you'd better pray the odds are still as good,' and she laughed, 'because they'll need to be.'

Still laughing, she kicked her horse and it went cantering along the road, the man only a pace or two behind her.

It was only then that I realised that the horse she was riding was the one that had so enthralled the grey-cloaked man.

EIGHT

THE FOLLOWING MORNING, we were up at first light and it took little time to pack our few belongings, eat a filling breakfast of porridge and warm bread and take our leave of the busy innkeeper.

I had not slept well. My mind kept returning to the two drunken brutes we had encountered at the inn and Lilith's and my powerlessness. Five against two, Alexa had said, but three against two would have been more to the truth, for despite the fact both Lilith and I carried working knives, we would have flailed about uselessly if forced to respond. It was a depressing and disturbing thought. Even Carly had only laughed when I had expressed surprise at the sight of her twin daggers, 'Knives can dance too, Ashil,' she had said and laughed again, as though it was all that simple.

Now, in the crowded stable, the dawn light filling the sky as we made ready to ride to the palace, I pondered my despondency while Carly, tending to Flir, commented that the brutes had been no commoners, full of too much drink.

'They were professional fighters,' she said as she settled the saddle on Flir's smooth back. 'I saw enough of them in Netla to know the type. They size up their opponents and only enter an unforced fight if they know their chances are good. Those two last night knew they were too drunk to fight well. They also knew that, sober, they would've had us.'

Alexa had been checking Drella's hooves but she looked up at Carly's last words. 'As did we,' she added. 'They had swords.'

'So many weapons,' Chandra exclaimed. 'Cynal's not at war.'

Carly nodded, pulling Flir's girth tighter. 'Tools of the trade for professionals, Chan.'

Alexa agreed. 'They're probably working in Cynal as guards.' She released the last of Drella's hooves and reached for her saddle blanket. 'With the enthroning so soon, all types of people and cargo are flooding into Cynal. Undoubtedly some are important or valuable enough to require guards. Those two are probably in somebody's pay and had the night off. No matter how tempting the situation was, they weren't stupid enough to get themselves hurt. A wounded guard is of little use to anybody.'

'They weren't from Cynal,' Chandra said.

'How do you know?' Carly asked, smiling at Chandra's assuredness.

'They wore boots. No-one in Cynal wears boots in summer.'

I turned away as the three laughed and continued to blithely discuss the previous night. It was obvious that none of them were the least disturbed by what had occurred and, all at once, I felt naive, craven and unseasoned.

219

Needing space to confront my inner demons, I led Lukar out of the stable and into the small rough court-yard, where I stood silently, one arm looped casually over his neck, taking comfort from his warmth. I heard the clop, clop of hooves behind me, then Timi leant over and nuzzled Lukar.

'I don't think they realise how we feel,' Lilith said, her voice soft and hollow in the still morning air.

'No,' I agreed.

There was no need to say more, and as the silence between us lengthened the faint murmur of voices and movement came to me from the stable.

'If you saw a woman who could not swim dive into the ocean to save another, what would you think of her?' Lilith asked.

I frowned and looked at Lil. 'She would be a fool. Now there would be two drowning women.'

Lilith smiled. 'Do you remember you once told me that it's the doing that makes you strong?'

'Yes.' I smiled wryly at the memory. 'We'd just climbed our first mountain.'

'At the time, I couldn't swim,' Lilith said. 'Now I can. I still can't defend myself, but I can learn, even if it's only a few moves that don't require a knife. I want to become strong, Ashil. I'm tired of feeling weak and scared, and of feeling guilty because of it.'

'Ah, Lil, you're right,' I said, standing tall. 'What can't we learn if we set our sights on it?' Already I felt much better, buoyant almost, for I had a goal, and it would make me both stronger and happier. I took her hand and squeezed it tight. 'We'll learn and next time, when our friends need us, we won't have to stand by and watch. We'll be ready to help.'

She grinned at me. 'And won't they be surprised.'

The sun was still low in the cloudless sky as we rode slowly towards the palace, but we could already feel the heat in the day. The people of Cynal rise early and the streets were beginning to hum with purpose. Out on the calm water were myriad fishing boats, their brightly coloured sails an eye-catching parade against the dark sea. Most would be almost ready to turn for shore to deliver their first silvery hauls, and I squinted, searching for boats that belonged to Laibi's family. He had told me his family's sails were green with a purple stripe and I thought I saw two with such colours far out upon the water.

As we rode, all around us Cynal shimmered with gaiety as preparations for the enthroning began. Normal routine was suspended as people planned, bought, and sold food and drink, cloth for special party outfits, pretty silken and tasselled decorations and huge scented candles to wave during the dusk procession. It was impossible not to be affected by the glorious feeling of anticipation that swirled through the city streets. Voices were loud and boisterous, faces wreathed in smiles and everyone had a hundred things to do and a hundred places to be, and stood around telling their friends about it on every corner.

And of course, the centre of all this activity was the palace itself. As soon as we rode onto the road leading to the main outer gate, we found ourselves behind a long line of heavily laden carts that creaked and groaned with almost comic loudness as the drivers nodded and bade us cheery good mornings while urging their mules on with good-natured abuse. The dull animals, blithely unaware of their destination and the purpose to which the goods they carried would be used, ignored the loud cajoling and threats and continued to plod on at their own sluggish pace. Finally the lead driver waved us on and with relief we were able to kick our horses into a trot and pass by, leaving them well behind as the gate came into view.

At first glance it was mass confusion, animals, tradespeople, entertainers, drivers with carts piled high with crates and sacks and flagons all attempting to pass through into the palace. I felt a moment's sympathy for the guards who were trying to make sense out of the shambles before them, then I turned my attention to finding our way in.

In fact it was not as chaotic as it first appeared, just incredibly busy. No sooner had one group been dealt with than another two would come to take its place. With little alternative, we stood patiently waiting our turn when we spotted Nikol coming towards us, a broad welcoming smile on her face. Delighted to see her, we greeted her warmly.

'Good morning,' she replied. 'How are we all feeling in the brilliant light of day?' And she slanted an amused look at Carly, who had consumed so much of the fine Cynalese wine last night.

Carly chuckled. 'Hale and hearty, and keen to begin.'

Nikol raised an eyebrow in admiration. 'Well and good,' she said and she opened her mouth to add something more when Flir, tired of standing still in the midst of such excitement, butted her impatiently. Nikol pushed the muzzle away with a gay laugh. 'Such eagerness!' she said. 'All right, follow me then and I'll take you to the captain.' She turned then and began weaving her way through the crowd with us following close behind.

Once through the gate the going was slightly easier. We no longer had to fear some small creature or child running out before us and under our horses' hooves, but still the paths ahead of us were teeming with people and carts and livestock and the palace grounds thrummed with vigorous activity.

Nikol caught my amazed eye and guffawed. 'Ever seen anything like it, Ashil?' she asked, idly patting Lukar's neck. I shook my head in reply. 'Today is the first day we've opened the gates to traders since mourning began. At first we hoped to restrict them all to the postern gatehouse but the queues became too long, so we're letting them in before noon at either gate. After noon, the main gate will be kept clear for the arrival of the guests and messengers. Most plan their arrivals for the afternoon.' She shrugged. 'It's not always like this, but you'll find the excitement is contagious.'

There was a hold-up in front of us on the path leading to the right, past the training ground, and Nikol excused herself to go and see what was causing the delay. She returned shortly, a sturdy, erect figure striding towards us, the cuffs of her trousers striking against her calves with each step. 'A cart lost one of its wheels and the driver behind wasn't paying attention,

223

so she drove straight into it. It'll take a while for the mess to be cleared, so I'll take you through the garden.'

We turned our horses around, Nikol ordering the people behind us to make room as we made it back to the gate. She took us up the central path that led to the main entrance of the palace. I regarded the queues ahead and was just thinking that this was not such a good idea, when Nikol shot off suddenly to the right and, following, we were soon surrounded by greenery and unbelievably and delightfully alone.

I looked around and sighed with pleasure at the natural and cleverly cultivated beauty of the gardens. Everywhere was a profusion of growth, low trees and bushes rustling with birdlife and brilliant flowers lining the narrow white paths of crushed shells and pebbles that meandered gracefully in all directions. We had ridden for several minutes before we spotted another person and he was clearly a palace servant, also using the garden paths as a short cut to run his errand. How my father would love this, I thought. He could lose himself for days here, studying the plants and talking with the growers, planning changes to his own small garden at home. I would make an effort to describe it as best I could in my next letter.

Small crossroads were formed where two or more of the white paths converged, and in their centres this time I not only heard but saw several fountains. They were eye-catching works of great genius. Playful sea creatures of stone spurting water down upon their cavorting cousins, carved so skilfully in the white stone that a quick glance could bring them to life.

We heard the eastern path that had been blocked by

the carts well before we could see it from the gardens and then our path widened and there ahead of us, slightly to our right, was a low, long white building, the palace guard house.

We picked our way over to the guard house, our horses' heads high, their ears twitching as they picked up our mounting excitement.

Nikol indicated a wooden rail. 'Tie your horses here. We'll settle them into the stables later.'

She waited as we dismounted, shouting greetings to several passing soldiers, then led us inside.

The low building consisted of a wide central corridor, full of seated groups of soldiers at low tables, and rooms that lined either side. The burble of conversation was lively despite the early hour and many of the uniformed women and men looked up curiously at our passing, some calling out friendly hellos.

Nikol nodded and grinned in reply but did not stop. Instead she steered us towards a middle room that was closed off from the corridor by a woven screen. She tapped on it and a deep voice bade us enter.

Smiling broadly at us, Nikol pushed open the screen and stepped in to the room, the five of us behind her. 'Captain,' she said, saluting, 'the cartographers.'

Captain Varl put down the parchment he was reading, dropping it onto the large pile of papers, parchment rolls and writing tablets before him on his workbench, and stood up to greet us. As Nikol introduced us by name, he clasped our wrists, his steady gaze running over each of us, studying us intently.

'Welcome to the palace,' he said brusquely, waving us to stools and returning to his own seat. He was a tall, well-built man, hard with muscle, his skin a dark tan with a thick, glossy braid falling down his back, between the blades of his shoulders. Without preamble, he began. 'We've placed you in the west wing, a work-room has been set aside for your use.' He turned to Nikol. 'Tell Ricah to put their horses in blue stable. We can move them again after the enthroning, if necessary.'

She nodded, obviously accustomed to the captain's curt manner.

'Because of the guests arriving for the enthroning, I can spare few of my soldiers,' the captain told us. 'Nikol and Rarnald have expressed interest, so I have assigned them shared duty in seeing you around the city. You are unlikely to encounter any difficulties during daylight hours, even in the rougher areas, though I caution you to be careful at night near the harbour.'

Without pause for our reaction, he continued. 'His lordship wants both the palace and the city mapped, but until all the guests have left it will be best to con-centrate solely on the city. Should there be any prob-lems report them to Nikol and Rarnald and, if necessary,' and he glared pointedly at Nikol, leaving her in no doubt that he was not to be disturbed for just any small matter, 'they will be passed on to me.

'I will meet with you once a week in your work-room to check on the progress of the maps and answer any queries you may have.' He then flicked over a piece of parchment, his dark eyes quickly scanning the contents. 'You are familiar with the contract you signed in Nalym?'

He paused for a moment and we answered that we were.

'Good,' he nodded. 'In short, the contract is for six maps, to be completed at the latest by mid-winter. One map of the palace and immediate environs, four maps of the city quarters, and one overall map of the city and surrounding area for the distance of half a league north, south and east. Should any delays occur, you will remain in Cynal until the maps are completed unless formally released from the contract by his lordship or his chancellor. Payment will be made in two lots, half upon arrival, which will be paid you this week, and the rest upon completion. Agreed?'

'Yes,' we replied and he nodded.

'Nikol will take you to settle in. Please avoid the south wing of the palace as much as possible until after the enthroning as it is full of guests and, unless expressly invited, the north wing, which contains his lordship's private chambers. It is out of bounds at all times. When it is time for you to map the palace, an escort will be arranged to take you through the north wing.' He paused. 'Do you have any questions?'

There was none and he stood up. We followed suit. 'I will come to see you in a few days to check how you are going. Good luck.'

Nikol saluted once more, then pushed back the screen. With a final nod to Captain Varl, we left the room. I was second last to leave and before I had stepped from the room he had already reseated himself and begun writing, his mind clearly on other matters.

With the five of us remounted, Nikol took us back through the gardens and over the main central path to the gardens on the west side. 'There are five stables in all,' Nikol explained as she walked beside us.

'We saw them yesterday,' Carly told her. 'Not that you could really miss them with those doors.'

'Yes,' Nikol laughed, 'but it makes it easier for Ricah, the keeper of the horses, to keep a tally.'

As we walked free of the gardens we stood in front of yellow stable, the middle one, and then turned left. Blue stable was the last, closest to the tower, and I smiled to myself as I realised that meant it was also furthest from the palace. Cartographers cannot compete in importance with royal guests.

Grooms were busy leading mounts to and fro, while others were seated in the shade rubbing and polishing leather and metal and chatting furiously to each other, their high, ringing laughter occasionally breaking out to fill the air with its happy sound.

Nikol waved over one of the grooms, a young girl of about twelve, who gladly dropped the bridle she was cleaning and came running over. 'Where's Ricah?' Nikol asked her.

'Over at green stable, preparing for the King of Eustape's arrival.'

Nikol pursed her lips in thought. 'Go and tell her I'm putting the five horses that belong to the cartographers in blue stable.'

The groom nodded and, long dark hair flying, ran off to do the errand.

'Come on,' Nikol said. 'Green stable is where Lord Tarn's horses are kept, along with those of the most important visitors. The captain decides on priority and Ricah has to follow it as best she can. I've never met anyone who can handle a horse better than Ricah. She has a charmed way with the creatures that even the most difficult of horses responds to.' The soldier chuckled. 'But she must be just about ready to tear her hair out by now, trying to accommodate them all.'

We led our horses inside the stable and Nikol found us vacant stalls near the rear. They were wide and well-aired and she called to another groom to fork in fresh hay. We settled our horses in and left them with their noses buried in the dry grass, munching away as though they had not eaten for days. With our packs on our backs, we turned to leave just as a small, wiry woman entered the stable.

'Ricah,' Nikol called, giving the woman a jaunty wave, 'how goes it?'

The keeper of the horses rolled her eyes in an eloquently disgusted motion as she approached us.

'Cheer up, Ricah, and meet the cartographers—Ashil, Lilith, Chandra, Alexa and Carly. And best of all,' Nikol grinned, 'they have only one horse each.'

Ricah welcomed us with a neat bow and a small smile at Nikol's teasing. 'Glad I am to meet you,' she said. 'Don't fret over your horses. Those in blue stable aren't forgotten just because they're at the end of the line. I take care of all my charges.'

'So we have heard,' Alexa replied. 'Nikol was just telling us she has seen none better when it comes to handling horses, even the troublesome ones.'

The little woman puffed up with pride and shrugged slightly. 'It's the troublesome ones that need the most attention. A bit of care and less use of the whip sees them right in no time. Now, let me meet yours.'

We walked back to the stalls and told her their names. She murmured gently as she stroked each one in turn, running an expert eye over them and nodding as though satisfied with what she saw. After she had seen the last one, she faced us and grinned suddenly, lines fanning out from around her eyes and mouth.

'You can tell a lot about people by their animals,' she said simply, and nodding briskly at us once more she turned on her heel and strode quickly away.

Nikol guffawed as we watched the receding figure move out of sight. 'That was Ricah. Come, and I'll show you the palace.'

Alexa and I fell into step beside the soldier as we left blue stable. 'How long has Ricah been with the palace?' Alexa asked.

'Ever since she was apprenticed here as a groom over thirty years ago. They say she had the gift even as a child, and that all she ever wanted to do was be with the horses. The old king, may his spirit soar, offered her an apartment in the palace when she was made keeper but she declined, saying she would rather stay close to the stables. She lives in a small house beside green stable and rarely enters the palace.'

We entered the palace through the same arched doorway as yesterday, passing the armed guards. As we followed the wide cool corridor with its numerous workrooms I wondered which one we would be given. We reached the staircase, so busy with the traffic of people that it appeared as lively as Binet's theatre on first night, and Nikol moved towards it.

'I'll take you to your rooms first,' she said over her

shoulder as she began to climb, 'so you can put down your packs.'

There were people everywhere and we walked for what seemed an eternity, climbing two flights of stairs then striding along several busy corridors, all beautifully decorated with silken hangings. Many of the hangings were just swirls of colour, but so wonderfully blended that they were a delight to behold, drawing the eye back for a second glance. The rooms around us abounded with talk and activity and, peering in, one could see clerks sitting hunched over parchment and writing tablets scrawling figures and words as they checked palace accounts while others with scrolls hurried past in the corridors, intent on their errands. Scribes carrying impressive-looking manuscripts strode by, talking about their latest tasks and arguing over what the records said, disputing this author or that, their voices rising as they became more and more involved in their discussions. It was all very stimulating and I could not wait to begin our own work.

Nikol noted our interest in the rooms and their occupants. 'This wing is filled entirely with workrooms and meeting chambers,' she told us. 'Most of the day-to-day running of the palace is accomplished here, except for the kitchen and the army. As well, there is an excellent library which draws visitors from distant cities, and of course the Mecla use it often.'

Just then, following on the heels of her words, a Mecla priest turned the corner in front of us, his startling scarlet robes vibrant against the muted colours of the palace. He was instantly recognisable for his greying hair and lined face.

'Greetings, cartographers,' Damin called cheerfully. 'You were obviously up with the sun.'

'In Cynal, the sun refuses to let one sleep in,' Carly responded. 'That and Chandra combined are a force too powerful to resist.'

Chandra's inability to linger in bed beyond the first hint of morning gold was a common source of amusement and good-humoured vexation amongst us.

Chandra shrugged. 'That is what the sun is for,' she replied easily. 'To tell the world it's time to wake. Even the birds know that.'

Damin was grinning broadly. 'You have a point, Chandra. There is much we can learn from animals that live free. They never war for instance. A fight only lasts until submission or flight, a far quicker and more harmonious solution than many mortals accomplish.'

Before anything more could be said, another Mecla appeared from around the corner, seeming almost to glide to Damin's side, so graceful were the priest's movements. There was something very familiar about this priest, and my memory teased me with the thought, like a juicy ripe fruit on a branch dangling just out of reach. It was only when Damin greeted her by name that I realised she was the Mecla I had seen at the king's funeral.

Rianne was a striking woman. Her features were strong and decisive, a broad square jaw, a wide mouth beneath a straight nose and wide, piercing brown eyes, the kind that looked out upon the world with almost terrifying keenness yet reveal nothing of the owner's thoughts. Unusually for a Cynalese, her dark hair was straight, falling below her shoulders like a bolt of dense shiny cloth.

'Good morning, Damin, Nikol.' Her voice was like her appearance, strong but pitched low, though I knew without a doubt it held such power that she could make herself heard by barely raising it.

Nikol returned her greeting and then introduced us. Rianne turned those eyes, dark like the rich earth, upon each of us, and her mouth curved as she spoke a pleasant welcome.

'We were just admiring the ability animals have to live together so happily, with the minimum of dissension,' Damin told her.

'I see,' and she smiled fondly at him. 'It may be that soon we will have the chance to study such traits at close hand.' Before elaborating on this enigmatic statement, she looked back to us. 'I understand you are quite well travelled, coming from Nalym and the camp of the Tamina to do this job.' She nodded when we agreed and then she smiled again, though her eyes were still and serious. 'Then perhaps you can help the Mecla. Do any of you know where we can find the Lakiya?'

I gasped. Lilith paled and Carly barely stifled a laugh. Chandra stood looking confused, repeating the name with a baffled frown, and Alexa was studying the priest carefully, her face expressionless. Finally, it was she who voiced what we all were thinking, except Chandra who did not know the name at all.

'The Lakiya are said to be a myth,' Alexa answered with imperturbable directness. 'A glorious legend of what mortals might have become had we chosen a different path to walk upon.'

'Often myths have a foundation in truth,' Rianne said calmly, smiling in a way I found unsettling. 'The

Lakiya exist, not perhaps as legend has them, but they and their beast friends live. Somewhere.' The cool smile lingered on her lips as she regarded Alexa.

With a jolt, I understood where I had seen that smile before. It was the same one I had seen Alexa wear so often. I stared at both women and saw the resemblance. It was not a physical thing, for no blood tied them. Alexa was fair where the priest was dark and Alexa's face and features were more curved and less bold, but the spirit in both faces was the same. A fierce fire of great strength and confidence burnt in both women, fuelling minds of amazing power, though I suspected greatly different persuasions. They were like the wind and the great tree, the former touching lives as an uprooting gale, lifting and setting down things in a different pattern than before, or passing over as soft and indiscernible as the gentlest hint of breeze, barely felt on the skin, while the other was there for all to see and shelter under at all times, magnificent, unabashed, solid and fixed.

'Somewhere,' Alexa repeated, one golden eyebrow raised. 'If you can say with such assurance that they exist, can you perhaps narrow the location down in some way?'

Unperturbed, Rianne answered, 'You are right of course. But now is not the time to discuss it. I only asked on the off-chance you might have heard where they reside during your travels. But it can wait. You have only arrived in the palace and have not yet had time to relinquish your packs. We can discuss this later when you are settled.'

It was an infuriating answer. First, we were told that

tales we had heard as children about people with amazing powers and their wonderful beast friends are, at least in part, true. And just when the discussion was becoming interesting it was called to a halt.

But Alexa accepted it gracefully. 'I would like that,' she said.

'Good,' Rianne replied, 'I look forward to it.' She and Damin bade us good day then and moved on down the corridor.

In time, we came to a wide open passage that cut across our path and as we stepped on to it, our feet sank in the thick cushioning of the floor rugs. 'We're now in the west wing,' Nikol said. 'It contains the permanent apartments of the palace officials and of course,' and she winked at us, 'people like yourselves who will be residing here for several months on business. You're very lucky,' she told us, as she crossed the passage, nodding politely as she passed several small groups of people, and continued along another slightly smaller corridor. 'Your rooms look over the ocean. There's no lovelier sight morning or night than our ocean, though I'm afraid Chandra will have to content herself with watching the sunset not the sunrise from your windows.'

'With that I will be very content,' Chandra replied happily, 'and so will Carly.'

'Have you heard talk of the Lakiya before, Nikol?' I asked, my mind still dwelling on Rianne's amazing declaration.

The soldier frowned uncertainly, 'There is much talk in the palace, the arriving guests and their servants stir it up like dust in a storm. The Mecla will deal with any trouble should it arise.'

235

I saw Alexa glance over sharply.

'Trouble? What trouble?' I demanded quickly.

Nikol shrugged. 'When a ruler is to be crowned, there is often talk of trouble,' she said evasively. 'Usually there is no truth to the words. It is a time that gossipmongers and troublemakers love. They have their chance to shine.'

'What does this have to do with the Lakiya?' Alexa asked.

We were all listening now, alerted by the soldier's reference to possible strife. The more one knew, the better one could react in a difficult situation.

'I do not know,' Nikol said slowly and I knew she was choosing her words carefully. 'Like you, I believed them to be a mythical people but the Mecla say they exist and the Mecla do not lie, so ... ' And she shrugged again.

'So?' Alexa prompted.

'So we will wait and see,' Nikol replied. She strode ahead, passed several doors, then stopped and nimbly stepped down a wide marble step into an arched doorway. She pushed open the double wooden doors and turned to us with a smile that I thought contained a hint of relief. 'Your rooms,' she announced.

Our apartment was sumptuously appointed. There was a central salon, spacious and comfortable, with a small balcony that did indeed offer a splendid view of the sea. From the salon it was possible to enter the other four rooms that comprised the apartment, three sleeping chambers, containing two beds each, and a large washroom.

'It's delightful,' I said, as I crossed the salon, avoiding

236

the white sheepskin rugs on the marble floor as my sandals were dusty. The room was cool and the tang of the sea air filled my nostrils as I looked around me with pleasure.

Two long low couches, white like the walls, sat facing each other, filling up one end of the room. They were adorned with silk-covered cushions in varying shades of blue ranging from the blue-green of the sea to pale sky blue to the dark indigo of sapphires. Against one wall was a large wooden chest, its key resting in the lock, and above it was a long, narrow shelf. Upon the shelf was a vase of blue flowers, the petals like splashes of bright ink against the white walls, and plates and goblets, all made in the Cynalese style of pottery. It was soon clear what they were for when one looked beyond the couches and saw across the room a round wooden table, well polished to bring up the grain, surrounded by six chairs of the same rich wood, with indigo silk cushions. On the occasions we chose not to dine with the palace inhabitants, we could have our meals here in great comfort.

'Ah, an amusement board!' Chandra exclaimed with enthusiasm, crossing to the low table set between the couches and picking up one of the playing pieces. Wearing an enormous smile, she held it up high to show Alexa, who grinned in reply.

Chandra had discovered such a board in Nalym and had asked Alexa to show her how to play the games. She had learnt with amazing speed and had since become extremely proficient, so much so that Alexa was the only one of us who remained able to offer her any challenge. They had been known to spend entire evenings immersed in the ever-changing pattern of the board, matching their wits, and I had no doubt it was a scene that would often be repeated here in Cynal.

Carly had made her way to one of the sleeping chambers and I followed her in. The room was large with a wonderful view of the ocean seen through a large west-facing window. It was light and airy with plenty of space for us and our belongings. There were two wide beds, covered with a pair of woven cotton blankets, one thick and one light, and a clothes chest at the foot of each bed. Small white rugs lay on the floor beside each bed, though the rest of the marble floor was bare. Against one wall, a cotton curtain hid several wide storage shelves.

Carly sat experimentally on one of the beds, bouncing lightly. She grinned at me. 'Feather-stuffed mattresses.'

I dropped my pack on the floor, glad to be free of its considerable weight. Moving to the other bed, I sat down then flopped backwards, my arms outflung, my knees bent over the edge. I twisted my head around.

'You're right,' I said.

Carly laughed and stood up, staring out the window. 'One of us will have a room all to herself,' she said after a moment. 'Only two of the rooms have windows, so if everyone agrees, I'll take the room without a window and you four can share.'

'Fine with me,' I nodded, as I sat up. 'I'd much prefer a view.' Politely, I refrained from mentioning Lindsa's name.

'Good. Let's see what the others think.'

Chandra, Lil and Alexa had been examining the

other chambers and were quite happy with Carly's suggestion. Lil would share with Chandra and Alexa and I would take the room where I had left my pack.

Nikol had been waiting patiently while we looked about. 'If everything's all right here, I'll leave you to unpack and wash up,' she said after a while. 'I'll come back for you in an hour or so to show you your workroom.'

We nodded and thanked her and began to unpack. It did not take long. We were adept at travelling with the bare minimum and at settling in to a new place quickly. We took turns to wash our hands and faces in the clean cool water provided for us in the washroom. I was first and was delighted to see the huge tub that filled one corner. Between that and the ocean, bathing would not be a problem. I finished at the basin and dried my hands, then walked out to the salon and sat down on one of the couches, a sky blue cushion behind me, and gave a contented sigh.

Minutes later, Alexa stepped from the washroom and walked to the balcony. She removed the woven screen from the doorway, so the view was unobstructed, and stood for a moment framed against the brilliant blue of the sky.

'It would be quite easy to just be, in Cynal,' she said without turning around. Her voice was low but I caught the pensiveness of her tone and the soft sigh at the end of her words.

Carly had finished in the washroom and joined me on the couch. She kicked off her sandals and tossed the hair from her face, but her eyes were on Alexa and I knew she had heard what she had just said.

Alexa still did not turn, but I could hear the smile in her voice, a pale smile barely there, as she went on. 'The sun, sea, the colours, all conspire until you feel you are ripe and loose and lazy and quite safe from harm and care. If I was very old, I think I would like to live here.'

Carly tucked her legs up under her and regarded Alexa. 'What about now, while you are young?'

Alexa leant back against the frame so she was in profile to us, her head still turned towards the sea. 'Now?' she said. 'I could live here quite happily for a short while. Then I would remember the smell of a forest after rain, and the play of the morning light through the leaves. I would miss the sound of water dripping from trees and trickling down amidst moss-covered rocks, on towards mighty rivers, white with action, and roaring in their beds. I would long for the warmth not of the sun but of a crackling fire, while all around me snow fell, white and crisp, with no print in it yet and I would desire that feeling of aloneness that often comes to you when all around the world is ice and cold and you can watch your breath steam, with the grey sky hanging heavy overhead.'

She inhaled deeply, as though she could indeed smell some of the delights of which she spoke, instead of the ocean's breath, and hear sounds other than its soft whoosh and the cry of the seabirds. She tilted her head back so that her curls pressed against the frame and she peered up at the sky, unseeing.

'And I would want to see the mountain birds flying, soaring above me while I stood high up above the earth, with vistas of rolling land about me and pure, thin air in my nostrils. I would crave the sight of enormous trees, heavy-headed, below me and the raw mountain slopes under my feet.'

Her voice had softened so that it was little more than a murmur and she looked back out to sea. Lilith had slipped into the room quietly to sit with us on the couch. We all stared at Alexa with astonishment and some envy. Alexa had seen much that we had not, and for a moment she had taken me from Cynal and with her on her journey. Although we had just arrived in the city, I felt restlessness stirring within me as though I was once more at home in Binet, a young inexperienced apprentice still smudging her ink. But I had it all ahead of me. How I loved the life of a cartographer!

In the silence, I could hear Chandra pouring water in the washroom and the gentle splash as she dipped her hands into the basin. Perhaps Alexa heard it too, for she seemed to recall where she was and she smiled at us, stepping away from the frame and slipping her hands into her pockets.

'And my thoughts would dwell also on those paths that I have not walked yet, the creatures I have not seen, the peoples I have not met and I would no longer be content with my place here.'

She chuckled deeply, suddenly, tilting her head back, her eyes shining with mirth. It was a startling sound, changing the mood instantly.

'Besides,' she added, her earlier wistfulness entirely gone now, 'I don't care for the idea of feeling completely safe all the time. A little danger or just the thrill of the unexpected can be an invigorating thing. So I'll enjoy Cynal while we're here and I'll let the sun and sea mellow me a little for that short while. Maybe when I am old and it is just that warm, mellow feeling that I crave, I will return.'

Chandra strode in on the end of Alexa's words. 'Planning the end before we've even begun?' She plonked down on the opposite couch, and Alexa left the balcony and walked over and joined her.

'You may be right, Chandra,' Alexa said with a smile. 'Anything could happen before it is time to leave.'

Chandra nodded. 'Don't roast the game until it's caught,' she quoted. 'I've always thought mellow was a strange word anyway, ever since Skar Linon told me about his wines. Now I can understand how casks can sit and the wine mellow, but no person is ever that still.' She glanced at Alexa. 'Maybe Cynal won't be as uneventful as you think. Maybe it won't give you the chance to slowly mellow in the sun, like a piece of fruit ripening undisturbed on the branch.'

Carly laughed loudly and jumped up, facing Chandra, her green eyes brimming with warmth and merriment. 'You know something, Chandra?' she asked. 'You are one of the most mellow people I've ever had the pleasure of knowing.' She leant over and gave Chandra a loud kiss on the cheek. 'But no more talking of wine or fruit or you'll make me both hungry and thirsty. We got up so early I feel as though breakfast was days ago and it's still only mid-morning.'

We agreed to drop the subject so that Carly would last until our midday meal.

'Good,' Carly said, moving to where one of the sheepskin rugs lay beside the couches, just in front of the

242

balcony. She ran one bare foot gently through the soft wool before folding her legs under her and stretching out upon it, her body cushioned by the creamy springy softness while the sea breeze gently caressed her skin.

Lilith had been quiet through all of this, sitting composedly beside me, enthralled by Alexa's words, then amused by Chandra's, but she spoke up now, her soft voice full of concern. 'Chandra may be right. Perhaps the enthroning will give Cynal more than a new king if what Rianne and Nikol spoke of earlier is true. Perhaps the calm will be disturbed.'

With a jolt, I realised I had forgotten the priest's astounding statement made less than an hour ago and Nikol's mention of possible trouble.

'Certainly there appears to be more happening here than we're aware of,' Alexa agreed. 'We'll find out more when we have a chance to speak with Rianne. I'd dearly like to know how or why this interest in the Lakiya has arisen and what the Mecla intend doing.'

'In all the tales I've heard, the Lakiya feed their beasts human flesh. I wonder if it's true?' Lilith asked nervously.

Chandra's eyes opened wide. 'Their beasts?' she queried, but Alexa shook her head.

'No, Lil, I don't believe it's true. I've heard tales in the north of the merfolk, that they like to pull mortals under and drown them and that they send sharks to harass divers. As we know, they are all false, spawned from ignorance and fear. I imagine it is much the same with the Lakiya. They've been so well hidden for so many years it's now impossible to tell the truth from the fabrications.'

Chandra opened her mouth to speak but I stared at Alexa with surprise. 'You speak as though you believe the Mecla,' I said to her, 'as though you are certain the Lakiya do in fact exist. Until this morning I had only ever heard them mentioned in legends.'

Alexa rested back against the couch, her arm a pale, pale gold alongside Chandra's ebony skin. 'I do believe Rianne, though I wonder how much she knows of their true nature. I have heard it said before that the Lakiya exist and we mortals are a curious bunch. We like to solve the riddles that are placed before us, for good or ill.'

'Yes,' Carly said from the floor, her voice slightly muffled. 'For good or ill.' She rolled onto her side, resting her head on one arm and idly tugged at the wool with her fingers. 'I was at a large party in Sach one year, when a rumour came that several Lakiya had been spotted near the mountains. The party was attended by many of the well-off youth of the city and they decided to get a hunting party together to catch one and bring it back alive.

'Six of them left, all strong and well equipped but inexperienced at hunting anything other than deer and rabbit. Ten days later, none had returned and rumours began to fly around the city that they had been murdered by the Lakiya, fed alive to their pets. Then a body was discovered floating in the river that flows from the mountains. It was mutilated and torn open and the city was suddenly afire with purpose. Trackers and hunters were hired and sent out and the city waited. Less than a week later, the hunters returned. They had solved the riddle of the Lakiya appearing in Sach.'

Carly paused and glanced up at us, drawing out the suspense, making us wait.

'Well?' I prodded. 'What happened?'

Carly grinned and lay back on the rug, her hands behind her head as she stared up at the ceiling. 'The hunters carried remnants of the clothing the six had worn and they also carried several large wolves' pelts. It seemed the spotted Lakiya was nothing more than a large, hungry pack of wolves. Now, thanks to the accuracy of the hunters, all dead.' She looked over at us. 'I'll believe these magical, powerful people exist when I see them, not before. Who's to say that the myths and legends did not start in exactly the same way? Someone did not see a wolf or a bear or some other large creature clearly enough and, lo and behold, the Lakiya are born.'

Chandra gave an exasperated sigh just as I was about to comment on Carly's tale and, seeing me about to speak, she quickly held up her hand to me. 'I've listened to you all talking about these Lakiya,' she said loudly, her brow creased with frustration, 'wondering whether they exist or not. I've heard Carly's story and now I am very confused. So will someone please tell me, who has never before heard the word Lakiya, exactly what they are.'

'Excuse us, Chandra. We sometimes forget that our experiences of life are not all the same.' Alexa paused, thinking carefully of her next words. 'The Lakiya are said to be a great people, strong and intelligent, with powers greater than those of mortals. No-one really knows where or how they live. Some say they live in a magnificent city, hidden from mortal eyes. Others believe that they live in mountain caves and come and go so silently that they are never seen.'

Enthralled, Chandra sat quietly listening. She had the ability to remain motionless for long periods of time and now she was as still as a statue, her breathing barely discernible.

'Yet on one point all the tales concur,' Alexa continued. 'Where the Lakiya go, go wonderful beasts. It is not clear whether they are the Lakiya themselves: many believe that the Lakiya are shape-changers. Others say that the beasts are their friends or pets and that they communicate without words. Some sceptics believe the beasts are just people dressed in animal skins and the Lakiya a band of wanderers with strange rites.' Alexa shrugged. 'We don't know much more. There are grisly stories, like the one Lil has heard concerning human flesh, and there are charming tales of lost children being returned to their towns saying they had ridden on the backs of huge animals, and wounded travellers waking to discover their wounds tended and food beside them.'

'No-one knows more?' Chandra asked.

Alexa shook her head. 'There are as many tales as there are towns and people in them, but no-one has ever been able to prove the Lakiya exist. And those who claim to have seen them have always been alone.'

The room fell silent and, far off on the water, I caught the sound of sails flapping in the wind and the cry of a sailor giving directions, the wind snatching most of his words away before I could understand them. After a while even that faded as the boat pulled away, heading out to sea, and I could hear it no more above the calm rhythms of the ocean as it played beneath the balcony.

Chandra had been mulling over Alexa's words, her head lowered in concentration, so all I could see was a sprouting of tiny black curls and the smooth dark satin of her brow. Carly was still lying on her back on the rug, her eyes closed now, softly breathing, her mouth curved in repose as though her thoughts were pleasant.

Lil rose from her seat and crossed to the water jug to pour herself a drink. She stood silently sipping the water, both hands cupping the clay goblet. Opposite me on the other couch, Alexa was gazing at the flowers across the room. Chandra finally broke the silence.

'If the Lakiya do exist then by their own choice they have stayed apart from mortals. If they play no role in mortal lives, why would the Mecla seek them out?'

Alexa smiled coolly. 'Indeed why?'

Before anything further could be discussed, there was a knock on the door and then it was pushed open to reveal a smiling Nikol.

'All finished?' she asked as she stepped into the room, chuckling when she saw Carly on the floor. 'It's good to see you feeling relaxed in Cynal.'

Carly grinned and stretched.

Nikol turned to the rest of us. 'Come on then, if you're ready I'll show you where you'll be working for the next few months.'

We all rose with alacrity and collected our work materials. The choice of room where we would draw the maps was an important element in the speed and efficiency with which we would work, far more important than our sleeping chambers as far as I was concerned. One could sleep almost anywhere, but one needed room to spread out the parchment, a firm even workbench to lean upon, light to draw by, quiet to concentrate, shelves for supplies and a drying area for the freshly inked maps. All this, plus a large enough area for five cartographers to work and discuss the maps and sketches together. Understandably then, it was with great purpose that we all followed Nikol out the door of our apartment, keen to discover what lay in wait for us.

NINE

Our workroom lay on the ground floor, not far from the room where we had first spoken with Neesha. This time, however, we did not return the way we had come. Instead Nikol led us towards the centre of the palace.

As we walked further into the west wing, Nikol allowed time for us to look around as we passed room after room of apartments.

'Is this a faster way?' Chandra asked, studying the passages we took. Of us all, her sense of direction was the most unerring.

'No,' Nikol answered, 'it's not. But because of the size of the palace, it will take you some time to familiarise yourselves with its layout, so I'm taking you downstairs by the central staircase.' She nodded her head in an easterly direction, where obviously the stairs lay. 'The staircase fills the centre of the palace and gives on to every wing, except the servants' chambers in the south-east corner.'

She turned to us, 'When each new recruit joins the army, one of her first tasks is to learn the rooms of the palace.' She shook her head. 'You'd be amazed at how long it takes some of them to get a picture in their minds. They wander around lost like mewing kittens, continually taking wrong turns, but the captain won't let them on full duty until they know it all. As he says, what use is a palace soldier if during an attack she cannot move at speed from one wing to the next?'

'How long did it take you, Nikol?' Carly asked.

'Less than a month. Both my parents were soldiers and I was in and out of the palace from a very young age,' she admitted. 'Particularly the kitchen.'

It was a fair distance from the west wall of the palace, where our apartment was, to the centre, so we chatted about the delicacies to be tasted in the palace kitchen and learnt the names of the cooks most receptive to interruptions and the pleading of a hunger that could not last until the next meal. We walked along more corridors, bustling with people, until finally we turned a corner and there before us was a wide landing. Rising above and stretching below it was the greatest, and busiest, staircase I had ever seen.

'It's huge,' I gasped, astounded, as we all paused, stepping aside so as not to halt the flow of people moving up and down the very heart of the palace.

'Yes,' Nikol agreed. 'When I first saw it, I was sure it must reach the sky.'

'Does it?' Carly asked with a straight face.

Nikol flashed her a grin. 'Almost. It comes as close as I ever want to get.'

Alexa stepped forward, her eyes flicking over the creamy marble, flecked with touches of pale grey. The stone had been carefully curved at the edges of each step and a bannister of polished wood stood at chest height along its inner edge.

'Come,' Nikol said, and we began to descend the stairs, our hands gliding over the smooth bannister. At each landing, it was possible to take six corridors, each heading towards a particular wing, and when we finally reached the ground floor we encountered yet another wondrous sight.

The stairs halted thirty paces from two huge wonderfully worked doors in a rich brown wood. The doors stood the height of two tall men and were flung wide open as servants and craftspeople hurried in and out, preparing the room beyond for the enthroning celebrations. Even before Nikol spoke the room's name I knew it had to be the Great Hall, that which filled the entire north-east wing of the palace, the room where we and countless other palace inhabitants, guests from far away, soldiers, Cynalese nobles and priests, would dine in nine days time.

Of one accord, we crossed the open space and peered in to the room, mute before its splendour. The ceiling was way above us, with delicately painted scrollwork in soft gold and pale blue flowing along its lines and gently intertwining as they ran towards the centre. Dozens of elaborate candelabra were suspended from the ceiling and, as we watched, one was carefully lowered and fresh scented candles fitted in place.

I turned to the left and let my eye run along the inner walls. They were pure white and covered with exquisite silken flags representing Cynal's allies. Towards the far end, on one side of the raised dais where the king and a select few would sit, was an enormous Cynalese flag, a golden sphere surrounded by green and edged in white. Beside it was the royal crest, the seahorse and the foaming wave below a gold and scarlet crown, its three points representing Cynal's strength, the moon, the sea and the royal bloodline, and the three beliefs of the Mecla, humility, generosity and peace.

At Nikol's insistence, we walked into the room, moving straight ahead in absorbed silence. When we finally paused, the furthest wall, that which faced the ocean, was still a great distance away. The features of the workers who laboured there were indistinguishable. They had thrown open the many doors that lined the wall, and appeared to be busy scraping and polishing the wood. The smell of the wax mixed with the clean salt air that blew in.

Beyond these doors was a broad marble terrace fit for dancing, with a backdrop of the sea that was breathtaking in its wideness and clarity. Far to the right, similar doors opened and the marble terrace continued around the eastern side, this time backed by the glowing green of the palace gardens.

Empty, the Great Hall was stunning, filled with people and laughter it would be mesmerising. Such grandeur took my breath away. I stood silently, momentarily forgetting our as yet undisclosed workroom, anticipating the gaiety of the enthroning. I tried to furnish the Hall with tables and chairs, with musicians and dancers, food and drink, elaborate evening clothes, candlelight and, of course, the presence of the new King of Cynal. It was an impossible task. Despite the many parties and dinners I had attended during our travels, nothing could compare with the celebration that would animate not only this room, but the entire city, and create a place for itself in Cynalese history.

Finally, Nikol roused us and we quit the room. 'Such a sight will have stirred your senses,' she said as she stepped around servants now beginning to work on the enormous entrance doors. Proceeding to bypass the stairs, Nikol turned us to the left. 'Come and I'll see if you can't sample some of our excellent palace food right now. It will give you a taste of what to expect. We can't have you beginning work on an empty stomach.'

She strode down the short corridor, pushed open a swinging door and held it open so we could precede her. Once past her, we were immediately over-whelmed by heat and the smell of food roasting, sim-mering, baking, cooling, and the sight of dozens of servants basting, chopping, carving, stirring, rolling and peeling. The long benches where they worked were covered with foodstuffs in varying degrees of prepara-tion, and stores lined the wall-shelves near pots and pans of every shape and size. A light, chirpy buzz of conversation filled the air, accompanied by the back-ground sounds of meat spitting, trays sliding, spoons mixing and knives falling.

A few servants looked up momentarily at our appear-ance. Nikol hustled us along the benches towards one side of the kitchen where a plump man in a large apron was checking the roasting meat. He nodded to another man who stood beside him, silently watching.

'It's ready, carve it up,' the plump man pronounced with a satisfied nod.

'What wonderful timing!' Nikol exclaimed, as the

plump man spun around with surprising swiftness and raised his thick eyebrows at the six of us.

'Nikol,' he drawled with an air of amused forbearance that told us she was not an unusual sight in his kitchen, 'you always say that. You have a better nose for food than a hog searching out truffles.' He glanced at us. 'Though you don't usually bring half your regiment with you.'

'Baki,' Nikol scolded good-naturedly, obviously accustomed to his ribbing, 'these aren't soldiers but cartographers recently employed by his lordship.'

Baki was one of the cooks Nikol had earlier recommended and it was clear that he was a favourite of hers.

He pursed his lips and emitted a low 'Mmm' as he nodded thoughtfully at us. 'In that case, good day to you all. Maps are handy things, though I don't know how you manage to get all the streets to join up so perfectly. Still, I suppose you have your secrets just as we cooks do.'

'Yes,' Nikol agreed, 'and one of them is that hungry cartographers draw dismal maps. Can you spare us some food? I've been showing them around the palace and it's left a hole in my belly.'

The cook dropped his eyes to Nikol's stomach. 'Not the same one that was there a few days ago?' he said dryly.

Nikol gave a loud laugh. 'No, this one is larger.'

Baki shook his head in mock resignation. 'Go and take a seat then, in the corner, and I'll see what I can spare. I don't know why we bother with a Dining Hall here.'

'Thank you, Baki,' Nikol said. 'If ever you want to work off that paunch, the exercise lessons are on me.'

With a horrified expression on his face, the cook hugged his considerable stomach. 'This is no paunch, it's a sign of my dedication to my work. Everything that leaves this kitchen is first tasted and approved by me. Lord Tarn will receive no second best while I'm in charge of his kitchen. Now go and sit down, you impudent rascal, and let me get back to my cooking.'

Nikol followed Baki's instructions and found us a spot at a corner table. Moments later, the cook came over carrying a large platter piled high with juicy slices of roasted pork, its outer skin a crisp, salted crackling. Directing a servant to put plates and goblets before us, he set the platter on the table. He strode off and soon returned with an equally large platter of vegetables— squash, carrots and steaming potatoes—and another containing cooked apples stuffed with nuts and dried fruits.

The servant laying our places brought us bread still warm from the ovens and pats of creamy yellow butter. It was a feast! Baki even added a flagon of cider, then to my surprise pulled over a stool and joined us.

'It's nothing grand today, friends,' he said as he passed the vegetable platter to Carly, 'but it should fill any of those holes Nikol was complaining of.'

I forked several pieces of the meat onto my plate and a selection of the vegetables. My mouth watering, I bit into the pork and exclaimed at its exquisite flavour.

Baki inclined his head in acknowledgement of the compliment. 'Thank you. And because it's useless expecting good manners from Nikol, I can see we're going to have to introduce ourselves.'

Nikol quickly swallowed her mouthful. 'I apologise, Baki, but the sight and smell of such food overwhelmed my senses and I was unable to think of anything else.'

She sat up straight, waved a hand at each of us and told Baki our names.

'Where are you all from?' he asked, eyeing the differences in our colouring.

'From all over,' Carly replied, goblet in hand. 'But our last job as cartographers was with the Tamina and before that in Nalym, near the Burrnayi Desert.'

'Ah, down south,' Baki said. Clearly he had only a general idea where that was.

It was a common enough reaction. Most people of non-travelling professions were familiar with little other than their own small part of the world. Maps, though available to anyone who had the coin to pay, were foreign things to such people, rarely if ever seen, and even then not always understood. Not that Baki seemed at all disturbed by his ignorance in this matter. He had no need to understand cartography to live his life well.

'I've a sister who's a sailor,' he told us, 'and she travels to amazing cities. Once she took me to Eustape on her ship.' Baki sat back and gave a dismissive shake of his head, evidently not all that taken with the island country. 'It's quite pretty,' he admitted, 'but then so is Cynal, and in Eustape I wasn't allowed to cook anything that had once lived.' He scowled at the memory. 'Now I can make vegetable dishes that delight the palate, but not every day! Do you know how much those people have to eat at each meal because they've no meat to fill them up?' Without waiting for an answer, he told us. 'Huge amounts, and that when they've got some of the finest fishing water at their doorstep.' He shook his head again. 'My sister loved it, thought it was a great adventure and visits the island quite often. For me, though, once was enough. Cynal has everything I need, I don't have to look elsewhere.'

'Cynal is an easy place to just be,' Carly said, sliding her gaze sideways to smile at Alexa.

'Yes, definitely,' the cook agreed. 'That's why I love it. Everyone is free to be themselves.'

Chandra had been following Baki's words intently, her natural interest in everything and everyone never flagging. Now, she pushed her empty plate away and leant her elbows on the table.

'In my tribe, I too had everything I needed,' she said seriously, drawing our attention. 'But sometimes you don't realise there is a lack or a different and better way of doing something until you leave the familiar and discover the unfamiliar.'

Baki's dark brown eyes were watching Chandra with fascination and I recalled my first encounter with her, her impressive stature, her straight-backed bearing and her plain-spoken, perceptive observations. For Chandra would never say what she did not mean, or move with the pack in order simply to be accepted. In her quest for knowledge she never sought confrontation, but nor did she actively avoid it. Chandra was well aware of her own ignorance in many areas, but she never lacked self-confidence or doubted her own worth. It was for precisely these reasons that we all sat quietly waiting for her to continue. Regardless of the topic under discussion, she was usually illuminating and always interesting.

'Before I went to Binet,' Chandra said, 'I had never paid for food before, nor seen such a variety. Instead I had either been a part of the hunt myself or I had known the hunters who had caught it and the cooks who had prepared it. There, I had my first bath indoors, with heated water, and slept within solid walls that did not move with the wind. I learnt to read and write letters, so now I can label my maps and I can read books and leave messages. And all the while I was surrounded by people I did not know and would never know. I did not even know which family they belonged to.'

A servant paused by my shoulder and began to clear away our dishes, though I noticed he sensibly left the flagon of cider. I sat back to allow him room while Chandra continued.

'Sometimes I saw things I did not like.' She frowned, creasing the dark skin between her brows. 'Things that would never happen in the tribe. I saw people who liked to own everything they saw, in Nalym, people even own other people, as though these "slaves" do not breathe and have minds and wills of their own but are like a blanket or necklace you might call yours. Even in Binet, people planned and saved their coin so they could have more clothes than they could possibly wear in a season and smelly oils and lotions that added to the city's reek and other ridiculous, unnecessary items. It was the same in Delawyn, where beggars sat unhappily in the streets while rich people with fat bellies and empty rooms in their houses walked by without stopping. Yet despite all the wealth and the comfort, the gods, those who give it all to us and deserve our thanks and praise, are almost forgotten.'

Her frown deepened. 'It was very strange for me,' she admitted. By now I was feeling slightly uncomfortable and I sipped my cider quietly. After all, one of the places she was describing with such unfavourable frankness was my birth city. Far worse was the fact I could appreciate all she said. Yet her next words had me breathing a sigh of relief.

'Sometimes I saw things which were wonderful. There were schools where all the children could learn to read and write, and if they asked a question their tutor could not answer, she would look it up in a book and find what they wanted. People could work at one thing all day and become skilled at their job without having to stop to do other tasks because there were other skilled people who did that. And the most beautiful music could be played on many different instruments, the like of which I had never heard before.'

Surprising us all, Chandra suddenly smiled, giving Baki a good look at those perfect teeth. 'And then I learned things that I just hadn't known.' She laughed at the memory. 'I did not know that the sun could turn skin red and make it blister and hurt and I did not know that people would build fences around their homes as though to keep them in. I did not know that buildings could be so high or that people will make themselves run and jump on special tracks because their bodies grow weak from being inside all day.' She threw open her hands, 'And until I came to Cynal, I had never swum in the sea, or met the merfolk, or heard of the Mecla.'

Still smiling broadly, she turned her attention to Baki. 'The tribe had everything I needed and I didn't have to look elsewhere, but I'm glad I did, and every new thing I discover, good or bad, makes me even gladder. Because if I find there are many ways of doing the one thing, then I can choose which way I like best and that means I'm no longer just Chandra of the tribe, but Chandra of Tirayi and that's why I love being a cartographer.'

'Ah, Chandra,' Nikol murmured into the silence that followed Chan's words, 'you make me want to give up soldiering.' She gave herself a little shake and grinned. 'But that will pass.'

'Chandra,' Baki said, 'all I can say is that if staying in Cynal and cooking for his lordship makes me happy and if going off to map the world makes you happy, and we are both free to do so, then we're two very lucky people and we should make the most of it.'

The servant who had cleared the table was approaching with a huge bowl and Carly cooed in pleasure. 'Well, all I can say, Chandra and Baki, is that right now I'm the one feeling lucky if those are stewed apricots I can smell.'

'Indeed they are,' the cook replied. 'Fresh apricots from the palace gardens with thick whipped cream on top.'

Carly smacked her lips together. 'If you call this meal "nothing grand" then I can't wait to taste what you have prepared for the enthroning.'

'Dishes as splendid as our new king. What else would

be suitable to celebrate the beginning of his lordship's reign? For he and his bloodline are one of Cynal's strengths.'

The apricots and cream were delicious and not even Nikol could complain of still having a hole in her belly as we rose from the table, fortified against an afternoon of vigorous mapping.

'Thank you, Baki, for a lovely meal,' I said and the others echoed the sentiment.

'It was a pleasure. Come again. The usual interlopers,' and he threw Nikol a pointed look, 'could learn much from your manners.'

Nikol was not in the least upset. 'I'll make a point of studying them next time we come, and the time after, and the time after that, and the time after that.'

Baki threw up his hands in mock horror. 'Out! Out!' he cried. 'I have work to do. You can study their manners elsewhere. Good day, cartographers.' And he strode quickly back towards the ovens to check on a batch of sweet tarts that had just finished cooking.

We left the kitchen and its warm, multifarious odour and re-entered the great stairwell. Cutting to the left, well behind the enormous stair base, we walked over the cool marble floor for many minutes, passing the Dining Hall, and finally came to a passage that would take us into the south-west wing, where we would find our workroom.

Nikol brought us to it quickly and as soon as I stepped into the room, whatever apprehensions I may have had fell away. The workroom was perfect. It was large and, because of the need for light, had an enormous window that faced south-west. A wide workbench ran under the window from one wall to the other, with four stools before it. Individual sections of the bench could be raised by lifting the wooden cover by a pull-ring to reveal a well underneath. A sturdy wooden tail was connected to the window-side end of the cover and this could be wedged into niches of varying heights and the cover adjusted to the preferred height for drawing. There were two more individual workbenches against the right wall and a large couch that joined with another on the east wall to form an 'L'-shaped sitting area for discussions. A low, wooden table sat before the couches.

On the left wall there were storage racks and shelves and, much to my relief, a large drying bench with clips to hold the skins down while the ink dried. The racks, shelves and benches were empty, so we would not need to work around other people's clutter. This was just as well, as we would create enough of our own as we went along.

'Now as to supplies,' Nikol said once we had finished inspecting the room, 'do you have enough to begin?'

'Yes,' Carly replied, 'we stocked up yesterday.'

'Good. If you run out of anything, let me know. There's always a supply of ink cakes and parchment in store for the scribes.'

While Nikol talked, we were unpacking. Out came the prepared skins which we placed, still wrapped carefully in their covers, on the shelves. Beside the skins we placed the ink cakes that we would dissolve in water in the ink wells on the benches. Pots of coloured dyes went alongside for the occasions we were asked to colour portions of the map. The dyes were very expensive and added considerably to the price and preparation time of our maps, though the results could be stunning.

We each selected a workbench, with Lilith and me being given first choice as we did the most drawing. Naturally, we chose the two centre positions under the window, with Chandra and Alexa on our sides. Because she did not draw, Carly took one of the benches against the wall.

Nikol was watching us, fascinated, as we walked around setting out materials and equipment. Now we had our seating arranged, we were placing the drawing styluses, brushes and sand shakers we would not use in the sketching on the benches and Nikol picked up one of the fine bone styluses and examined it closely.

'Why so many?' she asked, pointing at my collection of half a dozen that I had assembled in Binet.

'Some are spares for when the others break or go blunt, and some have different size tips so I can draw finer or thicker lines.'

She gazed down the bench at the collections of the other three. 'You don't share?'

Alexa grinned and put a hand on Nikol's shoulder. 'Do you share your sword with other soldiers?' she enquired amiably.

Nikol frowned and shook her head. 'Never.' Then she gave a soft murmur of understanding.

Alexa gave the soldier's back a friendly pat and stepped back to the bench. 'We cartographers are the same,' she said to Nikol. 'We'll share everything but drawing stylus and brush. After a while they come to suit our hand and no other, so if there is a change and someone else must use one of your own, your own drawing suffers.'

Nikol gave a brief nod and raised one of her eyebrows reflectively as she replaced the stylus carefully. 'There's a lot more to this map drawing than I'd realised.'

Carly was busy checking the contents of our two large mapping packs. She scanned our knotted measuring ropes, cross-staffs and the long and short wooden stakes we would need for the sketching. She examined our surveying frames, with their plumb-bobs, peep sights and notched horizontal bars and satisfied all the equipment was in working order, she replaced it in the packs. Finally she opened each of the two thick segmented wooden boxes that were packed tightly with wool. From each of the three segments within each box, she removed one item. The first was a small, shallow wooden dish, the second, an iron needle, and the third a small lodestone. These stones, when rubbed against the needles, would pass on some of their magical property so that the needles, floating on a piece of straw in water, would always point north. Carly fingered each item gently but all were undamaged and she repacked them carefully, closing the packs.

In the initial stages of each project, Carly would assist by carrying one of the packs and taking down notes and measurements. This helped to familiarise her with both the city and our work, and although she had no great understanding of cartography, she always knew what we were doing. This was useful for later, when her job would begin. Thanks to Carly, our entire working routine had become smooth and efficient since Nalym. While we sketched and drew, she saw to supplies, to any queries or problems regarding the contract, to the functions we were asked to attend and, of course, to our next project. She might not have been a cartographer but she was an integral part of our team and our success.

Carly handed me one of the packs and looped the other across her shoulder while Lilith, Chandra, Alexa and I gathered our small sketching kits. Now we were ready to begin the first stage of the mapping.

'Good,' Nikol said, nodding in approval. 'That didn't take long. Where do you want to start? The captain has asked us to leave the palace alone for the time, so you can begin anywhere in the city.'

We had already discussed the possibilities and knew we wanted to draw our baseline, the first line of many triangles, along the southern wall, near the lower harbour. Cynal is level with the sea only at the upper and lower harbours. Beyond here the land rises both northerly towards the palace and easterly across the city, levelling out at the marketplace. The ground we had chosen along the southern wall was flat and accessible and the harbour wall made a natural and easy second line. We had just explained this to a blank-faced Nikol when we heard footsteps in the corridor coming our way.

'Is it that time already?' Nikol asked as she peered out the window up at the sky. 'How I love day rounds, they just fly by.'

The footsteps became louder, and we all turned to the doorway just as Rarnald, glorious in his casual uniform, stepped through. He smiled brilliantly at us all, particularly Alexa. 'Good afternoon, carto-graphers,' he said. 'I'm here to relieve you, Nikol.'

Nikol inclined her head in acknowledgement. 'I've shown the cartographers their apartment and we've had a brief walk around the palace. Their horses are in blue stable. They want to begin this afternoon at the harbour.'

Rarnald smiled. 'Fine.'

'That's my work over for the day,' Nikol said merrily. 'I'll see you all here tomorrow morning after breakfast. Have fun at the harbour.'

'We're ready,' Carly told Rarnald. 'Lead on.'

Once again, we followed Rarnald's bare back as he took us out into the gardens. The white walls of the palace were now gleaming under the strong glow of the Cynalese sun as it sat high in the cloudless sky. The crowds on the paths did not seem to have thinned much and I wondered what havoc must be existing at the postern gatehouse now that entry through the main gate was restricted.

Rarnald had slowed his pace so that he walked amongst us or, more specifically, beside Alexa, and I hid a smile when Alexa spoke to him. He swung his head around quickly, his delight evident for all to see.

'How many soldiers' rounds are there in a day?' she asked.

'Three,' he answered. 'The night round, which begins two hours before midnight and lasts until dawn. The day round, which Nikol has at the moment, and the late round, which starts two hours after noon and lasts until two hours before midnight. There's also always two companies on special duties and intensive training.'

'So you're on the late round,' Carly noted. 'Does that make you one of the poor sods Nikol referred to last night who will be working the night of the enthroning?'

Rarnald nodded and smiled at the teasing light in Carly's eye. 'Yes, I'm afraid so. Rounds last for one month, and this is the first day of the new roster, so I'll miss the dinner but not all of the dancing.' As he spoke he turned back and smiled at Alexa.

Carly looked away and our gazes met. I could see she was biting hard on her lower lip so as not to laugh out loud. She was genuinely enjoying the soldier's attempt at flirting with Alexa and his abysmal lack of success.

Nikol's comment that the guests tended to arrive after noon proved to be true and the stables were busy. We weaved our way through the crowds of animals and people, trying not to stare curiously at each new arrival, with their fine clothes and bevy of attendants and piles of belongings. We slipped inside blue stable and Rarnald went to hustle up a groom but Chandra told him not to bother. It would be faster if we saddled our mounts ourselves.

Rarnald nodded and chose one of the army horses, carefully adjusting and checking the straps with a thoroughness that suggested a lack of practice. I went over on the premise of admiring his horse and ran a quick eye over his handiwork, for it would be a pity if that gorgeous face and chest were to suffer disfigurement from a fall. Satisfied with what I saw, I returned to Lukar and we mounted and rode out into the sunshine. Stepping onto the white path and turning in the direction of the main gate, his coat shining in the sun, Lukar gave a happy twitch beneath me that sent a shudder through his entire body. I smiled, knowing he would enjoy a pleasant afternoon walk through the city, and watched as he moved his ears about, alert but not nervous.

Following Rarnald, we were permitted to ride out through the main gate. Our progress for many minutes after was slow as we moved against the flow heading towards the palace, but we were finally free of the worst of it and able to ride at a swift trot.

Cynal's large lower harbour is on the west coast, at the southern corner of the city. If one could travel south in a straight line from the palace in the north-west of Cynal, one would, after many leagues, reach the harbour. It is not a pretty area but it has vitality and much colour and we rode towards it by passing through the well-kept area below the palace where merchants and the well-to-do lived. In most cities proximity to the ruler's house is an indication of rank and social status. In Binet only the very wealthy could afford to live near the Plaza of the City Guardians, and this was true also in Cynal. Those without the means to afford the luxurious and expensive area to the east of the palace settled for living below it, where they formed a buffer against the outlying inns and poorer housing of the harbour district.

We were not yet so familiar with the city that we could select the shortest path, so we trusted to Rarnald's superior knowledge in this as we took our horses through the pleasantly bustling streets. White houses, most of only one storey, crowded up to the very edge of the roadways, their blue and green shutters and doors startlingly bright by contrast. Occasional pots and tubs of plants and herbs sat near entrances but most of the houses, I knew, had inner courtyards hidden from view where decorative, edible and medicinal plants grew.

Children scampered in the streets, running up to pat and watch our horses, their small faces glowing with health and excitement as their dark curls flew around them with their wild, unrestrained movements. From time to time we encountered members of the city guard on patrol, their swords dangling from their hips, their gait relaxed and unhurried. They greeted Rarnald loudly and he flashed back his charming smile. Looking down at them from the back of his mount he teased them about all the wear and tear they must be experiencing on their feet. They denied this fervently with shakes of the head and mock frowns and told him that walking with a few blisters was better than not being able to walk at all.

Slowly the quality of the houses declined and we soon found ourselves amongst inns and shabby crowded tenements filled with family after family of the city's poor. It was noisier and ruder than the district further north but for all its loudness and rawness it held little that intimidated, unlike the poor areas of other cities I had seen.

Alexa moved up beside me, watching with interest the activity that surrounded us in the streets. She smiled at me and nodded at the edges of the road that were surprisingly free of refuse. 'Kira told me there were no beggars in Cynal. She was right.'

Rarnald, as ever alert where Alexa was concerned, nudged his horse up to join us. 'The Mecla have free-houses all over this district. So everyone in Cynal has food and blankets.'

He indicated the road edges. 'The Mecla also organise cleaning teams for each main block. Most people are more than willing to help the priests in any way they can, including those who use the free-houses. They feel they are working in return for their keep.' He glanced around him, eyeing the people who scurried or plodded past and who seemed more interested in our horses than in us. 'The Mecla can't stop the poor being poor but they can stop them from being hungry and keep the streets from breeding sickness.'

We walked on further, answering the occasional 'hello' from curious passers-by and looking up as people yelled down to us from their windows. 'Where are you going?' they called, or 'What are you doing?' 'They're cartographers working for Lord Tarn,' Rarnald shouted back to them. 'They'll be mapping the city, starting at the harbour.' Heads were pulled sharply in, like so many rabbits scuttling back into their holes, for there was news to be circulated and no time to be lost in doing it if they were to be the first to tell.

Rarnald pointed to a small, neat building across the road. It was white but with a scarlet door that made it appear to have been dipped in blood. 'A free-house,' he explained. 'Only the Mecla paint their doors scarlet. That way their buildings are instantly recognisable even to those who cannot read.'

A simple sign hung above the door with the three

beliefs of the Mecla—humility, generosity and peace—inscribed in the wood.

'Can anyone enter?' I asked.

'Yes, the Mecla will turn no-one away.'

'What about travellers newly arrived in the harbour?' Alexa queried. 'Can they stay in the free-house too and not pay for a room in an inn?'

'Yes,' Rarnald nodded. 'Anyone can use a free-house. It may sound surprising but few abuse the generosity of the Mecla.'

Alexa smiled and turned away, saying nothing.

Small shops selling everything from rope and sandal straps to sweetmeats and pickled vegetables and oil and cooking pots were squeezed between tenements or rimmed the ground floors, the vendor's tiny living quarters squashed in behind. The shops were busy, humming with business and bargaining and I knew we would have an interesting time mapping this area.

Not much farther on the rear of warehouses came into sight and I could hear the slap-slap of the sails of the large trading ships as they blew in the breeze and the lapping of the water against the harbour wall. Seabirds wheeled overhead, searching for scraps, their familiarity with people making them bold as they hovered, looking for easy pickings. Rarnald turned us into a long alley that ran between two huge warehouses, our horses' hooves ringing loudly in the confined space. Ahead the aqua sea and pale horizon beckoned and Lukar snorted happily. Leaving the alley, we halted in front of the warehouses that surround the lower harbour on three sides and there, before us, was the deep water of the ocean filled with ships of all sizes from cities far and near.

It was difficult to know where to look. Many of the warehouses were open as goods were being either stored away or packed onto carts, heading for the market or shops, private owners and merchants, or perhaps even the palace and the enthroning feast. The calls of the workers were loud and rough as they lifted and stacked the crates, their hands callused and cut, their clothing and skin stained with dirt and grime. Down at the water's edge customs officials checked each ship as it docked, their searches more thorough than usual because of the enthroning, their efforts supported by the dozen or so Cynalese soldiers standing armed behind them. Sailors milled around, waiting for their goods to be cleared before they could disappear into the city, eager for the delights being once more on land could offer.

A passenger ship had arrived and the people had begun to disembark. As one, families ran up to meet loved ones, frantically waving and calling while they hoisted young children onto their shoulders for a better view. Forced by the crowd to wait a little further back were horses held by servants and shiny curricles ready to collect their wealthy owners and bring them into the city in style. I watched the passengers cross over the wooden gangplank, the sun catching the colourful array of their bright clothing so that they looked like so many gay fluttering flags moving in the wind.

We had come to a standstill as we studied the harbour and its people, standing back out of the action to let our eyes roam, but we soon recalled our reason for being there. So, turning our attention back to finding a path through the melee, we headed for the far line of warehouses that nestled close to Cynal's southern wall.

We set up quickly, tying our horses in the shade and pulling out our equipment. Rarnald looked on, genuinely fascinated, and we paused long enough to thank him and say that we would be able to find our way back to the palace.

He grinned and shook his head. 'I have no doubt you could, but it is my responsibility to escort you around the city and the captain would be most annoyed if he heard I had left you alone at the harbour of all places.'

We shrugged and he stayed, keenly listening to our quick discussion as we divided ourselves into measuring groups and determined the scale to which we would be working. In addition to the land being flat, one of the reasons we had chosen this area to begin was that it was one of the few places in the city where we could measure along the actual city wall. Although the warehouses seemed to crowd around the harbour, right up to the wall, the southern warehouses all had rear doorways that opened onto a narrow alleyway. Rarnald might shake his head and mutter that such a design had been built to offer a quick escape from customs officals but we were thrilled. All we saw was that the alleyway was long, a cartographer's dream.

We had roughly paced the alleyway out while searching for sites in the city and knew it to be close to one-sixth of a league long, 'Or,' as Chandra explained to Rarnald, who had made the earlier mistake of asking her to explain what a baseline was, 'almost half a haul long, and there are ten furlongs to each haul, Rarnald, and three hundred paces to each furlong, and three hands to each pace and ten fingers to each splayed hand.' She smiled brightly then, sure now that Rarnald must understand it all.

No doubt she would have gone into further explanation had Carly not quickly handed a rope to Chandra and tugged her away by the arm to join Alexa.

The first thing to do was set up the iron needle in its wooden bowl of water. Lilith rubbed the lodestone against the needle, then placed the needle carefully upon a short piece of straw from the small bundle we carried. Once in the water, the straw quickly spun around, the needle now pointing north. Upon each mapping sheet, we would record the direction of the line we followed relative to north. This would be particularly useful later, when it was time to fill in the details within the framework of triangles.

Now Lilith and I were ready to establish the baseline. To measure this, we would need our long rope. It had three hundred knots in it, at distances of one hand apart, and was two and a half times the length of the short ropes. At the first corner of the triangle, the start of the baseline, we pushed one of the long wooden stakes into the ground. Alexa, Carly and Chandra would also use this as the starting point for their measurement of the harbour wall. Lilith took one of the wooden handles of the long rope and stood beside the stake with the handle touching its top. Holding the other handle and ten short stakes, I walked on along the alleyway. When the rope stretched taut, I turned and faced Lilith.

The end of our baseline was a large, odd-shaped tenement building that broke with tradition, having been built to the wall and so ending the alleyway.

From where Lilith stood, the tenement, though distant, was clearly visible. Looking along a wooden ruler Lilith aligned me with the corner of the tenement and the wall, for the wall we followed was not entirely straight, and when she was satisfied with my position, I pushed one of the short stakes into the ground to mark the end of the rope. Lilith then walked towards this stake and placed the handle she held to it and again I moved on.

We continued in this way. I would walk until the rope stretched taut and Lilith would align me so I could place another stake in the ground, then Lilith would move to the stake and once again place her handle to it. As each new stake was placed, Lilith collected the one she stood beside. The total stakes she held when we reached the tenement plus the number of knots remaining gave us our distance.

Yet our progress was not so fast or simple, for we had to stop and record numerous details along the way. When we came back to sketch this area in more detail, filling in even smaller triangles, we would make note of the number and types of buildings. Only the most important would be marked upon the final maps but we needed this information to make sense of the city. Now, however, we restricted the notes and sketches upon our mapping sheets to offsets to the wall where it bulged and records of the alleyways. To do both we required our cross-staff.

The cross-staff was a simple flat piece of wood carved

with a cross upon its surface, dividing the wood into quarters. One of these carved lines was blackened and was always aligned with the roped line, the remaining cross-staff line was then at a right angle to the rope and pointing directly at the object. Sometimes if the offset to the wall was a short distance, Lilith or I paced it out and recorded the measurement. At other times we used our short rope to measure the distance. Although we did not yet stop to measure the other alleyways, the cross-staff enabled us to note where each alleyway met our baseline.

Rarnald divided his time between the two groups, checking we were safe and well then following us about as we moved ropes and equipment. He managed to be unobtrusive and inquisitive at the same time, a rare skill, and was more than happy to hold stakes while we made notes or keep the rope taut for us while we measured offsets. He was handy too because he brought us reports on how the others fared along the harbour wall. Their progress was greatly impeded by the harbour traffic but was otherwise going smoothly.

Lilith and I had completed well over half the base-line, an amazing feat considering the size of the city, when we decided to stop for the day. We packed up and went to rejoin the others on the dock, the sun now lying low and dazzling upon the water before us. Together again, we exchanged notes, as we would do each day, to keep our mapping sheets current. This done, and chatting contentedly, we made to return to collect our horses, left in the care of a young soldier Rarnald had poached from the harbour guard.

Before we had reached the far end where our horses

were, a loud cry went up of 'Ship, ship,' and people rushed to the edge of the harbour to peer out at the approaching vessel, still only a small moving blur on the water, too far to discern clearly. The dock around us buzzed with speculation as to who it could be, as almost miraculously people flooded in from all directions, drawn by the excitement and the noise. The ship was moving at a great speed and was soon the size of a tiny toy but still unrecognisable to my eye. Suddenly one of the sailors from a nearby trader spied the flag.

'It's the flag of Eustape,' he yelled for all to hear. 'It must be the king.' A mighty roar went up as people began to cheer and stamp their feet.

'Come on,' Rarnald said above the noise, gently tapping Alexa's and my arms. 'You'll want to see this.'

He pushed forward, clearing a path for us and we followed until we stood directly behind the harbour guards, who quickly sent a messenger to the palace. Now, with something constructive to do, they began ordering people away from the edge of the harbour.

The ship seemed to be flying towards us now. We could see clearly the movement of the oars as the rowers raised and dipped them in unison and sailors scurried amongst the sails, bringing the great ship under control as it headed for the harbour. The flag the sailor had spotted was visible to me now, half purple and half orange, and as others saw it too another great cheer went up. It may have reached those aboard, for in reply we heard the pounding of drums and the blowing of trumpets announcing the arrival of the king.

The messenger must have ridden at full gallop to the palace for the welcoming party, headed by Neesha, soon rode onto the harbour and an aisle was quickly cleared through the crowd and petals of welcome strewn across it for the king to walk upon. The entire harbour area was full of people, right up to the warehouses, and there was a feeling of expectancy in the air as we watched the ship finally slow as the oars were lifted and the ship eased in to bump gently against the harbour wall. A cacophony of yells, cheers, clapping, whistles and stomping greeted it and continued for many minutes, growing louder as the gangplank was lowered. Aboard the ship, sailors and guards were lining up, well-disciplined and quiet, yet the grins on their faces revealed their pleasure at such a warm, heartfelt welcome.

Rarnald was beaming. 'Eustape and Cynal have always been the closest friends,' he yelled to us, over the din. 'There has never been a war between the two. We welcome them happily to our city.'

Neesha stepped forward into the prepared aisle and held up her arms for the crowd to quieten. When the noise had finally died down, she turned and walked with her small group of honour guards to the very edge of the gangplank and stood silently, her hands neatly clasped before her.

The ship had been quickly secured and the lines of sailors stood straight-backed and proud, waiting for their king to appear. She did not take long, stepping into their midst and staring across at the mass of people welcoming her. Her appearance brought another resounding cheer and she smiled and raised her hand in greeting. Neesha bowed and held out her hands as she spoke the formal words of welcome, then invited the king and her followers to cross over and enter Cynal. The king acknowledged Neesha's words with another serene smile. Two of her guards quickly crossed the gangplank and stood on either side of it as the king herself began to descend.

I watched her with wonder. The Eustapeans are a small people, with skin even darker than Chandra's, a true black. The king moved with amazing grace and composure and one felt that no task would be too great for her or too demeaning. She reached the bottom of the plank where Neesha stood and they grasped hands with true warmth and I knew I had never before seen such an aura of calm and tranquillity as I saw about the King of Eustape.

Her officers and senior attendants came up behind her and were in turn greeted by Neesha. Like their king, they were short and slender, and they were dressed from head to toe in the most splendid silks. The formal introductions completed, Neesha and the king began to walk along the flower-strewn aisle towards the waiting horses and the carriage of state.

As the king walked, she smiled at the crowd clamouring to see her, and as she passed us by we bowed low. She was dressed in a flowing silken robe of red and turquoise over loose silken trousers and I saw that her wrists and fingers and neck were hung with gold. Her black hair, rippled with tight curls, was pulled back from her face and held in a neat knot above her head. The lobes of her ears were lined with tiny earcuffs of jewelled gold. Her features were strong and decisive, her eyes calm and gentle. I liked her immediately.

With the king walking slowly and nodding at the

crowd, it was some time before they reached the carriage. And when they did the crowd was so thick it took many minutes for the driver to negotiate the horses through the people and away down the largest of the roadways leading from the harbour. As I had seen happen before, the crowd that had grown so quickly dispersed almost as fast. Crossing the dock was once more possible and, with a quick curious look at the Eustapean sailors still aboard their ship, we went to collect our horses.

The guard was sitting by Flir's legs, sunning himself. He smiled at our approach and stretched lazily as he stood. We thanked him and he nodded and gave Flir a farewell pat as he strolled back to his post at customs. We mounted and headed back to the palace along the harbour front. The Eustapeans were busy unloading crates and baggage, the dock in front of their ship quickly filling up with their goods. We were almost level with the ship when suddenly Lukar reared up beneath me, whinnying loudly as he shook his head and snorted with excitement. His sudden movements took me by surprise and I had to concentrate hard on staying in the saddle, leaning forward and holding onto the reins, while all around me the horses of the others were acting in the same way. Lukar reared again, nearly bumping Timi, who was bellowing frustratedly as Lilith clung to the reins, his eyes rolling to show the whites, his nostrils flaring as he tried to turn towards the Eustapean ship.

Beside me, I could hear Chandra trying to calm Bragan and I wondered at the strain on her shoulder. Ahead, Drella and Flir were whickering impatiently, shaking their powerful necks, lifting their legs and pawing at the ground, their ears twitching in all directions.

I could not see Rarnald, who was behind me, but I could hear the loud screams of his horse and the frantic striking of its hooves on the ground as it reared repeatedly. Then there was a cry and a dull thud, followed by a deep groan and I knew Rarnald had fallen.

Chandra urged Bragan around. His coat was glistening with sweat and his head was up but he was obeying her, and as I managed to turn Lukar, I saw her grab the reins of the army horse and try to tug it away from where Rarnald lay on his back. The horse fought, rearing and trumpeting, its hooves hitting the ground less than a hand's distance from Rarnald's head.

I slid from Lukar's back, holding tightly to his reins, and crossed to where Rarnald lay. Alexa joined me and he stirred just as we reached him, pulling himself slowly to a sitting position.

'Are you hurt?' Alexa asked, bending down before him, Drella's reins wrapped around her hand, though already the horses were beginning to quieten.

Rarnald shook his head, too winded to speak. Alexa offered her arm and he took it, standing up unsteadily.

Chandra had succeeded in pulling Rarnald's horse away and came up on foot with Bragan and the army horse and nodded towards the ship.

'Look,' she called out.

With all the horses once more under control, we all turned towards the ship. The Eustapeans had laid another board next to the gangplank so that it was now the width of four sailors and, across the plank, two

Eustapeans, equerries I gathered by their garb, were leading a pair of the most magnificent horses I had ever seen. It was a fearsome task for the beasts were huge and one was clearly a stallion, but they followed obediently behind their handlers, showing no concern for the glinting water beneath their hooves and holding their heads and tails up proudly.

The stallion reached the dock first and neighed loudly. It was all that was needed to unsettle our horses again and Lukar nearly pulled himself free of my grip so eager was he to run to the stallion. Chandra still held Rarnald's mount as well as her own and she tried to calm them both with gentle words, the straining muscles in her arms belying her gentle tone.

The mare reached the dock. A beautiful chestnut, her dark mane and tail were full and long. Her sleek coat shone in the sun. She was led over to join the stallion, a stunning creature as black as night who stood patiently waiting for her. As she stepped up to him, he nickered a welcome and, at that moment, Rarnald's army horse screamed furiously, a high piercing call, and bucked, narrowly missing Carly as he yanked free and galloped towards the pair.

It was chaos. All the horses pulled, straining against our grips, and I knew that if something was not done quickly we would have a dangerous situation on our hands.

Rarnald's mount had reached the pair. As the great black turned to look at him, all the fire went out of the army horse and he slowed, took a small step forward, then stopped and stood meekly. The same change came over our own horses. Lukar stopped fretting and stood as though nothing untoward had happened. Timi, Drella and Flir settled quietly and Chandra's Bragan nuzzled her affectionately. Dumbfounded, we watched unbelieving as one of the Eustapeans stepped up to the army horse and picked up the reins.

The black and the chestnut glanced over at us and, although they no longer strained to be away, our horses lifted their heads and whickered softly as though replying to some unheard question. The Eustapean pair snorted and lifted their heads up and down until their muzzles almost touched the ground. Suddenly all the horses were silent, seeming to lose their interest in each other as quickly as it had appeared.

The equerries quickly saddled the horses and swung onto their backs while Eustapean soldiers formed an escort around them. The equerries effortlessly kicked the horses into a trot and rode off out of sight down an alley, the soldiers jogging alongside. I breathed a deep sigh of relief and patted Lukar.

'They're gamer than I am,' Carly said, speaking of the equerries as she fondled Flir. 'Did you see the size of that stallion?'

'They must belong to the king,' I said. 'A pair like that would be worth a fortune.' I turned to Rarnald and asked how he was feeling.

He nodded. 'I'm all right. Nothing worse than a few bruises.'

'You fell badly,' Alexa said. 'I heard the air leave your lungs. Let's get your horse and we'll walk slowly back to the palace.'

I doubted that sounded very appealing to Rarnald, but he nodded without complaint and walked beside us as we went to retrieve his horse.

The Eustapean holding the horse saw us coming and began to walk to meet us.

'Thank you,' Rarnald said, holding out his hand to clasp the other man's wrist in greeting, then taking the reins.

The soldier grinned. 'I saw you fall. Horses have real minds of their own at times.'

Rarnald raised a very expressive eyebrow and muttered an unimpressed 'Mmh.'

'The stallion and mare were certainly very cooperative,' Alexa said. 'I didn't know Eustape bred such fine horses.'

'They're the finest we have,' the soldier told us. 'They belong to the king. She'll ride the black in the enthroning procession.'

We bade him goodbye and mounted, keeping an eye on Rarnald as he eased himself into the saddle. The fall had obviously hurt him a great deal more than he was saying, for I saw him wince and put a hand to his lower back.

'You'll need a hot bath, Rarnald, to soak out the soreness,' Chandra told him. He managed a small smile and took up the reins.

In consideration of Rarnald, we took our return to the palace very slowly, as even a light trot jolted him painfully. So the sun had sunk well into the west, a fiery ball melting into the indigo ocean, by the time we reached the main gate and were passed through.

'I wonder what sort of fun they had at the stables

when those Eustapean horses arrived,' Carly speculated dryly.

Chandra nodded grimly. 'Let's just hope they're settled in by now, for the sake of the skin on our hands.'

We need not have worried. All was peaceful at blue stable and we saw to our horses, rubbing and brushing them down, then checking they had enough feed and water. Rarnald tried valiantly to follow our example but both Alexa and Chandra told him to leave his horse and quickly saw to it themselves.

Outside the stable, the gardens were hung with the dulcet light of dusk, giving it a softness and mystery it lacked by day. I could smell the gentle perfume of the flowers and already several stars flashed and twinkled above us, like fireflies around the steady pale glow of the moon. The white paths were less busy than usual as we shouldered our packs and kits and turned ourselves towards the palace.

Rarnald left us as we drew equal to Ricah's house and we bade him good night. He disappeared along a garden path, a tall, slim figure, and we continued on, entering the palace and walking to our workroom. We quickly put away our equipment, taking care to lock the room after ourselves, and climbed the stairs and walked along the passages that would take us to the west wing and our apartment.

I was tired when we reached our room. Gladly, I stripped off my crumpled clothing and washed away the day's sweat. A servant knocked on our door and asked if we would like dinner sent to us and we gratefully accepted, marvelling at the efficiency of the palace.

The others bathed and when the food arrived we ate hungrily, saying little. Afterwards, Chandra, as straight and strong as ever, challenged Alexa to a match at the amusement board. Alexa agreed readily and they settled in for a friendly contest.

Carly, Lil and I lounged on the couches, drinking wine and speaking occasionally, our voices low and easy. When the flagon was empty, I rose and wished them all good night, then slipped off to bed, sliding under the light cotton blanket and falling instantly into a calm, dreamless sleep.

TEN

THE FOLLOWING MORNING we found Nikol waiting for us outside the workroom.

'Good morning, cartographers,' she greeted us cheerily. 'No bruised backs or sore backsides amongst you, I hope.'

'So you've seen Rarnald,' Carly said, with a wry smile.

'Yes, seen and heard. The silly duffer, he's never been much of a rider. Still, I can't say that if my horse reared up under me I'd stay in the saddle either.' She gave a quick, sharp laugh. 'I suppose that's why we're both foot soldiers.'

Alexa unlocked the door and we stepped inside.

'Besides the mishap with the Eustapean horses, how did it go at the harbour?' Nikol asked.

'Very well,' Alexa said. 'Today we'll complete the baseline and begin on the area filled with tenements and inns surrounding the warehouses.'

'Well and good,' the soldier replied. 'Though I don't think it will be any less chaotic than the harbour itself. And I can say for sure that you will draw a crowd.'

We smiled. This would not be anything new for us.

The novelty of our work always drew an audience, of both adults and children. Many followed us from street to street, fascinated by our equipment and note-taking. It had never bothered us before and I doubted it would today.

With the packs and kits once more on our shoulders, we left the room and walked to the stables.

'So now we'll be able to assess your riding,' Carly told Nikol with dry amusement as we stepped through the blue doors.

The soldier laughed. 'Yes, and this afternoon it will be Rarnald's turn to laugh at my soreness.'

For all her jokes, Nikol proved a competent rider, if a little stiff, and our ride to the harbour district was uneventful.

Lilith and I returned to the alleyway behind the southern warehouses and set to work quickly. By mid-morning we had all the measurements we needed and, proud of our speed, we went to join the others.

Mapping an entire city meant walking through innu-merable streets and squares. The harbour district, with its jumble of tenements and inns and shops, was filled with thin alleyways, wide pathways and long crooked roads that snaked out in all directions. I met Lilith's eye as we rode and we both grinned. This area, we knew, would be a challenge.

Alexa claimed me as soon as we appeared. We had two lines drawn and ideally would now be working on the third and final line of our first large triangle, a line which would run straight from the tenement building at the end of our baseline to the end of the harbour wall. Yet this was no open field or unsettled plain where it was possible to align both end points and measure the angle. This was a city, with buildings of every shape and size forming uneven city blocks. A visual alignment over such a distance was simply impossible, so the other three, accompanied by Nikol, had been working from a fourth point from which both the harbour wall and the tenement were visible. We would then move to another point and so forth until the lines of our different sized triangles could be drawn in. If we had two angles and the length of one side of any triangle, we could calculate the other two lengths by use of the mathematical charts we carried in our kits.

So far that morning, the south-eastern line from the fourth point to the tenement had been successfully measured. Now Lilith stayed with Carly, Chandra and Nikol, certain Chandra could use her help in measuring the western line from the fourth point to the harbour wall. Alexa had already marked with a long stake another point from which we could see both the fourth point and the tenement. I would help her calculate the two angles and it would give us our first complete triangle.

As the others left Alexa and me, a segment of the crowd that had lightly ringed us all morning broke off to follow them. Alexa and I smiled at the people who remained and took out a protractor and ruler and set up our iron needle in its bowl. Using it, we found north and recorded its position on our mapping sheets and the direction of the line we would be following. It was a particularly hot day and I could feel the sun burning through the thin cotton shirt I wore and, as we took up our positions, aligning the distant stake with this point along the ruler, I was glad of my wide-brimmed hat.

Shortly after noon, having long since completed the angle calculations of our first triangle and moved on to the next points, I stood up to ease my cramped muscles and blew air from my cheeks with a loud sigh. We had lost some of the crowd through boredom or the demands of work or home, but many had remained and their numbers had been bolstered by new arrivals. Glancing at them, I wondered at their fortitude in such heat. I removed my hat and wiped the sweat from my forehead with the back of my hand. If I had the day free, I thought, I would be far away from the city's warm streets, lazing somewhere on the white sand of the beach, letting the cool ocean air caress my skin. With another sigh, I replaced my hat and turned to Alexa.

She too had stretched her muscles, loosening those of her neck and back, but she was now facing the crowd, her expression beneath her own hat serious and intent as she scanned the many faces before her.

'What are you looking for?' I asked.

She gave me a small smile before flicking her blue gaze back to the crowd and continuing her search. 'I don't know,' she answered. 'Lately, I've had the feeling that we're being watched.'

'Well, we are.' I laughed and waved a hand at the crowd. 'But that's nothing unusual. They're just curious.'

Alexa shook her head. 'No, this is something different. Something secretive.' She ran her eyes over the far edges of the crowd one more time, but discovered nothing. Frowning, she turned to me. 'And if we are being watched, Ashil, I can't understand why.'

I shrugged. 'Maybe it's just children, playing a game.'

Alexa was unconvinced. 'Then they are very talented children, making little sound and staying well hidden, while never losing track of us.'

I looked at the crowd once more, but the many tanned faces that stared back at me were openly inquisitive and free of artifice or subterfuge. I shrugged again. 'Well, if you're right, they'll either grow bored and stop or they'll show themselves.'

Alexa's smile held little amusement. 'It's the showing themselves that I'm worried about. A friend has no need of furtiveness.'

I could think of no reply. Just then Carly appeared ahead of us from one of the many small streets that joined ours.

'Ashil, Alexa,' she called, waving as she approached.

Leaving the mystery of our pursuer unsettled, we moved to meet her. Carly had twisted her hair up under her hat to cool her neck and long dark tendrils were floating around her face. She grinned at us and idly pushed the tendrils behind her ear. Her face was glowing. Like Chandra, Carly loved the heat.

'We thought we'd stop for a meal now,' she told us happily. 'Nikol says there's an inn nearby that serves good meals and,' her green eyes gleamed with pleasure, 'good Cynalese wine. Are you ready to stop?'

Alexa and I nodded our approval.

'We've just finished these angles. We can work out the calculations later,' I said.

'Good. The others are waiting.'

We met them in the next street and, with a telling pat to her stomach, Nikol led us quickly to an inn a few streets away.

The inn where we had stayed our first weeks in Cynal was typical of most in the city and, in the heat of the day, I could well understand why the eating room was situated on the lower level. Here, patrons were served for most of the day while the rooms for rent above were occupied mainly during the cooler hours of the night.

With a grateful sigh for such an arrangement, I pulled off my hat and stepped down into the inn's deep belly. Even full of people and cooked food, it was deliciously cool, and in the moment it took for my eyes to adjust to the dimly lit room, my nostrils were filled with the assorted smells of food, sweat and wine. We found a table and sat down. Almost immediately a server appeared. I had developed quite a taste for Cynalese seafood so I ordered fresh fish, then sat back to survey the room.

The small solid tables were already more than half-full and conversation was loud and lively. To judge from the appearance of the many patrons, the inn was popular amongst the harbour workers and sailors. The server promptly set a wine flagon and water jug on our table and Carly reached for the flagon and began to fill a goblet for each of us.

Regretfully, Nikol declined. 'It's not permitted,' she explained with a sad glance at her empty goblet. 'My round isn't over yet and if the captain caught me drinking I'd have to do an extra half-round for the next month.' She shook her head mournfully. 'I'll just have to wait until Rarnald relieves me.'

'Well, it's not much longer now,' I said.

Nikol looked at me and raised one expressive eyebrow. 'That's easy to say when your own goblet is full to the brim,' she said dryly as she reached glumly for the water jug.

Lilith laid a hand on her arm. 'It could be worse, Nikol. If you had the late round, you couldn't have any wine with your dinner. You'd be forced to drink it early in the day or in the first hours of the morning when your round had ended.'

Nikol raised her head and looked at Lil in astonishment, then laughed suddenly. 'You're right! It's Rarnald who I should be feeling sorry for, not myself. You're a smart lot, you cartographers.'

Chandra nodded and flashed her stunning smile, making Nikol laugh even harder until Lil and I joined in.

The hum of conversation was growing as the inn filled up, and there was as much clinking of flagons on goblets as the clicking of knives on plates. We paid it no heed. Our attention centred on our table, effortlessly blocking out the background noises until, above the din, we heard a joyful voice call 'Carly!' and we all looked to see Lindsa weaving her way eagerly towards us, delight written all over her face.

'Good day,' she said, nodding at us. Then her eyes sought Carly and she smiled warmly. 'May I join you?'

'Of course,' Carly replied, returning the smile and moving her chair to make room beside her.

'How goes the map drawing?' Lindsa asked, as she

sat close to Carly and accepted a goblet of wine.

'It's only our second day, but we've encountered no problems so far,' Carly answered. 'What about the sailing?'

'Ah,' Lindsa waved a hand, dismissing that notion. 'There's little to do while we're in harbour. A bit of maintenance and we take turns guarding the ship, but we still have plenty of free time.' She shrugged and looked sidewards at Carly. 'We just have to find ways to entertain ourselves.'

Carly chuckled. 'That could be fun.' Lindsa beamed.

'Tonight a friend of mine is having a private party,' the sailor said. 'Some of the musicians who are performing at the enthroning celebrations are staying with him and will appear. If you're free, you're all welcome to come.'

At the word musicians, Chandra's eyes had lit up. 'I'll come. Do you know who is playing and what instruments they will use?'

'No.' Lindsa gave a short laugh. 'I've no idea.'

'It'll be a surprise, Chandra,' Carly said. 'The best parties always have some surprise or delight in store.'

'It would be a delight to see you dance,' Lindsa murmured softly, her eyes fully on Carly. I looked away, biting the inside of my mouth to stay silent, and noticed Alexa hide a grin as she raised her goblet to her lips. Her eyes met mine over the rim and they shone with laughter. It was almost my undoing. She had been preoccupied since entering the inn, glancing around several times at the occupants of the other tables, her eyes narrowed and thoughtful, but Lindsa had brought her attention back to our group and she was clearly enjoying herself now.

Unruffled by Lindsa's obvious adoration, Carly answered easily, 'Well, if the musicians are as good as you say, it will be my pleasure to dance.'

Our meal arrived and we ate hungrily, our appetites stirred by the labour of the morning. Afterwards, as we sat enjoying the last of the wine, I caught Lil's eye and she nodded towards Nikol. I inclined my head in answer. I would speak to the soldier once we were free of the inn. We hoped she would agree to teach us some basic fighting moves, but as Lil and I had no wish for the others to know of our plans, the conversation needed to be private.

When the wine was finished, we paid for our meal and rose to leave the inn. Lindsa gave Carly the address of her friend's house and we waved goodbye to her.

As we began to walk back towards the streets where we had been working I moved up alongside Nikol.

'How's your dancing?' she asked.

'Fair, but nothing like Carly's.' I smiled and glanced at the dark-haired figure ahead of me. 'She really is superb. She was in a dancing troupe before she joined us.'

'I'm not surprised, she walks like a dancer. Most of us bear the signs of our profession, in a soldier's case it's the scars.'

'Do you have many?' I asked, genuinely interested.

'A few.' She pulled her shirt from her belt and showed me a thick white scar that ran across her right side. 'I got that on patrol a few years ago. We were chasing a group of market thieves and while I was dealing with one, another snuck up on me from behind and stuck me with his dagger. I was off duty for two months.' She shook her head, her lip lifted in distaste. 'It was hell.'

'It must have hurt,' I commiserated and Nikol gave me a strange look.

'The wound healed quickly. I was up and about at the end of three weeks, but I couldn't use a sword.' She sighed loudly. 'I can understand the captain's view, but inactivity is a heavy burden for any soldier.'

There had been a time when I would have thought that such was the soldier's lot, and believed that the only scars a cartographer would ever wear were calluses on the fingers. However, I was now beginning to have my doubts.

'What did you do?'

'Oh, I helped train the recruits. My side might have been stiff and I couldn't wield a weapon, but there was nothing wrong with my voice.' She laughed. 'As they soon learnt. Some of them had difficulty telling the hilt from the blade when we began, but they picked it up fast enough.'

I glanced around but the others were all out of earshot. Even so, I lowered my voice when I spoke, 'Nikol, speaking of training novices, Lilith and I have a favour to ask you.'

Nikol looked at me curiously.

I dropped my voice even further. 'We'd like to learn how to defend ourselves. We know we'll never be soldiers or make any adversary tremble at the sheer sight of us, but we would like to learn a few basic moves. We were wondering if you'd teach us?'

A grin of delight spread slowly over Nikol's face and she threw an arm around my shoulders and squeezed me tight. 'It'd be a pleasure, Ashil, and with the right moves, you can make any adversary tremble. A killing blow is a killing blow, no matter who delivers it.'

What I thought of such words must have shown on my face, for she laughed loudly and gave me another squeeze. 'Never fear, we'll begin slowly and hope you will never need to use what I have to teach you.'

'That would be good,' I replied, with such wistfulness that she grinned broadly. 'There's one more thing. We want to keep it as a surprise for the others.'

'Easily done. Now when do you want to train? While I'm on day rounds, the early evening is best.'

'Fine.'

'Then shall we begin tomorrow? At the training ground? Wear something comfortable.'

I nodded. 'We'll look forward to it.'

At my words, Nikol raised one eyebrow. 'Liar,' she rebuked me softly. Then she left me to join Chandra.

We had reached the road where our two groups would part. Alexa and I left the others and resumed our work and, not much later, Nikol rode up to say goodbye. It was time for her to meet Rarnald and finish her round. We waved to her and she rode off to the arranged spot. Not long afterwards Rarnald came up to us, mounted, I noticed with a small smile, on a different horse from yesterday's.

The afternoon passed quickly and without incident. Our work was going well and when we came together to exchange measurements we were satisfied with our day's tally. Riding back to the palace, I asked Rarnald how he was feeling.

'Cautious,' he said and indicated his horse.

I like Cynal near sundown, the long shadows, the strips of light that dapple the roadways, the cooler air. It is a pleasant time, when one's work is finished and a night, be it of revelry or rest, lies ahead. That day, while we had worked, others had been busy decorating the city in preparation for the enthroning and the royal procession through the streets. In contrast to the mourning silks, colourful flags and ribbons of green, white and gold adorned buildings and hung from windows. In the calm of the evening they seemed to sigh daintily in the gentle breeze.

Small clusters of bells tinkled on street corners beneath large tasselled banners containing the royal crest with its seahorse, wave and three-pointed crown. Gold thread had been used for the crown and it flashed whenever touched by light. Through open windows and doors we could hear the light murmurs of conversation sprinkled with laughter and on the streets around us people walked, bound for home or the nearest inn.

Flir was restless and Carly patted her neck affection- ately. 'I'll ask Ricah tonight if we can put the horses in the pasture.'

I nodded and we turned towards the palace gates.

When we finally reached the stables we were sur- prised to discover a small retinue of guards outside green stable. They were Eustapean and were standing patiently and quietly by the doors. Before we had time to dismount, they came to attention and formed two neat lines. Into the centre of these lines walked King Charissa, her head turned as she talked to Ricah.

The king and the keeper of the horses stopped just outside the stable, deep in conversation. After a few moments, the king stepped away, bade Ricah farewell and walked back towards the palace, followed closely by her guards. Ricah rose from her bow and turned to re-enter the stable when she spotted us. She raised a hand in greeting and ambled over.

'Good evening,' she hailed us as she came close, pausing before Lil and Timi and running her hand over the gelding's chest.

'Good evening, Ricah,' we replied.

'Why was King Charissa walking?' asked Alexa. 'I would have thought she would dismount at the palace entrance and have someone bring her horse back to the stable.'

The keeper nodded and looked towards Alexa, but her eyes did not rise above Drella, who she examined while she answered. 'That's true, but she wanted to see where her horses are being stabled.' Satisfied with Drella's condition, Ricah finally raised her eyes. 'She told me that she likes to ride every day when she can. If she's unable to, her equerries take the pair out.' This behaviour of the king's had obviously impressed the keeper. 'She knows a lot about horses,' she said approvingly as she glanced back at the stables.

Carly asked if we could make use of the pasture.

'Yes, any time. Just make sure you shut the inner gate.' She grinned. 'And make sure your horse will come when called. It's a big pasture.'

We left Ricah and gave our horses a good brush before letting them loose. They trotted away happily, sniffing the other horses, then finding themselves spots where they could stand and tear at the grass.

Rarnald departed and we headed for our apartment,

only to meet Damin and Rianne on the marble walkway before the palace.

'Ah,' Damin exclaimed at the sight of us, 'I was hoping to see you.' He smiled, the lines of his face folding upon one another like a fan. 'I want to invite you all to a noontime meal this free-day. Laibi has promised to prepare something superb.'

Rianne stood gracefully beside him, watching us. 'Those at the House are most keen to meet you,' she said. 'It's not very often we get cartographers in Cynal.'

We accepted cheerfully.

'Good,' Damin nodded happily. 'Then this trip was not a total waste after all.'

People passing along the walkway had noticed the Mecla in their scarlet robes and stopped their conversations to bow and greet the priests warmly. Rianne and Damin returned their smiles with accustomed ease.

'Were you here to treat a sick animal?' Lilith asked with concern.

'I thought I was, but the poor creature only needs to be fed less sweetmeats and more food fit for a dog and he'll be just fine.' He frowned. 'Not that I haven't told royal cousin Leah that many times before, but she always ignores my advice.' Damin gave his head a little shake and sighed. 'Ah well, she is a blood relative of his lordship's, and if she sends to the House I can only come as bid.'

We stepped aside as a large group of guards strode by and entered the palace.

'Chandra,' Damin said, turning to her, his face lightening once more, 'Laibi has not forgotten your request to go net-fishing and he says if you are still interested

300

then you can go with his family on free-day morning. They will work that day as the whole of Cynal needs food for the celebrations.'

A broad smile spread over Chandra's face. 'I will go and I will enjoy it,' she said in a pleased tone, 'and I will bring Laibi plenty of fresh fish.'

Damin nodded, laughing softly. 'I will tell him.'

The priest had just finished describing where Chandra would find the fishing boats when a page wearing the royal colours approached. The girl bowed politely and turned to Rianne. 'His lordship would like to see you, Rianne. In his chambers.'

A slight frown skipped across the priest's brow but was quickly gone. 'Very well,' she told the page with a smile. 'Excuse me, cartographers, I must go. I look forward to sharing Laibi's meal with you at the House.' She inclined her head at us in farewell, then turned and followed the page through the archway and into the palace.

Damin watched her leave. 'It is a busy time not only for the fishers,' he said curiously. He caught us looking at him, our faces full of questions, and laughed. 'And no doubt a busy time for cartographers, so I too will be on my way. Good evening, and I will also see you at the House in three days time.'

He walked off along the path and after a moment we stepped under the arched entrance that took us inside the workroom wing and went to deposit our equipment. Once that was done, we climbed up to our apartment, Carly asking as we went if we wished to attend the party that night.

'I will go,' Chandra told her. 'I want to hear the musicians play.'

301

Alexa shook her head. 'No, I think I'll stay here. I'm curious as to whether Lord Tarn's wanting to see Rianne has anything to do with the Lakiya. I may hear something in the Dining Hall.'

'Ash?' Carly asked, looking at me, knowing better than to try and change Alexa's mind.

I was tired after our day in the sun and wanted to eat and rest, but I knew that Carly and Chandra would return with fascinating tales and I would regret not having been there myself. So I agreed.

'Good,' Carly nodded. 'What about you, Lil?'

Lilith hesitated, lowering her eyes. I could almost hear her internal battle, her shyness and insecurities warring with her desires and curiosity.

Carly watched for a moment as Lil pondered the question, then she stepped over and wrapped an arm around Lil's waist and pulled her close.

'Say yes. It will be fun and we can leave at any time, that's the beauty of parties. And Chandra, Ash and I promise not to leave you standing alone at any time.' She gave Lil a gentle squeeze. 'No matter how gorgeous the other guests are,' she whispered.

A small chuckle escaped from Lilith's lips and she nodded. 'All right,' she ceded, 'I'd like to hear the musicians too.'

'Wonderful,' Carly said with approval. 'We'll have a quick wash and a change and dine there. If Lindsa's friend is able to play host to such famous musicians, no doubt his tables will be groaning under the weight of culinary splendours just asking to be devoured.'

Over an hour later, clean and dressed in party finery, we set out. Alexa had wished us a good night and left earlier, planning to eat with the other palace inhabitants and hoping no doubt to see Rianne again.

The address Lindsa had given us was in the prosperous district to the east of the palace. We exited the palace by a side entrance near the kitchen.

The sun was down now and, once outside, the soft grey-black of night surrounded us. Insects called to one another in the palace gardens and the air was full of night scents. At regular intervals along the white paths, torches blazed, creating pools of light whose edges did not quite meet, so that one moved continually from light to shadow to darkness and back again.

As we approached the postern gate, far ahead of us we could see movement at the guard house and barracks. Activity in the palace may be slowing down but the guard house would always be occupied, accepting reports from soldiers on duty and ready to raise the alarm at any time should danger threaten the palace.

We turned to the gate and passed through with a quick hello for the guards. They wore light shirts against the cooler night air. The sight of them made me think of Rarnald and I wondered idly where he was. He would have only a few more hours left of his round.

Walking along the first of the city streets, Chandra began to hum softly. The song was vaguely familiar though I could not place it, but Carly joined in.

'You remember it!' Carly exclaimed in delighted astonishment when they had finished.

Chandra smiled and nodded. 'Yes, it has stayed in my mind. It is so very beautiful.'

'What song is it?' Lilith asked, her voice soft and curious.

Chandra turned to her. 'We heard it in Nalym. Demran played it on his gitar.'

I recalled the day of Carly's arrival amongst us in the desert city and how we had dined that night with Lord Maltra. Casting my mind back, I could faintly recollect the musicians who had played amongst us.

'I think your people should have given you drums not stylus as a child, Chandra,' I teased. 'Then you could have had music wherever you go.'

'Ah,' Chandra grinned, 'but when one without skill hits the drums it does not sound like music.' Her grin broadened, her teeth glinting in the dim street light. 'I am content to draw my maps if I can listen to truly talented musicians like Demran and carry their music with me in my head.'

A few paces ahead of us, a group of fashionably dressed Cynalese stepped onto our street, laughing and chatting, their expensive perfumes floating to us on the night breeze. When we reached the street Lindsa had named they turned onto it and we followed.

Lindsa had told us her friend was called Regi and his house was immediately recognisable. The front wall was festooned with torches and the orange flames flickered and danced like snake tongues, the thin wafts of smoke drifting up to merge with the dark heavens. In the wall was a wide and heavy door where an attendant stood, strong and imposing, passing people through. The night was still young but already a steady stream of guests presented itself and moved eagerly through the open door. As we drew closer, the sound of much gaiety reached us and Carly nudged me, her face alight with pleasure.

'Remind me to give Lindsa a big kiss,' she said.

'I hardly think she will let you forget,' I replied.

The group who had preceded us on the road greeted the attendant happily and stepped through the door; unchallenged, we followed them, entering Regi's magnificent house. Beyond the door was a long, marble colonnade, the columns intricately worked with delicate masonry and hung now with floral garlands. In the colonnade, people hailed each other, some pausing to speak with friends, their fine, brightly coloured clothing rustling and susurrant as they hugged and kissed in greeting, not caring that they slowed the passage of the other guests and the other guests not minding that their progress was delayed. We returned the warm smiles and hellos of friendly strangers as we moved along, passing the numerous doors to the living quarters set in the walls beyond the columns on both sides, our eyes taking in the many animated, gay faces and the breathing, rippling mass that was the crowd in the courtyard ahead of us. Beyond and above them, reaching up into the still indigo sky, rose the fine spray of a fountain and the outstretched branches of several richly blooming trees. From time to time a slight breeze would stir the branches and soft pink and white summer blossoms would gently fall upon the guests, settling on their shoulders and in their hair.

As we reached the edge of the enormous courtyard we saw that the colonnade divided left and right, running on to enclose the open space. We followed it no further, but stepped from it into the genial crush of people and looked ahead at the breathtaking beauty of

Regi's garden. It was in the very centre of the courtyard, an island where the small flowering trees, thick
green shrubs and tiny pathways edged with flowers sat
calmly, encircled by an outer ring of soft grass and then
the cobbled stones where most of the guests stood and
would later dance. In the middle of the garden island
was the fountain, its base wide and round, its water
tinkling blithely, a low, cushioned seat running around
its edge.

'Glad you came now?' Carly asked Lil.

'Yes,' Lilith replied, her shining eyes on the blossoms. 'It's lovely.'

Pleased, Carly smiled, but her eyes had left the
garden and were now on the guests. There must have
been well over two hundred people in Regi's courtyard and still more were arriving through the colonnade. They were elegant, perfumed creatures swathed
in rich clothing, their skin and hair smooth with health.
They stood around us in ever-shifting clusters, their
talk a relaxed, indistinguishable hum like a slowly sim-
mering pot over fire. Many, by their dark curly hair
and bronzed skin, were clearly Cynalese, but I also saw
fair heads, blonde and light brown, with eyes blue like
my own and green as new grass. Over by the garden,
by one of the flowering trees, stood four men with hair
and beards like flame. In Nalym I had grown accustomed to the sallow tan of the desert people and their
almond-shaped brown-black eyes and I saw that several
of their people were also here tonight, a large group
stood in discussion with three dark-skinned guests,
darker even than Chandra. All in the courtyard spoke
the Middling Tongue, but when one listened carefully

one could hear the different accents. To me, it was as beautiful to the ear as any song. I glanced around me, wondering who, amidst the crowd, was our host, for it seemed Regi had a wide and varied circle of friends. I wondered if he was a traveller.

Beside me, Carly spoke in a soft, musing voice. 'To judge by the silks and jewels, I'd say the cream of Cynal's society and friends have come to keep us company tonight.'

'And when they see your beauty they will be glad they came.' The voice came from behind my shoulder and we all turned as Lindsa laughed. 'As indeed I am,' she said as she stepped closer and made a small, neat bow.

We all bade her good evening.

'It appears your friend Regi knows how to throw a party,' Carly said.

'Aye, indeed. He likes nothing more than to make new friends and entertain his old ones. I'll introduce you. He is always pleased to meet interesting people with stories to tell, especially if they are gorgeous as well as entertaining. And you,' she grinned, 'are more gorgeous than most.' Admiration and desire shone from her eyes and she nudged Chandra, who happened to be standing next to her. 'Don't you agree, Chandra?'

Chandra frowned at the sailor. 'Carly is very beautiful,' she stated, her brow wrinkled as though wondering why Lindsa insisted on stating the obvious, 'but so are Ashil, Lilith, Alexa and I. We are young and healthy and happy.' She shrugged, an eloquently dismissive motion. 'Beauty alone means nothing. You have to look it in the face to see its value. Its worth is gone once the light fades or you turn a corner and leave it behind. If I turn my back on Carly she does not cease to have value or bring me pleasure because she also has a strong mind and voice, and with those she can reach me. If she was only beautiful I might want to look at her for a short while, but I would not want to work with her.'

Lindsa's blue eyes had widened as Chandra began her answer and the sailor appeared momentarily stunned. When Chandra had finished, Lindsa nodded.

'You are right,' she said seriously. 'I did not mean to imply that Carly's mind was pitted.' She turned back to Carly. 'Only that her character and appearance together are a mesmerising combination.'

'Enough!' Carly cried good-naturedly, raising her hands. 'Let's talk of some other matter.'

Movement to our left drew our attention as people moved aside to allow servants carrying platter after platter of delicious smelling delicacies to pass. They laid the platters on several long tables that had been set up between the flower-hung columns, then returned to the kitchen for more. The smell was mouth-watering and my stomach rumbled, our last meal now seemed so long ago. Many of the guests had already advanced on the tables and begun to pile plates high with food.

'Must we talk?' I said in what must have been such a plaintive voice that the other four all laughed aloud.

Carly grinned at me. 'Food,' and she said the word with relish, 'what a brilliant idea, Ash. It's both divert-ing and satisfying. And, of course, where there is food there is also wine.'

So we weaved our way through the guests towards

the tables and their delectable burdens. It was an enchanting evening. Tiny, glowing stars were scattered prettily through the sky and the moon shone palely above us, like a smooth, luminous pebble. Torches had been artfully placed high on the columns and in the garden and threw their warm light on faces with sometimes garish effect. We reached the tables and stared in amazement at the feast laid before us. My only thought before I began to fill my plate was mild disappointment that I would not possibly be able to taste everything.

I was adding a juicy slice of venison with a parsnip and apple relish to my already laden plate when I saw an extremely tall, stylish man approach Lindsa.

'Regi!' she cried with delight and threw open her arms to hug him tightly.

He laughed, a surprisingly deep sound. 'How is my favourite sailor?' he asked, and returned the hug, kissing her cheek.

'Well rested and on the way to being very well fed.' He chuckled and Lindsa turned to us. 'Let me introduce my friends, Regi. They are cartographers working for Lord Tarn.'

Regi greeted us all, taking our wrists in his hand and welcoming us to his house. His manners were smooth and charming and he looked at each of us with avid interest. Lindsa had been right when she said he enjoyed making new friends. He was, I thought, a collector of people.

'I employed a cartographer last year,' Regi said, 'to map my farm holdings and I followed his progress with fascination. Now, knowing a little of your style of work, I have a great respect for the cartographer's skill.'

'Thank you,' we replied and he smiled and leant slightly forward.

'It is the measuring that fascinates me. Tell me,' he began, but he got no further with his query, for one of his servants appeared at his side and politely excused himself to us before whispering softly in Regi's ear. Regi nodded, murmured a reply, then both men turned towards the colonnade entrance just as a small group of superbly dressed Cynalese emerged from between the columns.

A servant immediately moved to their side and addressed the young and very beautiful woman at the head of the group. She inclined her head in an imperious manner and the servant stepped down and began to lead the group forward through the crowd.

Regi turned to us and bowed. 'It was a pleasure meeting you, cartographers, but now, I'm afraid, I must excuse myself. Perhaps we will be fortunate enough to speak again before the night ends. Until then, good evening.'

With his servant at his side, he left us and walked gracefully forward to greet the woman and her group. The other guests had quietened and were watching the woman with an unmistakable curiosity mixed with awe. Carly asked Lindsa who she was but the sailor shook her head and said she did not know.

There was a Cynalese couple standing near me at the table and they looked around at Carly's question. 'She is Leah of the royal house,' they told us softly, their voices lowered, 'cousin to Lord Tarn.'

'Ah,' Carly smiled, 'Leah of the sweetmeats.'

Lindsa frowned. 'You know her?'

'No,' she chuckled, 'but we have heard of her.'

Regi and Leah were deep in conversation and the talk of the other guests was beginning to revive, though most kept one eye on Lord Tarn's cousin.

Chandra, however, had not forgotten our reason for being there. 'Let's eat now,' she said. 'Our food grows cold and soon the musicians will begin. I want to find a place close to the dais so I can see them clearly.'

'Good idea,' I agreed, for my stomach had reasserted its claim on my attention.

'Perhaps we can sit by the fountain,' Lilith suggested. 'The blossoms smell so lovely.'

We were in luck, for the arrival of royal cousin Leah had drawn the guests from the garden and the fountain seat was unoccupied. We sat on the cushions and ate and drank while the soft voice of the fountain whispered behind us. Before long, other guests began to wander in amongst the cool greenery. They approached us in their friendly manner and began to chat to us. Servants came around, taking our empty plates and refilling our wine goblets. Well-fed and mellow, we rose to our feet and mingled, enjoying the light conversation and the new faces and the attention we, as strangers, received.

The dais Chandra had spotted earlier was to our right, behind the fountain. She was with me, speaking with two of the flame-haired men, when she saw servants beginning to prepare it for the musicians. Eagerly, she excused herself.

'I will ask them when the musicians will begin,' she said to me, 'and if they know their names.'

Smiling to myself, I glanced across at Lil, who was

standing with Carly and Lindsa amongst a small group of people. Carly shone at parties. She was just wicked enough, smart enough and gorgeous enough to dazzle whomever she met. Tonight, to judge by the interest on the faces around her, was proving no exception. Yet she had not forgotten her promise to Lilith and was including her in the talk. Not far from them stood Lindsa, her face revealing both her delight in the witty conversation and her despair at the growing number of Carly's admirers. A number I was only going to increase, for the flame-haired men were keen to meet Carly too, so I led them over and they greeted her with broad, eager smiles and glittering eyes.

Lilith soon separated herself from the group and came to stand by me with an unvoiced look of relief. If Carly was rich honey, I was the bread. 'Where's Chandra?' she asked.

I indicated the dais. 'Hovering impatiently,' I replied.

Lilith nodded and looked towards the dais. A moment later, she grabbed my arm. 'Look! I see her now. Isn't that Demran she's speaking with?'

Incredulous, I turned and spotted the familiar erect figure of Chandra speaking with a slim man of medium height. His dark brown hair was cropped short and he wore a neat sleeveless shirt of dark cotton over loose trousers. As we watched he raised the large leather bag he held in one hand and tugged it open. From it he pulled a familiar-looking instrument. He smiled and held it out for Chandra's inspection.

'It's his gitar,' Lil gasped. 'It *is* Demran.' She looked at me, her eyes wide open in astonishment, her lips rounded in surprise, and we both burst out laughing.

Oh, what ecstasies Chandra would know tonight!

We were not the only ones to notice the musician. The crowd was slowly beginning to drift towards the dais, aware that the performance would shortly commence. Many obviously recognised Demran, for he and Chandra were interrupted often as guests stopped to speak briefly with him, their faces reflecting their pleasure at meeting such a distinguished and talented musician. There was a ripple amongst the crowd as Regi and Leah approached and I saw Leah smile for the first time as she took Demran's hand. Regi turned to introduce Chandra, but although Leah nodded she did not deign to take Chandra's hand. I thought I saw Demran's face tighten at the rebuff but from such a distance I could not be sure.

As Regi led Leah to a row of chairs that had been placed before the dais for important guests, I turned to Lil. 'Come on,' I said. 'I'd like to meet him too.'

Lil grinned and we headed for Chandra. Despite all the interruptions, she and Demran had not moved one pace further apart than when we had first spotted them and, now, during a brief respite, they were once more deeply immersed in a private conversation.

As we drew closer, Chandra caught sight of us out of the corner of her eye. She raised her head and smiled joyfully. There was no need to ask if she was enjoying herself tonight. We stepped up beside her and she stretched out an arm towards us, as though to pull us into the circle of warmth that surrounded her and her companion.

'Demran,' she said happily, 'these are my friends, Ashil and Lilith.'

'I am very pleased to meet you both.' His voice was a delightful rich baritone, deep and mellifluous, the words so beautifully shaped and spoken that both Lilith and I paused in appreciation before replying.

'We are looking forward to hearing you play,' I finally told him, repeating, with little imagination, what several dozen others had no doubt already told him that night.

He bowed his head slightly in acknowledgement of my words. 'I am glad to have the three of you amongst my audience.' His eyes flicked to Chandra and he smiled. Beaming, she looked back at him.

There was a pause, unnoticed by either Chandra or Demran, who seemed to have forgotten there was a party taking place around them. Lil, who had been just about to ask something, hesitated, looked at both their faces and blinked. Then, as the pause lengthened, she finally asked, in a delicate, tentative voice if he would sing tonight as well as play.

Demran turned to her and nodded. 'I have already promised to sing at least two songs.' He looked back at Chandra as though recalling a secret shared. 'I must make amends for my performance in Nalym.'

Chandra frowned. 'It was not your fault. Lord Maltra chose to waste your talents by having you play for only a short while.' She looked unhappy with the memory, almost grumpy. 'She should have let you sing that evening.'

I had never seen Chandra in such a mood and while I was coping with the novelty of it Demran took one of her hands and smiled into her eyes.

'Well, this evening there are no such constraints and

314

it will be with great pleasure that I will both sing and play for you.'

As he lifted her hand towards his mouth, Chandra turned it so that instead of kissing the back of her hand, his lips met the softer flesh of her palm. A beatific grin spread over her face as her eyes met Demran's. He lingered for a moment over the kiss, then he straightened and squeezed her hand gently before releasing her and stepping forward onto the steps that led to the dais.

Chandra, Lilith and I moved too, until we stood at the front of the crowd, close enough to rest our hands on the edge of the waist-high dais. It was draped in a smooth, dark cloth, bare of all but three chairs and two other musicians who stood, one holding a pipe, the other a small drum, quietly talking. As Demran mounted the steps they broke off and moved towards the chairs.

Demran settled himself on one of the seats, chatting softly with the other two. The piper sat beside him but the drummer moved her chair away and returned to stand in the same spot. Demran dropped his leather bag on the floor behind him and began to fiddle with his gitar, strumming and tightening the strings. From time to time the piper or drummer would play a few notes but it was clear they were not quite ready to begin, so I let my eyes wander until my attention was caught by movement at the rear of the dais in the shadowy darkness of the colonnade.

Two tall torches had been carefully placed to illuminate the musicians, so that all beyond the dais was thrown into a deep, black darkness. Yet, in that darkness, I could see figures moving. I knew who they must be, standing in the dark. With only a back view of

Demran and his friends, Regi's servants were quietly gathering to hear the celebrated musicians who were to play at their lord's enthroning.

Yet, suddenly, Alexa's words came unbidden into my mind. 'Lately, I've had the feeling that we're being watched.' Inexplicably I felt that way now and chill-bumps ran over my flesh, causing me to shiver in the warm night air. Of course, I was being foolish, I told myself. No guest would stand behind the dais and it was hardly likely that any of Regi's servants would be interested in a group of cartographers. Still, the feeling persisted and would not leave me as I peered futilely into the dim gloom between the columns.

It was Chandra's loud cry of pleasure that brought my attention back to the dais. The musicians were ready now and, at Demran's sign, Regi climbed onto the dais and turned to face the crowd. 'Friends,' he announced in a loud, proud voice, 'the musicians will now begin.'

There was a tittering of delight and anticipation amongst the crowd, who were now all clamouring to see the dais and its occupants. Beside me, upright and intent, her face glowing with rapture, was Chandra. Turning to face the subject of her fixation, I forgot my fears and then the music began.

At first it was just the piper playing a slow, languid melody, cool and clear like a gently running stream. Then, like the heartbeat of all living creatures, came the regular boom-boom of the drums and finally, like the whispering of the leaves on the trees and the tall grasses on the bank, Demran began to softly strum his gitar and then to sing:

'Come sail with me, I'll take you far,'
He grinned and said with glee.
'My boat is fast, the water's smooth.
Come sail, come sail with me.'

My feet were sore, the trail now dead,
The water's song was sweet.
I looked into his dancing eyes.
'I'll go with you,' I said.

The wind blew strong and off we flew,
We had no need of oar.
Above us, in the clear blue sky,
I watched an eagle soar.

The sun sank low, I slept in peace,
Untroubled by the night.
I woke to see in dawn's pale blush
My sweet capt'n shining bright.

'What do you seek so far from home?'
He asked me with a smile.
'The famed Mahara to catch and claim.'
He frowned and asked me why.

I showed him rope and chain and whip
I carried in my pack.
'I'd hold him tight to me with these
And share his secret pact.

'He has mighty knowledge, old and wild
Of ways to heal all ills.

With such a treasure of my own
I'd head home to my hills.'

I sighed, with voice and heart so low
At the thought of all I'd left.
How I missed them as I travelled.
Now I must return bereft.

I saw a sadness in his eye,
A frown upon his face.
'Mahara causes no pain,' he said.
'Why force him from his place?

'Take wings from birds, they cannot fly,
No legs, a wolf can't run.
Enslave Mahara, he will fade away
Like clouds that hide the sun.'

I knew him then, my heart was sore
As I raised up high the rope.
He did not struggle, did not scream,
His face held all but hope.

I held him tight, as I had longed
And saw how he had paled.
Where now had gone the glee and shine?
I knew my task had failed.

He took me to a bank nearby,
And bade me warm farewell.
I hoist the pack upon my back.
'Goodbye,' I called. 'Sail well.'

I walked towards the quiet field,
My heart was light and gay.
I had no coin and no great prize,
Yet before me riches lay.

From atop the hill I heard his voice,
So sweet and pure and bright.
Beside him stood a weary hunter
I saw her rope coiled tight.

I grinned and strode on through the grass.
Each step was keen and strong.
My quest had ended here today.
Below I heard his song.

'Come sail with me, I'll take you far.
Come sail, come sail with me.
My boat is fast, the water's smooth.
Come sail, come sail with me.'

The drumming ended, there was a final flourish with the gitar and pipe and then they too ceased. The song was over. A great collective sigh of delight rose from the crowd, as we were all returned to Regi's party and forgot the river ride we had just taken and abandoned the quiet field we had walked in. Soft murmurings of appreciation for Demran's genius began but before they could build to any strength, the musicians suddenly struck up a lively dance tune, an invitation impossible for most to resist.

People spread out to clear a circle for the dancers

and Carly and Lindsa were among the first to take to the cobbled stones. Carly was laughing as she spun and stepped to the music, her long hair flying, the light material of her skirt lifting to reveal her slim golden calves. Her steps followed no formal pattern, yet she moved with an effortless fluidity, at one with the rhythm of the music.

She was surrounded now by other dancers, whose gaiety and energy seemed to fill the courtyard, along with the scent of expensive perfumes floating free of warmed skin. Now that Demran was no longer singing, an undercurrent of talk and laughter was bubbling around me and wine goblets were once again being filled. I glanced at Chandra, for normally she loved to dance, but this evening she was too enchanted by the occupants of the dais to think of moving. I smiled and turned back to watch Carly.

She and Lindsa had linked hands and were performing an intricate weave dance with another couple. Carly outshone them all. Indeed, there was no other tonight who could compete with her skill. The thought warmed me and I felt an inner glow of pride that she was my friend.

One of the men I had met earlier in the evening asked me to dance and we joined hands and found a space amidst the others. A few moments later I saw Lilith accept a young desertman. When the music changed to another jaunty tune, I changed partners and then once more again. I passed Carly several times as I spun around and she grinned at me encouragingly. At one time my over-zealous partner and I bumped into Regi and Leah. He laughed and she frowned and, abashed, my partner and I apologised and moved on.

By the start of the fourth tune my throat was so parched I knew I could dance no more, so I pleaded thirst and left the dance area in search of a goblet of wine. I found a servant and took three goblets, almost draining one before I returned to Chandra and offered one to her. She still had not moved, and though I doubt such mundane things as wine had been much on her mind, she took the wine with thanks. I looked around for Lil, the third goblet was for her, in case she too was driven by thirst to abandon the dancing. If not, it would be no hardship for me to consume its contents. Her flushed face appeared in the crowd before me and she headed towards us. I handed her the goblet unasked and she took it with a wide smile and drank deeply.

The next piece the musicians began was the second of the songs Demran had promised to Chandra. It was a tale of love between a woman and man, beautifully moving yet, as I was later forced to confess to Chandra, I missed many of the words as I was too intent on watching the dancers. Specifically, Carly, Regi and Leah.

At the beginning of the song, Leah was asked to dance by a young woman whose silk vest gleamed with precious gems. Whether because she was impressed by the woman's rank and wealth or because she genuinely liked her, I do not know, but Leah actually smiled and accepted and took the woman's hand. This left Regi free of his royal guest and he wasted no time in striding over to ask Carly to partner him.

Wanting to get a better view of the dancers, I stepped away from Lilith and Chandra as Regi and Carly moved to the centre of the dance area. Regi danced as stylishly as he dressed and he and Carly glided over the stones as though they had been dancing together for years. They were both clearly enjoying themselves, chatting happily as they twirled and spun amidst the other less talented couples. Their dance was interrupted when a guest's necklace unexpectedly broke, showering the cobblestones with jewels and sending the servants rushing forward to pick up the small but valuable stones. Until they had all been collected, the dancers were forced to pause and Regi took advantage of the time to introduce Carly to Leah and her friend.

By chance, when the necklace had broken, Leah and her friend had been dancing only a few paces from where I stood. So when Regi and Carly sought them out they discovered me standing close by and Regi waved me over.

I stepped forward, both curious and tentative, for what I had seen of Leah so far had done nothing to endear her to me. In fact I was startled by the contrast between her and her warm and charming cousin, Lord Tarn. It was at this stage, though this I did not admit to Chandra, that I ceased entirely to pay any attention to Demran's song.

Carly squeezed my arm in greeting as I fell into step beside her.

'Where's Lil?' she whispered.

'With Chandra,' I nodded towards the dais and she grinned and relaxed.

As the five of us came together, Regi spoke a few words of introduction, politely and diplomatically turning to each of us as he did so. It was immediately clear that I was considered the least important member of the group, for both Leah and her friend gave me only a cursory glance before returning their attention to Carly. While Regi spoke, I looked at the faces of the three women before me, aware as I did so of the unmistakable tension in the group. On the far left stood Leah's friend in her brilliant vest. She looked Carly over with an assessing eye, and impressed by what she saw she darted a glance at Leah full of barely suppressed amusement. Beside her and directly in front of Regi was Leah, stony faced and aloof. Unaware of her friend's pleasure in seeing her face-to-face with a worthy rival, Leah stood erect and proud, so beautifully cold she was like a sculptured figurine. By contrast, Carly appeared almost offensively unconcerned. The dancing had left her glowing and she was relaxed and amiable, smiling lightly.

Regi finished speaking and looked expectantly at Leah. I waited, knowing I would be dealt with only after Carly. Yet instead of acting promptly, Leah paused insultingly, as though first considering whether Carly was worthy of her attention. Then finally, slowly, condescendingly, she offered her hand. I was silently dismayed by her rudeness and turned shocked eyes to Carly, both angered and hurt on behalf of my friend.

But Carly was no-one's fool and she stood calmly, having read Leah's intent with precise, unruffled ease. Then I saw what Leah had failed to. The only other cartographer Leah had met that night was Chan, but Carly was no Chandra. Carly was neither immersed in the inchoate delights of a love affair nor too unfamiliar with social intricacies to miss such an obvious snub.

Indeed, Leah had made a grand error of judgment, for she had offered challenge in an area in which Carly excelled. So instead of immediately taking the hand, as Leah expected, Carly deliberately paused, reversing the situation so that it was Leah who became the suppliant, the inferior. Just as the pause was drawing to a painful length, Carly held out her hand and took Leah's. Their eyes met, Leah's hard with fury, Carly's alight with confidence. Then both clasp and gaze were broken as Leah abruptly turned away, taking her friend's arm without a word to either Regi or myself and stalking off into the crowd.

After a few moments of stunned silence, Regi blinked and drew a deep breath before turning to us and apologising. Then his face softened slightly with belated amusement at Leah's precipitant departure.

'I have never seen her react in quite that way,' he said, 'but Leah does sometimes forget that high birth is not an excuse for incivility.'

Carly raised her eyebrows. 'Being born into a particular family is no excuse for anything,' she replied. 'Netla taught me that.' Then, changing her tone and expression totally, she smiled wryly at me. 'I hope you weren't planning on becoming the greatest of friends with Leah, Ash, as I think I've just spoilt your chances.'

I laughed along with her. To tell truth, Leah's goodwill did not greatly concern me, but silently I could not help wondering if her cousin would hear of tonight's incident and what he would think of it.

'What about you, Regi?' I asked suddenly. 'Won't she make it difficult for you in Cynal?'

He shook his head. 'Leah and I have known each other for years. She needs people like me. She may not attend another of my parties in a hurry, but this will soon blow over.' He looked at Carly. 'I did not, after all, insult her.'

Carly shrugged, already bored with the topic of Leah. 'Let's dance, shall we?' she suggested. 'We can do a three star turn to this count,' and she nodded in the direction of the dais where, now that all the jewels had been collected, another rousing dance tune was being played.

We moved out into the centre of the dance area, where the three of us linked arms and skipped and twirled around one another, laughing happily.

When the musicians paused for a rest, I declined Regi's offer of wine and sweetmeats and moved instead towards Lilith. I could not quite smother a yawn as I came up before her and she laughed softly at me. Chandra was engrossed in conversation with Demran once more and scowled unhappily at anyone who dared approach the celebrated musician. Demran could barely keep his eyes from Chandra and was ignoring the crowd entirely.

'I saw you with Leah,' Lil said as I turned back to her. 'She didn't look very happy.'

'She wasn't,' I answered succinctly, then I chuckled at the look of curiosity on her face and threw an arm around her shoulders. 'I've had enough dancing and wine tonight.' When she nodded in agreement I suggested, 'Why don't we say good night to Regi and head back to the palace? I'll tell you all about it on the way.'

ELEVEN

At regi's, I had been far too immersed in the activity around me to spare thought for how Alexa was spending her evening. Even through the short walk back to the palace and Lilith's and my lazy chatter, not once did she or her reason for staying behind enter my mind.

As Lil and I entered the east wing I was feeling more wide awake than I had when we quit the party. Indeed, as we began to climb the huge central staircase, now brilliantly lit by many torches, I found I no longer felt any desire to sleep at all. Still, I would no doubt have continued on to our apartment and bed had Alexa not just then made an unexpected appearance below us and called our names.

Startled, Lilith and I turned and peered over the wooden bannister. Alexa was one flight below us and we smiled and waved to her, stopping to allow her to catch us up. As she climbed, I saw that she was holding something large and flat against her chest and my curiosity was immediately piqued. Alexa made the most wonderful discoveries and I waited for her eagerly.

As she drew level, she grinned and asked how the

party had gone. At once I wondered what she had been doing this night, for her eyes were bright and her face was radiant with excitement. I noted that slung across one shoulder was her sketching kit, from which the ends of three maps protruded.

'Good,' I replied, recalling her question after a moment's pause, 'the party was good. Demran was there.' My eyes rested on the large leather-bound tome she was cradling and I pointed to it. 'What's that?'

'Ah,' she said, patting it and smiling, 'this I found in the palace library. There is something in it I want to show Rianne.' She glanced up. 'Demran the musician?'

'Yes,' Lilith answered happily. 'He and Chandra have been together most of the night and, while he played, she didn't move from the edge of the dais.'

Normally, I would have been more than willing to describe the events of the party in detail but for now I was far more interested in hearing Alexa's account of her evening. So I interposed quickly, before the subject of Demran and Chandra could be pursued. 'Do you mean you've already seen Rianne?'

Alexa nodded, then glanced at a large crowd of people climbing up behind us. 'Come to the landing and I'll tell you all about it.'

We climbed to the next landing and sat on a long bench that had been provided, no doubt, to offer rest for those who were forced to climb many flights of the huge staircase each day. Alexa dropped her kit on the floor and placed the book in her lap, her hands resting lightly on the leather cover, and began to describe her evening.

'Once I left you, I met with some guard friends of

Nikol's who invited me to dine with them. The meal was relaxed and friendly. Gradually talk moved around to the white panther.' It was simply spoken but I raised an eyebrow, for it was not hard to guess who had brought the conversation around to such a topic. 'The guards don't know much,' Alexa admitted. 'They've been instructed to listen for and report any talk of the white panther and it's already common knowledge that Rianne is trying to contact the Lakiya.' She frowned slightly. 'Though the guards either don't know or aren't permitted to say why.'

'Does Rianne think there is a connection between the Lakiya and the white panther?' Lilith asked.

'I don't know, Lil. That's what I hope I am about to find out. Once dinner was over I thought I'd see what I could read about the Lakiya in the palace library, only to discover several Mecla there before me, intent on the same task. The priests were only too glad to have another pair of eyes and I set to work. But it is no easy project. The library is large and references to the Lakiya can be found in the most obscure places. Often, after an arduous search, the information only confirms what we already knew.'

She drummed her fingers over the book and flashed us a delighted smile. 'But the evening was not without some success. Midway through the search, Rianne appeared. She could not stay long, she had to return to Lord Tarn, but she wanted to know if anything new had been discovered. At that stage there was nothing to report and she left, after pausing for a moment to speak with me. If I found anything of interest, she said, bring it to Lord Tarn's chambers.'

I gasped. 'And that's where you're headed?'

Alexa nodded and I wondered if it had occurred to her just how rare such an invitation was. I also wondered if Lord Tarn would take the opportunity to question Alexa on cartography. The thought made me a little glum, so I quickly subdued it.

'The priests and I returned to work,' Alexa continued. 'But it grew late and we had found nothing of any importance. The Mecla finished for the night but I was still wide awake, so the librarian let me stay a little longer and, by chance, I found this journal by a Melcran priest.'

My eyes dropped to the book, wondering what it contained that would bring Alexa so effortlessly into the private apartment of Cynal's ruler.

'It is a listing of medicinal plants and their applications,' Alexa said, 'written while the priest journeyed from village to village, making note of local herbal treatments as she went. It was the travelling aspect that first attracted me. I did not think it very likely that a Melcran herbalist who had lived over a hundred years ago would have anything to say of the Lakiya, but I was wrong.'

Both Lilith and I looked at Alexa, eyes wide. 'She met them?' I asked, my voice rising with incredulity.

'She believed she did, while she was travelling in the far north, through low mountains. It had been over a week since she had sighted a village and she was beginning to fear that she had lost her way. She stopped in a small clearing on the edge of a forest to camp for the night when it happened. Listen.'

Alexa flipped open the book at a page she had

marked and began to read the priest's entry.

The attack was worse than anything I could imagine. They came at us from out of the shadows, their fangs dripping saliva, their dark wings flapping, their evil snarls filling the night air with horror. They flew at Braen first, he was larger and therefore offered a greater feed, and I was flung from the saddle. Braen's screams of pain and terror as the bloodsuckers bled him and tore him open almost ripped my mind apart and still more and more of the vile creatures came, until all around me were such visions of depravity and foulness that I prayed I would faint before they came for me.

The largest of the Hyish rose from Braen's still twitching carcass, blood smeared across its muzzle and chest, its narrowed eyes now glaring hungrily at me. It raised its head and screamed, a heart-stopping bestial cry of bloodlust and domination. There was nowhere for me to run. The Hyish surrounded me and I knew they would easily hunt me down, even if I could escape from the clearing. My end was near. As the beast strode towards me, followed closely by others, I watched as other of the Hyish grabbed my saddlebags and pulled them apart, scattering my carefully stored and catalogued herbs on the wind. I fell back, beaten. No-one would read my journal now or share my great discoveries, my work was all for naught.

The Hyish are long-lived but reproduce rarely and it is only this that keeps them from spreading their terror all over Tirayi. Few beasts can match them in the wild and only armed mortals can hope to defeat them. Alone and unarmed, I prayed that my death would be quick.

Then suddenly the Hyish paused, only paces from me, and raised its muzzle into the air, testing the breeze. I could smell nothing but all the Hyish quietened, standing still and alert. Then, to my surprise, their stillness turned to agitation and they began to back away from the forest behind me, onto the mountain path, moving their wings anxiously as though preparing for flight. I had enough time to wonder what sort of creature could frighten away a Hyish and if that same creature would look upon a mortal as an easy, tasty meal, and then the entire clearing erupted around me.

Some were winged and looked like giant eagles, others sprang from the forest, their great bear heads roaring a challenge to the Hyish. Trapped and unable to fly free, the Hyish were forced to fight, but they had met their match. The great bears and the giant eagles seemed to work together and their numbers and strength overwhelmed the vile ones. Some of the Hyish managed to escape but most lay dead on the clearing floor, their blood mingling with Braen's. I did not escape unscathed. Though ignored during the fighting, a Hyish fleeing the deadly combination of talons and beak above and claws and teeth before it scrambled past me, knocking me aside in its haste. I fell hard against a large rock and heard the sound of breaking bone as my arm hit. The pain was almost unbearable but I had time to see the Hyish vanquished and watch the victors gather and silently slip into the night as quickly and mysteriously as they had come, before the pain became too great and unconsciousness took me.

I had heard tales of the people of the beasts, the Lakiya, some call them, but had doubted their verity. Yet, when I awoke, I was in a strange place, my arm was nestled in a bed of soft moss and the pain had greatly eased. Pale figures moved about me and one lifted my head for me to drink and I glimpsed a face above me as pure and colourless as untainted marble. As the Lakiya rose, something soft, like fur, brushed against my cheek and I thought I heard a low coo, though the lips of the Lakiya did not move. Still weak, I rolled my head to the side and saw another of the pale figures stroking the head of a great bear and I thought, it was they who saved me. Then my eyelids grew too heavy to keep open and I drifted off into a sleep.

When I awoke I found a woven basket beside me containing my collection of herbs, once more neatly laid out and divided. I moved to examine it closely and discovered that my arm no longer hurt. I was healed. I looked around but I was alone and, I am sure, no longer in the place where I had rested the night before. Inside the basket there was food and water, my journal, and a small woven package that I unwrapped carefully. Inside, I found a thick lock of coarse brown hair. It had been cut from Braen's mane. With tears blurring my vision, I wrapped it up gently and began on my way.

Alexa closed the book and for a moment we were silent, letting our thoughts settle. I stared at the hanging

332

on the wall opposite, not really seeing it, my mind on the tale I had just heard. There was the possibility, of course, that the priest had been lying, or mistaken, but this I did not really believe. Her story had the sound of truth to it. I believed what I had just heard.

The corridor where we sat had fallen quiet, undisturbed by the passage of feet, and it was into the strange silence that Lilith finally spoke, whispering softly.

'So they do exist, just as Rianne said. And they are kind and gentle, not wicked as in other tales.'

'Yes, kind and gentle and mysterious,' Alexa replied, in a voice almost as low. 'I hope this will help Rianne locate them and I hope, as we are the ones bringing the journal to her, that she will tell us why she is so keen to contact the Lakiya.' She stood up, slipping her kit once more onto her shoulder and holding the book tight. 'I should go now. It is getting late. Do you want to come?'

That option had not occurred to me. 'Will we be let in as well?' I asked, both thrilled and alarmed.

Alexa shrugged. 'I don't see why not. Lord Tarn and Rianne are going to be curious about the area where the Melcran was attacked by the Hyish, and who better to discuss it with than cartographers.' She nodded at her kit. 'I already have our maps of Tirayi. I stopped by the workroom on my way here to collect them.'

I took a deep breath. 'All right,' I agreed. After all, it would not be the first time I had sat in conference with a powerful ruler, and of my skills as a cartographer there was no doubt. I had no reason to be so hesitant.

Lilith declined. The party and its excitement had been enough for her tonight.

333

So we returned to the staircase and climbed again, Lilith leaving us soon after as she headed for our apartment. Alexa and I wished her good night and continued on.

I knew the north wing was given over entirely to the royal family but I was unfamiliar with its layout.

'Where exactly do we have to go?' I asked.

'The third floor, to Lord Tarn's private living chambers,' Alexa said.

'Do you know what's on all the other floors?'

Alexa nodded. 'I asked the Mecla. On the ground level is Lord Tarn's study, his private library and several meeting chambers. The smallest of the meeting chambers seats no more than ten, while the largest is able to hold more than two hundred. Above this, on the first floor, are the private dining rooms and salons where special guests are entertained. According to the priest I spoke with, it is a great honour to be invited to dine there. The second floor is currently inhabited only by Lord Tarn's personal servants, though it also contains sleeping chambers for any royal children and finally, on the third floor, are Lord Tarn's sleeping and living quarters.'

When we reached the third floor and left the staircase to move towards the north wing we immediately discovered the difference between this and other sections of the palace. At every door there were two or more guards, fully armed, and had Rianne not had the forethought to alert the guards to Alexa's possible arrival we would certainly have been turned away. As it was, Rianne's message only mentioned one cartographer, so we were asked to wait while a guard went on ahead to ask if Lord Tarn wished to see us. When the answer came back in the affirmative we were led along many passages and passed glorious rooms of understated but delightful elegance and comfort. The few hours Lord Tarn would have alone to relax could not have been spent in more peaceful and calm surroundings.

Finally, we came to a pair of large, elaborately carved doors, flanked by two guards. We halted and one of the guards turned and rapped upon the expensive wood. He waited several seconds, then entered, closing the door behind him. He returned a few moments later and nodded to us. Both doors were swung open and Alexa and I were admitted.

We stood in a wide, open salon, calm and quiet. Enormous windows faced out over the ocean before us and to our right, filling the eye with a soft indigo-black view of the endless gently rolling water and the star-sprinkled heavens. The view was overwhelming, breathtaking. Then Lord Tarn stepped forward to greet us and I forgot all else.

I had thought myself better prepared for our meeting this time, hopeful that the awkwardness that had beset me previously would not resurface. After all, I had reasoned with myself, that response had been entirely due to the shock of such a sudden encounter. Yet as his eyes met mine, dark and glowing, I felt my breath catch and my heart beat faster and I was forced to confess to my own deception. Dazed, I dropped into a deep bow and murmured his name, vaguely aware that beside me, Alexa had done the same. I rose slowly, my lips still parted for air, my face pale, and then he smiled at me, a smile so personal and warm and so pleased that, without thinking, my mind dancing with wild joy, I smiled back, brilliantly and unreservedly.

Until this moment I had not noticed Rianne, but she now appeared at Lord Tarn's side.

'My Lord,' she said, her voice filling the silence, 'may I present the cartographers?'

At these words he lifted his eyes from me and looked at her. 'You need not trouble yourself, Rianne,' he said in that beautiful deep, rich voice. 'We have already met.' His gaze flicked back to us. 'And I'm delighted that Ashil and Alexa take their duties so much to heart that they will discuss their maps and share their knowledge at such a late hour.'

On hearing my name on his lips a sudden hot burst of pleasure washed over me and, for the first time since entering the room, colour filled my cheeks. Once more, his eyes sought mine, as though he too did not wish to look at anyone or anything else. Then he half-turned towards a pair of silk-covered couches behind him.

'Let's make ourselves comfortable before we begin.'

We settled ourselves on the white silk. Alexa and I on one couch and Lord Tarn and Rianne on the other. Another knock on the door announced the arrival of a servant bearing a tray of drinks which at Lord Tarn's request she left on the low table between us before silently departing. Rianne served us all drinks. Then Lord Tarn sat back.

'So, tell us what you have discovered of the Lakiya.'

Alexa spoke eloquently and concisely, explaining how she had picked up the Melcran journal by chance only to discover the entry that told of the priest's encounter with the Hyish and her rescue by the Lakiya. She read the entry aloud and Lord Tarn and Rianne listened intently. Afterwards, Alexa handed the book to Rianne, who studied it avidly.

'The area the Melcran refers to, in the far north amongst low mountains, does it give you any idea where she may have been?' Lord Tarn asked.

Alexa handed me a map and I unrolled it on the table so that it faced Lord Tarn. I pointed to the most northern range, above Sach.

'It is probably this range, Lord,' I said, 'but the mountains go on for leagues and it is impossible to be precise. Forest rings the mountains on both the south-east and south-west and while the priest may have been able to travel for a week without reaching a village a hundred years ago, there is no way of knowing how many villages have since sprung up. It would be necessary to visit all the villages in the area and speak to the inhabitants to see if they knew how long their village had stood, then try to plot an area that was once uninhabited and that a priest on horseback could cover in a week. It would be very time-consuming.'

Lord Tarn nodded. 'And not necessarily accurate.'

'It is not certain either, Lord, that the Lakiya are still in that area,' Alexa pointed out. 'They may have moved elsewhere or may have only been passing through when they encountered the priest.'

'Yes,' Rianne agreed, looking up and shutting the book, 'but it is good to know that the Lakiya did help a priest of Menlin, even so long ago.'

'Why would they not?' Alexa asked, turning immediately to the Mecla priest. 'Has there been trouble between the sects of Menlin and the Lakiya?'

Rianne sighed and gave Alexa a slight smile. 'Though I would dearly love to answer your questions, the only response I can give is that I do not know.' She glanced at the map spread before her and continued in a low voice. 'The only ones who can supply me with the answers are the Lakiya themselves.'

Determinedly, single-mindedly, Alexa asked if that was why she sought them.

Across from us, Lord Tarn chuckled. 'Curiosity is an admirable quality,' he said, 'and quite invaluable in a cartographer. I think in this instance we can satisfy it a little. It is no secret that we seek to make contact with the Lakiya, and we are asking all we can to help us in this quest. The truth is we have heard some disturbing reports about the re-emergence of the white panther and we need to discover the extent of the Lakiya's involvement, if any, before we can act.'

'Why do you think the Lakiya are involved, Lord?' I queried.

His brown-black eyes turned to me and, his attention fully on me, he explained. 'The value of the white panther, Ashil, lies in its association with the Menlin sects. It must appear with one of the followers of Meclan if people are to believe that like the first white panther it was sent from the gods. We know the rumours were not started by the Mecla and King Charissa has told us that the Melcran are just as perplexed by the talk as we are. That leaves only the Meran. As we do not believe the white panther being spoken of is truly from the gods and we know the Meran do not have the power or ability to create such a creature, we fear they have in some way coerced or joined with the Lakiya. But we need to be certain and for that we need to speak with the Lakiya.'

'I thought the Meran had little power now, Lord,' I said, puzzled.

'Yes,' he agreed, 'but only compared to the power they once held.'

Seeing Alexa's and my frowns of concentration, Rianne elaborated.

'They no longer have the power they had ninety years ago, when they broke with us and the people and so many of them were destroyed. But those that survived went into hiding and small groups of Meran still exist, planning for the day when they will regain their position and power. Their leader today is Nitma and we believe she is based in Delawyn. She is obsessed with re-establishing the Meran and their mind powers and her venomous hatred for the Mecla and Cynal is well-known. Should she gain such a powerful tool as the white panther, with which she could draw people to her unquestioningly, she could create havoc all over Tirayi. It is our greatest fear.'

'Still, you do not know for certain that the Lakiya are involved,' Alexa persisted.

Rianne shook her head sadly. 'If the rumours of the white panther are true, then there can be no other explanation. We know little of the people of the beasts. Nitma may have found something to tempt them with, perhaps promised them rewards when she holds power.' She shrugged. 'We only know we have no time to waste. Every day we wait brings us closer to the emergence of this white panther.'

I gave a small sigh that must have carried for Lord Tarn gave a crooked smile. 'You seem bedazzled, Ashil,' he said. 'What don't you understand?'

I smiled back, almost childishly delighted each time he used my name. 'It is all this talk of the Lakiya, Lord. I still find it surprising. Until a few days ago I believed them to be no more than a myth, and now I hear them spoken of with such certainty that it bewilders me.'

'And now you will discover that the little you do know will tantalise and intrigue you,' he replied. 'It will do so until you wish to know more, until you want to meet a Lakiya in the flesh and ask question after question.'

I nodded, then laughed, for it was exactly how I felt and because his smiling eyes were making me feel light-headed. Never had I met such a handsome man. I wanted only to look and look at him, to gaze at that face, so strong and proud, his royal ancestry carved into the firm, clean planes, his keen intelligence glowing in those dark, dark eyes, and I wanted to run my fingers through the glossy strands of his black hair and lightly draw a finger over the small scar on his top lip then down over the hard-muscled wall of his chest to the flat, taut planes of his belly, exposed under his open vest. I swallowed and raised my eyes to his once more and saw there a reflection of my own desire. Excitement, exultation and dread flooded through me, then beside me Alexa asked if there was anything we, as cartographers, could do and Lord Tarn's attention was turned to her.

'There are two things,' he replied, his voice calm and contained, allowing no hint of emotion to colour it.

'First, you can keep your ears open for news of the Lakiya or the white panther as you work in the city. As strangers, people may feel more inclined to speak freely before you and you may hear something that will help us with our search. Secondly,' and here he turned back to me and I thought his voice softened slightly, 'I would like a map of the northern mountains where the Melcran priest travelled, with as much detail as you have.'

'Certainly, Lord,' I said, very properly, and then his mouth quirked in a small smile and I tried unsuccessfully to bite back the one forming on my own mouth.

'If you could bring it to me as soon as you have finished it, Ashil,' he said gently. He turned to Rianne. 'I think that is all.'

Rianne nodded. 'Yes, Lord.'

'Then, as it is late, we will bid you good night, Ashil and Alexa, and thank you for your help.'

Lord Tarn rose and I collected the map from the table and stood with Alexa.

'Good night, Lord,' we said, bowing. 'Rianne.' And we nodded politely to the priest, who had moved around to stand beside us.

'Thank you for bringing the journal,' she said as she walked with us to the door. 'I will keep it and read it through.' She opened the door. 'Sleep well.'

Drawing on a mighty inner strength, I resisted the temptation to look back one final time at Lord Tarn and stepped through the doorway with Alexa. The guards stood attentively at either side of us and behind us I heard the soft click of the door as it shut. Our guide came forward and Alexa and I followed her silently through the quiet passages. She left us at the central staircase and as we climbed down I waited for Alexa to make some comment about Lord Tarn and me. Instead, she took a deep, delighted breath.

'The Lakiya, Ash!' she said, with exultant relish. 'Just think what excitement may be before us in the days ahead!'

I smiled and agreed, but it was not the Lakiya I was thinking of but Lord Tarn and the message I had read in his dark eyes.

TWELVE

' . . . And that was the final song for the evening. Everyone applauded and afterwards several people came over to ask Demran to play at their parties before the enthroning.' Chandra grinned broadly. 'He turned them all away but he has offered to come and play here for us one evening. Wait until you meet him, Alexa, you will like him very much.'

Alexa laughed softly. 'I'm sure I will.'

It was early morning and we were seated at the table in our apartment, eating breakfast. Chandra's description of Demran and his songs had concluded our tales from the night before.

'It sounds as if we all had an eventful evening,' Carly said, smothering a slice of bread with honey. 'Chandra met Demran, Lilith, Ashil and I danced the night away, Alexa discovered an important journal, then she and Ash dazzled Lord Tarn and Rianne with their cartographic knowledge.'

'You forgot to mention your encounter with royal cousin Leah,' I teased, filling a mug with milk.

'Ah,' Carly laughed. 'Yes, the delightful Leah.' She shook her head. 'What I can't understand is how someone as charming and pleasant as Lord Tarn can contemplate marrying someone so rude and arrogant.'

I gagged on a mouthful of milk. 'Marriage?' I squeaked.

Carly nodded. 'Mmm, Regi told me.' She licked a drop of honey from her fingers. 'The death of the old king delayed the announcement. They'll have to wait until after the enthroning now.' She crinkled her nose in distaste. 'I don't envy Lord Tarn.'

I was speechless. It was horrible, unthinkable. Morosely, I finished my milk.

'We'll have to work without Ashil today,' Alexa said, swiftly changing the subject. 'She'll be working on the northern map for Lord Tarn.'

I nodded and straightened, her words bringing me back to the work at hand. 'It shouldn't take me long,' I said, mentally reviewing our maps of Tirayi. 'It's a straight copy. I'll only need a day or two to complete it.'

'But first we get to fill our pouches with Cynalese coin,' Carly said merrily. 'We receive our half payment today. Captain Varl is meeting us at the workroom and will take us to the chancellor afterwards for payment.'

Not wanting to keep the captain waiting, we quickly finished breakfast and readied ourselves for the day ahead. I collected the three Tirayi maps from the shelf in my room where I had placed them last night and Alexa hoisted her sketching kit on to her shoulder. We joined the others in the central salon and, together, we left the apartment and headed for our workroom.

Captain Varl arrived moments after us and we showed him our mapping sheets with the measurements and rough sketches we had made so far of the harbour district. He looked them over carefully and was satisfied with our progress. He asked if we had any complaints or queries and we told him we did not and he led us to the chancellor's rooms.

We had not spoken to Neesha since our first interview and I did not doubt that her days were long with business regarding the enthroning, now only seven days away. Yet even Captain Varl seemed surprised to see the Eustapean guards standing side by side with the Cynalese soldiers before Neesha's door.

One of the Cynalese soldiers stepped forward and saluted. 'Captain,' he said briskly, 'the chancellor is expecting you, but King Charissa has made an unexpected visit and is with the chancellor now. Do you want me to announce you?'

Captain Varl frowned and shook his head. 'No, we will not interrupt the king.' He turned to us, just as a Eustapean attendant bearing what appeared to be flagons of Eustapean wine was admitted to the chancellor's room. Through the open door I caught a glimpse of the king and as she looked up I smiled and bowed. I saw her return the smile before the door shut.

'I apologise, cartographers,' Captain Varl said, 'but payment will have to be delayed. I will arrange another time with the chancellor as soon as possible.'

Once more the door opened and we glanced over as the Eustapean attendant reappeared and approached Captain Varl.

'Captain,' she said, tilting her head to look up at him, the top of her head barely reaching his shoulders, 'King Charissa does not wish to cause any disruption and asks that the cartographers be admitted to complete their business with the chancellor and share a goblet of Eustapean wine.'

The captain raised an eyebrow in surprise. 'The king is most generous.'

The attendant nodded and backed away. One of the Cynalese soldiers opened the door and the six of us entered. We bowed before King Charissa, who smiled serenely, enveloped in that aura of calm that I had noted at the harbour. 'I am pleased to meet you, cartographers,' she said, in a light, pleasant voice. 'Rianne mentioned your work this morning and aroused my curiosity.' She laughed softly and with such genuine enjoyment that we found ourselves grinning along with her. 'It appears you manage to combine the roving life with purpose and accomplishment and I confess to some curiosity and perhaps some small amount of envy for that which no king can ever have.' She waved a small, slender hand in the direction of the couches. 'Please sit and share some Eustapean wine with me and you can tell me a little of your tales.'

Neesha had risen at our entry and remained standing while we made ourselves comfortable on the couches. Once we were settled, she turned to the king. 'If you will excuse us, your majesty, Captain Varl and I will collect the cartographers' pay.'

King Charissa inclined her head. 'Of course, Neesha.'

The chancellor and captain crossed to the rear of the room where another door was set in the wall. Neesha plucked a key from the ring at her waist and fitted it in the heavy metal lock. The key turned smoothly and the door opened and she and the captain disappeared inside.

I eyed the flagons of wine, flanked by goblets, on the table before me and wondered who would pour now that Neesha had left the room.

As though able to read my thoughts, King Charissa leant forward towards me and asked if I would do so.

I lifted the flagon and filled six of the goblets, handing one first to the king, then one each to the others.

'Ah,' Carly exclaimed delightedly, as she accepted her goblet, 'before I came to Cynal I had heard only two things about Eustape, your majesty. One, that it is a small island to the south, and two, that its wines are some of the finest to be found on Tirayi.' She raised the goblet to her nose and inhaled deeply. 'Mmm, delicious.'

King Charissa laughed. 'What you say is true enough. Yet we do not exist on wine alone. We grow and export oranges, lemons, limes, olives, as well as wheat and barley and, for ourselves, we keep goats and cows for their milk and grow more vegetables than I could name for our tables. Yet such fare is rather dull compared to our wines and so it is for them that we are known.'

Alexa took a sip of the wine. 'Eustape is also known for the Melcran religion, your majesty,' she said evenly, 'and the fact you will eat no flesh.'

'Yes,' King Charissa nodded, 'our ways fascinate many and make, I am sure, for much interesting dinner conversation. Though it is mainly speculation.' She shrugged lightly, unconcerned. 'Our priests keep to the island so very few who are not Melcran know our religion well.'

'It must make it difficult, your majesty, to attract new followers,' Alexa commented.

'Religion should not be forced upon anyone,' the king replied, 'and those who wish to learn more are free to seek us out.'

'Do many, your majesty?' Lilith asked shyly, again exhibiting that surprising fascination with the Menlin religion.

'It is not a life that suits all,' the king admitted, 'but few who join the Melcran ever leave. Our ways are seen as strange and sometimes overly demanding by those who do not know the full delights of being Melcran. Yet we do not seek to convert our critics. Their lives are their own, just as ours are our own to spend rejoicing in Melcran.'

'Damin explained to us, your majesty, that the writings of Meclan are interpreted differently by each sect,' I said. 'Is this why the Melcran are the only Menlin sect not to eat flesh?'

King Charissa threw up her small hands in mock exasperation. 'I was warned of your voracious curiosity and here I was hoping that you would indulge my inquisitiveness.'

'Excuse me, your majesty,' I apologised hastily.

'There is no need for apology. It was not a reprimand, and, please, while we are meeting so informally, you may drop my title. For a full answer to your question you would have to speak with a Melcran priest. I can only say that for a Melcran to achieve harmony with the world around her, she must show respect for all living creatures. The Melcran, more so, I believe, than the other two sects, have an affinity for the natural world. So for a follower to kill an animal that is deranged or wounded beyond healing is painful, but to kill a healthy creature for food is abhorrent.'

Chandra frowned. 'Other animals eat animals. It is the way of the wild and if the kill is clean and swift and not to be wasted there is no dishonour.'

'But we are not animals. We have a choice.'

'What would happen if the Eustapean crops were blighted,' Carly asked, 'and your people starving, with only your cows and goats left? Would you eat the already dying animals to save yourselves, or all die?'

King Charissa nodded appreciatively. 'When I was a child there was a game I would play with the other childen. We would ask each other questions that by their very nature resulted in unsatisfactory answers. Listen.

'You and two others are stranded a day's walk from the nearest village. The other two people have been bitten by a deadly snake and will die before the night is out unless they have medicine. One of these is your dearest friend but she is a weak, sickly creature who heals slowly and it is not certain she will survive, even with medicine. The other is your fiercest rival, who you dislike and who dislikes you, but she is healthy and strong and likely to live with medicine. In your pack, you have enough of the precious herbs to keep one from death while you go for help. Who do you give the herbs to?'

Silence.

King Charissa laughed. 'Yes, that was often the

response while the other children listened gleefully and you squirmed, trying to think of a way out of the conundrum.' She turned to Carly. 'As for your question, I can only say that there is no actual law in Eustape that forbids the eating of flesh. It is the Melcran way but it is a choice that each must make alone.' She paused. 'Now tell me about the life of a cartographer. Where did you work before Cynal?'

So we spoke with King Charissa of the many jobs we had taken and the routes we had travelled and she followed our stories with undisguised enthusiasm, insisting we fill our goblets once more with the delicious wine while she questioned us on how well we came to know the places where we worked.

'It depends on the length and type of job,' I replied. 'Obviously the longer the job and the greater the area mapped the greater our familiarity becomes.'

'So, a city like Cynal, where you will be working extensively for several months, you will come to know very well. Perhaps even better than some of the inhabitants,' King Charissa said.

'Not necessarily better,' Alexa argued, 'just differently. What has become old and uninteresting to an inhabitant will be new and fascinating to us and we will fit it into an overall picture that we gain of the city, a picture that is placed alongside the others we hold of the many cities and places we have visited.' She shrugged. 'As a result, coming in from the outside we sometimes notice what the inhabitants are too close to see.'

'Yes,' the king murmured thoughtfully and was quiet for a moment. 'How does Cynal differ from the other cities you have visited? Have you seen or heard anything peculiar while here?'

'Peculiar?' Alexa echoed.

'We had never seen the Mecla before we came to Cynal,' Lilith said.

'And we met the merfolk,' Chandra called brightly.

King Charissa laughed. 'Yes, I know.' She must have seen my eyebrows rise in surprise. 'They often visit Eustape and tell us all sorts of news. We heard all about your games.'

'Oh,' I mouthed silently, wondering if it was to Eustape that the merfolk had fled.

'What I meant by peculiar was anything unusual that did not seem to belong in Cynal, anything or anyone out of place here.' She paused, looking at each of us, then she drew breath, obviously making a decision, for she went on. 'I know Rianne and Lord Tarn have spoken to you of the white panther and Nitma of the Meran. Well, the Melcran too are concerned. Our ways are not the Mecla ways and Cynal is their city but we too would like to hear any news of the Meran or the white panther. Rianne told me of the Melcran journal you found and the map you are drawing. Should you discover anything more, I would like to be informed.'

Alexa shrugged. 'We know nothing.'

'Perhaps not, but as you have said, you will sometimes notice what the inhabitants are too close to see.'

Carly shook her head, her goblet still in hand. 'If this priest Nitma is so much trouble, why not just arrest her?' she asked.

'Two reasons. Firstly, such an action would surely

incite the Meran to rise against us, and secondly, no-one has ever seen Nitma. Her face is unknown to us and we do not know where to find her. Only when she feels confident of victory will she reveal herself to us.'

I heard the door behind us opening and knew Neesha and Captain Varl were returning.

'We'll do what we can,' I promised. 'If we see or hear anything while we're working we will tell you,' then honestly I added, 'but I doubt we will be of much help.'

King Charissa nodded. 'Perhaps, but somewhere, somehow, Nitma will make a mistake. It is up to us to be watching for it.'

The sound of much clinking heralded the arrival of our half payment, divided into five very plump pouches in the hands of Neesha and Captain Varl.

'You are just in time,' King Charissa cried warmly as they stepped up to the couches. 'There is still one flagon of wine left.'

Both grinned and bowed, then Neesha handed us each a pouch. 'Your payment, cartographers.'

'Thank you,' we said.

'A word of advice,' Captain Varl said. 'Do not travel the city with that much coin upon you. Lock away what you do not require at the moment.'

'We will,' we said.

Neesha poured herself and the captain a goblet of wine and they seated themselves. King Charissa turned to us. 'It has been a most pleasant talk, cartographers. I hope you have a good day's work under Cynal's blue skies.'

'Thank you, your majesty,' and we rose to our feet. It was time we began earning the coin we had just been given.

Captain Varl looked up. 'Don't let us disturb you, captain,' I said. 'Enjoy your wine. We know the way back.'

He nodded. We wished good day to Neesha, then bowed again to the king, crossed to the outer door and let ourselves out onto the corridor. Our pouches attached securely to our belts, we turned towards our workroom.

'She is so nice,' Lilith said as we walked along. 'Strong and intelligent and powerful and nice.'

'People are generally nice when they want something,' Carly retorted. 'Either nice or intimidating.'

Alexa looked at her curiously. 'You didn't like her?'

Carly shrugged. 'I don't see what this business with the white panther has to do with us. We're cartographers, not priests, it's no concern of ours and I think we should keep our distance.'

'I don't think we should forget that we're here to draw maps,' I said, 'but if we happen to see anything unusual while we are working, what harm can it do us to tell the Mecla and Melcran as a courtesy?'

'That's a good question, Ashil. What harm indeed? We don't know. The Meran and Lakiya are obviously powerful and we know very little about them. That's how we should leave it.'

'They must have no hunters on Eustape,' Chandra said suddenly, seemingly amazed at the idea, 'and that means they would have no trackers.'

'Or furriers, or fishers,' Alexa added.

'Or parchment,' I gasped. 'What would they draw their maps on?'

'Maybe once an animal is dead, the Melcran don't object to using its skin,' Lilith suggested.

I nodded, considering, and Carly barked a laugh.

'Oh, Ash,' she exclaimed merrily as she threw an arm around my shoulders, 'I should have known better than to think any priest could distract you for long from your one and only love, maps. Nitma need only throw an interesting map of some unknown city or a flawless piece of parchment in your path and she'll be able to walk past you with no fear of being noticed.'

I smiled, accustomed to Carly's teasing. 'I don't think Nitma or any Meran is going to be in the least interested in any cartographer.' I paused. 'No matter how talented.'

Everyone laughed.

'If we're careful and don't take any unneccessary risks,' Alexa said, 'I can't see any harm in doing as we've been asked and keeping our eyes open. I'm curious about this white panther and the Lakiya, yet I can see Carly's viewpoint as well, especially as I feel King Charissa wasn't telling us all she knew.'

Carly nodded. 'It's one set of priests against another and I'm sure there are plenty of secrets being kept by all concerned. I'm staying out of it.'

We had reached the workroom. As I would be working in here alone today, I kept the key.

'We'll leave most of the coin with you, Ash,' Alexa said, untying her pouch. 'It'll be safe in here and if you get the time before we're back you can take it up and lock it in the chest in our apartment.'

'Fine. Have fun,' I said, just as Nikol arrived.

She gave me a friendly wave, then the five of them departed and I turned with a sigh to my workbench and unrolled the Tirayi maps.

Time for work.

THIRTEEN

With no distractions, I worked well and quickly and it was early afternoon when I finally rose from my workbench and eased my cramped muscles. It was too late to eat in the Dining Hall but, wanting to stretch my legs and satisfy the growling in my belly, I deposited our half payment in our apartment then went in search of Baki.

My senses reeled as I entered the kitchen. My nostrils were assaulted by numerous smells, layered upon one another in delicious randomness, causing my mouth to water and my stomach to gurgle in anticipation. The heat from the ovens scorched my skin as I walked past and so great was the variety of food being prepared and the number of servants working that my eyes could not take it all in. Yet, most of all I noticed the noise. After the calm and quiet of the workroom, the chatter of the servants and the sound of utensils rising and falling and the scraping of bowls and plates was both startling and shocking.

Baki saw me and waved, his face alight with good cheer. 'Good day, cartographer,' he called as he approached. 'On your own today, I see.'

I smiled broadly. 'The others are at work in the city, but I had a map to draw here in the palace.'

He nodded. 'It must be engrossing work to have kept you at it so late,' and he leaned towards me and said very seriously, 'and now I bet your poor stomach is protesting because it missed the noontime meal.'

I did not miss the teasing light in his eye and I grinned with delight. 'Yes, and protesting very loudly.'

He straightened. 'That's what we're here for. Take a seat and I'll bring you over some food and we'll see if we can't put to rest those hunger pangs.'

I moved to the same corner table where we had sat on our first visit and settled myself with a happy sigh. A large plate of stew was placed before me and a warm loaf of bread. I inhaled deeply, savouring the aroma.

'It looks good, smells good and tastes good,' Baki said as he pulled out the chair opposite me and lowered his considerable girth into it. He plonked a flagon and two goblets down. 'What craftsperson or artisan can say that about what they create?'

I was in no mood to dispute such a statement and the rich stew was, of course, superb. I gave a low purr of pleasure as I chewed slowly, drawing the flavour from the thick chunks of meat and vegetable.

Baki nodded in satisfaction. 'The greater the hunger, the sweeter the taste.' He reached for the flagon and unstoppered it and made to fill the goblets but I waved a hand at him.

'No wine for me,' I said, swallowing a mouthful. 'I've already had two goblets today and any more on top of this excellent meal will send me to sleep at my workbench.'

'Water then,' and he called to a servant nearby to bring a jug. 'I, however, have yet to taste this batch,' and he poured a small amount of the wine into his own goblet. 'It's just in from one of our better wine-makers. If it's good enough, we'll serve it at the enthroning feast.' He sipped the wine and seemed to roll it about his mouth, then swallowed. 'It is good,' he pronounced very seriously. 'Not good enough for his lordship's table, but it will do for the tables of his lesser guests.' And he replaced the stopper in the flagon.

'Do you have much wine and food ready for the feast?' I asked, murmuring thanks as a servant placed a water jug before me.

'Much?' Baki snorted. 'My storerooms are groaning at the edges and still more arrives. But better too much than not enough. Fortunately I have the finest cooks in all of Cynal working for me.' I noticed several of the servants nearest us look up smiling at his words and I did not doubt that Baki was as popular with his staff as with the soldiers who came to eat in his kitchen. 'It is exciting too, to put together such a grand meal. It is hard work for us all but all challenges have their rewards.'

'I agree with that,' I said emphatically, pouring my water. 'That's why I love my work. Each new job is a challenge and always different from the one before. It makes life thrilling.'

'As long as you don't forget there are other thrills to be had in life besides drawing maps. Now tell me what you have seen of Cynal.'

We talked while I finished the stew, tearing off a

piece of the fresh bread to wipe the last of it from my plate. Then I ended the meal with a crisp red apple Baki took from a passing bowl.

'We are still sketching the south corner of the city,' I said, the apple half-eaten in my hand, 'and as the city fills with celebrators for the enthroning our progress will slow but,' I smiled and shrugged, 'Cynal is so beautiful and welcoming that we will not begrudge a few extra days spent here.'

'I hope . . . ' but Baki got no further with his sentence for one of the servants waved over two dark-haired men in Cynalese uniforms who were carrying a crate filled with wine flagons. They inclined their heads politely to Baki.

'We have ten flagons of wine,' one of them said, 'a gift for Lord Tarn at his enthroning from King Charissa. The captain told us to deliver them directly to you.'

'Very well,' Baki frowned and pushed back his chair. 'I hope you have enjoyed your meal,' he said to me graciously. 'Now I must return to the demands of my kitchen.'

I thanked him and he walked away and led the soldiers through the door that led to the storerooms. Knowing I had drawn well that morning, I did not hurry the last bites of my apple and stayed at the table to finish my drink of water before taking my plate and goblet to a bench and leaving them with a servant.

Instead of turning back to the workroom when I left the kitchen I found myself wandering towards the Great Hall. The huge doors were open and I stepped inside, viewing once more the awesome space and size of the room. It filled me with delight to see it, delight and a soft delicious excitement whenever I thought of the upcoming enthroning.

Today servants were busy removing the silken allies' flags from the walls to wash and dry them so they would gleam brilliantly amidst the candles and lamps of the evening festivities. Others had begun to clean the immense walls. The servants worked with a zeal and jollity that transformed the room from one of toil to one of buzzing energy, for they knew that in a few days time their efforts would be rewarded when they became part of the glamour and jubilance of the celebration dinner.

I dawdled no longer. I had not forgotten that Lilith and I were to have our first fighting lesson with Nikol that evening and there was much I wanted to complete on the northern map before then. Quitting the Great Hall I walked alongside the base of the central staircase. As I drew level with the kitchen entrance, the door opened and the two soldiers who had delivered the wine stepped out. They did not appear to notice me but turned to the left and began making their way towards the long passageway that I would take to the south-west wing.

The passageway was busy with palace traffic but I paid it no heed, for my mind was too busy contemplating exactly how and what Nikol was planning to teach Lil and me. I told myself the uncomfortable twisting in my belly was only eager anticipation and to be expected. I just hoped Lilith and I would not prove too great a challenge for even Nikol's sunny temper.

The two soldiers had paused ahead of me before the

arched opening to the south wing. They were speaking softly but seemed to be deliberating over whether to enter or continue along the passageway. I kept walking, wondering just how heavy a practice sword was and if it was likely to leave my drawing hand blistered, when one of the soldiers called politely to me.

'Excuse me,' he said, smiling abashedly. 'We normally work the city rounds and we've forgotten if it's this archway or the next that leads to the main entrance.'

Wondering how I would ever explain such blisters to the others and if Nikol would allow Lilith and me to wrap our hands before we commenced our lesson, I answered distractedly.

'Ah,' they nodded when I had given them directions. 'Thank you. It is this one we want.' And they passed quickly under the archway.

Perhaps, I thought, Nikol would not even train us with swords. She might decide it was too impractical, with neither Lil nor I ever likely to carry one, and select instead a smaller, more mobile weapon. A dagger, I thought, trying to mentally weigh one in my hand, and wondering how the feel would differ from my single-edged working knife. Or perhaps nothing at all; hands and feet could be weapons all on their own if the right moves were known. With my mind busy pondering each option, I came to the south-west wing and left the passage, following the now familiar twists and turns of smaller walkways until I was once more at the workroom.

The northern map, though by no means a difficult task, did require my full attention and diligence, so for the rest of the afternoon I was able to put Nikol and the impending lesson from my head and immerse myself in the spreading lines of ink before me. I was still busily drawing when the other four returned.

Alexa peered over my shoulder and clapped me on the back. 'You've done well,' she said. 'The map looks more than halfway finished.'

I smiled. Alexa always had a positive word to say. 'How was your day?' I asked.

Chandra pulled out her mapping sheets and spread them on the workbench beside me. 'We too had a busy day. We've covered the entire baseline,' and she pointed to her rough sketches showing the mass of triangles jutting out from the original line Lilith and I had drawn.

'That's wonderful,' I said, bending over the sheets, my eyes tracing the new work. I straightened, glancing back at the northern map, and calculated. 'I should be able to rejoin you either tomorrow afternoon or, at the latest, the following morning.'

'Good,' Chandra replied. 'All is going well.'

'Yes,' Carly answered brightly, 'and that always makes me hungry. Why don't we eat in the Dining Hall tonight? They'll begin serving soon and my mouth is watering at the thought.'

Alexa and Chandra murmured agreement but Lil glanced hastily at me. 'Go ahead,' I said. 'I had a late meal with Baki and I'm far from hungry. I'll tidy up here and copy Chandra's notes. I might have something to eat later.'

'I'm not all that hungry either,' Lilith added, turning from me to the other three. 'I'll eat later with Ash.'

362

Carly and Chandra accepted our statements without question and quickly put away their kits and packs and crossed to the door, but Alexa gave us both a curious look. She paused, as though considering whether to speak. 'We'll be in the Dining Hall if you need us,' she said eventually. Then she too unloaded her kit and joined Carly and Chandra as they left the room.

Lilith gave a deep sigh of relief. 'We won't be able to plead lack of hunger every night.'

'No,' I agreed, 'or we'll starve.'

Lilith grinned, then, after a moment, her expression grew serious. 'I've been nervous all day,' she confessed, 'wondering what Nikol has planned for us.'

'So have I. We just have to remember why we are doing this and that it was we who asked Nikol to help and she has agreed to teach us as a favour.'

'I know,' Lilith said in a small voice. 'It's just that when I think of all those strong, eager recruits who want to be soldiers and then I think of us, my stomach quivers inside.'

I gave her a gentle nudge. 'We're young and healthy and determined. How hard can it be?' When Lilith did not reply immediately, I frowned and asked her to help me with my notes.

Before long, the notes were copied and the benches were tidy and Lilith and I had no further excuse to keep us from our meeting with Nikol. Taking deep breaths, we squared our shoulders and set out.

We left the palace and walked along the path before the stables, speaking quietly. As we drew near to green stable we heard the sound of horses trotting towards us and saw ahead of us King Charissa, mounted on her magnificent black stallion, returning from a ride. Beside her, one of her equerries was riding the chestnut mare. The king reached the stable and dismounted, leading the stallion inside, and the equerry followed with the mare. Two guards followed them in while the rest stood attentively at the door.

'King Charissa is certainly very diligent about exercising her horses,' Lilith said.

'She probably enjoys it,' I replied, recalling with a guilty twinge that I had not taken Lukar out that day.

'I don't think I'd like to be king,' Lilith said. 'You'd never be able to feel totally rested or safe or carefree and you would never know the satisfaction of walking away from a completed job because there would always be another task to take care of, another problem to solve, another battle to win in your kingdom.'

'Well, don't fret, Lil,' I said with some amusement. 'Unless there have been some amazing changes at the Plaza of the City Guardians, I doubt you have much to worry about.'

'Don't you understand?' she went on. 'It would be like a heavy cloak you could never take off. I'd feel weighed down.'

I shrugged, looking back towards the Eustapean soldiers before the stable door. 'The weight might make some stand taller, become stronger. Just as some people are suited to being outstanding cartographers, others are suited to ruling. Most are raised to it and there must be a lot of satisfaction in knowing you've made life better for your subjects or averted a catastrophe. As for the fact it's never-ending, that's just life. There's always going to be another good day and another bad day

364

ahead of you, however you earn your coin.'

Lilith smiled a little. 'Would you like to be king?'

'No,' I admitted, giving a little laugh. 'I'd be neither a good diplomat nor a good politician, but I can understand the attraction of power. The danger is when the love of power becomes greater than the love for the people.'

Lilith turned away to look out over the garden. 'I'd fear being asked to do more than I was capable of,' she murmured softly, 'and failing all those people.'

'You'd learn though,' I argued, 'as with everything. Remember your earliest attempts to draw?' I chuckled. 'I'm sure there were moments when my father despaired of ever having a cartographer for a daughter.' Lilith nodded, smiling. 'Now, we search for challenges, for jobs that are demanding, hard, and we think nothing of it.'

'Yes,' Lil said quietly, 'I suppose every sword-wielding champion started as a raw recruit under a more talented instructor.'

I gave her a quick sideways look and she grinned back. I smiled too. 'Exactly. Just think, even Nikol was once inept.'

'But not for long, I'm sure.'

We had long ago left the stables behind and passed the south-west tower, turning eastward along the path. The smithy was quiet now, its rooms dark, as the sun sank slowly in the west. Before us, torch-lighters weaved from torch to torch along the path edge, touching the tallow-soaked flax with their own fiery brands, leaving a blazing trail behind them as they moved quickly on. There was still some traffic at the main gate, so Lilith and I kept back, as close to the garden's edge as we could, our eyes peering forward, searching for Nikol amongst the muted activity of the training ground.

The torch-lighters had got there before us, so the training ground was rimmed with bright flickering light. To one side, speaking casually with another soldier, stood Nikol. She saw us approaching and waved. Her face was slightly flushed and sweat had dampened the edges of her curls around her forehead and cheeks. Both she and the other soldier held wooden practice swords. I glanced at Lil one final time and we strode forward.

'Good evening, Nikol,' we called, coming towards her, just as her friend excused herself and left.

'Good evening, Ashil, Lilith,' she replied cheerily. 'Ready to begin?'

We nodded.

'First, we need to warm and stretch your muscles. It will make it easier for you to work and keep them from being too stiff in the morning. I'm already warm from practice, but I'll run around the edge of the training ground with you.'

She propped the wooden sword against the wall and moved into a slow, easy run, beginning to head around the outer edge of the ground. After a moment's hesitation, Lilith and I copied her, our sandals crunching the shells and pebbles underneath, our arms swinging forward and back beside our bodies as our legs stretched out beneath us. After completing the first lap I was feeling sufficiently warm, but Nikol kept going, giving Lilith and me no choice but to follow. After the second lap, sweat began to trickle between my shoulderblades and on the third and, thankfully, final lap my breathing was coming shallow and fast.

Stopping to wait for us to finish the third lap, Nikol looked relaxed and seemed no more tired than when she had begun. She nodded approvingly when Lilith and I finally ran up to her.

'Well done,' she said. 'Cartography keeps you in good shape. Now, we'll stretch.' When she spoke her voice was even and unstrained, her breathing easy.

The stretches were a relief after the exertion of the run and I rose from them with my breathing normal once more and my muscles feeling pleasantly loose.

'To begin with, we'll work without weapons,' Nikol said. 'You need to understand the power in your own bodies first. We'll start with your arms. Ashil, I want you to step up and try to hit me.'

Clearly, I looked as stunned as I felt by such a request.

Nikol laughed. 'You won't be able to hurt me,' she assured me. 'Now try.'

I stepped up to Nikol and made a rather half-hearted attempt at hitting her jaw. She swatted my hand away effortlessly.

'No, Ashil,' she told me, frowning. 'You're here to learn and it means you must have faith in my ability as a teacher, so when I tell you to do something, do it properly. Now hit me again, hard.'

Rebuked, I faced her again and raised my hand to strike, feeling extremely uncomfortable with both the action and the intent, but I did as she had told me, swinging my hand forward to slap her face, hard. My hand got nowhere near her face. Instead it was deflected neatly by her forearm and the elbow of her other arm swung forward and up, striking my chest, her closed fist beside her own jaw. The blow was not meant to hurt, but I grunted and staggered back a step, rubbing the spot, knowing that tomorrow I would have a bruise there.

'That's what I am going to teach you. How to land a quick, hard blow that will knock over your opponent and let you escape. You don't look like soldiers and you're not the type who seek out trouble, so the sort of people who pick a fight with you will be looking for a bit of fun and an easy win. They won't be expecting you to retaliate with much skill. I'm going to show you how to look for an opening and deliver your blow so you can escape as fast as you can. With speed and surprise, you should be able to get away.'

Nikol paused and looked at us. 'If that's what you want to do,' she added, 'because there can be reasons for staying with a fight. You may be cornered and unable to escape, your companions may be under attack and in need of you, or you may wish to capture or kill your opponent.'

Lilith's eyes widened and I pulled a slight face.

'Let's begin with the move I just made. I'll do it slowly and you follow me.'

We stood facing Nikol, imitating her movements, stepping forward with the left leg and swinging with the right arm. 'Raise your left arm while you move forward, Lilith. It'll protect your chest from any blows.

'That's good, Ashil, but the fist should be lightly clenched and tuck your thumb in or you'll break it.

'Remember to aim your blow beyond your opponent, both of you. It will give the blow greater strength.'

From that simple, as Nikol referred to it, movement, we moved onto others. All of them appeared easy and straightforward when Nikol demonstrated them, but were awkward and difficult when it was time for us to attempt them. Lilith and I worked hard, hitting and bending and twisting and thrusting with all our might, mercilessly assaulting our imaginary foes. Nikol corrected and encouraged us, letting us feint towards her body to get the feel of a true opponent, all the while explaining why one move was better than another and how another, if done incorrectly, could do more damage to ourselves than any adversary.

When Nikol finally called an end to the lesson, my arms were burning with fatigue, I had no energy left, and I had never felt so exhausted. Yet I was grinning ecstatically. I felt wonderful. Just let any foe jump from behind a tree as Lilith and I walked back to the palace and they would soon regret it. We might not look like soldiers but we knew how to protect ourselves.

Nikol took one look at our proud faces.

'A word of caution,' she said. 'Sometimes after a recruit has had a few lessons, she becomes eager to try out her new fighting skills and goes looking for an opportunity. She picks a fight, gets beaten and becomes badly demoralised and believes she will never make a good soldier. You're both quick to learn and enthusiastic, but you still need more lessons before you can feel confident of surviving an attack. For the moment, keep your new skills to yourselves. Practise if you like, but do it privately.' She grinned at our sobering faces. 'I'll let you know when you're ready to challenge the Cynalese champion. Now when do you want your next lesson? Tomorrow evening?'

Lilith and I nodded.

'Good,' and she leant to pick up her practice sword. 'I'll see you both then. Make sure you wash the sweat off.'

'Thank you, Nikol,' I said. 'We appreciate the time you are giving us.'

'Ah,' she chuckled, 'it's a pleasure. Perhaps one day I'll be glad I trained you both.'

Lilith and I walked with Nikol to the edge of the training ground, then waved goodbye to her as she turned towards the barracks.

Once we were back inside the palace we climbed the staircase to our empty apartment where we stripped and washed. Feeling extremely pleased with ourselves, we dressed quickly and left the apartment once more, our spirits high, intending to treat ourselves to a fine meal.

FOURTEEN

I HAD NEVER known such agony, not even when I had sliced open my thumb, nearly severing it, while cutting parchment as an apprentice. Then blood had flowed thickly and I had paled at the ferocity of the pain, but this was a hundred times worse. I idly rubbed the thick scar on my left thumb, thinking that now it was one of the few parts of my body not burning with pain. I rolled over and groaned softly as the effort set more muscles alight. Evidently Nikol's theory about warming and stretching our muscles was flawed. Stiff and tortured beyond belief, I groaned again and sat up. When I remembered that we had another lesson that night I groaned again, louder.

Across from me in the other bed, Alexa raised herself on one arm and asked, 'What's wrong?'

I almost confessed the truth, then I recalled it was a secret. 'My stomach hurts,' I replied. 'It must have been the fish I ate last night.'

Alexa frowned. 'Do you want anything? A drink of water?'

'No, I'll be fine.'

'You sounded awful. Are you well enough to work?'

'Oh,' I gasped, for I hadn't thought of that, 'I'm not that bad.'

Alexa grinned and threw back her blanket, climbing from bed. 'No, of course not. It would take much more than a stomach cramp to keep a stylus from your hand.'

I smiled back weakly. Even my neck muscles ached. 'Did Lilith eat the same fish as you?'

'I think so,' I muttered, realising how difficult it was to maintain a lie and how I detested doing so.

Alexa drew on her robe. 'Then she might be feeling the same.'

Thinking it more than likely, I nodded.

Alexa stepped closer to my bed. 'Do you feel like breakfast?' she asked considerately. 'I can bring some in.'

'No need.' I shook my head, her concern making me feel even more deceitful. 'I'm sure I'll feel better once I'm on my feet.' Gingerly, I swung my legs over the side of the bed. It hurt but I refused to utter another groan in Alexa's company, so I ignored the pain and stood up. I even managed another weak smile. 'I'll just have bread and fruit,' I told her, 'and by mid-morning I'm certain I'll be feeling fine again.'

'All right,' Alexa said. 'But if you become worse, leave the map and come up here and lie down.'

'I will,' I promised.

One look at Lilith's drawn face at the breakfast table was enough to tell me that she too was suffering, though not from the malady Alexa told Chandra and Carly afflicted us. They were all very sympathetic and it was only because Lilith insisted that she was fit for work that they allowed her to accompany them shortly afterwards when they left for the city.

Poor Lil, I thought, as I wished them a good day's sketching. They would all be watching her so carefully for any sign of illness that she would be forced to move and act as though nothing plagued her. In the safety and solitude of the workroom, I would be under no such restrictions and could give voice to my discomfort when and how it suited.

In truth, concentrating on the northern map kept my mind from dwelling on the state of my body, and so it was with a satisfied sigh that I put my stylus down in the early hours of the afternoon, the completed map lying before me. I stretched, and groaned. The stiffness was still there, though it had eased a little since the morning, but I was too pleased with the map to be bothered by it. Clipping the map to the drying bench, I began to collect and tidy my equipment, humming softly to myself. I would let the map dry, then take it to the north wing and leave it for Lord Tarn. He would be pleased with it, I was sure.

When the ink was dry to touch, I unclipped the map and left the workroom with it, locking the door behind me. I remembered Alexa had said Lord Tarn's study was on the ground floor and it was there I headed, intending to leave the map with one of his staff. I was stopped and politely questioned when I reached the entrance to the north wing and once again I waited while a message was sent on ahead. The wait was longer this time and when the soldier did return he surprised me by leading me not to Lord Tarn's study but up the stairs to the first floor.

It was very quiet here, compared to the buzz and activity in the rest of the palace. The few servants we did see seemed to glide past silently and all was cool and very proper. The rooms were elegant and stately, their walls covered with impressive paintings depicting scenes from Cynalese history. I felt awed by my surroundings. It was so clearly a place for the powerful and influential to meet to discuss important matters and be entertained by Cynal's ruler that I wondered what I was doing here. After all, I had only come to deliver a map.

My guide had not spoken another word since we had climbed the stairs and the hushed, sober atmosphere kept me from questioning him on where I was being taken. I would know soon enough, I supposed.

As we traversed an extremely long hallway, servants came up behind us carrying tray after tray of delicious-smelling courses. The scent filled my nostrils and I hoped I would be free of the map soon for, thanks to my tale of deception that morning, I had been forced to take only a light breakfast. Now the map was completed I desired nothing more than a large, filling meal before I rejoined the others. Stepping aside to let the servants pass, I wondered if Baki would be happy to see me a second day in a row.

At the end of the hallway the servants ahead of us disappeared to the left. Moments later, my guide and I too turned that way, though the servants and their mouth-watering banquet were no longer in sight. Instead I saw a closed, guarded door and I was pleased to note that this was our destination, for my guide crossed to it and knocked lightly. The door was opened by a soldier and we entered.

Inside, the trays of food were now tantalisingly arranged on a side table and the servants were standing beside them, ready to serve. A long, wide gleaming table was at the centre of the room with places set for two though, as yet, there was no sign of the diners. Thinking they had better hurry if they wished to taste the food at its best, I turned to my guide, to ask who we were waiting for, when the door opened behind me. Finally, I thought, spinning around.

Of course, I should have known; the servants, the extensive array of food, the soldiers, it all suggested royalty, but until that moment when Lord Tarn and his escort stepped through the door I had not suspected it was him I was to meet. It was a surprise but by no means an unwelcome one, for once again the sight of him filled me with pure delight. I flushed with pleasure and smiled and I saw the way his eyes changed from brown to deep black and his face lightened on seeing me. Breathless, I dropped into a bow, murmuring, deliciously, his name.

His escort halted inside the door but Lord Tarn came forward until he was but a hand's distance from me. Then, his touch gentle yet firm on my arm, he lifted me up so that we stood facing one another, my face raised to him, his head bent to me.

'Have you eaten, Ashil?' he asked, very softly, so that no other could hear.

The question was so unexpected and the warmth of his hand against my flesh was so wonderful and the depths of his eyes so mesmerising that I gave a small, surprised, light-headed laugh.

'No, Lord, I haven't.'

He grinned and I wondered if he was aware that his thumb had begun to ever so delicately caress my skin, sending chill-bumps along my arm.

'Good,' he murmured, his eyes warm and intent, 'then we can dine together.'

At that moment I could think of nothing I would rather do, so as he moved towards the table, his hand still lightly caressing my arm, I walked beside him, trying to calm my frantically beating heart.

Ahead of us, two servants moved towards chairs but Lord Tarn paid them no attention. 'I was dealing with some unwelcome news when I was told a cartographer bearing the northern map I had requested had come to the north wing to deliver it,' he told me, smiling. I nodded, noting the small scar on his top lip pull taut. I wondered how he had got it. 'I knew it would be you.' I met his eye and after a short pause he looked away. 'I suspected that, just as I had stayed at my workbench during the noontime meal, you too had been busy in your workroom putting the final touches to your map. The thought of putting aside my troublesome affairs for a short while and dining in such pleasant company was too tempting and I instructed the kitchen to prepare a meal for two.'

Colour rose in my cheeks. This had all been arranged because he wanted to see me, be with me. The colour deepened as I felt his dark eyes return to my face. This time it was I who looked away. For although the hot delight was still there, as keen and pervasive as before, it was now arrayed beside the fact of his rank and my own inexperience. Confused, but feeling I should reply in some way, I resorted to propriety.

'You honour me, Lord,' I told him in little more than a whisper.

We had reached the table and the servants held the chairs for us but Lord Tarn did not sit. Instead he turned to face me fully, a frown etched deeply upon his brow. 'I hope it is not just that, Ashil,' he protested, his voice low and intense. 'I hope it is much more. I enjoy your company and I hope that you enjoy mine.'

Of that there was no question, though I knew life was rarely so simple. Yet, I thought, we are only sharing a meal and what harm could come from being honest with him, as he had with me? The rest I would deal with later, if necessary. His gaze had not wavered from my face and for a moment I wished he would not look so seriously, so penetratingly at me.

I tilted my head back and moistened my lips. 'I too enjoy your company very much, Lord,' I said honestly, 'and could think of no-one else I would rather dine with.'

He nodded, very pleased, and exhaled as though a great tension was leaving him. 'Then let us eat,' he said.

Lord Tarn sat and a servant relieved me of the northern map that I still carried, rather limply, then drew out my chair for me and saw me comfortably seated before withdrawing to resume his position beside the side table.

As though this was a signal for the other servants, they suddenly became animated, bringing a wine flagon to fill our goblets and carrying platters of food to the table, pausing first at Lord Tarn's shoulder and then at mine so we could select from the bounteous offerings. When we had taken our share and the aroma had once again stirred my appetite, Lord Tarn dismissed everyone, quickly and quietly. Without a word, the servants left, followed by the guards, who closed the door behind them. For the first time, Lord Tarn and I were alone.

Feeling strangely unprepared for this, yet also wanting it desperately to proceed, I darted an anxious glance at the man on my left. A meal was a long time not to make a fool of one's self. Following his example, I took my first mouthful.

'How are you enjoying Cynal, Ashil?' he asked casually as he reached for his goblet.

It was the sort of question any new acquaintance might ask and it calmed me considerably. I smiled a little at my own silly fears. 'We are all enjoying it very much, Lord,' I replied. 'It is a lovely city and we have been made to feel very welcome.' I was proud of myself. This was not so hard after all.

Lord Tarn nodded. 'Does it compare favourably with other cities you have visited?'

'Indeed, Lord,' I replied with enthusiasm. 'Cynal is prettier than most, the people are very friendly and, of course, you have the merfolk. No city they visit so freely can be all that bad.'

He raised an eyebrow at me and for one horrible moment I thought he had taken offence at my glib words. Then slowly he smiled.

'You are right, Ashil, sometimes the merfolk divine more clearly good and evil than many mortals.' What was the shadow I saw in his eyes? 'In all,' he murmured, 'I think Cynal is a good city.'

'Of course, Lord,' I said with much feeling, and a protesting frown as I struggled to understand. 'I did not mean to suggest otherwise. Your people are happy, they smile often, they are free. Cynal is a city to be proud of.'

'Free and happy,' he repeated, his smile askew, his eyes on his wine. 'How well you have put it.'

We ate for a moment in silence, I puzzled, and Lord Tarn clearly immersed in thoughts other than cartography and cartographers. Then, as though determined to throw off his queer mood, he sat back, straightening his broad shoulders and spoke brightly.

'So tell me all about your family, Ashil. Where were you born?'

The question was a simple one to answer and I welcomed the chance for easy, diverting conversation. I was not so vain or self-seeking that I desired his attention and thoughts to be fully on me all the time, but I did want for him to forget the trials of leadership for a short while, and relax like any common person. For that reason, I was glad to follow his change of topic.

'I was born in Binet, Lord,' I told him. 'My father is also a cartographer and my mother is a financier and I have a younger brother, Thoma.'

He was watching me closely, now, keen to note my responses and expressions. 'Do you miss them?'

'Ah, always, Lord,' I confessed, grinning. 'Almost, I'm sure, as much as they miss me.'

He chuckled. The earlier dark mood had lifted from us both. 'You are close then, it is easy to see.'

'Yes, Lord,' I agreed simply. There was no need to say more.

He nodded and seemed about to ask me something, then changed his mind. When he did speak it was to ask if it was because of my father that I became interested in cartography.

'Yes, it was, Lord,' and my face lit with pleasure as I remembered. 'He works for the army in Binet, and when I was young I would follow him to the army base and shadow his every move. I was fascinated by his maps, I loved the feel of the skins and the cold, wet smell of the inks and the shiny hardness of the styluses and tools. At first, when I was very young, he would tolerate my questions and exclamations for a little while. Then, needing to work himself, he would hand me a scrap of parchment and an old stylus and ink and send me off to a corner to entertain myself while he attended to his own drawing. I loved it and would sit happily drawing for hours, creating my own little maps. The other cartographers would come and admire them, letting me settle the ink with their sand shakers and offering me advice that I as a child took very seriously.

'Later, when I was older, I would go to the workroom after school and my father would give me old maps to copy, briefly explaining how best to copy and how to match the measurements. Occasionally, I was allowed to accompany him when he rode out to sketch, and I would help him with his notes.' I shrugged. 'It did not come as a surprise to anyone that I asked my father for a job when I left school. I studied and worked under him right up until I left Binet. My plan then was to see and map as much of the world as I could.'

'And how much of the world have you seen?' he asked.

'Not nearly enough, Lord.'

He smiled. 'Tell me.'

'Our first three positions were with landowners to the west of Binet. Then we visited Delawyn and were there only a short while before we were offered work by the Loban. Once we had finished the priests' map we went south to work for Lord Maltra in Nalym and then on to the caravans of the Tamina. We stopped at Binet to see Lilith's and my family before coming on to Cynal.'

'The other three are not from Binet?'

'No, Lord. Chandra is from a nomad tribe, Carly is from Netla, though she was living in Sach. I don't know where Alexa was born, she rarely speaks of her past.'

He considered this, his eyes falling to my plate. Seeing it was still half-full, he raised an eyebrow. 'I must let you eat. I didn't invite you to dine with me so that you could leave still feeling hungry.'

I nodded happily and took another mouthful, continuing to eat in silence until my plate was nearly empty. Putting down my knife, my hunger assuaged, I said, 'You have very skilled cooks, Lord.'

He laughed softly. It was a lovely sound to hear. 'Yes, but I imagine Lord Maltra in Nalym can claim the same.'

Thinking of Nalym, I frowned. 'Except those that work for you, Lord, do so from choice, not because they are slaves.'

Lord Tarn's face grew instantly serious and his voice sobered. 'You are right, Ashil. Slavery is abhorrent to everything my father and ancestors have ever fought for to make Cynal strong. It is only when your freedom is threatened that you come to appreciate how greatly you value it and how fiercely you will fight to protect it.'

A little startled by the gravity of his answer, I recalled the conversation Lilith and I had had the day before about kingship and its duties. Uncertain as to whether it was proper to question him in such a way, but curious to know his answer, I asked Lord Tarn if he wanted to be king.

'Yes, Ashil, very much,' he replied, not at all annoyed. 'Like you I was encouraged from an early age, in my case to study the skills and responsibilities of kingship. My father was a good king and a wonderful teacher. He taught me that ruling can be a challenge, a delight and, at times,' he nodded, 'an unbelievable horror. The Cynalese people are easy to love and I want to be their king and do all I can to keep Cynal safe and the people, as you said, free and happy.'

I watched him in silence for a moment, admiring him.

'I think you will be a great king, Lord,' I whispered softly.

'Thank you, Ashil. I will certainly be off to a good start if I bring to my duties half the enthusiasm you show for your maps.'

My cheeks tingled, pinkening, and, to cover my embarrassment, I reached for my goblet.

'Where do you plan to work after Cynal?' he asked me, lifting up his own goblet.

I shook my head. 'It will depend on what offers we receive, Lord. We haven't made any plans yet. This job is quite long, so we won't sign another contract until the maps of Cynal are almost completed, just in case there are any delays or extensions.'

'I see. And when you have had enough of travelling and mapping, does the tie to your family mean you plan one day to return and settle in Binet?'

'No,' I answered immediately, without pausing to think. Then I stopped to consider just what I meant. I opened my mouth and shut it again. 'I do not know, Lord,' I finally admitted. 'I have not planned that far ahead. I will continue to work and travel until it no longer holds me. Then,' I shrugged weakly, not yet able to foresee such a day, 'I will see.'

'Have you never been tempted yet to stay a little longer, to dwell in this strange, unknown place, and forget your maps for a while?'

'Never, Lord,' I answered truthfully. 'For who knows how exciting and wonderful the next place will be?' I opened my hands. 'Tirayi is so very large, I think it will always draw me on.'

He stared at me for a moment, a long, hard look, then turned from me. 'Perhaps one day it will be different,' he said, his tone very even.

'Perhaps, Lord,' I agreed, though I did not care to dwell on such thoughts. 'Who can tell the future?'

He smiled slightly and looked back at me. 'The Mecla believe that we sow the seeds of the future in the present, Ashil.'

'Yes, Lord,' I nodded, 'but we still cannot see how well they will take root.'

His eyes flicked over my face, my skin, my eyes, my mouth and finally lingered on my hair.

'No,' he said slowly, 'you are right. We cannot.'

I had gone very still and he must have noticed for he sat back and drew a deep breath. 'Are you still hungry, Ashil? I noticed some splendid desserts on the side tables but I'm afraid we must serve ourselves.'

I welcomed the change in mood and topic. 'Yes, Lord,' I replied, 'dessert sounds very tempting.'

'Good,' and he stood up. 'Let's see what there is.'

I stood also and we walked to where the dishes were laid out, picking up plates and filling them with the sweet fruits and pastries. Before we returned to the table, Lord Tarn paused to pick up the northern map that the servant had placed to one side of the food trays. He laid the map beside his place as we reseated ourselves at the table and began to eat.

'Have you or your friends seen or heard anything more of the white panther since we last spoke?'

I licked away a spot of sweet syrup from my lips. 'No, Lord, we have heard nothing.'

He gave a brief nod and pursed his lips thoughtfully as he unrolled the map. He stared at it for a long time in silence, his eyes travelling over every section absorbedly. Finally, he rolled it up and glanced at me.

'It is good, Ashil,' he complimented, 'very good, your skill is evident.'

'Thank you, Lord,' I murmured.

He put the map to one side and continued. 'Such skill is one of the reasons I have thought about employing resident cartographers in Cynal. Scribes, though comfortable with the stylus, are not familiar with the intricacies of sketching and drawing.'

'Yes, Lord,' I agreed wholeheartedly. Too numerous

were the times I had been forced to explain that, though I dealt with stylus and ink, I was not a scribe. Too often my explanation met with blank, uncomprehending faces.

'Perhaps you could offer some advice on how best to set up a cartography base in Cynal.'

I opened my eyes wide and grinned. 'It would be a pleasure, Lord.'

'A pleasure,' he repeated, contemplating me. 'You say it with such enthusiasm, Ashil. You must be a joy to work with, you are so naturally cheerful.'

Thrilled and embarrassed, I was saved from answering when a soldier knocked on the door and entered on Lord Tarn's command. She walked forward and bowed.

'The others are assembled, Lord.'

'Ah,' he nodded, 'good.' Then he smiled at me. 'It has been delightful dining with you, Ashil, but I must leave you now. Think about what I have said about cartographers for Cynal.' He rose and paused, turning back to me. 'And it would please me, Ashil, if you would join me at the royal table for the enthroning celebrations.'

Mute with shock, I could only nod, but he seemed content with that and left the room. Alone at the table, I was finally able to release the breath I did not know I had been holding.

I had no difficulty finding the others in the city, though I was surprised to see their numbers swelled by the presence of both Lindsa and Demran.

As I rode towards them, Carly came forward to meet me, Lindsa at her side.

'What's in the package, Ashil?'

I dismounted and, facing Lukar, fiddled with my kit. 'I stopped at the market and bought an outfit for the enthroning.'

'Ah,' Carly purred, stepping around so she could see my face, 'something gorgeous to tantalise Lord Tarn with,' she taunted softly.

'No,' I protested hotly and she laughed.

'Of course not, Ash. It's Damin you're trying to impress, isn't it?'

'I'm not trying to impress anyone,' I explained. 'I simply didn't have anything suitable to wear. I lost all my clothes with Cleo and the replacements I bought in Binet are too informal. I can't embarrass myself or our group by attending the enthroning poorly dressed.'

'Too informal!' Carly exclaimed, feigning surprise. 'I thought you bought some lovely plain evening shifts in Binet.' She smiled wickedly. 'Won't they do?'

She did not even quaver under the dark look I gave her so I decided if she would not let the topic alone, I would change it, and I turned to the blonde sailor by her side.

'Hello, Lindsa.'

'Hello, Ashil. Did you get your map finished?'

'Yes, I did, finished and delivered.'

Noting an alarming glint in Carly's eye, I made to move on, but I was not quick enough, for Carly fell in beside me.

'Who did you deliver the map to?' she asked, ever so casually.

I waved at Alexa, Lilith and Rarnald, who were working beyond a crossroad a little way down the street.

'I took it to the north wing,' I replied.

Carly nodded. 'And who did you give it to?'

I stopped walking and looked at her. She was alight with mischief and I knew it was useless trying to keep it from her.

'I gave it to Lord Tarn, Carly, and we ate together.'

'Ash!' she cried excitedly, slapping me on the shoulder. 'Now, you've impressed me.'

'It was just a meal.'

She calmed down and nodded. 'Of course, it was. After all, Lord Tarn eats several times a day. It means nothing to be invited to join him.' She grinned and hugged me close. 'I hope the outfit is suitably stunning.'

'What outfit?' Chandra asked, beaming, coming over with Demran.

'One I bought for the enthroning celebration,' I answered succinctly. 'Good afternoon, Demran.'

Demran grinned. Like Chandra he seemed full of barely suppressed excitement, as though he was having difficulty staying in the one spot. He looked torn between bursting into song and dashing off on a mad, crazy run.

'Good afternoon, Ashil,' he replied, making the three words resound with happiness. 'Have you had a pleasant day?'

Carly guffawed and looked away. Both Chandra and Demran frowned quizzically and gazed at me.

'I've had a lovely day, thank you,' I said, ignoring Carly. 'And now I'm ready to work. Who should I help?'

'We've established a point on the western edge of the crossroad,' Chandra told me, pointing to the long stake stuck in the ground beside a squat house. 'Alexa and Lilith are measuring to the north of the crossroad. Rarnald is helping them. Carly and I have been working on this side with Demran and Lindsa.'

I looked at the sailor and the musician. 'New recruits?' I asked brightly.

Demran laughed. 'Only for the afternoon. This evening I revert to being a musician.'

'He is going to play in our rooms tonight,' Chandra told me proudly, her eyes aglitter.

'Wonderful,' I exclaimed. 'I'll look forward to it. What about you, Lindsa?' I questioned. 'What do you think of cartography?'

She laughed loudly. 'I'm not too sure about cartography but I like cartographers,' and she looked directly at Carly, her gaze warm and intimate. Turning back to me, she explained, 'I only came over to talk to Carly, but before I knew it she had handed me a piece of knotted rope and told me where to stand with it. All I wanted was to ask her out tonight.'

I slanted an amused look at Carly. 'Well I hope she has something suitably stunning to wear.'

Carly grinned and shook her head. 'There's no need, Ashil, we've decided to stay and listen to Demran play in our apartment.' Then she tugged the measuring rope Lindsa held in her hand. 'Let's get back to it, it will be dusk soon,' and the two of them walked off.

Chandra touched my arm. 'Come and have a look at my mapping sheets, Ashil. There's something I want to show you.'

She began to speak of the day's work as I walked alongside her and Demran, who, to judge by the expression on his face, seemed more than content to just follow us, listening to Chandra speak.

As we neared the crossroad, Alexa broke away from Lilith and Rarnald.

'Did you complete the map, Ashil?' she called as she approached.

'Yes, this afternoon. Lord Tarn has it.'

'Good. Was he pleased with it?'

'Very,' I said, as she reached me. I stopped while Chandra and Demran walked on to collect the mapping sheets. 'He wanted to discuss setting up a cartography base here but was interrupted. I don't know how he manages to concentrate on so many things at once.'

Alexa nodded. 'He's a smart man. Did he say anything about the Meran?'

'No. He only asked if we'd heard anything.'

She nodded again, her eyes falling on Chandra and Demran chatting absorbedly together.

I followed her gaze. 'You've had plenty of company this afternoon, I see.'

'Yes,' she smiled at me. 'Lindsa came upon us while we ate and Demran decided to take a stroll through Cynal when he stumbled upon us.'

'A stroll,' I gasped. 'Isn't he staying at Regi's?'

'Yes.'

'He walked all this way?' We were leagues from Regi's place.

'Yes,' Alexa chuckled.

I shook my head in disbelief. 'He must be exhausted.'

Alexa grinned. 'I think "stumbling" upon us has

more than removed any vestiges of fatigue. And how are you feeling?' she asked, regarding me closely. 'Lil's much better.'

'So am I,' I assured her hastily. 'I feel fine now.'

'Good,' she nodded, then glanced back to Lilith and Rarnald. 'I'd better go back. We want to reach the next point before the light goes.'

She left and I joined Chandra and Demran and checked over the calculations on her sheets. Despite the arrival of the musician and sailor, progress was good. Keeping to this pace, we should have no trouble fulfilling our contract and delivering the maps on time. I handed the last of the sheets back to Chandra and opened my kit. No trouble, provided, of course, all went as planned and nothing untoward happened to delay us.

In the calm of the late afternoon, with the sun caressing my skin and the cool breeze tangy with salt, such a thought seemed almost farcical.

FIFTEEN

ONCE THE DAY'S mapping was completed, we gathered by the crossroad and discussed our plans for the evening. Demran explained that he would have to return to Regi's to collect his gitar, and he wondered if Chandra would care to join him for a meal there, alone. Regi, it appeared, would be out for the evening. Chandra agreed instantly and she and Demran rode off on Bragan, both glowing with happiness, having promised to return to the apartment after their meal so Demran could perform.

Realising there was no need to hurry back to the apartment, Lindsa invited Carly for a swim. Carly grinned and handed me her pack and, hauling Lindsa onto Flir's back, they rode off together.

So it was only Alexa, Lilith, Rarnald and me who turned homewards towards the palace. Traffic had been increasing each day as the enthroning grew closer, so we moved at a slow, easy pace through the busy streets, chatting idly. Alexa was saying she wanted to visit the library before Demran arrived to see if anything more had been discovered on the Lakiya. Beside her, Rarnald was listening attentively, not wanting to miss a single word Alexa spoke.

When we were nearing another, larger, crossroad I had to quickly pull Lukar back as a cart came rumbling around the corner, drawn by two very enthusiastic mules, no doubt aware they were heading home and keen to be where there was food and rest. The driver gave me a wave of thanks and the cart passed by. I patted Lukar and looked up to see how far ahead the other three were. Not far, about fifty paces, but already on the other side of the crossroad. I touched my heels to Lukar's side and moved forward, scanning the crowd for the fastest route through, only to stop suddenly in shock, for there, walking not twenty paces from me, a stranger upon her back, was Cleo.

As I looked again closely, I saw that the dark-haired, olive-skinned man was in fact familiar, though I could not think where I had seen him before. His companions, riding beside him, were the two brutes we had met at the Blue Dolphin.

Shock passed quickly. 'Alexa! Rarnald! Lil! Look, it's Cleo!' I yelled, fearful lest the thieves should escape again.

My voice was loud and faces turned towards me in the crowd. Alexa, Rarnald and Lilith swivelled and followed the direction in which I was pointing. I saw Alexa say something hurriedly to Rarnald and then they began to ride quickly back towards me. The three thugs would not have known Cleo's name, but it would have soon become clear that the riders making their way through the crowd, and one of them wearing a soldier's uniform, were heading for them. The woman yelled something urgently to the men and they wheeled their horses around and charged back down the street from where they had just come, the four of us in pursuit.

The thugs paid no heed to where they rode, knocking people and objects over in their haste. We were more careful and had to clear the mess they left behind and the distance between us began to lengthen. I was slightly ahead of my friends and when the thugs separated at the next street, the woman continuing straight ahead, Cleo's rider turning left and the other man going right, I ignored Alexa's calls and, without hesitation, followed Cleo.

The street was narrow and there were no other riders on it, though it teemed with pedestrians, they yelled at us as we raced past but I ignored them. An idea came to me and I pursed my lips and gave a sharp, clear whistle, the one I had always used to call Cleo before a ride. I saw her head come up and I thought she slowed, but then her rider kicked her viciously and she ran on and I cursed the worm to the deepest hell-pit.

He was leading me back to the harbour district and I smiled grimly. If he hoped to lose me there his task would not be an easy one. The turns and twists of the area we had so recently sketched were still fresh in my mind. Then he made his mistake, he headed Cleo down a small alleyway that I knew led back to the road I was on. Perhaps he knew this too and was counting on my continuing after him while he doubled back and escaped by emerging behind me, so I left the road and turned down the parallel alleyway, knowing we would meet.

The look of surprise on his face was almost comical as he rounded the corner before me and pulled up sharply. The alley was not wide, he could not ride past me and he gathered the reins to pull Cleo about, but had delayed too long. We were only a few paces apart and when I gave the high-pitched hoot, Cleo responded beautifully, rearing, her front legs pawing the air, and throwing her unsuspecting rider onto the ground.

He fell awkwardly, twisting to the side and landing hard on his hip. There was a loud crack and I heard him cry aloud in pain as he lay sprawled upon the hard cobblestones, his leg jutting out beneath him at a strange angle. I dismounted cautiously and he looked up, his eyes glazed with pain. He was moaning softly and scrambling for something at his side. It was only when I saw the gleam of a blade that I realised he had drawn a knife.

I drew my own nervously as I approached him, hoping my inexperience did not show, for I had never held it as a weapon before. His eyes focused on it and he gave another low moan, then, with a mighty effort, he pulled himself up onto one elbow. I stopped, wondering if he meant to throw the knife as it was clear his broken leg prevented any other form of attack.

He glanced once more at the knife in my hand then lowered his own to the ground so that the hilt, held in one hand, fitted between two cobblestones, the blade pointing up into the air. Suddenly, as he lifted his body above it, so that the blade was now below his heart, I grasped his intent and cried out just as he thrust his body down, impaling himself upon his own knife.

I groaned as the blood spewed out, running from his body to form a giant crimson pool. The only sound he made the whole time was a low grunt of exertion and then a soft sigh, almost of peace. Then he was still.

Taking Cleo's and Lukar's reins, I turned about, pale with shock, and went in search of a city guard.

Back at the palace apartment, Alexa and Lilith greeted me, their faces concerned. They had had no luck in their pursuit of the thieves and had returned to the palace, anxious for news of me. Recalling the vicious attack near the camp of the Tamina, they were relieved to see me return unhurt and listened to my tale in stunned silence.

'Why would anyone do it?' I said when I had finished my story. I was too unnerved to sit and had begun to pace. 'I was not going to hurt him, I only drew my knife because he had drawn his.'

'Evidently he preferred death to capture,' Alexa replied. 'It was not your fault, Ash.'

'But why? How could anyone?' I asked, frowning unhappily, swamped by confusion.

'Perhaps he feared what would happen to him if he was taken alive. Either that,' Alexa said, 'or he feared what he would disclose.'

I stared at her, taken aback. 'You mean like a pact?'

She shrugged. 'It's possible. One look at Chan's shoulder is reminder of the company he kept. I imagine there are some secrets amongst that lot that they wouldn't want spread around.'

It was all so much to absorb, I sat down weakly and Lilith came to sit beside me.

'At least you have Cleo back,' she said.

'Yes,' I agreed. Then I shook my head in disbelief as I remembered, 'He was still using my saddle.'

'They probably never thought to see us again,' Lilith offered softly, 'so when they came to Cynal, they wouldn't have seen the need to change the horses or saddles.'

I was nodding slowly in agreement with Lil, when, from across the room, Alexa laughed suddenly. Lilith and I looked up curiously.

'Lil's right,' she said, still laughing. 'You must've given them one hell of a scare, Ash, coming up behind them like that and screaming out Cleo's name to the world. They would've thought themselves far and away from any recriminations over the Tamina attack and, lo and behold, in the distant harbour city of Cynal the dusk calm is shattered by an outraged bellow from Ashil the cartographer and they're forced to flee.'

I smiled. It was rather funny to think of. 'It's a pity the other two weren't caught. I still remember their drunken stench from the Blue Dolphin.'

'Yes,' Alexa agreed. 'I doubt we'll catch them now. They will have recognised Rarnald's uniform and they'll either stay hidden or leave the city.'

'I wonder if the chestnut-haired woman is with them,' Lilith pondered, raising her eyebrows in query.

'I bet Chandra will wonder the same thing,' Alexa said wryly.

Afterwards, there being nothing more she could do about the thugs that evening, Alexa left for the library. Lilith and I were just about to quit the apartment for our lesson with Nikol when Rarnald and another guard arrived. Rarnald was pleased to see I was unhurt.

The thief's death had been reported by the city guard, he told us, and he had been sent by the captain to question me. The interview was brief and unilluminating. As yet the Cynalese had no clue to the man's identity.

'You're late,' Nikol said, as we walked up.

'With reason,' I replied and gave her a brief description of the evening's events.

'Death before dishonour,' Nikol said. 'It's the creed of many armies.'

'I wouldn't have thought horse-stealing was exactly honourable,' Lil observed.

'You have a point, though during war it's acceptable for a soldier to steal from the enemy to save her own life.'

'Last time I heard, neither the Tamina nor we were at war with anybody,' I commented dryly.

Nikol laughed. 'Well and good, let's forget him then, he's dead and harmless. Rarnald will spread the word and the guards will keep an eye out for the others. As for us, today we'll practise head blows and some kicks, in order to keep any living opponents at bay.'

Head blows?

Nikol laughed again. 'You've a face that tells all, Ashil.' She tapped me high on the forehead where my hair grew. 'You've got one tough weapon here. Now you're going to learn to use it.'

A certain mental shift is required to contemplate thrusting your head, like a battering ram, into another's stomach, or smacking them hard across the forehead with your own skull, but Nikol was there to bring the shift about. She had Lilith and me complete the exercises so many times that I began to feel dizzy and I collapsed with relief when Nikol finally called a halt.

'That's enough of those. Lil, I think you're a natural at them. Now let's move on to kicks. Ashil, on your feet. Feint a kick.'

Obediently, I came to my feet and prepared to kick.

'No, Ashil, don't look at my leg,' Nikol cried, before my foot was even off the ground,

I pulled up short and let out a loud, long breath of frustration. 'Why not?' I asked, puzzled and a little annoyed. I was still feeling dizzy from the head blows. 'That's where I'm going to strike.'

'Yes, but you shouldn't let me know that. All I have to do is step aside and then you'll be off-balance and I'll land a blow. Make your movement faster and keep your eyes on my face. If you must look at my leg, do it as you strike.'

Confused, and wondering where the exhilaration from the first lesson had gone, I nodded.

'Now try again,' Nikol directed. 'Keep both knees slightly bent and your feet spaced for balance. Now go.'

I stepped forward on my left leg and swung with my right, aiming the kick at her shin, while trying to keep both arms raised to protect my chest, my eyes on her face, and breathing out at the moment of contact. The kick went wide, my arms felt suspended uselessly in midair, I wrenched my side and I don't think I breathed at all.

'Much better, Ashil,' Nikol said. 'You're getting it. Now your turn, Lilith.'

Relieved to have a rest, yet angry with myself for being so clumsy, I moved aside so Lilith could face Nikol. I watched the intent look on her face as she too tried to remember all of Nikol's advice and saw the stiff, weak kick she threw. Seeing Lilith's lack of skill did not make me feel any better.

After we had repeated the exercise numerous times, with myriad variations, Nikol told us we were both doing well. She glanced at my face. 'Don't look so despondent, Ashil. I couldn't draw a map after only a few lessons, could I?' I shook my head in reply. 'Exactly. It will come to you, it's just a matter of persistence. That's enough for tonight. Already I can see a huge improvement in the way you're both moving. Now,' she continued, 'tomorrow's free-day, I'm not on duty but I'll be training in the morning. Do you want to have a lesson then?'

Want may have been too strong a word, but Nikol was right, we were improving, slowly, and neither Lilith nor I was prepared to give up. What we lacked in skill and strength we made up for in determination, so we both nodded.

'Come after breakfast,' Nikol said, 'and be sure to eat lightly.'

'We will,' and we bade her goodbye.

When Lil and I returned to the apartment, dripping sweat and thoroughly exhausted, it was still deserted, so, saved from explanation, we stripped and washed and changed into fresh clothes. Revived a little by the wash and the knowledge that nothing more strenuous than eating awaited us that night, we curled up on the couches in the salon, feeling pleasantly relaxed. Already the man's death was receding into the past and taking the worst of the horror with it.

Hunger was just beginning to make its demands known, causing me to contemplate rousing, when the door opened and Alexa came in, followed by two servants carrying food trays. Lilith and I both sat up straight as the servants placed the trays on the dining table.

'I didn't know who would've eaten, so I ordered enough for all of us,' Alexa said.

She turned to the servants and thanked them, seeing them to the door and shutting it after them.

Lil and I were already at the table, filling plates and pulling out chairs with their silk-covered cushions. We barely waited for Alexa to join us before we began eating.

We ate in silence, Lilith and I too intent on our food to waste time speaking or to notice Alexa's preoccupation. I might find Nikol's lessons torturous, but I always felt wonderful when I sat to dine afterwards.

'The Cynalese diplomat in Delawyn was found murdered yesterday evening,' Alexa said, very evenly, her food untouched on her plate.

Lilith and I stared at her in shock. 'Who killed her?' I asked in dazed disbelief. Murdering a diplomat was unheard of, except, I swallowed, in times of war.

'Him. No-one knows. The Ethnarch is denying all knowledge and has assured Lord Tarn that he is doing all he can to find the killer. The Cynalese are sending their own people over to join in the search.'

So now there were two deaths, I thought. Then a

chill ran down my spine as I thought how silly it was of me to group them as though the suicide of the thug and the murder of the diplomat were in some way connected.

'Lord Tarn seemed rather sad and preoccupied this afternoon when I dined with him,' I murmured wonderingly. 'He told me he had been dwelling on some unwelcome news.'

Alexa looked at me with interest. 'Did he say anything else?'

'He spoke a lot of the importance and value of freedom and how it is only when it is threatened that you realise how fiercely you will fight to protect it.'

Alexa nodded. 'I have the feeling this is related to the Meran. Remember Lindsa told us that Delawyn is abuzz with talk of the white panther and that the death of the king has stirred up the old trading rivalry between Delawyn and Cynal.'

Lil and I nodded.

'But why kill a diplomat?' I asked.

'As a sign, perhaps of warning, perhaps of strength, a way of saying that Cynal has much to fear but does not scare them. It may also be a way of testing the people of Delawyn, to see how they react to the news of the murder. Remember, Rianne said she believed Nitma was based in Delawyn. From our own visits we know it is a city full of much evil, some of it possibly due to the Meran. If Nitma and her followers have been inciting the people against Cynal, they would want to know how successful they have been before they make a decisive move.'

'Murder is a pretty decisive move,' I pointed out glumly.

'Not if you're never caught. If the Meran are responsible, they won't want to reveal themselves until they think they cannot possibly lose. The stakes are too high.'

'Do you think this means the Meran are ready to show the white panther?' Lilith asked anxiously.

Alexa shrugged, clearly frustrated by the lack of information. 'I'm just guessing, Lil, but I think it's all too much of a coincidence to mean anything else. We know from Rianne that Nitma and the Meran hate Cynal and the Mecla. It would seem a logical choice then to begin your bid for power by attacking your enemies, the ones you blame for your loss of power ninety years ago.'

'It was the Meran's own fault,' I protested. 'They were abusing their mind powers and the people turned against them. They can hardly blame the Mecla.'

'But they do. The Mecla would not help them so they became the Meran's enemies. Besides, you're overlooking the obvious. The Mecla did not support the Meran ninety years ago, appalled by the actions and intentions of the Meran, and the Meran know they will get no support from either the Mecla or Melcran this time. To win the people's support, the Meran will use the white panther, saying such evidence cannot be refuted, but they will not have forgotten the Mecla. They know that the Mecla will still be a dangerous threat, even if the people are fooled. A threat they will need to diminish or, preferably, remove entirely.'

I gasped as I finally understood what Alexa was saying. 'You're talking about the Meran declaring war on the Mecla, aren't you?'

'Yes, and the followers of Mecla, and it will be a bitter, bloody war. Once begun, neither the Mecla nor the Meran will be able to rest until their enemy is destroyed, for good.'

There was complete silence for several seconds as we sat trying to assimilate such dreadful, shocking news. Finally it was Lilith who spoke.

'Then the only way to stop it beginning is to prevent the Meran from displaying the white panther.'

'Exactly,' Alexa nodded, 'and in order to do that, contact must be made with the Lakiya.'

I shook my head, feeling sick with dread. 'No wonder Rianne and King Charissa are asking all for news and help. They're trying to avert a war.'

'But time is running out,' Alexa said. She glanced at Lil and me, her blue eyes hard and grave. 'Soon they may just be hoping to win it.'

Carly and Lindsa arrived first, their hair still wet from their swim. They came through the door noisily, laughing and chatting, and exclaimed in pleasure at the sight of the heavily laden table.

'Who died, Ash?' Carly asked brightly, looking at my pale face as she sat down, a full plate before her. I went even paler, but just then the door opened again and I was saved from answering her.

Chandra and Demran came into the apartment with faces so gay and merry that I felt a moment's qualm at having to be the herald of such bad news. Hesitating, I glanced across the table at Alexa but her eyes were fixed on the whitening scars on Chandra's shoulder, visible beneath her sleeveless shirt. Beside Alexa, Lilith was cradling a goblet and staring into its depths.

I took a breath and rose to my feet, wishing I did not have to reopen a wound so newly healed. 'Chandra,' I began, and I went on to tell the events of the evening while the room grew still and quiet around me and the cheer left Chandra's face.

'Did you see Ray?' was her first question, quiet and steady, her dark eyes intent on me.

'No,' I replied softly, 'nor the woman that cut you.'

Her head went back slightly and Demran stepped closer and put an arm around her shoulder, his fingers resting near the scars.

After a moment, Chandra nodded. 'How is Cleo?'

'A little thin, but she will be fine.' I shrugged. 'She was very happy to see me,' I added a little lamely.

For the first time, Chandra smiled. 'Sometimes you say the silliest things, Ashil.' She looked at the four seated around the table, back at me and then at Demran. 'I hope Rarnald and the guards find her, I would like to meet her one more time.' Then she tapped the leather bag Demran held and smiled at him. 'But for now, I would like to hear some music.'

Willingly, Demran obliged, and while he set himself up upon a chair in the salon and fiddled with his gitar I came and sat beside Chandra.

'I am well, Ashil,' she told me before I had even spoken. 'You are one who feels too much the pain of others. I am healed now, but I am angry, for what they did to us and because they are here in Cynal and have disrupted our lives once again.'

'If we had been one day earlier or later, or even arrived

at the Tamina camp at a different time that day, none of this would have happened,' I reflected with a little sad sigh. It was a thought that had occurred to me before.

'Who knows what else would have happened to us then? Perhaps something worse,' Chandra replied. 'The gods meant for it to happen. They must have a plan. It means nothing that we cannot understand it. In all things show care, do your best and move forward and the gods will reward you in this life and those to come, but the obstacles are theirs to choose.'

I did not think I believed this but, faced with Chandra's unwavering certainty, I remained silent.

'Ah,' Chandra exclaimed happily as Demran began to softly strum his gitar, 'this is a song he wrote for me, Ashil.' There was a brilliant quaver of excitement in her voice. 'No other has yet heard it. He played it for me earlier tonight. It is very beautiful.'

And it was, as indeed were all Demran's songs, all love songs this evening I noted with amusement and pleasure, for nothing could have been better designed to push the last vestiges of pain and anger from Chandra's mind. The rest of us might well have not been in the room, for Demran's and Chandra's eyes rarely strayed from each other and the heat coming off them both was so intense that I wondered at Demran's ability to concentrate on his music, amazed that his strings did not burn and shrivel under his touch.

It surprised no-one then when Demran had finished and we had all praised and thanked him that Chandra announced she was to spend the night at Regi's. She would leave from there in the morning to meet Laibi's family and go net-fishing. We watched them leave as gay and merry as when they had first arrived.

Much to my surprise and delight, when I awoke on free-day morning I discovered that the stiffness in my muscles had eased rather than worsened. Nikol was right, I thought happily, I must be improving.

Buoyed by this thought, I dressed quickly, careful not to wake Alexa, and joined Lilith for a small meal. Lindsa's sandals were lying by the couch in the salon, but there was no sign of either her or Carly. As I looked at the shut door to Carly's room, I smiled and thought it was unlikely there would be for hours. Quietly, Lilith and I left the apartment.

Outside, another beautiful day in Cynal was beginning. I inhaled the fresh salty air and glanced up at the brilliant blue of the clear sky above us. What a delightful setting for a day without work, I reflected happily, walking beside Lil, my spirits soaring.

This morning, Nikol wanted to practise yelling.

Both Lilith and I looked at her in astonishment.

She laughed loudly. 'It's not as strange as it sounds. I've told you to breathe out as you make contact and breathe in as you prepare to deliver the blow. Well sometimes it's best not only to breathe out but to yell at your opponent. It upsets them and it fires your blood. Let's practise.'

I did wonder what people passing the training ground must have thought when they heard the three of us releasing these strange, tortured roars, but after a few shy attempts I began to relax and concentrate on how Nikol managed to make her cries so deep and ferocious. Hearing that would certainly make me pause and reconsider attacking her.

'It's from the belly, not the throat,' she explained. 'Using those arm blows you've learnt, move forward attacking imaginary foes and scaring them with your battle cries.'

After several attempts, Lil and I started producing some admirable sounds and Nikol was right, it did heat my blood. I felt looser and stronger and more in control.

'That's great. Keep moving but now attack with that kick to the side of the leg I showed you yesterday.'

Lilith and I complied, knocking our imaginary enemies left and right before us.

'That's great,' Nikol called approvingly, as Lilith and I reached the edge of the training ground and stopped, panting heavily. 'Next lesson, I'll bring some hay-filled sacks for you to practise with, so you can actually make contact with your blows and kicks. Now go and enjoy your free-day. It's my son's name-day today and we're off on a picnic.'

There was a message for Lilith and me in our apartment saying that Alexa, Carly and Lindsa had gone for a swim at the cove. We could join them there if we wished, otherwise they would see us at Mecla House at noon.

We found them easily enough. Alexa was swimming, while Carly and Lindsa were lying close together under the shade of one of the largest trees.

'Ahoy,' Carly called when she saw us. 'It's the two mysterious ones, who disappear at first light.'

'How would you know what time we left, Carly?' I

407

asked as I sat on a corner of their blanket. 'You were still snugly tucked up in your room at first light.'

'Don't look so smug, Ash,' Carly rejoined easily, looking like some sort of large, sleepy cat as she lay lazily on one elbow. 'Alexa was up early and noticed that the two of you were nowhere to be found. Just what have you been up to?'

'We went for a run,' Lilith replied, looking as guileless and innocent as ever. I was impressed. It was a good answer, and honest. Nikol had made us run four laps of the training ground this morning. Yet Lil gave nothing away of our secret.

'Yes,' I said, 'it was such a beautiful morning.'

Carly was looking at the two of us in disbelief. 'You've had too much sun, running on free-day morning!'

'We wanted to work up an appetite for Laibi's meal. Are you coming to Mecla House, Lindsa?' Lilith asked, cannily changing the subject.

'Ah,' Lindsa sighed loudly. She had been stretched out comfortably by Carly's side but sat up now and shook her head. 'I cannot. Have you heard that a Cynalese diplomat was killed in Delawyn the day before yesterday?'

Lilith and I nodded, our faces carefully devoid of all expression.

'Mmm,' she said unhappily. 'It could not have happened at a worse time, with the Cynalese all worked up about the white panther and Delawyn upset over trading rights. Yesterday, some angry Cynalese began throwing refuse at the ship and calling for us to hand over the murderer. The captain is worried it may become worse and he has ordered double guard duty for everyone. I must return to the harbour before noon and remain on duty until late this evening.'

'Well I hope you have an uneventful shift,' I offered. She looked so sad at having her time with Carly disrupted.

'Aye,' she replied, a trifle grimly, 'so do I.'

'Enough gloomy talk,' Carly quipped, rising to her feet in one fluid motion. 'It's hot under here and I think we could all do with a swim.' Without another word, she pulled off her light clothing, dropping it carelessly to the sand. 'Come on, Lil,' she said holding out a hand to her, 'let's show these two how it's done.'

Lilith grinned and took her hand, rising to her feet while I laughed and even Lindsa managed a wry smile. Lilith quickly removed her own clothes and took Carly's hand again. Without a backward glance, the two of them walked leisurely to the water's edge.

Exchanging a resigned, amused look, Lindsa and I rose to join them.

Later, when Lindsa had already left for the harbour and the four of us were sitting, drying ourselves on the blanket, we explained to Carly the conclusions we had reached the night before. When we had finished, we paused, waiting for her reaction.

She nodded, running fingers through her damp hair to loosen the tangles. 'We're lucky then that we got our half payment,' she said. 'If war does occur, we are free to leave and do not have to return any coin we have already received, no matter how great the amount is. It's in the contract.'

409

'Carly!' I exclaimed, amazed. 'Forget the payment. Don't you care? It could mean a war, people will die.'

'I know what happens in a war,' Carly said, her voice hardening, 'and I've seen people die, quickly, slowly, fearfully, painfully. But this war is not mine and I won't be here if it does break out. Why should I stay or care? These are not my people, I barely know them, and there is nothing I can do to stop it happening.'

'I agree with Carly,' Alexa said softly.

'What?' I cried, spinning my head around to face her. 'How can you say that?'

'Because she's being logical. If war does break out, I think we should leave. We are not soldiers or priests and we could be of more use out of the city. All of Tirayi will be affected if Nitma gains power. If we are free then we are mobile.'

I sat staring at her, aghast. How could she and Carly be so cold?

'The real issue is what can we do now,' Lilith said.

Carly shrugged. 'Nothing.' She saw me glaring at her. 'We'll keep our eyes out,' she added, 'but unless we spy something of monumental importance, it's really up to the Mecla and Lord Tarn. I'm sure they're working on plans we're totally unaware of. This whole thing will probably be resolved before the enthroning.'

'Why don't we leave it there,' Lilith suggested, seeing me open my mouth to argue once more with Carly. 'We can talk of it again if anything new arises.'

'Good idea, Lil,' Alexa agreed, rising and stretching. 'It's time we were heading for Mecla House anyway.'

We dressed and rode back into the city, talking little, each occupied with her own thoughts.

My own thoughts were ominous. If Nitma had been responsible for the diplomat's death in Delawyn, who, I wondered, would be her next target?

Mecla House was south-east of the palace, spreading out in the fork formed where the main western thoroughfare from the city's gates split in two, becoming the Street of Lights and Market Way. All day traffic flowed up and down both roads. Along the Street of Lights people travelled to and from the harbour district, the palace and the wealthy northern section of the city. Directly across from the House, on the other side of Market Way, lay the marketplace. The area surrounding the two streets was one of continual noise and activity, with crowds, carts, livestock, all milling about from dawn till dusk, and at its very centre, standing tall and proud, was the scarlet-doored, scarlet-roofed, Mecla House.

As we rode up the thoroughfare, part of the free-day crowd, I wondered at the choice of such a location for a priesthood. Where was the peace and quiet they would surely require for their prayers and study? Today, being free-day, and this being Cynal, the marketplace was closed, yet even so the sheer number of people on the streets was startling. Why would the priests choose such a place?

As we approached the fork we could see the high walls of the House that spread to the very edge of the roadway. They were excellently maintained and appeared almost blindingly white in the sunshine. I stared at them, almost mesmerised. The building was double-storeyed and the walls rose strong and thick against the blue sky, yet the only windows visible were those on the second floor. Beneath them, as far as I could see on both sides, stretched a sheer blank face.

We turned left at the fork and rode a few paces along the Street of Lights until we came to a huge, gleaming scarlet door set into the wall and facing out to sea like an enormous red iris. Above it were etched the words HUMILITY, GENEROSITY, PEACE. We had arrived.

Uncertain where to find the stables, we dismounted before the door and held our horses while Alexa stepped up and rang the large, brass bell above which sat the word WELCOME. Moments later, the door opened and Damin stood there, a broad smile spread across his face.

'Welcome cartographers,' he said. 'Welcome to Mecla House.'

'Good day, Damin,' Alexa replied, smiling back.

The priest came forward, closing the door behind him and waved to us all. 'Come, I will show you the stables. It will be cool there for your horses.'

'Has Chandra arrived?' Alexa asked as she walked beside him, leading Drella.

'Ah, yes,' he chuckled, 'with so many fish that Laibi's eyes grew round in disbelief. Laibi's brother says Chandra has a natural skill. She is with Laibi now as he prepares the meal.' He laughed. 'She wanted to see how one cooked fish.'

Damin was taking us further along the Street of Lights and I marvelled at the size of Mecla House. To my right ran the impressive white wall. At street level, still unbroken by door or window, it seemed to continue forever.

Several hundred paces later, we came to a single, wide gate with a heavy, simple handle at waist level. Damin turned it with ease, pushing the gate open. A skilfully laid path lay before us and I could hear the whinnying and nickering of horses to our left, but I did not turn to seek the stables, for my eyes were held by the green paradise that spread out before me.

'It is delightful, is it not?' Damin asked, seeing our rapt expressions. 'Several of the priests are growers,' he explained. 'The flowers, there,' and he pointed to rows and rows of beautiful flowers that grew to our right, 'they sell to market vendors. Ahead,' and he pointed towards the green centre of the yard, 'is where many of the priests come to relax and meditate. At the centre is a large circular bench that surrounds the largest tree. Smaller benches are scattered throughout the rest of the garden. Many of the trees bear fruit, for the growers believe that functional can also be beautiful.'

We led our horses into the cool, comfortable stable and Bragan gave a small whinny of welcome, lifting his nose from a pile of hay to watch his friends enter. Other horses watched us curiously, their noses over their stalls, but our own paid them little attention— they had smelt water and wanted only to reach the troughs. We left them secured and drinking happily, and turned with Damin towards the House.

A stone path ran straight from the stables to the rear wall of Mecla House and we followed it, the fruit garden to our left, like some small fertile island. As we neared the back of the House I saw that the building was in fact U-shaped and in its centre, open to the sky, was the Dining Area.

Numerous priests in scarlet robes were gathered about the long wooden tables, some setting places, others standing chatting idly or already seated. All looked up curiously at our arrival and murmured words of greeting when Damin gave our names in a general introduction. The full glare of the midday sun fell on the priests, lightening their robes to an almost blood red, and as I counted fifteen tables, lying neatly in rows of three, I wondered at such an arrangement. No doubt it would be charming to sit outside both morning and night when cool breezes blew and the sun's strength had ebbed, but now, with the sun's fierce rays seeming to eat into my back, I was sceptical about the pleasure to be obtained dining fully exposed to such heat.

Damin was steering us towards the far table in the front row and I glanced up, puzzled, at the two tall wooden beams that stood at the end of each row, like huge fingers pointing up at the sky. High up on each beam I could see a thick iron ring, but before I could pause to wonder at their purpose Damin was hailing another priest and I turned to see Kira coming towards us.

She grinned, her beautiful olive skin glowing, her eyes shining with excitement. 'Welcome, cartographers, we have all been looking forward to your company on free-day.'

'Thank you, Kira,' Alexa replied, for us all, 'we are all pleased to be here.'

'Good. Please sit and we will bring drinks.'

While we sat and Kira left to fetch drinks, two priests came to our table carrying what looked like large, thick hessian mats with large hooks at each end. Laying all but one mat down, they smiled and excused themselves as each climbed onto a stool and slipped the hooks through the rings on the wooden beams. They gathered the mat and stretched it over our heads and repeated the procedure at the other end of the row. Pulled taut across the table, the mat offered instant shade, allowing only weak, diffused light through. Yet as the beams stood several paces from the outer wall, sunshine still spilt to the stone floor close to the wall and flooded through the windows that rimmed the area. I had my answer to the mystery of the windowless outside wall. By looking out into the Dining Area, the ground floor rooms would receive plenty of light but little of the noise from the busy streets. It was a clever solution and I smiled at its simplicity. I should learn to have more faith.

Kira returned with wine and water and she and Damin sat with us, handing us a goblet each, while around us the tables began to fill as more priests arrived. Lilith asked Damin how his animal healing was going.

'Well, I have had no disasters or deaths this week, though it has been a week for horses, infected eyes, damaged frogs, strained legs. Still,' he smiled, contentedly, 'none of it irreparable.'

'It has been a week of horses for us also,' I said. 'My stolen mare was recovered here yesterday, after I was sure I had lost her forever.'

The Mecla were interested in my tale and I briefly

described the events surrounding Cleo's theft and recovery. Not only Damin and Kira listened attentively, but numerous other priests seated at our table.

'And only a few days before,' I added, when I had completed my story, 'we had a strange experience with King Charissa's horses as they were unloaded at the harbour.' Turning to Damin, I asked if he had seen them.

His eyes had lit up with interest and he shook his head. 'No, Ricah has been singing their praises. She says the king has them taken out every day and often rides the stallion herself. If all Eustapeans are so enthusiastic about exercising their horses, they must have a fine herd on their island. I am curious to see such creatures. Tell me about them.'

Willingly, I related the story of the pair's arrival and our own horses' response. 'It was very strange,' I commented when I had finished, 'and as quickly as it began it stopped, just like that, as though a flame had been quenched.' I shrugged lightly. 'It was a novel introduction to the Eustapeans.'

'Ah,' Damin exclaimed, enthralled, sitting back and tapping his fingers on the table, 'now I am even more fascinated. Of course, we all know that animals communicate differently from mortals, but I have never heard of such a thing happening before.' Eager astonishment animated his features. 'I must make a special trip to the palace stables.'

'A word of warning, Damin,' Carly put in, her voice heavy with mock seriousness. 'Go on foot.'

The tables had all filled now, though three vacant seats had been left near us. As Laibi and other priests

416

who had been helping him in the kitchen came out carrying trays of delicacies, Rianne arrived, to be hailed by many of the priests and finally coming to sit with us.

She greeted us, then turned as Laibi placed a steaming platter in the centre of the table. 'You have excelled yourself as usual,' she complimented him.

He smiled. 'I cannot take all the credit, I had some extra help,' and he nodded towards where Chandra was expertly balancing one of the long trays on one hand as she walked towards us.

She beamed at us. 'Good day, friends. See what I have caught you to eat.'

The meal was superb. Chandra regaled us with explanations and descriptions of her time at the nets. It had been a great pleasure, she said, we should all try it one morning.

The first course completed, I sat back. Pleasantly relaxed from the fish and the wine, I was feeling too lazy to speak any more. Instead I listened to the words of those around me.

Lilith was chatting to Laibi about being Mecla. 'It is wonderful,' I heard him say, 'because I am always myself and I need never be alone. I have my fisher family who love me, love the child they raised and respect the man I have become, and I have my Mecla family who love and understand me, the priest. They know of my striving, of the continual need to learn, and their understanding gives me strength. It was Meclan's belief that inner strength leads to outer gentleness.'

Rianne, across from me, was telling Alexa that

messages had been sent by trained birds to Mecla in the north, who would see what they could discover of the Lakiya. The map I had drawn Lord Tarn had been sent and the priests would begin their search within that area.

Kira was laughing as Carly replied to the priest's query about her feelings on the white panther with an undignified snort. 'I am sick of hearing about it,' she said. 'Such talk is like a dog chasing its tail. Around it goes, amusing for a short while, then one becomes bored with it and turns away. Lord Tarn speaks of it to us, and Rianne and King Charissa. We know nothing, they know nothing, Nitma has yet to do anything to prove she has any real power. I mean no offence, Kira, but until something happens it will all seem the same to me, boring.'

'What would it take to convince you of her power? A white panther walking through the streets of Cynal?'

'That might be proof of her power, yes, but common thugs can have power. It wouldn't convince me she has the approval of the gods.'

'With many people the sign will be enough.'

Carly snorted again. 'Many people in this world are stupid. We five are not. If Nitma was truly keen for us to support her, and I cannot see why she would be, it would have to be through coercion, not conversion.'

'The sign of a good meal is that it induces in the participants a desire to listen as well as speak,' a deep voice murmured in my ear.

I smiled as I turned towards Damin. 'Then I would have to say that Laibi's meal so far is a truly great success.'

The old priest nodded. 'Sometimes it can be nice to just sit and let life flow over and around you, like cool water. It can be just as refreshing.'

'Chandra would say I was sitting here "mellowing."'

Damin laughed softly, his face creasing along well-worn pleasure lines. 'How do you plan to spend the rest of free-day?' he asked.

'We were thinking of taking the horses for a run outside the city, to give them a chance to stretch their legs.'

SIXTEEN

A WEEK FOR HORSES indeed, as we discovered shortly after we left the House, our bellies pleasantly full, our minds pleasantly relaxed.

Timi had gone no more than two blocks when we heard the unmistakable sound of a loose horseshoe striking the cobblestones. Lilith dismounted and lifted his hind foot to see the shoe hanging crookedly.

It was a long walk to the palace but Lilith had little choice, as there were no blacksmiths working in Cynal on free-day. She would lead Timi back and have the palace blacksmith shoe him early tomorrow.

'Don't stop for me,' she said, looking up at us. 'Go for your ride and I'll see you back at the apartment later.'

'Are you sure?' I asked. 'I can come with you.'

'No,' she shook her head, 'give Lukar a run. He'll be sharing you with Cleo soon enough.'

I smiled and we left her. Ever since our arrival in Cynal we had been planning on visiting Mount Rittoy, the fire mountain that reared up behind the city like some imposing crouching beast.

Once free of the city, we set the horses to gallop.

Ecstatically, Lukar stretched his legs and raced over the rough grassland. For a short while I gave myself up to the sheer, physical pleasure of being on his back. I moved with his rhythm, listened to the regular drumming of his hooves as they touched earth, felt the wind on my face and lifting my hair, and inhaled the smell and warmth of the wild land.

The other three were spread out around me and their presence only added to my contentment. It was already late afternoon. Across the water sea diamonds sparkled in the wake of the setting sun. Around us, shadows were lengthening.

Lukar had begun to slow. The land had been slowly rising as we came nearer to Mount Rittoy and I stared up at it, for the first time close enough to see it clearly. It was the first fire mountain I had ever gazed upon, and I looked at it with wonder.

Rittoy means flames in the old language of Cynal, when it was only a fisher village and had yet to learn the Middling Tongue. The village was gone now and its people long dead, but their name for the mountain and their story of its fiery reign had survived. Glancing up at its flattened peak, I could not imagine a mountain spewing fire and ash, or burning rivers running over the earth. It must be a glorious and fearful sight.

Yet we were safe. The priests who understood such things said the mountain's voice would be heard no more. Rittoy had fallen silent before even the first stone of the new city of Cynal was laid and now the earth that had once been scorched black and lifeless was rich and fertile with prosperous farm holdings spread about the mountain's northern and eastern flanks.

'Shall we climb it?' I asked the others as they grouped around me.

'Yes,' Chandra called, excitedly. 'Regi told me there are two small hot lakes on the seaward side, and cracks where hot mist rises from the earth. I want to see them.'

Our interest sufficiently aroused by Chandra's words, we loosely tied the horses and continued upwards on foot. The base of the mountain was wide and easy to climb and finding purchase in the thick tufts of grass and weed was not difficult. However, as we moved further up the southern flank the way steepened and became so riddled with unexpected holes and ditches and rocks we had to place our feet carefully.

At one time I paused and peered up at the peak, still so very far ahead of us, then turned and stared across at Cynal. From such a distance, the domes of the palace appeared like some huge white resting bird, making the rest of the city look like a beach on which it sat, a beach casually strewn with shells and debris of many colours. It all seemed so very innocent and harmless, a city all light, no shadow.

About halfway up the mountain the earth suddenly formed a small, natural ledge about two paces wide that ran off towards the west. Thinking it unlikely that we would find an easier route we followed it.

As we rounded the seaward side it was immediately clear that the worst of the mountain's wrath had been felt here. Although shrubs and grasses grew wild as elsewhere on the lower flanks of the mountain, they sprouted in uneven gullies and along long, broken ridges. Even the peak on this side looked different, for it was jagged and ugly, like a face half torn away.

We wandered on, our noses twitching at the strange, unpleasant smell which we soon discovered came from one of the two steaming pools. It was surprisingly small and looked innocuous enough, but when Alexa picked up a long twig and plunged it into its depths she met with no resistance and had to pull her hand away for fear of scalding it.

'Look,' Carly said, pointing to where hot jets of steam hissed from the earth. 'I wonder why it does that.'

'It's like the earth's cooking,' Alexa murmured wonderingly, getting as close to the jets as was possible.

The second of the steaming pools was below us and we gave up any thought of climbing further up the mountain as we clambered down towards it.

'It may have been a ferocious, terrifying mountain at one time,' I said loudly, getting slightly ahead of the others as I increased my speed, 'but not any more.'

'Be careful, Ashil,' Chandra called. I turned to wave a reproving hand at her and went tumbling straight into a long, deep gully. I landed with an undignified thud and a startled cry, but was luckily uninjured. It was very dark and I looked up to see the springy growth that had covered the gully already back in place above me. I pushed it aside and climbed out, feeling a little sheepish, particularly as Carly was laughing so hard she was almost doubled over.

'What were you saying, Ash?' she managed to splutter out.

I threw her a dark look and continued slowly forward. This time heeding Chandra's words.

This low down on uncultivated land small hardy trees grew, their branches gnarled and dry, buffeted as they were by the sea winds. We had almost reached the pool and had just pushed past one close clump of trees when both Alexa and Chandra tensed and spun around suddenly, knives flashing in their hands.

Alexa darted back up around the trees while Chandra moved quickly to the other side, pointing for Carly and me to spread out. Carly drew her daggers and reluctantly I drew my knife. I could feel my heart begin to race. Whoever or whatever was amongst the trees was now trapped between the four of us.

Suddenly the trees erupted, branches shaking as they were pushed aside, and a tall, pale, grey-clad figure dashed towards where I stood, frantically trying to escape. Bending my knees as Nikol had taught me, I leant slightly forward. I got a glimpse of huge, terrified, pale, pale eyes and then I grabbed him, tensing as I waited for his first blow.

It did not come. He stood quietly in my arms, his body shaking, gazing at the other three as they approached, his head moving from side to side like a cornered animal.

'We won't hurt you,' I whispered, aware of his fear. His face turned to mine and I knew him.

'You're the man from the Blue Dolphin,' I exclaimed, loosening my grip slightly, 'the one who was staring into the horse's eye.' The others were closer now, studying him curiously. I turned to Alexa. 'He must be the one you've felt following us.'

Alexa nodded but she was not looking at me. Instead she was staring at the pale, smooth face of the man, the flesh so clear and colourless it was like marble.

'Who are you?' she asked. Her tone was one of soft wonder.

I wanted to release him so I could see him properly. His head was above mine and he was very slim, but in a tall, drawn-out way, like an afternoon shadow. His hair was several shades lighter than Lilith's and grew soft and long. His fine, delicate features had the look sometimes seen in young ascetics, whose faith sustains them and has never been shaken, but at the moment they were pinched with fear and uncertainty. Strapped beneath his ribcage was an empty wool-lined pouch.

He still had not answered Alexa. 'If you mean us no harm,' she said gently, 'you have nothing to fear from us.'

A little of the tension seemed to leave him and I knew he had understood. He looked at Alexa and I saw his lips part and move as though he was trying to speak but did not know how. Finally, after several seconds, he gave a soft sound, like a sigh.

'I am Tilyya,' he said.

It was as though he had breathed the words, or they were borne on the wind. If I had not seen his mouth move I would have thought the sounds part of the breeze that stirred the leaves around us, and I knew with a certainty that no mortal voice could have produced such a sound.

Alexa had gone very still. 'Lakiya?'

He frowned a little, drawing his delicate eyebrows together, though no lines appeared to mar his skin. He seemed to have trouble with speech, as though it was a strange, forgotten talent. 'Yes,' he sighed finally. He paused, searching for more words. 'So your people call us.'

Lakiya! It was tremendous. I laughed a little and released him, sheathing my knife. They did exist. Here was the proof! He must have wondered at the huge grin on my face as I danced before him but then Chandra stepped forward eagerly, looking about the mountainside.

'Where is your beast friend?' she asked curiously.

He winced, an expression of incredible pain crossing his face and I stopped dancing. 'I seek him. The Evil One has him.' He pointed at Carly and demanded in great anguish, 'Where is the Evil One?'

Now it was we who frowned.

'I don't know any Evil One,' Carly replied suspiciously.

'You bear the scent.'

'Carly?' Alexa asked. 'Have you any idea what he is talking about?'

'None.' She shook her head.

Tilyya raised his head and his nostrils flared. He lowered his head and glared at Carly, his pale eyes hard and cold, and he pointed at her again. 'You smell of the Evil One, who has taken my mla. At first I could follow the cries of my mla as he called for help, but since we have been in this place the Evil One has silenced him and covers their scent. It is only the servants of the Evil One who I can follow now, so that they will lead me to my mla. Where is he?'

Carly, I could see, was beginning to be annoyed. 'I don't know what you are talking about. I don't know any Evil One or this mla you speak of and the only scent I carry is my own.'

426

'No,' he breathed, 'your scent is strong and living. The Evil One's is weak upon you.'

'Then show me where it is,' Carly challenged.

Tilyya walked gracefully towards her, his movements lithe and light. As he reached Carly, Chandra moved to Carly's side, her hand resting on her knife.

'She is our friend,' Chandra warned him. 'Do not harm her.'

The Lakiya studied Carly quickly and his eyes darted to her left wrist, where she wore the thick, silver wristband she had purchased in Nalym.

'There,' he said.

Carly's eyes widened in a sudden flash of understanding. She pulled off the wristband and the chestnut braid fell out. Picking it up she offered it to the Lakiya.

'Is it this?'

The Lakiya took it between his long fingers and looked at it with revulsion and pain. 'Yes,' he murmured, 'this is from the Evil One. Are you a servant?'

Carly's outraged 'Ai' was loud and expressive. 'If this came from the Evil One who stole your mla, then the Evil One is the woman who attacked us,' she explained angrily. She pulled aside Chandra's shirt to reveal the scars. 'This is what she did to us and she stole from us too, two horses. I carry that braid because she is our enemy and because we one day hope to meet her again.' She glared up at Tilyya. 'And I am no-one's servant.'

The Lakiya looked momentarily stunned by Carly's explanation, then he smiled at her, a beautiful smile.

'Then we have a common enemy,' he said. 'We can help each other.'

'Perhaps,' Alexa said, 'but first we need to understand certain things.' She indicated a patch of coarse grass nearby. 'Let's sit and we will tell you what we know of this Evil One and you, Tilyya, can tell us about your mla.'

'You called him my beast friend,' Tilyya began, once we were seated, 'but that is a vile name mortals use. Amongst us they are called mla and there is one for each Lakiya.' As he spoke, his hand had drifted to the pouch beneath his ribs and he began to stroke it idly. 'They are small,' and he cupped his hands as though holding a bowl, 'and we carry them with us.' His hand returned to the pouch. 'When they are born, they are tiny and covered in white fur, and totally defenceless, as is my mla. As they grow, they lose their fur and begin to take the glow. When a mla glows, it is the time for the first change.'

His face hardened. 'A mla can assume the shape of any animal and although we know that mortals speak of us with great confusion and curiosity, and some envy us our "beast friends," the ways of both people are very different and the Lakiya choose to stay apart. In all our history, though we meet mortals from time to time, we never harm them and no mortal has ever become our enemy nor ever sought to hurt or steal our mla, until the Evil One.

'When the mla are still hatchlings in fur, it is common to leave the Nahaar, where the Lakiya live, and go out alone to strengthen and explore the mind bond. My mla and I were far from the Nahaar when the Evil One struck. We were deep in rapport and the

Evil One was strong and took me by surprise. The Evil One has power and cunning and I was defeated, yet the Evil One does not know my people. I lived when the Evil One thought I died. My mla was stolen, hurt greatly as he was torn from me. Days later, when I recovered, I could hear his screams of pain and I began to follow the Evil One. First inland, then to a horrible city by water and finally over the water to this place.'

I gasped. 'This must have been what the merfolk felt, the great evil crossing the water the morning of the funeral. It must've been the woman with the mla.'

'Yes,' Carly said, 'and I bet right here we have Lindsa's stowaway.'

'Did the Evil One and her servants have horses with them on the ship?' Alexa asked.

'Yes,' Tilyya replied. 'Six horses. One for each servant and one for the Evil One.'

Alexa raised an eyebrow. 'Does this Evil One have a name?'

Tilyya paused to think, staring hard at the ground. I saw the moment he recalled it, for his face lit up and he looked at Alexa.

'I heard one of the Evil One's servants once use the word Nitma. Could that be it?'

'Yes,' Alexa nodded grimly, 'that could indeed be it.'

Tilyya wanted to hear the story of our encounter with Nitma and I told it to him briefly. He was disgusted that any mortal would want to hurt their own. Hearing the name Nitma had stunned me but I was aware also of a growing excitement as I realised that here was the solution to the problem that so occupied Lord Tarn and Rianne. The Lakiya had been found and the war could be averted. Nitma seemed already defeated in my mind. That thought and the thrill of actually speaking to a Lakiya were enough to keep my spirits high.

'What were you doing staring into that horse's eye?' I asked.

'It was a horse of one of the Evil One's servants. I was trying to touch its mind to see if it could tell me where to find the Evil One.'

'And did you?' I asked in wonder.

'We touched but the horse's mind was cloudy and slow and could not understand what I asked. I was going to follow the servants when they reappeared but then the five of you came and I could smell the Evil One's scent upon you and I was confused, so I ran. I followed you afterwards.'

I smiled. 'You were at Regi's party, weren't you? Behind the dais.' He looked confused so I shook my head and waved a hand, dismissing the question. I was already sure of the answer.

'Why haven't you gone to the priests, the Mecla?' Carly asked. 'They've been sending out messages all over Tirayi saying they wish to speak with the Lakiya. Nitma's their enemy and they're fearful that Nitma and the Lakiya have joined forces.'

Tilyya was aghast. 'The Lakiya would never join with an Evil One.'

'Well the Mecla seem to think it's a possibility. They don't know Nitma has stolen your mla.' Carly paused momentarily. 'Would it be possible for your mla to change into a white panther?'

430

'Yes,' Tilyya answered, 'when he takes the glow, if he wished it or I asked it.'

'Would he do it for Nitma?' Carly questioned.

Tilyya seemed to close in upon himself. 'The Evil One would have to force him, to break him. My mla's screams would fill my mind.'

'Would you like us to take you to the priests?' Alexa asked. 'They may be able to help you find your mla.'

'No,' he hissed, recoiling. 'The Evil One's servants are amongst them.'

That shook us. My earlier certainty of a quick resolution abruptly deserted me.

'Which of the priests serve her?' Chandra asked, astounded.

'I do not know. As with the Evil One, there is a shield amongst the priests. Tell them nothing,' he implored, 'or the Evil One will know I did not die.'

It was growing late. Soon the sun would set and Mount Rittoy would be in darkness. It was time to return to the city.

'We must discuss what you have told us,' Alexa said to Tilyya, as we rose from the ground, our minds battling to absorb all we had learnt. 'Can we meet you tomorrow?'

Tilyya nodded. 'I will come to you early near the palace,' and, without another word, he slipped off silently into the trees and was gone.

'So what do we do?' Carly asked, as we returned to our horses. 'If all Tilyya says is true, then, unchecked, Nitma may well raise this white panther and win

431

power for the Meran. Do we ignore Tilyya? Do we help him? Or do we tell the Cynalese that we have made contact with a Lakiya and let them deal with it?'

'It depends on how badly we want Nitma ourselves,' Alexa said. 'It's likely she still has Ray and she has the Tamina attack to answer for. Yet the problems facing Cynal and the Mecla are far greater and should perhaps be given a higher priority.'

'Perhaps if we told Lord Tarn personally,' I suggested. 'He could stop it from reaching the ears of the false Mecla.' Worriedly I muttered, 'I know it's a risk.'

Chandra was scowling heavily. 'Nitma must be caught and stopped. Tilyya will try whether he has help or not. We must decide if help is to come from us or Lord Tarn and his soldiers.'

As we swung up into our saddles, Carly spoke, 'If either way, Nitma will be crushed, and one way holds no danger for us, I would take that way. I want to see Nitma pay but I don't care if the blow comes from me or another.'

'But as Ashil said,' Alexa pointed out, 'it's the risk. The risk of telling the wrong person and Nitma being warned.'

'Yes,' Chandra agreed. 'The more ears that hear the tune, the more mouths to sing it.'

Undecided, our minds busy with such thoughts, we rode from the mountain.

It was dark when we entered the palace and released our horses into the pasture. Timi heard us ride up and came to greet us, snorting happily on seeing his friends.

Ricah was coming out of her house as we closed the gate and she ambled over towards us.

'Greetings,' she called. 'Did Lilith find you?'

'Find us?' I repeated.

'Yes, she got your message to meet her beyond the postern gatehouse. She was pretty tired after walking Timi back all that way, but it seemed so important, I got one of the grooms to see to Timi while Lilith set out.'

'Who delivered the message?' Carly asked.

Ricah shrugged. 'A soldier, not one I knew though. Ah, here's King Charissa and her horses, I'll leave you now.'

'Let's get up to the apartment and talk,' Alexa said hastily, and we turned our back on the Eustapeans and hurried inside the palace.

My heart was pounding inside my chest and I kept taking deep breaths to calm myself. Lilith was fine, I told myself. There must have been a mix-up with the message and it had not been for her after all. She was sitting safe and comfortable in our apartment.

The apartment was empty and there was no sign that Lilith had even returned that day. Beginning to feel slightly ill, I moved towards the salon and saw the small parchment roll lying on the amusement board. I gave a loud whoop of relief. Lilith had been back and had left word telling us where she was. She had probably tired of waiting and had gone to find some dinner. I scooped up the roll and opened it out.

It was brief and to the point: 'Speak no more of the Tamina attack and do not describe the faces of the riders or identify them to anyone or the small blonde,'

433

and there was a lock of Lilith's hair enclosed, 'will die, painfully. Stay silent and she will be returned to you.' It was unsigned.

I must have made a small groan for Chandra came over and asked, 'What's wrong, Ashil? What does Lilith say?' Carly and Alexa were only a few paces behind her.

'It's not from Lil,' I whispered. 'Nitma has her,' and I handed over the roll of parchment. 'They've kidnapped her.'

'We have four things on our side,' Alexa was saying a few minutes later as we sat together on the couches. 'Nitma did not sign the message. As far as she knows, she is still just a thug and horse thief in our eyes. She is unaware of our meeting with Tilyya so she does not know that we have learnt of her theft of the mla, nor does she know that we are aware the reason she waits before unveiling her white panther is because the mla must reach maturity and take the glow. Finally, we have Tilyya's warning about the Mecla. We know we cannot risk trusting any of them with information about the Lakiya or our plans to rescue Lil.'

'She must be terrified,' I mumbled.

'She knows we'll come for her,' Chandra said forcefully. 'Cynal is not that large. We will find her and this evil Nitma.'

'That little piece of toad gut,' Carly snarled, coming to her feet. 'Because it suits her ends she steals Lil, terrorises her, throws our lives into disorder. The arrogant, corrupt, power-obsessed toad! Too bad if the world doesn't want her, she's going to force herself into people's lives no matter how much it hurts. That's all these people know. Force. Well this is one time the pain felt isn't going to be by the innocent. Nitma is going to be wishing she'd chosen a different day to visit the Tamina before this is all over.'

'I take it you no longer want to leave the search up to Lord Tarn and his soldiers?' Alexa asked.

'No, we'll do it. With four cartographers who know Nitma and several of her servants by sight, and one very determined Lakiya who can track by scent, we shouldn't have any trouble finding where they're hiding. But we won't tell anyone. I don't want to give any conniving Mecla the satisfaction of warning Nitma before we arrive to show her her plan has failed.'

I nodded earnestly. 'I agree. Now all we can do is wait until Tilyya meets us tomorrow.'

Already I wished the night gone.

SEVENTEEN

I DID NOT FEEL much like eating but Alexa had impressed upon us the need to appear as though nothing had happened, especially in the palace, so we made our way to the Dining Hall. Lilith, we were to say, had taken a bad fall while out working and had wrenched her back. She would not be able to move for several days and would keep to the apartment. We hoped that within that time we would have found her and brought her back safely.

The Hall was filling quickly and we took the last seats at a table where several Cynalese and Eustapean soldiers were talking merrily. They greeted us cordially, and then the first of the platters came around. I served myself then handed the dish on. The Eustapean beside me was one of King Charissa's equerries.

Somehow, Alexa and Carly managed to carry out a conversation with the rest of the diners and Chandra's and my quietness went unnoticed. Neither Chandra nor I were good at keeping our feelings from our faces or voices, so we stayed silent, appearing to concentrate on our food.

The more I thought of Lilith's incarceration by

Nitma, the more my anger grew. For the first time, I understood how anger could buoy a person and carry her along, even strengthen her, I only hoped Lilith was not too deeply immersed in fear and misery to feel a little of the same angry heat inside her.

Consumed as I was by thoughts of Lilith and our predicament, I flinched slightly when the Eustapean beside me knocked over his goblet and sent its contents running over the table and into my lap. I turned to him, smiling and ready to laugh away his apology, but he was staring hard at the table, his eyes strangely unfocused, his forehead creased as though perplexed, his hand limp on the table top where it had just fallen. Wondering if he was ill, I leant over, only to jump back quickly as he thrust himself to his feet, his face contorted with pain and shock. Then, horrendously, shockingly, he threw back his head and began to scream. Shriek after shriek of high-pitched, agony-filled screaming filled the air, then I became aware of the shouting and calling in the passages outside and the sounds of running feet. The Dining Hall doors were flung open and a guard hurried in, calling to all soldiers to report for duty at once. There was trouble at the stables. There had been an attack and the pasture was on fire, all hands were needed. She reeled off a list of officers' names and where they could be found and was gone, on to deliver her message elsewhere.

All was chaos. Chairs were pushed away, swords were grabbed, voices were loud and questioning as the Cynalese soldiers rushed from the Hall. The Eustapean beside me collapsed in his chair, whimpering slightly as he sat staring vacantly at the wall.

'Come on,' Chandra said, tugging at my arm. 'Let's get down there.'

My thoughts were on Cleo and Lukar loose in the burning pasture, but as I glanced up into Chan's face, I understood. If Nitma was in any way involved, this may be the opportunity we were seeking. On my feet, I looked once more at the Eustapean but others of his people were with him now and would take care of him.

Outside, the passage was full of people and guards shouting orders. All guests and servants were being asked to stay inside the palace. The soldiers would attend to all horses and the outside paths must be kept clear for their passage. We raced on, through the crowd, ignoring the soldiers, and I could feel the blood pounding in my veins. Fearfully, I wondered just what we would see at the stables.

It was full night outside but an eerie orange glow lit the sky. Despite the soldiers' pleas, people filled the path, their fear and tension as palpable as the foul breath of some living beast. We ran forward and soon we could hear the crackle and roar of the flames and feel the searing heat upon the air. The stables were before us, lit from behind by the hungry fury, and then I became aware of another sound, loud and piercing, heart-rending—the terrified screams of the trapped horses.

The rear of yellow and red stables was alight and soldiers were racing to free the horses inside, leading the sweating, trembling beasts from the burning pyre, throwing shirts and vests over the animals' eyes to calm them. It was frantic work. Other soldiers rushed buckets of water and shovelled manure over the flames, hoping to keep the fire from spreading to the other three stables, while others battled the blaze in the pasture.

With the pasture burning and the stables unsafe, soldiers were forced to gather the horses in the garden, unable to prevent the crushing and tearing of the beautiful flowers and plants by twitching, careless hooves. Out of sight of the flames, the horses calmed, until the next gust of wind brought the smell of smoke and their nostrils flared and their eyes rolled anxiously.

Some of the crowd, unasked, had begun to assist the soldiers as they stood in rows, passing bucket after bucket of water along through the open pasture gates to be thrown onto the raging inferno inside. But the fire was too great. None of the pasture horses had yet been saved. The soldiers were trying to open a path through the flames but the ferocity of the fire forced them back each time. I wanted to help desperately— all six of our horses were trapped behind that wall of flames—but first we needed to know if there was any sign of Nitma that could lead us to Lilith.

Green stable was not on fire but a small group of soldiers stood guarding the entrance, and as we came as close as was permitted we heard the single bellowing of a horse inside. It was a tremendous trumpeting, loud, angry and pain-filled, but none of the soldiers moved to help it. A soldier came running along the path to the officer overseeing the work at the stables and spoke quickly to him. The officer listened in silence, nodded curtly, then ordered a small number of his soldiers to spread out and form a passageway.

Moments later Lord Tarn, Rianne and King Charissa walked up, surrounded by a small retinue of guards who looked about warily, their hands on swords and bows, poised for action.

The three leaders looked strained. Although Lord Tarn was expressionless, in the dancing firelight his skin looked strangely pale and his eyes were hard and glittering. Beside him, Rianne had drawn herself up tall and straight but her lips were parted, as though caught in a sudden shocked gasp, and her breathing was shallow. King Charissa, so much shorter than the two, seemed weighed down by an inestimable sadness, her face despairing and drained. As they reached green stable, the officer stepped forward, saluted and bowed.

The outraged screaming of the horse in green stable seemed to become louder and King Charissa stared at the stable in horror. Without waiting to hear what the officer had to report, she walked on with her Eustapean guards towards the open door of the stable, her face a mask of grief. She passed through the doors and the screaming seemed to reach a fever pitch. It continued for several more moments, then suddenly, abruptly, it stopped. I swallowed, for my throat had become thick. I knew how the Eustapeans hated to kill.

Lord Tarn and Rianne spoke a few more words to the officer, looking at the fire and the crowd around them, then they moved to the stable and disappeared inside. Clearly, Lord Tarn had made comment on the number of people on the path, for the soldiers imme-diately returned to the task of dispersing the crowd. Reluctantly, people obeyed, either joining the bucket line or returning to the palace to sit out the fire. We were torn. We did not wish to leave. We needed to know what had happened in green stable and what had caused the fire.

Carly spotted Rarnald and called to him. He frowned on seeing us and rushed over. 'You must return to the palace,' he said quickly. 'It is dangerous out here and we need the path cleared.'

'What happened, Rarnald?' Alexa asked. 'We heard there was an attack.'

'Yes.' He nodded and he glanced at green stable. 'We are not sure whether it was an attempt to get into the palace and the intruders sought to escape by horse, or whether they came simply to cause trouble in the stables. All we know is that a struggle occurred in green stable and one of King Charissa's horses was killed and the other was badly injured.'

He paused and we waited, knowing there was more.

'And?' I asked softly, though I dreaded what his next words would be.

He turned back to us, his voice low and sad. 'And Ricah was killed, run through by a sword. She often keeps her shutters open at night and she must have heard the intruders and come out to investigate. She was found beside the body of King Charissa's mare.'

Ricah dead! I could feel tears beginning to form. 'Oh, Rarnald,' I whispered.

'Yes,' he murmured softly. Then he seemed to recall his duty. 'Now you must leave. One of the grooms cleaning up in white stable heard the struggle and alerted the guards. They came quickly and saw the flames and sounded the alarm. A search for the intruders has already begun. Go back to the palace and stay there.'

Lord Tarn, Rianne and King Charissa had still not come out of green stable, where there lay three to mourn. Evil One, Tilyya called Nitma. How right he was. I refused to think how one who could kill so easily was treating Lilith.

There was a triumphant shout from the pasture behind us. The flames had been beaten and a gap cleared for the horses. The first of them were being brought through now, shuddering over their ordeal.

Smiling with relief that at least it seemed our horses would be safe, we began to move away when suddenly there was a commotion at green stable. King Charissa came out, calling for the officer. She had discovered blood on the stallion's hooves. One of the intruders had been wounded. Lord Tarn stepped out beside her. The power of the stallion had been great and the intruder could not have gone far. Lord Tarn ordered all but soldiers from the grounds. A thorough search was to take place and Ricah's murderer would be found.

This time we had no choice but to obey the order and we made for the safety and privacy of our apartment. The west wing was quiet. Soldiers passed us from time to time, patrolling, but most doors were shut and the people sequestered inside.

'What I don't understand,' Carly murmured, so as not to be overheard, as we reached the apartment door, 'is why anyone trying to steal a horse to escape would kill one and wound another? No thief or murderer could be so clumsy, so it can't have been accidental.

Or, if the intruders were just looking to cause trouble, why would they choose to attack two of the largest, most ferocious horses in the stable, two which clearly fought back?'

I was just as perplexed. 'Why did the Eustapean equerry scream in the Dining Hall? How could he have known of the attack?'

Alexa had unlocked the door and we stepped inside. 'It's . . .' but Alexa never finished her sentence, for she had turned around and was now facing the salon.

Surprised, we all followed her gaze and saw what had silenced her. Seated on one of the white couches, clutching his chest, was the beefy, lank-haired thug from the Blue Dolphin, one of the two who had escaped the day I had regained Cleo.

'Good evening,' he said, his voice short with pain, his eyes malicious. 'A warm night out?'

'How did you get in?' Alexa asked calmly, moving towards him and ignoring his question.

The man held up a key. 'A present from Lilith,' he said and gave a small, unpleasant laugh. He dropped it next to him on the couch where a small square of parchment lay. 'She even drew me a map,' he added, smiling, and I suddenly wanted to hit him very hard.

Alexa was before him now and she sat herself on the couch opposite.

'You're wounded?' she asked.

'Yes, the stallion was too cunning, but we got the runt in the end. Unfortunately the alarm was sounded before we could escape and I knew I'd never scale the walls with my ribs broken, so I praised Meclan that the Blessed One had thought to give me this.' He tapped the map. 'After all, we've had two kits full of materials since our visit to the Rovers. Why not use them?' He grinned nastily. 'Now we get to spend the night together.'

'Or you get to spend the night in the dungeon,' Carly spat. 'What makes you think we'll hide you?' Her voice was incredulous.

'In a word—Lilith,' the man replied with offensive relish.

'Where is she?' Chandra demanded, stepping forward quickly.

The man laughed. 'I'm hardly going to tell you, am I?' The laugh became a sneer. 'My friends who escaped know I had the map and was planning to come here. They lit the fire to give us all cover to escape and I hid in that little house beside the stable until I saw my opportunity to enter the palace. With people getting under the guards' feet, it was easy to slip inside the palace and into this room. Should I be turned in, my colleagues will kill your little friend.'

'If the Cynalese imprison you, your friends will have no way of knowing if we handed you over or you were caught on your way here,' Alexa pointed out.

The man nodded. 'True, but are you prepared to take the risk? The Blessed One doesn't like people who interfere with her plans. Lilith wouldn't die pleasantly.'

'The Blessed One?' I repeated. 'You mean . . . ' but Alexa shot me a warning glance. It was in Lilith's best interest that we not reveal our knowledge of Nitma's identity. I swallowed. 'Who do you mean?' I asked instead.

'You'll know soon enough. Everyone will when she

takes her rightful place. She's going to change the world.'

'She'll be busy,' Alexa replied dryly.

The man smiled. 'She'll succeed, too. She's magnificent.'

Alexa raised an eyebrow but said no more about the Blessed One. 'What's your name?'

'Zerak.'

'Why did you kill Lord Tarn's horses?'

Zerak frowned. 'They were Eustapean horses.'

'No,' Alexa shook her head, turning to us ever so guilelessly for confirmation. 'They were two of Lord Tarn's best. King Charissa's horses were moved to another stable yesterday. Was it an attempt to upset Lord Tarn before the enthroning?'

I could see Zerak was rattled, unsure whether to believe us or not.

'I saw King Charissa riding the black this afternoon and another Eustapean was on the mare,' he argued.

'They are different horses,' Chandra said. 'Didn't you notice that King Charissa's stallion has different coloured eyes? It was Lord Tarn's black that broke your ribs.'

Zerak looked worried. He still had one arm wrapped around his chest. There was little blood, the stallion's hooves must have just grazed him on impact, but I well remembered how a blow to the chest felt and knew that even sitting he must be in pain.

'You're lying,' he whispered.

Alexa feigned surprise. 'Why would we?' she asked. Then she stared at Zerak with obvious speculation. 'Are you saying it was King Charissa's horses you were after?'

445

'I'm not saying anything,' Zerak snapped back.

Chandra shrugged. 'Well, everyone will be happy the Searchers are safe.'

The Searchers? Bemused, I glanced at Chandra, then saw the way Zerak's face had drained of all colour. For one fascinating moment I thought he might faint.

'How can you possibly know about the Seekers?' Zerak hissed.

Chandra shrugged again and I could see how it infuriated Zerak. 'The Eustapeans do not hunt or trap animals, so who would learn to track? At the harbour, when the Eustapeans were unloading the Searchers, they spoke with our horses, calming them. The Searchers are the beast friends of the Melcran. They are their trackers.'

A slow smile of delight was growing on Alexa's face. 'Chandra's right,' she said to Zerak. 'The Melcran eat no flesh. They respect all that lives and keep to themselves on their peaceful island. What is to stop them following Meclan's path and communicating with animals without interference or fear of opportunism? Was that why you wanted to kill them ... because their search this time was for the Blessed One?'

'Why would they be seeking the Blessed One?' Zerak asked defiantly, though his eyes were wide with fear. Great Ruler of the Skies, I thought, Chandra had been right. The Eustapean horses were Searchers.

'Why have you not killed yourself?' I asked cruelly. 'The man I caught with my horse did. Don't you fear the anger of the Blessed One for failing?'

'We did not fail,' he screeched. 'We killed the Seekers. The black did not have different coloured eyes

and they were in green stable. I saw them this afternoon and they were the horses we killed. They were
King Charissa's.' Then as he realised what he had just
admitted, he stopped abruptly, glaring at us with
hatred. 'It makes no difference what you know,' he
snarled. 'We have Lilith. Whisper one word to anyone
and she'll die.'

'Should that happen,' Carly retorted swiftly, 'there
won't be any reason for us to put up with your stinking
company any more, so we'll send you back to your
Blessed One, in chunks.'

Zerak's head flew back but Alexa had stood up and
the exchange went no further.

'Tonight, Zerak, we'll give you Carly's room,' Alexa
said. She looked at Carly. 'Take what you'll need, and
we'll put Zerak in there.'

Carly moved to her room and shortly after reappeared with her pack. Alexa then demanded Zerak's
weapons. He refused at first, but acceded grumpily
when he saw the blades in each of our hands.

'Do you want to strap your chest?' Alexa asked but
Zerak only sneered once more; it appeared his fine
spirits of earlier had departed. Without a word, he
came slowly to his feet, holding tightly to his chest,
and began to walk to the door, ignoring the four of
us. Once inside the room, Carly took out her key and
locked the door. Zerak would be going nowhere
without our permission.

'Chan, I'm impressed,' Alexa said, patting Chandra
on the shoulder as we regrouped on the couches. 'How
did you know about the Eustapean horses?'

Chandra smiled broadly. 'I started thinking about it

447

the morning we spoke with King Charissa. Then, as we learned more about the Lakiya, I remembered Damin had said the Melcran had the mind powers too. I was not certain when I spoke to Zerak but I suspected the Eustapean pair were not ordinary horses.'

'And Zerak confirmed it,' Alexa finished with a grin.

'So,' I said, amazed, 'it could have been the horses who called to the equerry for help this evening.' What would it be like hearing such a call inside your mind and feeling the death blow?

'If King Charissa has brought these Searchers to Cynal she must have known or suspected that Nitma was here,' Carly pointed out.

Alexa nodded. 'Yet from what Lord Tarn and Rianne have said to us, it appears they do not share the knowledge. I wonder why King Charissa hasn't spoken to them of it?'

'The false Mecla?' I asked. 'Perhaps the Eustapeans are aware there is a traitor and sought to catch Nitma on their own. Or Nitma has silenced the king in the same way she has silenced us.'

'No,' Chandra said. 'Then Nitma would not have needed to kill the horses. She could have just threatened the king as she has threatened us with hurting Lil.'

'This is good news then,' I crowed. 'We can speak with the king and seek Nitma together.' Then I noticed the worried expression on Alexa's face. 'What is it?'

'The secrecy with which the Melcran have used the Searchers suggests that Nitma was unaware of them until now. She thought us silenced and Tilyya dead.

She probably thought her path clear. Wait for the mla to glow, then reveal herself as the gods' chosen one and call the people to her. Now Nitma knows the Melcran seek her in Cynal, she is no longer safe. With the Searchers dead, King Charissa will have no reason not to speak to Lord Tarn and Nitma's quiet waiting period is over. Lord Tarn will pull Cynal apart looking for her. The greatest danger for Nitma is that there are five people in Cynal who can identify her. Whether Nitma believes we know who she is or not is unimportant now. We have seen her face. She will hold Lilith to keep us quiet, but I wonder how long it will be before she starts to think that the five of us dead is a far better solution. When it was important not to alert the Cynalese to her presence here our deaths would have been too risky. But now, while she waits desperately for the mla to glow, she will be prepared to take any action necessary. The first and easiest kill is close at hand, Lilith.'

'No,' I moaned in protest, 'you must be wrong. They couldn't kill her.'

'They didn't have much trouble with Ricah,' Carly said. 'The Meran sacrifice the living, Ash, and we've been a nuisance from the start. They'll probably enjoy it.'

Chandra was quiet for a moment, then she spoke firmly. 'We must give the Cynalese a description of Nitma before we search for Lilith. Should anything happen to us, they must know who to look for.'

'We can leave behind a sealed message for Lord Tarn,' Carly suggested. 'That will give us some time to try and rescue Lil.'

449

'We need Tilyya,' I said, thinking ahead. 'If we release Zerak, we can follow him.'

'He'll be expecting it, it may even be what Nitma planned when she gave Zerak the map and key,' Alexa mused, 'but there's little else we can do. Let's sleep now. Come morning we'll be busy.'

When we rose we sent word to Nikol that we would spend the day in the workroom and would not need her assistance. Her reply said that she was needed in the search for the intruders and would be out of the palace the length of her shift. She wished us a good day.

Over a quick breakfast, we discussed what we would tell Zerak when he awoke, then I slipped away, hoping to meet quickly with Tilyya outside the palace.

There was a palpable tension within the palace. People I passed moved quietly, their eyes anxious, their faces revealing feelings of disbelief, fear and outrage. The intruders had not been caught and the palace was uneasy. The enthroning was now only four days away and most of the important guests had arrived. It made everyone nervous to know that such an attack had occurred and gone unpunished. For King Charissa, who was much adored by the Cynalese, there was sympathy over the death of her much prized horses, and for Ricah, much loved and admired, there was genuine sadness and mourning. It was a melancholy morning.

The acrid smell of smoke reached me as I stepped from beneath the low portico onto the path from where we had first seen the fiery glow of the blaze last night. The fire was dead now, successfully quashed by the determined effort and sweat of the Cynalese soldiers. There remained only the charred remnants of the two middle stables and the desolate blackness of the once-rich pasture. I wandered to the pasture gate and stared at the scorched earth. The fire had burnt over half the grass, and the contrast between the tough, living blades, bending in the wind, and the blackened stubs was unsettling. Moving over the damaged pasture were growers, beginning to turn the burned waste in preparation for the new growth.

A fence had been hastily constructed around the undamaged end of the pasture and it was here, grazing contentedly, their memories enviably short, that the pasture horses and those from the damaged stables were being kept. A small group of people surrounded the fence, each peering anxiously into the crowded pasture, searching for a familiar coat or muzzle, eager to discover the fate of their horses. I thought of our six and quickened my pace.

Fifteen horses had died, a woman beside me at the fence said, nine in the stables and the rest in the pasture. Plus, she added, King Charissa's pair in green. She shook her head, repeating 'fifteen' as she wandered off.

I saw Timi first, then Drella and Lukar and Bragan. Flir and Cleo I had to search for but I soon discovered them standing together in the far corner. All were safe. Relieved, I called Lukar over and he nuzzled me affectionately. Stroking him, I led him from the pasture and returned to the path.

More growers were tending the rows of battered and

trampled flowers along the path's edges, while others saw to the damage in the garden. They were silent and absorbed, many on their knees, their deft fingers righting the bruised plants or placing seedlings in the dark earth with delicate swiftness.

I moved on to blue stable to collect Lukar's saddle and stared up at the craftspeople swarming over and around yellow and red stables. In contrast to the growers, they were loud and active and the sound of their hammering and shouting and wood-hauling seemed to echo in the mild early morning air. Even the blacksmith was busy this morning, hard at work at his anvil as Lukar and I passed, and I wondered suddenly about Timi's shoe. Ricah could not see to it now.

Traffic was banked up at the main gatehouse as soldiers checked each entrant to the palace. It was not as difficult to leave, but getting Zerak out undetected would clearly not be an easy task.

I did not know where I would find Tilyya but, recalling his ability to follow us, as he had done for days, I did not doubt he would soon appear. So I walked Lukar free of the crowds, heading west through the streets, the light blue sea ahead of me, lightly scanning the faces of those who passed me. When I came to a quiet corner, shadowed by a tall building, I dismounted and bent over, pretending to fiddle with my sandal. When I straightened up, Tilyya stood before me.

'Good morning, Ashil,' he whispered shyly, his smile tentative.

'Good morning, Tilyya,' I replied, giving him a broad reassuring grin. 'We have news.'

His expression grew attentive. 'About the Evil One?'

I nodded. 'Yes,' I told him, keeping my voice low. 'When we returned to the palace yesterday we discovered that Nitma has kidnapped our friend, Lilith, and is holding her to keep us from speaking with the Cynalese or Mecla. Then Nitma sent several of her servants into the palace last night to kill two horses belonging to King Charissa of Eustape. The king is Melcran and the horses were Searchers. One of the servants was injured and could not escape. We have him now.'

Such joy that shone from his eyes! 'And he will tell us.'

'I am afraid not.' I shook my head. 'He believes in Nitma.' I told Tilyya our plan. 'If it works you must promise that if you find Nitma's hiding place you will not try and enter it alone but will come back for us. We cannot risk Lilith being hurt. Do you understand?'

Tilyya stared at me for a moment with his pale, clear eyes. 'I understand,' he murmured. 'You love Lilith, I love my mla, we will save them both.'

With that I was in full agreement. 'We will leave by the main gatehouse and head out of the city. Can you follow us?'

'Yes, I will follow you.'

'Good. I have to go to the market before I return to the palace, but we should leave the palace by midmorning. The man is broad and strong with lank blond hair. He is wounded in the chest and he mustn't see you, Tilyya, for we can't have Nitma warned. She would have been unhappy to learn of the Searchers. She will be alert now, watching for trouble. And she is powerful.'

453

'I have not forgotten the Evil One's sting,' he replied. 'I will watch for you at the gate.'

He turned to leave but I remembered something Alexa had told me to ask and I reached out and caught his arm. A sudden, startling shock ran through my hand and along my arm and I broke the contact quickly. It had not exactly hurt but it was far from pleasant and for a moment all thought left my mind.

I must have gasped for Tilyya stepped up hastily to me and breathed my name, an expression of solicitous perplexity on his smooth, eerily beautiful face.

'What happened?' I murmured.

'I am sorry,' his voice was tinged with regret, 'I am near my mla and my body seeks to speak with him. Our language is strange to mortals and because you cannot communicate that way it sometimes causes pain.'

I nodded. The bones in my arm were aching and I folded it across my chest. I shook my head and recalled my question. 'I wanted to ask you when your mla will take the glow. We need to know how long Nitma must wait before she can call the white panther.'

Tilyya's face seemed to grow long with perturbation. 'My mla reached maturity late last night,' he admitted, very softly.

I gave a small, fretful groan, Lil!

Tilyya's expression lightened and his own eyes glowed. 'For the briefest moment he was aware of me as he felt his own power.'

'Does Nitma . . . ' I began tremulously.

'No,' he looked at me, 'the Evil One does not yet realise that he has attained his full glow, and he will not help the Evil One to learn. He knows I am near and he awaits me. Should the Evil One discover my mla is ready for the change and force him, my mla is lost to me.'

And Lilith to us. 'We must hurry,' I said, feeling my breath come short as my heart began to pound. 'Watch for us,' and I grabbed Lukar's reins.

My trip to the market was short but Lukar's coat had begun to shine with sweat by the time I reached the palace, for I had pushed him hard. With the white panther at hand, Nitma would fear no-one, and then Lilith's life would surely be over.

EIGHTEEN

A STIFF AND SURLY Zerak was sitting at the table chewing on his breakfast as I entered.

'Where have you been?' he demanded.

'Making arrangements to get your ugly face out of here,' I snapped back, dropping my morning's purchases on the table. 'Or did you plan on walking out of the palace all on your own with half your chest caved in?'

He raised his lip in a sneer but said no more. Carly gave me a friendly pat on the back as I walked past, her face lit with amusement. From a couch, Chandra was regarding me with concern. She knew something had to be wrong for me to speak that way, and Alexa raised one eyebrow in query. I gave her a brief nod, indicating I had met Tilyya. Time to tell them of the mla's maturity when we were free of Zerak.

Alexa stood and faced the thug. 'We have discussed our position and have decided that it is in Lilith's best interests to get you out of the palace.'

Zerak gave a smug snort. 'Smart decision.'

If only he knew, I thought, but that would come later. First we had to clean him up and dress him in the nondescript clothing I had purchased from the market. His chest was badly discoloured and we could not risk it being seen. Sensing freedom, he cooperated, washing and grooming himself, then standing quietly while I tightly strapped his chest and helped him into a new shirt. Remembering Chandra's earlier observation, I had bought a pair of sandals for him to wear instead of his boots.

'My weapons,' he ordered, once dressed, not bothering to look up as he slid an exploratory hand over his strapped chest.

'You won't need them,' Alexa replied equably, though today she wore her own short sword and Chandra had her bow and quiver laid out ready.

'I want them back,' he growled, glaring at her.

'No,' Alexa said. Ignoring his angry cursing, she asked Zerak if he was well enough to sit a horse.

Zerak grunted. 'I can ride,' he told her sourly.

'Good,' she nodded. 'Let's go.'

Carly was last to leave and I knew that she was placing the sealed letter with Nitma's description and all we knew of her plot upon the dining table. It had been written that morning while I met with Tilyya and was addressed to Lord Tarn. If we did not return, we knew Nikol or Rarnald would come looking for us in our apartment. Neither would dare open a letter for Lord Tarn, but would take it to him immediately.

A few people in west wing glanced curiously at Zerak as we passed.

'Stop scowling,' Carly reprimanded him, 'you're drawing attention.' After that Zerak relaxed his face and attempted to participate in our light, contrived conversation about Cynalese restaurants.

All went well. We got Zerak out of the west wing and into the south-west and slowly down the stairs, though we had to pause on a step from time to time, as though engrossed in conversation, to allow him a chance to rest and catch his breath. Even so, by the time we reached the workroom his injury was telling and his forehead was wet with sweat. Once the door was shut he collapsed weakly against a workbench. Without comment, Carly handed him a rag and he wiped his face. We were halfway there.

Chandra picked up Lilith's kit and, after removing the more valuable items, passed it to Zerak. He took it mutely and watched as we slung our own kits over our shoulders. Delicately, imitating us, he eased the kit up his arm and over his shoulder, using his hand to keep the kit from bumping his chest. The four of us stepped back to examine him. For this morning, for the benefit of the gate guards, Zerak was to play a cartographer.

Satisfied that we had done our best in the short time available, we left the workroom and had almost rounded the first corner when a voice behind us called our names and steps hurried towards us. I swallowed nervously, cursing our luck, for I knew the voice, and we turned and faced Rianne.

'Good morning, cartographers,' she greeted us, her eyes falling straight away upon Zerak, and I wished he was dark, instead of bearing the blond hair and ruddy skin so common amongst the Delawese.

'Good morning, Rianne,' we each replied and Carly

sidled up next to Zerak and slipped an arm around his waist.

'Rianne,' she cooed, smiling up at the beefy thug beside her, 'this is Zerak, a friend of mine.'

The emphasis she put on the word friend made it seem that he was much more and the priest smiled and nodded politely while Zerak encircled Carly's waist with one arm and bowed stiffly. Looking away from the couple, and Zerak's kit, Rianne asked where Lilith was.

'She hurt her back yesterday,' Alexa replied, with a deprecatory smile. 'She's resting upstairs.'

'Should I send a physician?'

'No,' Alexa answered, 'she just needs rest. She'll be fine in a day or two.'

Rianne paused for a moment, absorbing this. 'I was coming to see you in your workroom. Lord Tarn and King Charissa will be meeting this afternoon, after Ricah's funeral, and they would like two of you to attend with the sketches you have so far made of Cynal. Will you make yourselves available?'

It was impossible, of course, we would be midway through our search for Lilith, but Alexa nodded. 'Of course.'

Rianne's gaze skipped over Zerak once more before she nodded curtly. 'Come to the north wing. An escort will be waiting to take you to the meeting room.' Expressionless, she bowed to us and left.

With Zerak present we were unable to discuss this turn of events, though the implications were clear. If Lord Tarn and King Charissa were meeting, it could only be to discuss one topic. King Charissa would tell

Lord Tarn that Nitma was in Cynal and the hunt for the Meran leader would begin. When that happened, Lilith's value as a hostage would swiftly decrease.

Outside, in the bright sunshine, the growers and craftspeople still worked, adding their numbers to the busy pathways. Despite last night's attack and murder, preparations for the enthroning could not cease and everywhere people raced with important tasks to complete. We hoped the bustling palace crowd would work to our advantage by providing us with extra cover.

At the pasture we called our horses. With Timi still unshod, I had no choice but to allow Zerak to ride Cleo. She was still a little thin from her ordeal but was moving well and did not object to the saddle. Her ears twitched uncertainly when Zerak moved towards her but she stood unmoving as we helped him mount. It was a difficult task, and time-consuming, but he was finally in the saddle and sitting quite straight. We swung up into our saddles and began the walk to the gate.

I peered at the guards' faces, immensely relieved not to recognise any. If they did not know us, they would not know that Zerak was not normally of our party. A large group of guests had just arrived and were being courteously passed through, though even they had to submit to a carriage-by-carriage search and account for each of their numbers. The wait was long and the sun grew hot. I had forgotten my hat and sweat gathered between my shoulderblades.

Finally, the last of the carriages passed by and we were waved forward. The officer looked us over quickly, taking in every detail, and I felt the sweat trickle down my back, light as a feather touch.

'What's your business?' she asked.

'We're cartographers, drawing for Lord Tarn,' Carly answered brightly. 'We're off to sketch more of the city.'

If our faces were unknown to the officer, our task was not.

'Pass along,' she said, pointing an arm in the direction of the gate.

I only hoped Tilyya had seen us, for we did not stop. Chandra took Cleo's reins and we trotted through the city. Zerak spoke out once, wanting to know where we were going and ordering us to let him down near the market, but we hushed him and said we had to find a quiet place to talk first. He was having difficulty staying astride Cleo. Otherwise I am sure he would have protested more. When the city's gates were in view, we slowed the horses to a walk.

'I don't want to leave the city,' Zerak hissed. 'I'll only have to walk back.' His eyes had the glassy look of unremitting pain and his mouth was tight with the strain. We ignored him.

There was a large group of soldiers standing to one side of the city gates, briefing each other on their morning's news, I supposed, but the gate guards did not stop us. Keen to leave the city and its danger of exposure behind, I only glanced over the soldiers. When next I returned, I hoped to be on the trail of Nitma.

Zerak did not canter well and, despite all the evil I knew he had done, I found his cries to stop hard to block out. But the rough handling suited our purpose and when the horses began the climb up and around Mount Rittoy we finally eased our pace until we came to a rest halfway up the seaward side.

'You turd-mites!' Zerak screamed, almost over-wrought, as he pulled futilely at the reins, still held firmly by Chandra.

'Relax, Zerak,' Carly said, smiling. 'The ride's over now, dismount, we're going to have a talk.'

'I don't want to talk,' he yelled. 'Let me go now or your friend, Lilith, will suffer.'

'Shut up and get off the horse,' Carly told him. 'There's only so many times you can use the same line.'

A flicker of doubt crossed Zerak's face but was soon gone. He did not believe we would risk Lilith's life, but with no other choice at hand he slowly dismounted, jarring his chest as he landed and half-falling to the ground.

The four of us came and sat around him.

'We have considered all options,' Alexa said, enviably cool, 'and we want to propose an exchange with the Blessed One.' Her ice-blue eyes stared directly at Zerak. 'You for Lilith.'

Zerak's mouth hung open in shock. 'You're mad!' he cried, both arms wrapped around his chest, his face now haggard with exhaustion.

'The Blessed One has what we want, we have something she wants,' Alexa continued, opening her hands eloquently. 'The solution is simple.'

'She'll never agree,' he rasped. There was fear in his eyes now.

'No?' Alexa asked. 'She doesn't want you back?'

'Not enough to trade,' he growled defensively. 'So,

I've admitted it, we've an agreement. Nothing is to jeopardise the Blessed One's rise to power. She wants to keep you silent so she'll keep Lilith, and there's no way, without me, that you can even contact her.' He seemed pleased with himself for pointing out that fact and relaxed a little.

Alexa nodded. 'Then we kill you. Carly?'

With evident delight, Carly stood and drew her twin blades from where they had been concealed beneath her clothing. Zerak's eyes grew wide.

'No,' he spluttered. 'Then Lilith will die.'

'But you're quite right, Zerak. Without you we cannot contact the Blessed One, so she will not know whether you live or die. Nor, apparently, will she care. You are a nuisance to us. We cannot give you to the Cynalese for fear the Blessed One will learn of it, though perhaps it would not matter, and if you are of no value to her then you are of no value to us. We promise your death will be quick and, afterwards, we will not leave you to rot but will bury you.' And with that, spoken in such a reasonable, almost friendly, tone, Alexa indicated to Carly to proceed.

'Wait,' Zerak cried, his voice high. 'Perhaps I've been a little hasty. Perhaps there is another way.'

'Yes?' Alexa prompted.

'I could take you to the Blessed One. Maybe she would trade me for Lilith after all. I'll lead you there.' He was almost gushing now, so keen was he to convince us.

Alexa paused to consider it, cruelly extending the moment while Zerak watched her face intently for any sign of reprieve.

'No,' she concluded. 'I don't trust you. You'd try and lead us into a trap. The Blessed One would love to silence us all, whoever she is. She is not keen for others to know her face. It is easier for us to kill you. We will find Lilith some other way.'

'But . . . ' Zerak began to protest as Chandra stood and joined Carly and they began to advance upon him. He tried to stand, awkwardly coming to his feet, one hand fumbling at his waist for the weapons that he usually kept there.

'In cold blood,' he wailed.

'There will be no blood,' Alexa promised. 'Chandra can kill with one blow. It will be painless. Should you struggle, Carly will use her daggers and there may be pain. Goodbye Zerak.'

He stared at Alexa in disbelief and Chandra kicked his legs out from under him. He landed heavily on his knees, pain from his ribs lancing his body. Before his mind had time to clear, Chandra dealt him the blow. It was quick, smooth and painless, as promised, and he crumpled at our feet, inert.

Tilyya came to us as we lay hiding behind a ridge. He greeted us silently and lay down beside us. Together we watched the gully below us.

A strong gust of wind blew and the smell from the steaming pool beneath us reached me and I wrinkled my nose. It was still unpleasant.

Suddenly Tilyya pointed ahead and we crouched lower. There was a stirring amongst the springy growth that covered the gully, a prodding, a testing, then it was roughly pushed aside and Zerak thrust himself up. He turned his head from side to side, fearfully, his eyes darting all about him. When he saw nothing, he lifted his hand to his head and tentatively felt the lump there. He dropped his hand and laughed triumphantly, for he believed he had just cheated death, then he climbed from the gully.

He moved slowly, hampered as he was by his broken ribs and a very sore head. After his hours of unconsciousness he was bound to feel a little disoriented, though no doubt his euphoria at being alive would help keep him moving. If he believed, as we hoped he did, that he had survived a clumsily delivered blow intended to kill, and been thrown into the gully grave and left to rot, then he would not be concerned with being followed. It was our only hope. We needed Zerak to return to Nitma in order to find her ourselves.

When Zerak reached the base of the mountain we started to move. We passed the gully into which I had fallen only yesterday, and kept low amongst the small trees. Not once did Zerak look back as he shuffled eagerly towards the city.

When we paused again, to keep the distance between Zerak and ourselves safe, Tilyya whispered that he would leave us now. He appeared almost feverish with excitement, like a candle's brilliant white flame.

'Remember,' I told him, 'if we lose him, return for us.'

'I promise,' he breathed and he was gone.

In short, careful bursts, we covered the ground between Mount Rittoy and Cynal, close on the heels of Zerak. The toll on his body was beginning to show and his shuffle had slowed a little. When we next stopped, I glanced up at the sun. It had already begun its afternoon descent. Ricah's funeral would be over and the meeting between Lord Tarn and King Charissa would begin shortly. I wondered what Lord Tarn would make of our absence. If it was permanent, no doubt Leah would be ecstatic.

Entering the city could be difficult. We needed to be far enough away from Zerak so as not to be seen, yet close enough to see which direction he took.

Just short of the roadway, Zerak halted and made an attempt to dust himself off, straightening his shirt, tidying his hair with his hands, and licking his fingers to try and scrub the dirt and sweat from his face. He rubbed at his chest, then eased his shoulders back so he stood as straight as possible and strode out.

He was stopped almost immediately, the guard looking Zerak over and asking him to step aside to be questioned. We were too far away to hear the conversation, but whatever explanation Zerak offered it was acceptable to the soldier for he nodded and let Zerak through.

The four of us crossed to the other side of the gates. A guard began watching us and when I caught her eye, I smiled. We did not want to be stopped and lose sight of Zerak. She smiled back and turned away. We walked on. Inside Cynal, Zerak was moving along the western thoroughfare.

Carefully, we followed the tiring Zerak as he continued along the Street of Lights. We halted at the corner of a building.

'He's so slow!' Carly exclaimed frustratedly, flinging herself against the building wall.

'Patience,' Chandra remonstrated. 'Better too slow than too quick.'

'I wonder if Nitma has discovered the mla's secret yet,' Alexa mused. I had told them of the mla's maturity while we waited for Zerak to emerge from the gully.

'We'll know if we're greeted by a white panther,' I replied humourlessly.

'If we are, remember to stay back, Ash,' Alexa said, staring intently at me. 'Chan will have her bow ready and Carly and I will go in first. We know there are at least three thugs with Nitma, plus Zerak, and there may be more. We'll try and get Lilith out without alerting them but it may be impossible. If there's a fight, leave it to us while you try to free Lilith. Keep your knife out but only use it if you have to.' She looked along the street, following Zerak's progress. 'I hope Tilyya has a fighting trick or two,' she murmured.

Zerak turned a corner and we began to move again. It was harder to keep an eye on him in the busy streets but easier to hide ourselves. The streets were beginning to change as we drew closer to the harbour district and Zerak seemed to be putting on an extra display of speed, like a horse nearing home. Nitma and Lilith could not be far now.

As the streets narrowed, we had to be more careful, the four of us were hard to miss. Carly and I were following Chandra and Alexa's lead, trusting to their experience. We saw no sign of Tilyya.

467

The tenements began to crowd around us and we slowed, darting into doorways and small alleys and under shop awnings, shaking our heads at the children who came running up, hoping for a game. Adults watched us pass curiously, some wishing us a good day, others holding up wares from their small shops and waving to us to come and buy. They were loud and friendly and gay, as though they were free of all troubles, and their noise and raw, rough energy only added to the tension building inside me. We were north of the great harbour warehouses now. It would be soon.

Zerak was approaching another corner and Chandra waved us into an alley. I could not see what Zerak was doing, but from the way Chandra drew back quickly it was clear he had begun to check his surroundings.

'He's scanning,' Chandra whispered.

'We must be close,' Alexa replied.

Chandra took another cautious look. 'Come, he's gone.'

We trotted to the corner and around it, where Zerak had turned. It was only a short street, fewer than fifteen paces long, and Zerak was nowhere in sight. Carly cursed as we ran to the end. One of the district's largest roads was before us and there was no sight of the blond thug anywhere amongst the traffic.

'We've lost him,' I cried in soft despair.

'He can't have gone far,' Alexa said, looking up and down the street. 'He's probably in one of the tenements.'

Carly glanced at the dozens of tall, squashed buildings. 'Yes, but which one?' she asked dryly.

'Let's see what we can find out,' Alexa said. 'We'll

split and take a stroll along both ends of the street.'

'Wait,' Chandra ordered, taking a tight grip on Alexa's and my sleeves. 'Tilyya is across the road, beside the yellow awning, and he is waving us back.'

I had to narrow my eyes and search hard before I spotted the Lakiya. 'He's pointing at something to our right.'

We stepped back and peered along the street. There was a large tenement beside us, a small, run-down collection of busy, colourful shops, another tenement and . . . I gasped, for the irony was extraordinary. The scarlet door was shut, looking bright and solid in the afternoon sunlight, and the words of belief were large for all to see, swinging on their sign.

'A free-house,' I exclaimed in wonder, giving a small, dazed laugh. 'Tilyya's pointing at a free-house.'

Carly shook her head. 'That cunning piece of toad gut. She's been plotting and attempting the Mecla's downfall while they've been feeding and sheltering her.'

Alexa watched as Tilyya crossed to us then flicked her eyes back to the free-house. 'Nitma can't have every room in the house at her disposal,' she reasoned, 'so we'll have to tread carefully. It will be impossible to judge who her servants are until they make a move against us, and any warning we give Nitma of our presence is time she has to kill Lilith.'

She turned to Tilyya. 'Can you reach your mla?'

'No, this place is shielded.' He smiled beatifically. 'So he must be there.'

Alexa nodded. 'Then let's go find them.'

There was a small bell at the door but we did not wish to announce our arrival, so when the door opened to our touch we stepped inside, closing it quietly after us. A ceiling window allowed the bright sun to fill the small, square entrance area and splash on the corner staircase as its steps rose and fell before us. An open door on the right revealed an empty workroom—the Mecla guardian's, I presumed. All the other visible doors on this level were shut.

The sound of several voices came to us from behind the staircase and we walked forward, finding two large open doors giving on to a large, table-filled room. A small kitchen could be seen at the rear and a scattering of people sat at the dining tables, talking and playing at amusement boards. A few looked up and smiled vacantly but none seemed to find our appearance threatening, nor were any of their faces familiar, so we smiled but did not enter. Back at the staircase we considered our next move.

'Maybe we should just take it one room at a time,' Carly suggested softly.

'I would hide downstairs, if I had the choice,' Chandra said. 'No windows.'

Apparently Tilyya agreed with her for he had already begun to descend the stairs. With no better option at hand, we followed him.

The stairs ended after just one flight and we were surrounded by four closed doors. Two on the left, one on the right and one behind the stairs. Tilyya crossed to the left and stood beside the first door, tilting his head as he pressed it close to the wood. He dismissed it instantly, shaking his head at us. Alexa drew her sword and moved to it, opening it gently. It was a washroom, unoccupied.

At the second door Tilyya paused again, his eyes wide and unfocused as he leant towards it. He held the pose for much longer and as the waiting grew I saw Chandra draw an arrow from her quiver and notch it to her bow. Carly's twin daggers were already in her hand. Resignedly, I took my own knife from my belt, regretting the fact Lilith and I had not yet reached the weapon fighting section of our training with Nikol. Actually, to think of it, we had not even reached the hay-filled sacks section. That was to have been today.

Tilyya stood straight. He was perplexed. 'I am not sure . . . ' he began and the door opposite burst open.

The first woman who charged through, waving her sword, fell to Chandra's arrow. Then a dark-haired man and a short, sturdy woman rushed out, to be met by Alexa and Carly. Blades flashed, cutting through the air and crashing noisily. Chandra reached for another arrow just as movement on the stairs caught my eye.

'Behind you, Chandra,' I shrieked and she spun and drew her hunting knife. Zerak was in no shape to fight but his sword gave him extra reach. Angry and hungry for revenge, he launched himself at Chandra, who danced effortlessly away.

Tilyya was trying the door but it was locked. Lilith had to be in one of the two remaining rooms. The wood was thick but old and I called out, 'Lil, if you're in there, move back.' Raising both my arms and still clenching my knife, I took a deep, calming breath. Then I stepped back and made a small jump with my left leg, swinging back with my right leg as I landed, and kicking the door with all my might. I aimed beyond the door and let out a loud belly-cry. To my utter amazement, there was a sound of tearing wood and the door flung open. I grinned. Who needed hay-filled sacks?

Lilith was lying tied to a small bed, her mouth stuffed with rags, her eyes shining with joy at seeing me. I smiled ecstatically. She was safe, and I gently pulled the rags from her mouth.

She wet her lips. 'Ashil,' she whispered, her eyes filling with tears.

'You're safe, Lil, we've come to rescue you,' and I began to carefully cut the rope that held her ankles and wrists.

'Ash, the chestnut-haired woman is Nitma . . . who?' she gasped suddenly and I jerked around.

'That's Tilyya,' I said, calming myself and returning to the rope. 'He's Lakiya. We know about Nitma. She stole Tilyya's mla, his beast friend, that's how she's going to create the white panther. A mla can take any animal form.'

'Lakiya,' Lilith repeated in wonder, then the sound of fighting seemed to grow louder outside. 'The others?' she questioned, looking towards the door that had swung back over, blocking her view.

'Yes, they're outside, fighting the thugs. Can you stand?'

I slipped my knife into my belt and helped her sit up. She drew breath as the blood began to circulate freely once more. The ropes had been so tight they had left deep ridges in her skin. She rubbed her wrists while I took an ankle in my hands and massaged it, then swapped it for the other. When she placed both

472

feet on the ground and stood, she was unsteady but managed an awkward hobble.

'Are you hurt at all?' I asked, concerned, looking her over.

'No,' she shook her head. 'They've been ignoring me.'

Tilyya stepped forward. 'My mla?' he asked her.

Lilith stared at him and blinked. It was the first time she had heard his strange voice. 'What does it look like?'

Tilyya cupped his hands. 'He is tiny and he glows.'

Lilith frowned. 'Nitma came to see me once and the whole time she had her hand in her pocket, fondling something. It was round like an apple.' She shrugged. 'Perhaps . . .'

The Lakiya nodded with excitement and pivoted gracefully and was gone. There was only one door left unopened and still Nitma and the mla to be found.

There had been several unpleasant groans and cries from outside while I had been cutting Lilith free and as I pulled back the door, the first sight I saw was Zerak lying sprawled across the floor, blood staining his shirt front. This time, Chandra's blow had been true.

Yet three more thugs had appeared and Chandra was struggling now against a lithe, fair woman who moved her sword with frightening speed. Chandra had dropped her bow and knife and was wielding Zerak's sword, but her unfamiliarity with the weapon was showing as the fair woman tried to back Chandra into the corner between stairs and wall. There was an evil smile on the woman's face as she slowly forced Chandra back.

Alexa was now fighting the scarred woman from the Blue Dolphin. I heard the woman mutter something about the odds being to her liking this time as she struck Alexa with a barrage of quick, skilled blows. Yet Alexa matched her blow for blow and did not seem unduly fearful. Not far from her, Carly was whirling her twin blades with intimidating speed before another blond man. The short, sturdy woman and the dark-haired man, whose face was strangely familiar, lay dead on the floor.

Lilith came up beside me, leaning against the door, twitching her ankles with a grimace on her face. Together, we looked at the other three. Alexa had an ugly gash at her neck and both Carly's arms were bleeding. Chandra was splattered with blood, though I could see no wound on her.

The scene was eerily paralytic and, not knowing what to do, I stood doing nothing. Suddenly Carly gave a cry, bending over in pain, clutching her side. Blood streamed through her fingers. As her opponent laughed and raised his blade I felt rage wash over me like a sudden dousing in hot water and I charged forward. From behind him, I bent my knees and swung one leg out, whipping it around to crack against his thigh. He screamed in shock and pain and as he toppled forward I stepped around him and thrust my elbow up under his jaw. It was a beautifully executed blow, with a straight fist, thumb tucked in, and an accompanying yell. Carly looked at me in astonishment as the man slumped unconscious at our feet.

Chandra was now in a desperate situation. Backed up against the wall, she was heaving the sword in front of her, simply parrying blows and not even attempting to attack. I made to move to her but Carly signalled no, and she raised one of her daggers and with a deft flick of the wrist threw it across the room. The blade dug itself into the woman's back, deep between her ribs, and with a soft, strangled cry, the woman fell. Chandra lowered her sword in relief and leant back against the wall. We all turned in time to see Alexa pull her sword from the blonde woman's body. She wiped the sweat from her brow and saw Lilith and she smiled. 'How are you, Lil?'

'Much better now, and soon I'll have feet I can walk on again.'

We paused to regain our breath, the torrent of thugs seemingly halted, at least for a while, and then we heard the soft moaning.

'Tilyya,' Carly said, trying to stand upright.

The Lakiya was nowhere in sight and then I saw that the fourth door, the one behind the stairs, was slightly ajar. The moan sounded again, coming from behind it, and this time we could distinguish a word, a soft, pain-filled, 'No.'

'My dagger,' Carly said, reaching out towards the dead fair woman. Chandra braced one foot against the woman's back as she leant down and pulled the blade free. I winced at the sound it made. Chandra handed the dagger to Carly and we turned towards the door, knowing what we must face behind it.

Nitma of the Meran. Nitma of the mind powers.

NINETEEN

CHANDRA LED THE way, still gripping Zerak's sword. She pushed the door open and darted inside, closely followed by the four of us. We all stopped short, fearing to move.

There must have been more than eight of them ranged across the room, huge, heavy-pelted, with yellow eyes and long, sharp fangs exposed as they curled their lips in low, threatening snarls. Wolves. Behind them, seated beside a fire and laughing at us was the chestnut-haired woman we had met in the forest, so long ago and so very many leagues away. Nitma.

'Welcome, cartographers,' she said expansively. 'You have saved me considerable trouble by walking to your own deaths. My pets have been horribly deprived since they arrived in this detestable city and are delighted to see their dinner. They do so enjoy a fresh kill.' She laughed again and stroked a small glowing sphere that lay in her lap only fingers away from the fire.

Tilyya was kneeling before her, trembling, his eyes fastened on the mla.

'We had thought to find a white panther,' Alexa spoke coolly.

Nitma glared at her. 'And indeed you will see one,' she said, raising her chin as she answered. 'Before I set my wolves to kill you. The mla glows. There is nothing to stop me creating the panther.' She looked disparagingly down upon Tilyya. 'Nothing at all.'

He gave a despairing groan. 'Not the fire,' he pleaded. 'It will burn him.'

Nitma smiled exultantly. 'It will sear him, setting him in the form I demand, and he will be mine forever. Look upon him the last time, Lakiya. It would have been better if you had died where I left you, or had the sense to return to your people once you recovered, for your journey has brought you naught. The mla is mine and soon all of Tirayi will ring with the sound of people calling my name. I will be acclaimed as was Meclan and all will follow me. There will be only one religion, Meran, and all others will fade into obscurity. Nitma and her panther will make history.'

Alexa laughed. 'Of course,' she pointed out, 'Meclan did truly receive a white panther from the gods, while yours is stolen from the Lakiya and is unwilling. You will never rival Meclan's name. The people will see through you, you are a fake. Isn't that what Brai the seer told you?' Her tone was derisive.

'Silence!' Nitma screamed, rising from her chair. 'The blind fool knew nothing. My mind power is every bit as strong as Meclan's, stronger, for I have learnt more,'

She began to stare at Alexa, her face held in an ugly grimace. At first Alexa's arms began to tremble, then her legs and her whole body. Her breathing came fast and shallow, her legs gave way and she fell to her knees. Sickened as I watched, I searched frantically for a way to help. Carly yelled at Nitma to stop.

Alexa was having trouble breathing now and her hands scrambled uselessly at the neck of her shirt. She wanted air. We were helpless. Alexa was suffocating before us and there was nothing any of us could do. Then Tilyya leapt suddenly through the air, a high, long graceful leap, his slim fingers reaching desperately for the mla in Nitma's lap. Nitma flicked her gaze to him and he fell to the floor with a small sad cry. At the same time, Alexa drew a large breath and fell to the ground, the contact broken, gulping in mouthful after mouthful of air.

Nitma's laugh rang with satisfaction. 'You puny creatures,' she cried, looking from the shaking Lakiya to Alexa. 'See how I can control minds. I can tell a body to stop breathing, slow a heartbeat to nothing, tell muscles to seize. No-one will defeat me. The Meran were not strong enough last time and I have not made the same mistake. I have studied hard. This time it will be different. You have interfered in my business for too long. Zerak tells me that Lord Tarn is meeting with King Charissa this afternoon, no doubt to discuss me, but their attempts to find and stop me are laughable.' She looked down at the mla in her lap. 'For now it is time. Watch, cartographers, and be happy that your last vision in this life will be of Nitma's white panther. Watch the new power begin.'

Having spoken, she threw the glowing sphere into the fire.

Tilyya stood with his head thrown back. He did not scream but a heart-piercing, keening sound came from

478

his mouth. An answering shrill cry came from the mla amongst the flames and the transformation began.

How such a small, shapeless creature could change into anything so glorious and fearful as the gleaming white panther that emerged from the flames was inexplicable to me. It was beautiful and ferocious and wild as it stepped clear of the flames and snarled, opening its mouth to reveal perfect white teeth. It dwarfed the wolves, standing at waist level, and I felt tears sting my eyes as I looked at it. It was so beautiful and was to be used so vilely.

Nitma looked up. 'Do you see?' she said triumphantly, over our heads.

I swivelled quickly and saw the traitor, Kira, as she entered the room, her eyes fastened upon the panther.

'Why?' I whispered and she turned to me.

'Nitma will unite the people, make them strong, stop their suffering.' While she spoke Kira's eyes glowed with her fanaticism. She watched the panther lie down before Nitma. 'She will do more than Meclan in spreading his word.'

'It is hard to be strong without freedom,' Carly told her sourly, holding her bleeding side, 'and hard to feel joy in life when you live in a way not of your choosing.'

'Meclan's way is right and Nitma is the right person to bring the change. With Nitma, there will be no more barriers to Meclan's word, everyone will be happy, and it will happen swiftly. The Mecla are too slow to act, too many opportunities to make a difference pass them by. Nitma, with her panther, will change it all.'

She is mad, I thought. How could she not see the contradiction in her own words?

'Was it you who warned Nitma of the Eustapean horses?' Chandra asked.

'Yes. When you described their arrival I became suspicious. The Melcran have their own mind powers. I told Nitma and she organised for the horses to be killed. They were a threat.'

'And Ricah?' Alexa asked softly.

For a moment, Kira looked pained. 'That was an accident. Her death was not meant to happen.'

'What about our deaths?' Carly asked. 'Is this all a mistake too?'

'I . . .' Kira faltered.

'There are always teething problems,' Nitma intervened smoothly. 'Once I hold power, such actions will be unnecessary. Come, Kira, let us watch my white panther obey my first command.'

With relief, Kira left us and passed beyond the wolves to stand at Nitma's side. Both the panther and Tilyya were still, Tilyya appearing to stare at the floor, the panther lying quietly, not even its tail moving.

'Panther,' Nitma cried, her voice resounding with authority, 'I give you your first command. Kill her.' And her finger pointed directly at me.

'No,' I whimpered, as the panther stood and curled its body so it could see me over its shoulder. It gave a snarling growl and launched itself, straight at Nitma.

Nitma screamed, Kira screamed, I screamed, the wolves howled, suddenly released from Nitma's mind control, and Tilyya smiled. The panther tore out Nitma's throat, bringing her rule to an end on the cold basement floor as her blood flew from the white fangs, speckling the walls and the coats of the wolves.

Disoriented, reverting back to their natural state, the wolves smelt the blood and eyed us hungrily. We began, very slowly, to back towards the door. Our chances were not good. It did not seem fair that we had come so far, had rescued Lilith and seen Nitma die, only to be killed ourselves by wild beasts we could not even blame. I felt cheated. There were still so many maps to draw, so many places to see, and Lord Tarn to kiss. In despair, I realised I did not even know what he tasted like.

The largest and heaviest of the wolves stepped ahead of the pack, singling out Alexa. He dropped to a crouch and the muscles in his body tensed, ready to spring. He gave a bestial growl of hunger, rage, and bloodlust and flew through the air, only to have an arrow sail deep into his chest.

With a mournful cry, the wolf fell and I turned to see Rarnald in the doorway fitting another arrow to his bow. He called to us to stay down and then he, Nikol and other Cynalese soldiers began to rain arrows down upon the wolves until all lay dead. Weak with relief, I sat down, my legs unable to support me any longer. I was numb. Even the sight of so much blood did not have the power to shock me any more.

Then Lilith darted past. She was racing towards Nitma's chair, her blonde hair flying, her speed belying her ordeal. A small door had been opened behind the chair and Lilith caught the traitor who was trying to escape through it. Kira struck Lilith across the cheek but Lilith only grabbed Kira tightly by the shoulders and pulled her close. Lilith thrust her head forward and her forehead hit Kira's with a booming crack. Kira crumpled to the ground.

As the Cynalese soldiers began to enter the room, Carly looked from Lilith to me. 'What have you two been up to?' she asked with incredulity.

Nikol patted Carly on the shoulder. 'They've been taking lessons. Self-defence means self-respect,' and she winked at me and passed on.

I closed my eyes for a moment and leant back against the wall, not wanting to think or see any more. Then a soft, deep voice above me said my name. I opened my eyes to Lord Tarn's concerned face. He was smiling and asking me how I was.

A thrill ran through me and I came to my feet. 'I am fine, Lord.'

'I understand I owe you all a great debt of thanks,' he murmured.

'No debt, Lord,' I replied. 'Nitma had Lilith. She was our enemy too.'

'How . . . ?' he waved a hand at Nitma's body. 'Was it a wolf?'

'No, Lord,' and I grinned and leant closer. 'It was a Lakiya,' I whispered, 'and his mla.'

I saw the wonder that lit his features and my grin broadened as I recalled the glamour and enchantment of Tilyya.

'He must have gone,' I said, looking about me and seeing Rianne speaking with Alexa but no sign of the

Lakiya, 'but,' and I looked back up at him, 'I'll tell you all about it.'

'When you did not attend my meeting with King Charissa I became worried,' Lord Tarn was explaining to us, as we sat in his chambers that evening, bathed and fed, our wounds tended. 'Rianne mentioned that you had left the palace in the company of a stranger, a Delawese she thought, and passed the word to Captain Varl. He asked his soldiers if they had seen you and Nikol admitted having seen you pass through the city gates when she was making her morning report, and that you were with a blond man. She thought it strange at the time as you had sent her word earlier that you would be working in the palace all day.

'Rianne suggested we ask Lilith, who you had told her was resting in your apartment with a sore back. But instead of Lilith we found a letter explaining all you knew of Nitma and your plans. We sent soldiers out asking for a sighting of you. When a disturbance in a free-house was reported to the city guard we knew we had found you. We arrived just in time, though I was denied a sighting of a Lakiya,' he concluded with a wry smile, 'but we were very glad to see you all alive.

'Now tell me,' he said, leaning forward enthusiastically, 'how did you meet this Tilyya and what is he like?'

Carly's side was paining her so she excused herself shortly after our story was told. To my surprise the other three stood as well, each with a different excuse. Alexa said she wished to go and find Rarnald and thank him for his timely arrow. Chandra wanted to check on Ray, who had been recovered from the free-house, and see our other horses that the Cynalese guards had retrieved from Mount Rittoy, along with our kits. Lilith wanted to go with her and have a quick word with the blacksmith about Timi's shoe. I glanced out the window. It was dark, the blacksmith would have finished for the day long ago, but I did not argue, nor did I offer any reason to leave. In fact I was delighted to be the only one staying after Rianne excused herself on the premise of checking on Kira.

Lord Tarn watched them all leave, receiving their polite bows with a warm smile, then turned to me once they had gone.

'Ashil,' he said softly, 'there is something I would like to ask you.'

'Yes, Lord?' I answered, feeling excited colour fill my cheeks.

'When Rianne brought me the letter and I realised what you had planned to do, I was scared at the prospect of not seeing you again.' The room seemed very still as he spoke and I realised I was holding my breath. 'As the Mecla say, "Today is the future of yesterday." I do not want to go through life wondering what it would be like to kiss you or hold you and . . .'

He paused, sighing as he sought the right words.

'And you never know when there will be a raid on your farm,' I finished for him.

He frowned and smiled. 'What farm?'

'It's just a saying,' and I moved to sit beside him. 'I

don't want to go through life wondering what it would be like to kiss or hold you either.'

His eyes softened and he stroked my face. 'You are very beautiful,' he murmured!

'So are you,' I whispered and I leant forward to taste his lips.

Later that evening, we strolled together along the stone gallery of the palace.

'I am glad you're to map all of Cynal,' Tarn said, encircling my waist with his arm. 'It will keep you here for many more months.'

I smiled. 'I'm glad too.'

He chuckled softly. 'To think I had been worrying because I had heard nothing from the north on the Lakiya, when all along, one was under my very nose.'

I raised his hand and kissed it.

Below us the fluid darkness of the sea reflected the silvery trail of the moon. I looked out over the lit city. It was a stunning view, and I inhaled the salty breeze with pleasure. It was almost as though I could hear my name whispered upon it.

'Ashil,' it called, and then I knew. I spun around, my mouth open with delight.

'Tilyya?' I spoke back into the breeze. 'Is that you?'

He appeared before us and I heard Tarn's small exclamation of wonder.

'Ashil, I have come to say goodbye.' He was different tonight, less earthly, more one with the night and the breeze and the stars.

'You're going home?' I asked.

'Yes, it is time,' his voice breathed. 'We miss the Nahaar.' I heard a soft coo. 'My mla would like to thank you,' and he opened his pouch and brought out the glowing sphere.

It was like a tiny star in the dark night and he held it out to me in both hands. I touched it gently and it pushed up against me, warm and soft, cooing and sighing happily as I stroked it, its colour intensifying.

'He likes you,' Tilyya said and I laughed joyfully. Then he held the mla out to Tarn. 'He wishes to greet you. We know you are our friend.'

Tarn touched the mla and I watched it roll in Tilyya's hands towards the caressing fingers.

'Have you seen the others?' I asked.

'Yes, we have said goodbye.'

'Tilyya, why did Nitma fail? This has puzzled me since Nitma's death. I thought she controlled your mla?'

'It was the fire. The Evil One's power could not reach my mla through the flames. She did not know enough about us. Once free of the Evil One's control, my mla and I could speak again and I formed a shield around him. The Evil One's power was familiar to me now and I could prevent the control happening again. When my mla emerged a panther, it was to deceive and kill the Evil One, so we would truly be free.'

I looked down at the vocal sphere, now rocking merrily in Tilyya's hands.

'We'll all miss you,' I said.

'We will miss you too, but now we must go,' and already his voice had begun to fade as he began to move slowly away until we lost sight of him upon the gallery. 'Goodbye, Lord Tarn.' His words floated back to us, soft as a blossom fall. 'Goodbye, Ashil.'

And he was gone.

Tarn sighed and pulled me back against him, hugging me close as we gazed out on the city lights. 'What a night,' he murmured against my hair. 'Two dreams have come true.' His breath tickled my ear as he spoke. 'Did you know, I have never been to Binet?'

'Well,' I said, turning in his arms to place my hands against his chest, 'if you ever need a guide.'

He smiled and kissed the tip of my nose. 'Perhaps after the enthroning.'

I thought of what else was to happen after the enthroning. I did not wish to ruin the night but jealously won over prudence.

'Tarn, are you to marry your cousin Leah?'

He did not even move but answered easily. 'No, there was some talk of it when my father was alive but neither Leah nor I am keen on the idea. She is a talented musician and wishes to travel with a troupe. Both our parents objected when they were alive, and Leah grew very bored here. Now I have given her my permission to leave and she is very happy. She will stay for the enthroning but after that . . . ' I felt him shrug.

After that! What a wonderful night it had been!

EPILOGUE

THE ENTHRONING FIRES lit the city, their heat and brilliance reflecting the mood of the people of Cynal. Everywhere there was dancing and singing and celebrating, for the new king had just been crowned and the dusk procession, with the king at its head, had begun to wind its way slowly through the city streets.

King Tarn sat upon his horse, waving to his people, his green robe stirring softly about him in the gentle breeze. He was flanked by the Mecla priest, Rianne, who had performed the ceremony, and his chancellor, Neesha, and the captain of his guard, Varl. The escort wore their finest uniforms, walking proudly behind their king, their swords bumping against their legs as they moved in time, their faces glowing with importance.

The crowd roared to see the magnificent man who was their ruler and he smiled to hear their adoration. Yet he was not fooled. He was as much theirs as they were his and he knew he would have to work to keep the love and respect that flowed towards him now. He waved again and hundreds of tiny scented candles were waved in reply, like so many dancing fireflies.

The procession halted at the upper harbour where the fishing boats were moored. Here where Cynal's three strengths met—the moon, the sea and the royal blood—Rianne stepped forward for the final rite of the day. The people were hushed, watching as she rose to the platform that had been erected only that morning. She spoke the ritual words, hands outstretched to the pale moon and the never-silent sea and King Tarn stepped up beside her. Drawing a small bucket from the water, Rianne dipped a hand, filling it with the cold salt water and dripped three drops upon his head. He was anointed.

Wild ecstasy ran through the crowd and their cheering grew as the King of Eustape went forward to honour the new King of Cynal. King Tarn welcomed her warmly and he formally invited her to join him as he returned to his palace for the enthroning celebrations.

Inside the palace, the Great Hall lay ready, adorned with its silken flags and the royal crest and the tables groaning under the weight of silver plate and goblets. All gleamed and shone and as the guests began to arrive, the food was brought out. By royal decree, all inhabitants of the palace were permitted to attend the celebrations, the servants who carried the platters having only to work a short while before they were relieved and freed to enjoy the festivities.

King Tarn took his place upon the dais with his important guests, both Cynalese and foreign, and among them were five cartographers, Chandra, Lilith, Alexa, Carly and myself.

Only two of our friends were not present—Rarnald,

who was on duty for several more hours, and Baki, the cook. The rest were there. King Charissa, Rianne, Neesha, Varl, Damin, Laibi, Nikol, Demran, Regi, and even the king's cousin, Leah. Thanks to Carly, Lindsa the Delawese sailor had also been invited.

Nitma was dead, Kira was imprisoned, and Cynal could breathe easily.

Later, the exquisite meal over, King Tarn rose to mix with his guests and I stood quietly, enjoying the spectacle around me. The horror that had so consumed me only days ago was already beginning to fade like a hollow fever-dream.

'It is a sight we thought at times never to see.'

I turned at the voice and bowed. King Charissa smiled pleasantly, then returned her gaze to the crowd of guests. 'When she killed Fletya, I feared she had won.'

Fletya, the chestnut mare. Since the deaths of the Eustapean horses, the king had appeared to shine a little less brilliantly. Tonight I thought I saw a return of some of her earlier luminance.

'Did you suspect Kira?' I asked, for it was only in looking back that I saw the many hints of her fanaticism.

'No.' She shook her head. 'It was only by chance that we discovered one of the Mecla was false. A message we were later to cancel was sent to King Tarn's father through the House. When the Meran acted upon it, we knew the information could only have come from a Mecla, but which one? Never having had reason to suspect a Mecla, we had become too careless. We pretended bafflement at the Meran's interference while we thought about what it all meant. Nitma would move soon, we knew, and then the old king died. We guessed Nitma would see no better time to make her bid for power so we brought Fletya and Karrha with us on our official visit to Cynal and began to search the city.'

'We would never have found Nitma without the Searchers,' I told her.

She lay a hand on my shoulder. 'You are very kind.'

I could see Nikol weaving her way towards me with two goblets of wine and King Charissa saw her also. 'Perhaps one day you and your friends will visit us on Eustape,' she said in a lighter voice. 'We would all look forward to such a visit.'

I grinned, truly pleased. 'We would be delighted.'

She squeezed my arm and left me. Moments later, Nikol came and stood beside me, offering me a goblet.

'All this time with kings, Ashil. I hope you still find time enough for your lessons.'

I feigned innocence. 'Definitely, Nikol. Who knows, I may actually learn something.'

Nikol punched me playfully in the arm, then raised her goblet and quickly drained it.

The servants came around with Cynalese wine flagons and she waved one over to refill her goblet. 'Poor Baki,' she mused, after taking another long draught. 'What a time to get sick. He's missing all the fun.'

'Sick from what?'

She shrugged. 'I passed through the kitchen on my way here and they said he had fainted. Probably the heat—that kitchen is one enormous oven. He's asleep

491

in his room.' She saw my worried expression. 'It's not the food,' she reassured me. 'It's all been tasted by the other cooks and he's the only one who got sick.'

A servant poured wine from a Eustapean flagon and offered it to King Tarn and Rianne and something niggled at my mind. I suddenly recalled the servant of Nitma who had killed himself before me. His dark hair and eyes had appeared familiar and now they returned to haunt me. Where had I seen him? As King Tarn and Rianne raised the goblets to their lips, a second face came to mind. The dark-haired man that Alexa had fought in the free-house. Why did their faces tease me so? The goblets were tilted and I remembered Nikol telling me all Cynalese soldiers had a mental map of the palace and I began to scream, the wine from my own goblet splashing the floor in a brilliant pool as I rushed to where King Tarn had spun about in bewilderment.

'The wine's poisoned,' I yelled, panting anxiously. He and Rianne hastily lowered their goblets, glancing at the dark depths suspiciously.

'It's Baki,' I gushed, reaching them. 'He tastes all the wines, just a small sip but he tastes them all. I was in the kitchen when two of Nitma's servants delivered some Eustapean flagons they said were a special gift for the royal table. They were acting the part of Cynalese soldiers but they had to ask me for directions. I didn't think anything of it at the time. When I saw both their faces later, in connection with Nitma, I wondered how I knew them. She wanted to poison you.'

King Tarn waved over a guard and sent him to check

on Baki. The goblets were collected and the Eustapean flagons removed from the Hall.

King Tarn bent to me. 'My saviour,' he whispered.

I gave him a shaky smile as I tried to calm my breathing. It had been far too close for my comfort.

Not to let the incident shadow the evening, King Tarn asked the musicians to begin playing and Demran and his friends came out and began a dance tune. Soon people spun and twirled on the dance area and on the marble terrace and Nitma was put from their minds.

The guard returned to say that he had wakened Baki. The cook had fetched the Eustapean flagons late that afternoon and tasted the smallest amount. An hour later he felt ill and collapsed in his kitchen. He still felt a little nauseous and would spend the evening in bed.

The flagons were destroyed and the celebrations continued. Demran sang his love songs to Chandra and I danced with King Tarn several times. When we stopped to rest, he moved to speak with more well-wishers and I joined Lilith near the marble terrace.

'It's a good night,' she said.

'Yes,' I agreed simply.

Her eyes fell on Alexa taking to the dance area with Damin. 'It's strange,' she reflected, 'when I first met the Mecla I thought they were everything I wished to be. Strong, content, driven, complete. The more I saw of them, the more I liked. Then Nitma kidnapped me and for a while there was only fear, but it soon passed and I began to feel anger and determination and I discovered I was stronger than I had thought. I could bear more than I had realised and I discovered that I was happier than Kira.' She looked at me and smiled. 'I discovered I like who I am because I'm only getting better.' She glanced at Damin as he swung over the marble floor with Alexa. 'I don't need a scarlet robe, after all.'

The dance ended and I saw Chandra striding towards us. 'Did you like the song?' she asked happily.

'It was wonderful,' I told her.

'Demran has already received many offers to play over Tirayi, but he has decided to stay in Cynal until Carly finds our next job. He has said he can play where we work.' She was brimming with joy.

'So we'll have music wherever we go,' I quipped, enjoying her excitement.

'Yes,' Chandra replied and there was rich satisfaction in that single word.

'Ashil, let's dance,' Alexa called, coming over and taking me by the hands. She pulled me gently onto the terrace and held me in a light embrace. 'I wonder if anything during the rest of our stay here will match the excitement of the past week,' she mused.

I gave a half-laugh, half-groan. 'No, it mustn't.'

'King Tarn looks radiant this evening.'

I turned to see him dancing with Leah. 'He's hoping we'll agree to stay on once the maps are completed and help set up a Cynalese cartography base.'

Alexa nodded. 'Anything's possible,' she replied easily.

'You wouldn't fear becoming too mellow?' I asked her.

She raised an eyebrow in amusement. 'A little bit of mellowing can be a good thing, before one's next adventure.'

I grinned. 'Alexa?'

'Yes,' she answered, looking at me, her blue eyes relaxed and friendly.

'I've always wanted to ask you, where were you born?'

'Ah,' she replied softly, 'this is a night for King Tarn and Cynal, Ashil. Another night I will tell you my story.'

Rarnald came forward then, his round over. 'Alexa?' he spoke tenderly, almost reverentially.

She smiled at the soldier. 'I promised Rarnald his first dance,' she said to me. I nodded and slipped from her arms.

I turned to leave, then stopped. 'You will tell me, won't you?' I asked.

Alexa looked at me. 'Yes, Ashil,' she promised gently. 'One day.'

The evening grew late and I joined King Tarn on the dais where he sat with his important guests. His eyes softened with love as I approached, and for the moment I forgot my friends and my maps. Alexa had been right, this was a night for the king and the city and I put all else from my mind.

As dawn began to break in the sky, I kissed Tarn's sleeping form and climbed silently from his bed. At the window I could see the fishing boats dotted upon the water and I suddenly wanted to be down there. I left the palace swiftly and saddled Cleo.

I had thought to find the cove deserted but there was another there before me.

'That's her ship,' Carly said, pointing to a large vessel

that was slowly sailing towards the horizon. 'We said goodbye last night.'

I sat beside her on the sand and hugged my knees. 'Will you see her again?'

The only sound in the cove was the lapping of the water and the harsh, hungry cries of the seabirds. The sky overhead was streaked with gold and rose.

Carly shrugged. 'If ever I'm in Delawyn, perhaps. She wanted me to go with her.'

'Yes,' I said and we both fell silent.

'I brought something of yours with me,' Carly announced, turning. 'Here,' and she held out the pig's bladder.

I bit my lip and shook my head. Had it really only been such a short while ago? Where were the merfolk now?

'Thank you,' I murmured, chuckling softly as I lightly tossed the bladder in the air. Then I jumped to my feet and raced to the water's edge, tossing the bladder higher and higher as I went. 'Come on,' I called, 'let's play.' I threw the bladder slightly away from me and chased it over the sand, catching it before it fell to the ground.

The water behind me sloshed and whooshed, its voice never quiet, and I saw Carly walk towards me. She opened her mouth to speak but the words I heard were not from her lips or from any mortal voice. I spun around and there was Rayi, floating only paces away, smiling gleefully, her eyes on the bladder, and she spoke the words again, gaily, merrily, words I had thought never to hear again.

'Throw it, Ashil, throw it.'

Beverley Macdonald
THE MADIGAL

For forty years the Madigal has slept, travelling the very fabric of time and space. And now the Madigal wakes ...

All is not well in the Madigal's city, the city whose streets she mapped and whose laws she framed six centuries ago. The winters have grown longer, colder. Crown Prince Harry tyrannises the people, and ice-bear ravage outlying settlements.

For many the Madigal is only a distant memory, the stuff of legends; others have no desire to see a newly awakened Madigal meddling in their affairs ...

Even her own tower feels strange to her. What has her Keeper, Wixwyn, been doing while she slept? Has he been dabbling too deeply in the Old Arts?

As the Madigal acts to ensure the future of her city and its people, she must also preserve the strange paradox that binds her future and her Keeper's past ...

Shannah Jay
QUEST
Book One of the Chronicles of Tenebrak

At fourteen, Katia is *chosen* to serve her Brother the
God at the Sisterhood's great temple in Tenebrak.
Once *chosen*, there is no turning back.

But Discord is spreading across the face of Katia's
planet, its violence threatening the very existence of
the 20,000-year-old Sisterhood.

Far above Tenebrak, Davred, a brilliant young xeno-
anthropologist, studies the Sisterhood from the Confex
observation satellite. Risking everything, he decides to
help the Sisters in their quest against Discord.

However, as the quest enters its most critical stage, it
becomes clear that neither Davred nor the Sisters
know all the secrets of this mysterious planet …

Shannah Jay
LANDS OF NOWHERE
Book Two of the Chronicles of Tenebrak

Can the Kindred truly find sanctuary in the Lands of
Nowhere?

They desperately need refuge from Those of the
Serpent, whose incense-choked shrines worship pain
and suffering throughout the Twelve Claims, and from
Robler, the increasingly unbalanced Exec in charge of
the Confederation satellite that circles above them.

The Lands of Nowhere are the legendary lands of the
deleff, told of only in children's tales. The mysterious
deleff have already saved the Kindred twice, but are
they really allies in the Kindred's quest against
Discord? And why are the deleff so reluctant to let
them leave the closed community of Dsheresh Vale?

As the Kindred encounter new threats to their quest —
and new allies and new Gifts — the planet Sunrise
reveals itself as more baffling than ever...